PRIVATE PARIS

PRIVATE PATHS

PRIVATE PARIS

by

James Patterson & Mark Sullivan

Magna Large Print Books
Long Preston, North Yorkshire,
BD23 4ND, England.

British Library Cataloguing in Publication Data.

A catalogue record of this book is
available from the British Library

ISBN   978-0-7505-4343-9

First published in Great Britain in 2016 by Century,
part of the Penguin Random House Group

Published in Large Print 2017 by arrangement with
Random House Group Ltd.

Magna Large Print is an imprint of Library Magna Books Ltd.

Printed and bound in Great Britain by
T.J. (International) Ltd., Cornwall, PL28 8RW

Pour La Ville Lumière

PROLOGUE

TAGGER

18TH ARRONDISSEMENT, PARIS
APRIL 6, 12:30 A.M.

The messenger bag pressed tight to his hip, the hood of his black sweatshirt up, and a black-and-white checked kaffiyeh scarf looped around his swarthy neck, Epée walked quickly down the Rue Marcadet.

His name meant *sword* in French – more particularly, a duel sword, which is how he thought of himself that night.

I am declaring war here, Epée thought. The Sword marks the first battleground.

The shabby area around him was sparsely traveled that late, and he was careful not to look up at the few people who passed him on the sidewalk near the corner with the Boulevard Barbès. The shops that lined both sides of the boulevard were dark, but lights flickered in the apartment windows above. Somewhere a baby was crying. Somewhere Middle Eastern music was playing.

Epée looked to his north beyond an Islamic bookstore, a tailor's shop that sold robes, and the storefront office of FEZ Couriers, a messenger service. She was right where he remembered her from his scouting trip the week before.

She's big enough, he thought, *and her shin is flawless.*

In fact, she's perfect. I couldn't find one better.

Seeing that the sidewalks were vacant for

blocks in either direction, Epée reached down, tugged the kaffiyeh scarf up over his lower face, and began to jog toward his target. Just past the closed doors to a mosque, he skidded to a stop, reached in his messenger bag, and snatched two cans of spray paint.

With a can in each hand, he sprayed the mosque wall in big, looping movements that started high over his head and finished at his toes. In seconds, he was done and feeling the bittersweet ecstasy of the spent artist.

The graffiti was his design, bloodred and dripping. Despite the swooping, stylized letters, there was no doubt what the tag said:

AB-16

A car engine started down the street to his south. Headlights flashed on and found Epée, who dropped the cans and took off like a spooked deer.

The engine roared. Tires squealed. Headlights slashed. A Klaxon began whooping, and the scene was cast in flashing blue.

Fucking Paris police were watching the place!

Epée sprinted diagonally across the boulevard, between two parked cars, and onto the opposite sidewalk. The tagger was uncommonly fast, but no man could outrun a police car in a straight-line race.

Then again, Epée had no intention of moving in a straight line. An expert in parkour, the French art of urban obstacle course running, he saw everything in the street, high and low, as a potential ally.

The police car was almost abreast of him. Another patrol car appeared from where Barbès meets the Boulevard Ornano. It raced right at Epée. His remarkable brain saw angles, vectors, and converging speeds as if they were opaque readouts on a jet fighter pilot's visor.

The unmarked car behind him now came into his peripheral vision. Epée cut hard off the sidewalk toward the vehicle's front bumper. He jumped fluidly, gracefully, but full of intent and precision. Tires screeched.

The tagger's rubber soles found the bumper. His body and legs coiled into it, and then sprang off. The move threw him forward through the air, tucked like a downhill ski racer off a jump.

Epée landed, chest forward, his legs churning in perfect cadence with the momentum he'd created, not in retreat at all. He charged the oncoming car, played chicken with it as his mind spun. Would they run a guy down for tagging? He didn't think so. But stranger things had happened.

Stranger things did happen. Instead of braking, the cop accelerated. Epée could hear the other car coming fast as well, as if they meant to hit him front and back, cut him in half.

Epée leaped into the air like a triple jumper. His left foot tapped the hood of the oncoming police car, his right foot caressed its flashing blue lights, and both feet absorbed the landing a split second before the two police cars crashed head-on and just behind him.

Epée had made his escape look as elegant as a ballet solo, but he wasn't taking any chances and sprinted hard for blocks before slowing on a quiet street.

He saw a brand-new white BMW parked in the middle of the block, saw that the street was deserted, and took the opportunity to spray-paint the hood with the same bloodred graffiti tag.

AB-16

Two down, the Sword thought as he moved on. Only forty-eight to go.

PART ONE

APRIL IN PARIS

Chapter 1

1ST ARRONDISSEMENT
APRIL 6, 3:30 P.M.

'The secret to understanding Parisians, Jack, is to see that they are almost the exact opposite of people in Los Angeles,' said the big bear of a man sitting across from me. 'In L.A., children are raised to be optimistic, full of life, friendly. People who grow up in Paris, however, are taught the value of melancholy and an unwavering belief in the superiority of suffering. It's why they have a reputation for being rude. It's to make you as uncomfortable as they are, and they honestly believe they are doing you a favor.'

It was late afternoon, a warm, gorgeous spring day in the French capital, and Louis Langlois and I were sitting outside Taverne Henri IV in the Place Dauphine, well into our second glasses of excellent Bordeaux.

I smiled and said, 'It can't be that bad.'

Amused, Louis shook his head and said, 'It is a fact that having fun, laughing, and generally enjoying life in Paris is a clear indication of latent insanity, or at least that you are visiting from an inferior place, which means anywhere outside the city limits.'

'C'mon,' I said, chuckling now. 'People seem genuinely nice. Even the waiters have been great so far.'

With a dismissive flip of his hand, he said, 'They seem nice because, at long last, they understand that Paris is the number one tourist destination in the world, and that tourism is the biggest money-maker in the city. At the same time, they know you are a tourist from America – the land of the absurdly obese, the absurdly wealthy, and the absurdly ignorant – and they hope you give them an absurdly big tip. You must believe me, Jack. Deep inside, Parisians are not enjoying themselves and find it upsetting when others appear overly happy.'

I raised my eyebrows skeptically.

'Don't believe me?' he said. 'Watch.'

Louis threw back his head and began roaring with laughter. The laugh seemed to seize control of him, and shook down through his entire body as if he were scratching his back with it.

To my surprise and amusement, the patrons around us, and even the waitress who'd just delivered our wine, were now glancing sidelong at him. That only encouraged Louis, who started howling and slapping his thigh so hard tears streamed down his face. I couldn't help it and started laughing too. The people around us were gaping openly or sniffing at us now, as if we were refugees from a funny farm.

At last, Louis calmed down and wiped away the tears, and when the café had returned to normalcy, he murmured, 'What did I tell you? I use this – laughter – to upset suspects many times. To the people of Paris, a policeman who sees humor in everything, he must be crazy. He must be dangerous. He must be feared.'

I held up my hands in surrender. 'Your city, Louis.'

'My adopted city,' he said, holding up a finger. 'I do not think this way, but I understand it well.'

Thirty years ago, Louis left his home in Nice in the south of France and joined the French National Police. His extraordinary emotional intelligence, his understanding of the French people, and his unorthodox investigative instincts had propelled him swiftly into a job in Paris with La Crim, an elite investigative force similar to the major case units of the New York and L.A. police departments.

For twenty-nine years, Louis served with distinction at La Crim. The day before his retirement, I offered him a job at three times his old pay. He now ran the Paris office of Private, a global security and investigative agency I founded and own.

You'll hear people refer to Private as 'the Pinkertons of the twenty-first century.' I don't know if we warrant that high praise, but it's flattering, and the reputation has helped us grow by leaps and bounds over the last few years, especially overseas, which causes me to travel more than I'd like.

I'd been visiting the Berlin office for a few days and arrived in Paris the evening before. After a series of meetings with the local staff during the day, Louis suggested we go out for a few drinks and then a fine meal. That brilliant idea had brought us to one of his favorite cafés and led him to begin to explain to me the intricate mysteries of Paris, its citizens, and their way of thinking.

Before Louis could move on to another subject, his cell phone rang. He frowned and said, 'I asked them not to call me unless it was important.'

'No worries,' I said, and took another sip of wine.

Even if the Parisians weren't happy, I was. Louis Langlois was a funny guy and Paris was still one of the most beautiful cities on earth, filled with interesting and sometimes shocking people, art, and food. In an hour or two, I'd no doubt be eating an incredible meal, and probably laughing a whole lot more. Life, for the foreseeable future, looked very good.

And then it didn't.

Louis listened to his phone, nodded, and said, 'Of course I remember you, Monsieur Wilkerson. How can Private Paris be of help?'

Wilkerson? The only Wilkerson I knew was a client who lived in Malibu.

I mouthed, 'Sherman Wilkerson?'

Louis nodded and said into the phone, 'Would you rather talk with Jack Morgan? He's right here.'

He handed me the phone. Now, the last time I'd heard from Sherman Wilkerson like this, out of the blue, there were four dead bodies on the beach below his house. I admit that there were nerves in my voice when I said, 'Sherman?'

'What are you doing in Paris, Jack?' Wilkerson demanded.

'Visiting one of my fastest-growing offices.'

Sherman Wilkerson was a no-nonsense engineer who'd built a wildly successful industrial design company. By nature he dealt with facts and often understated his opinion of things. So I

20

was surprised when he said in a shaky voice, 'Maybe there is a God after all.'

'You've got a problem in Paris?' I asked.

'My only granddaughter, Kimberly. Kimberly Kopchinski,' Wilkerson replied. 'I just got off the phone with her – first call in more than two years. She's in an apartment outside Paris and says there are drug dealers hunting for her, trying to kill her. She sounded petrified, and begged me to send someone to save her. Then the line went dead and now I can't reach her. Can you go make sure she's safe? I've got the address.'

'Of course,' I said, signaling to Louis to pay the bill. 'How do we find her?'

Wilkerson read me out an address.

I wrote it down and said, 'Can you text me a photograph? And tell me about her? College student? Businesswoman?'

Louis laid down cash on the table and gave me the thumbs-up during a long pause.

'Sherman?' I said, standing. 'Are you there?'

'I honestly don't know what Kim's been doing the past two years, and I know little of her life over the past five,' Wilkerson admitted as we left the café and Louis called for a car. 'Her parents – my daughter, Pam, and her husband, Tim – they died in a boating accident six years ago.'

'I remember you telling me that,' I said. 'Sad.'

'Very. Kim was in her senior year at USC, and back from a junior year in France, when it happened. She was as devastated as we were. Long story short, she inherited a bit of money along with a trust, and she turned wild child. She barely graduated. When she did, she went straight back to France. For a time I know she was working for the Cannes Film Festival organizers. We tried to stay in touch, but we heard from her less and less. Before today, there was a Christmas card from Monaco, and before that, a condolence card when my wife died.'

The car pulled up. Louis opened the door, and I climbed in, saying, 'Don't worry, Sherman. We're on our way.'

'Thank you, Jack. You'll call when you have her?'

'I will.'

'Protect her, Jack. I beg you,' Wilkerson said. 'She's my only grandchild – my only living relative, really.'

'You've got nothing to worry about,' I said, and hung up.

After filling Louis in on the conversation, I pushed the address I'd written on a napkin over to him. 'Know it?'

Louis put his reading glasses on and studied it, and his nostrils flared as if he'd scented something foul. Then he looked up at me and with a definite edge in his voice said, 'Look up *trouble* and *danger* in a French dictionary, and you get a picture of this place.'

Chapter 2

PANTIN, NORTHEASTERN
SUBURBS OF PARIS
3:45 P.M.

How can I make you burn?

How do I make you come alive like a creature from hell's fire?

In what used to be a linen factory along the Canal de l'Ourcq, these questions consumed the woman standing on scaffolding, absently stroking her long braid of mahogany hair, and studying the giant's skeleton.

She was in her mid-thirties, with dusky skin and haunting pewter eyes, and she wore clothes that were completely at odds with her exotic beauty: black steel-toe work boots, double-faced and riveted canvas pants, and a flame-resistant cape and apron over a heavy denim shirt.

She turned from the skeleton, still unsure how it was all going to work, and looked for answers among the various materials she'd bought or salvaged and transported to the building. In the last month she'd amassed two tons of number 9 rebar in twenty-foot lengths. She had sections of battered steel conduit torn from culverts during a big highway job out toward Reims. And she had stacks of scrap sheet metal, angle iron, and galvanized pipe gathered from junkyards and metal

23

recycling plants across northern France.

The massive steel posts came from an old engine repair shop in Orleans. They were already standing, four of them anchor-bolted into the cement floor. I beams had been hoisted and pinned in place as well, forming an open-sided rectangular box forty-five feet long, twenty-five feet wide, and thirty feet high. From a structural point of view, the heavy work was over. The superstructure of the skeleton was standing. And already she could see the vague dimensions of what was to come forming in her–

'Haja!' a man's voice called.

Haja startled and looked around to see a rugged man in his late thirties emerge from a door in the corner. Thick neck, bronze skin, short black hair. He carried a gym bag and was dressed in a sweat suit. Cleats hung around his neck.

'Up here, Émile,' she called.

Émile Sauvage spotted her and said, 'Shouldn't you be getting ready for your date?'

'Henri won't be ready until nine,' she said. 'I have plenty of time.'

'You'll text when you're inside?'

'I remember the plan,' she said.

'I'll see you there.'

'I look forward to it, *chéri*,' she said. 'AB-16 at last.'

Sauvage smiled. 'AB-16 at long last.'

Haja blew him a kiss and watched him go out the main door. She heard the bolt thrown before she turned again to look at the skeleton.

Seeing it from this new angle, she had a sudden, intense inspiration, saw how she might begin the process of creation. Rushing about now, feeling feverish, Haja climbed down off the scaffolding. She grabbed a pair of heavy bolt cutters and snipped off several lengths of rebar. She set them on the floor next to the near post, and then wheeled over the welding tanks, hose, and torch.

Putting on the helmet and shield, she took up the torch and the striker, and then turned on the oxygen and acetylene gas and ignited the hissing mixture. Even through the smoked glass, the flame was searing in its intensity.

I can sculpt you, she thought. *I can create you from scrap.*

But how do I make you burn like this welding torch?

How do I create an apocalyptic vision that France will never, ever forget?

Chapter 3

MONTFERMEIL, EASTERN SUBURBS OF PARIS
4:45 P.M.

Shortly after Louis Langlois and I spoke with Sherman Wilkerson we headed east out of Paris in workmen's blue jumpsuits that featured the logo of a bogus plumbing company. Louis drove a Mia electric-powered delivery vehicle, which looked like a minivan back home, only much smaller. The tiny van had the same fake plumbing logo painted on the rear panels and back door.

Louis said he used the Mia and the plumbing disguises often during surveillance jobs, but tonight we were using them to stay alive.

'The areas around the Bondy Forest have always been places of poverty, crime, and violence,' Louis explained. 'You've read *Les Misérables?*'

'Years ago,' I said. 'But I saw the movie recently.'

'Okay,' he said. 'That scene where Jean Valjean meets Cosette getting water? The inn where the Thénardiers robbed their customers? All in Montfermeil. It looks different today, of course, but the dark spirit of the place continues. Montfermeil is like your Bronx was in the nineteen seventies, or South Central L.A. in the nineties: high unemployment, high crime rate, and lots of gangs, drug dealers, and violence. Add an angry Muslim and young immigrant population, and it's unimaginable to me why Mademoiselle Kopchinski would take refuge in Les Bosquets – one of the worst housing projects in France.'

I shrugged. 'We'll find out, I guess. You're sure about the plumbers' gear being the right way to go?'

'*Bien sûr*. Everybody needs the plumber at some time, in some emergency. *Non?* Plumbers can come and go at all hours and no one thinks anything of it other than some poor bastard has a backed up toilet. And plumbers tend not to get hassled even in places like Les Bosquets. 'Why is that? Because everyone needs the plumber! Someone shakes the plumber down, and soon no plumbers will come, and no one wants that. Not even there.'

'This wouldn't fly in the States,' I said, gesturing at the full jumpsuit. 'People would know we weren't plumbers.'

Louis seemed taken aback by that. 'How would they know?'

'No American plumber would wear a coverall like this. If they did, they couldn't show their ass crack, and that's a requirement in the States.'

Louis glanced, and then laughed. 'This is true?'

'No.'

My cell phone buzzed, alerting me to a text. It was from Sherman Wilkerson and included a photograph of a pretty young woman with sad eyes sitting at a bar. At a red light I showed it to Langlois, saying, 'It's the most recent picture of her Sherman's got. He said it's at least four years old.'

'As a rule I don't like babysitting jobs,' Langlois said.

'Neither do I,' I agreed, pocketing the phone. 'But when a client like Sherman asks Private to look after his granddaughter, we answer.'

Twenty minutes later, and less than eleven miles from the chic streets and genteel parks of central Paris, we entered a world apart. Out the van's window, the area didn't look too bad at night. It kind of reminded me of East Berlin, with big clusters of drab, uniform, state-designed high-rise apartment buildings – a communist's decaying vision of ideal housing.

Then I started seeing the graffiti. 'Fuck the police' was a common theme. So were images of faceless men in dark hoods with flames painted behind them and Arabic scrawled above them.

'Was this project part of those riots a few years back?' I asked.

'Les Bosquets was in the thick of it,' Louis confirmed. 'And it's home to a vicious gang that specializes in targeting tourists who take the train from de Gaulle to Paris. A few months ago, they put a car on the tracks to stop a train holding more than a hundred Japanese visitors, then went on board and robbed everyone at gunpoint.'

'Brazen.'

'Yes, but there are reasons,' Louis replied. 'Back in the sixties and seventies, when France was on the up economically, we needed labor, so they allowed anyone from a current or former French colony to immigrate here. They built the projects, and a generation later the economy busts, and the immigrants stay on, having children, lots of children. Fifty percent of the population out here is younger than twenty-five. And they can't find jobs. So they live in terrible conditions, with no purpose. It's a recipe for disaster for everyone involved.'

'Can't they work their way out of it through school?' I asked.

Louis wagged a finger at me and said, 'You are thinking of the States again, Jack. In France, it is not the same. There are proven paths to power here – the right schools, the right friends – and these paths are shut off to the immigrants. Worse, there is no public transportation in these areas. Without a car, you go nowhere. You're trapped. You get angry. You explode.'

Louis flicked his chin toward the windshield. 'There it is. Les Bosquets.'

28

The project consisted of eight decaying high-rise apartment buildings. Clotheslines hung from windows, as did immigrants of all ages and skin colors. Louis pulled over on the Avenue Clichy-sous-Bois.

He opened the glove compartment, got out a Glock 19, and handed it to me.

'I'm not licensed to carry this in France,' I said.

'You're not a licensed French plumber either, Jack,' Louis said. 'Put it in your pocket, and let me do the talking.'

It's hard to argue with a guy who knows his turf as well as Louis. I decided to trust his judgment and nodded. We got out and grabbed toolboxes and flashlights from the rear hatchback. Men across the street had checked us out when we pulled up, but now they were ignoring us.

'You see?' Louis muttered as we headed down the road that ran north into the complex. 'Everyone needs us, even if we don't show the butt cracks.'

Chapter 4

7TH ARRONDISSEMENT
5 P.M.

The hooker, the props, the locks, and the flankers were tight in the scrum when the eighth man joined them, and the battle began.

On a pitch in the shadow of the Eiffel Tower,

the scrum half player snatched up the rugby ball and pitched it to the fly, who sprinted madly to the outside of a defensive mob in full pursuit. The fly passed the ball to the inside center, who took a hit, but not before he lobbed the ball on to Émile Sauvage.

Sauvage snagged the rugby ball out of the air, tucked it, and accelerated right at his enemy. He smashed the heel of his palm into the face of the first defender and broke into the open field. Out of the defensive pack a big coal-black guy appeared. Moving laterally with tremendous speed and agility despite his bulk, he seemed sure to flatten Sauvage.

But a fraction of a second before he could, Sauvage laid down a stutter step that suggested he'd change direction. The feint worked. His pursuer planted a foot so hard to cut the other way that he tripped and sprawled while Sauvage loped on toward the in-goal area.

A whistle blew. Sauvage slowed to a stop well shy of the try line and went back to help the big guy to his feet. 'You didn't roll that ankle, did you, Mfune?'

Mfune smiled, shook his head, and said in the clipped French of West Africa, 'Nice move, though.'

'Keep them guessing, embrace the chaos,' he said. 'It's the only way to survive and win a battle. Any battle.'

'Best tactic,' Mfune agreed.

The other players were drinking water and gathering their gear. Practice was over.

Sauvage said, 'I think we have time for a few

rounds before the lecture, don't you?'

'If we're quick about it.'

They grabbed their bags and water bottles and hurried off the field, crossing an equestrian track and parking area to get to a three-story, tan-colored building. They passed through double doors, went to a locker room, stored their cleats and practice jerseys, and retrieved their pistol cases.

After signing into the fifty-meter range in the basement, they received 9-millimeter ammunition, ear protection, and shooting glasses.

They set human assailant silhouette targets at thirty-five meters, loaded their MAC 50 pistols, and fired in five quick, two-round bursts until their weapons were empty. When they called back the targets, they saw that four of Mfune's shots were to the forehead, and six clustered over the heart.

All ten of Sauvage's bullets, however, had patterned tight between the eyes. They cased their pistols, turned in their protective gear, and returned to the locker room. Drying off after a shower and shave, Sauvage moved to his locker, already forcing his complex mind to compartmentalize.

The uniform helped as it always did.

In short order, he was dressed in French Army-issued khaki shirt and trousers, a black tie, and a green commando sweater with epaulets. Polished black shoes and a green garrison cap completed the transformation.

He shut his locker door. Mfune was dressed and ready as well.

Mfune gave him a crisp salute and said, 'Major Sauvage.'

'Captain Mfune,' Sauvage replied.

'I don't know why these guest lectures always occur at night,' Mfune complained softly. 'And tonight of all nights.'

'At ease, Captain,' Sauvage said. 'We've got a few hours before AB-16 is launched.'

The French Army officers left the locker room and walked outside across a cobblestone court-yard. Other men and women in uniform were already hurrying into a two-story buff-colored building through light-blue doors in need of paint. Next to the door, a brass plaque read, 'École de Guerre.'

War School.

Chapter 5

5:15 P.M.

Louis was right about plumber being the perfect disguise.

We passed four or five small groups of menacing-looking types, and as soon as they'd had a hard stare at our plumber's logo, they relaxed and looked away. The last group was out in front of the entrance to the address we'd been given, a building at the rear of Les Bosquets.

I remembered enough from high school French class to understand when one of the guys asked where we were going. Louis never broke stride, just went past him saying something I couldn't follow. It seemed to do the trick, however, because no one trailed us into the lobby, which featured poor lighting; a wall of mailboxes, many broken; and a cement floor that was cracked and offset in several places.

'What did you tell those guys?' I asked.

'I said that the toilet in 412 was backed up and there's shit all over the place. It shuts down their curiosity every time.'

We didn't have to use a buzzer, because there was no buzzer or security of any kind. A young Muslim woman in black robes and head scarf came down the stairs and glanced at us with enormous brown eyes that showed suspicion until they focused on the logos on our jumpsuits. She nodded and went on. Two Asian teenagers came bouncing down the stairs as we climbed, and never gave us a second glance. Nor did the African woman carrying a load of laundry.

'I've got to remember this,' I muttered to Louis as I followed him toward a cement staircase.

'Plumbing is a beautiful thing,' he replied.

When we reached the fourth floor of the tenement we opened the door into an empty hallway with a rug frayed down to the floorboards. The smells of the place hit me all at once: lamb cooking in garlic and onions, cigarette smoke, marijuana smoke, and the odor of too many people living in tight quarters.

The apartment walls and doors could not have been very thick or insulated, because a general din filled the passage: babies crying, pots banging, men shouting, women shouting back, televisions and music blaring in Arabic and other languages I couldn't identify. It all felt depressing – suffocating, even – and I'd been in the building less than three minutes. Louis said there were people who'd lived in Les Bosquets their entire lives, and I began to understand some of the pressures that contributed to the riots.

But why had Wilkerson's granddaughter come here of all places?

Louis knocked on the door to 412. Several moments later, a woman's voice asked who we were, and Louis replied that we were from Private and had been sent by Kim's grandfather.

A minute passed before a dead bolt was thrown. The door opened on a chain, and a wary woman who looked Polynesian and was wearing a blue skirt and floral blouse looked out at us, and asked to see our identification. We showed it to her, and she shut the door.

Nothing happened for several minutes, and Louis was about to knock again when we heard the chain slide, and the door opened. Louis stepped inside a dimly lit, narrow hallway, and I followed.

The door shut behind us, and I turned to find myself face-to-face with Kimberly Kopchinski. In her late twenties now, wearing jeans, a black blouse, and a rectangular silver thing on a chain around her neck, she was undeniably beautiful in person. But I could tell by the color of her skin and the way she held herself that she'd been through some terrible physical ordeal recently, and that she was very, very frightened.

We introduced ourselves and showed her the badges and identifications.

'How do I know my grandfather sent you?' she asked.

I showed her Sherman's text and the picture of her. Kim stared at the picture for several moments as if she barely remembered the girl in it.

'He says you're in danger,' I said.

'I *am* in danger,' she said.

'He said something about drug dealers?'

'I just need somewhere to go, to disappear for a while,' she said in a strained whisper. 'Can you help me do that?'

'We can,' I replied. 'But it helps if we know who we're hiding you from, Kimberly.'

Her face twisted with inner pain, and she said, 'Call me Kim. And can we have this conversation later? Once I'm somewhere safe? I can't stay here anymore. My friend's husband is coming home from Lyons in a few hours. He doesn't know I'm here, and if he did I'd be...'

Her lower lip quivered.

'Don't worry, Ms. Kopchinski,' Louis said. 'You are under the care and protection of Private Paris now. Already you could not be safer. We'll take you to the same hotel where Jack is staying.'

'A hotel?' Kim said, alarmed. 'No, that's too public.'

Louis said soothingly, 'This hotel is the most discreet in Paris. Already I have you registered there under an alias.'

The Polynesian woman emerged from a doorway at the other end of the hall carrying a canvas bag. She set it down and tapped on her watch.

Kim appeared to be torn, but nodded, and went to the woman. She talked quietly to her for several moments before hugging her. Both women looked distraught when they parted.

Grabbing the bag, Kim said, 'Let's go.'

We got more scrutiny leaving with her than we had when entering, and plenty of hostile glances, but no one challenged us directly. With Kim in the backseat and Louis starting the Mia, I thought we were home free. Thirty minutes from now we'd have her safely in a suite at the Plaza Athénée and I'd be talking to Sherman Wilkerson, trying to figure out a way to get her quickly to L.A.

Louis threw the Mia in gear and was pulling a U-turn to head west toward Paris when head-lights went on a block in front of us. Another set went on half a block behind us.

I didn't think much of it until the car in front of us, a black Renault, pulled out and stopped side-ways across the street. He couldn't block the entire avenue, but there wasn't a whole lot of room to get past him either.

'*Merde*,' Louis said, locking up the brakes on the electric van and throwing us in reverse.

'What's happening?' Kim cried.

'We're not waiting to find out,' I said, twisting around in the seat to look out the rear window and see the other car, a blue Peugeot, coming fast in the other lane.

A bald, pale man in a studded, red leather jacket hung out the passenger-side window. He was aiming a rotary-magazine shotgun.

Chapter 6

Sauvage swelled with pride as he climbed to the second floor of France's fabled War School, the history of the place flickering in his thoughts. In 1750, at the suggestion of Madame de Pompadour, Louis XV founded a military academy for poor young men so they might have a vehicle for bettering their lives. The most prestigious course of study was and is War School.

Almost every major French military figure of the past 225 years has been through a variation of the program, including Napoleon Bonaparte and Charles de Gaulle. Officers who've attended War School have effected radical change before, Sauvage thought, and we will again.

They moved toward a small amphitheater already filling for the day's special lecture: 'Psychological Warfare.'

Though not his specialty, the major looked forward to the talk.

Entering the amphitheater, Sauvage scanned the room and his fellow students – an old recon habit. He thought that even within this elite group of military minds, there was no one here, except him and Mfune, who had the vision, courage, and conviction to attempt something like AB-16.

The rest? They were sheep.

The lecturer that evening was Eliza Greene, a U.S. Army colonel assigned to NATO in Brussels and an expert in the fine art of fragmenting the will of the enemy and turning the hearts and minds of civilians caught up in war.

A few of the techniques and examples the American described fascinated Sauvage, but he ultimately found the lecture lacking and raised his hand to say so.

'Colonel Greene,' Sauvage said. 'Those seem like excellent tactics, but with all due respect, wouldn't psychological warriors such as yourself do well to adopt the techniques of modern marketing, especially the art of branding?'

A short, stocky woman in her forties, Colonel Greene crinkled her brow in response. 'You are...

'Sauvage,' he replied. 'Major Émile Sauvage.'

She nodded, watching him intently. 'How would you do this, Major?'

'By standing for something, Colonel,' Sauvage said. 'Maybe only one thing, but selling that position, that one thing, with a logo, perhaps, to the enemy and civilians long before combat ensued.'

Colonel Greene tilted her head, thought, and said, 'That's really the job of politicians, isn't it? The selling of a war? It isn't until you have troops on the ground and combat begins that psychological techniques really work. Defeating the enemy in battle repeatedly goes a long way toward winning civilian minds.'

Sauvage stood his ground. 'Again, with all due respect, Colonel, have you been on duty in Afghanistan?'

She stiffened and said, 'I have not.'

'I spent four years in Afghanistan with NATO,' Sauvage replied. 'And I can tell you for a fact that the U.S. message there – the branding, if you will – was mixed, garbled, and the old country will just revert to its ingrained ways the second you leave.'

Colonel Greene smiled at him without enthusiasm and said, 'Perhaps you can run a war your way, with branding, logos, and all, when you're a commanding general, Major Sauvage.'

Sauvage found her smugness infuriating. He wanted to tell her off, inform her in no uncertain terms that he already was the commander of a growing army.

But then he felt Mfune's slight elbow nudge, and understood. He couldn't appear to be a fanatic in any way, shape, or form. That was the key to staying undetected as a scout, as a spy, and as a guerrilla warrior.

'I look forward to it,' the major said, sounding reasonable.

But as the colonel returned to her lecture, Sauvage was thinking that someday, after it was all over, he'd track down smug Colonel Greene and spray-paint 'AB-16' all over her know-nothing face.

Chapter 7

The shotgun roared. The rear driver's-side window exploded, throwing bits of glass and causing Kim to scream in terror, and me to dig for the Glock 19.

Louis reacted by showing us his mad skills behind the wheel.

At another time and another place, the head of Private Paris might have driven for a bank robbery crew or as a stuntman in the movies, because that shotgun blast caused him to unleash a series of maneuvers over the course of the next fifteen minutes that left me speechless and shaking.

The second after the side window exploded, Louis ducked down and threw the delivery van into a series of S turns, as if he were a skier in a slalom course, only going backward. Kim's screams had died down to whimpers even as the Peugeot locked up its brakes and came after us in reverse. The Renault, however, was in third gear, in our lane, and coming at us at full throttle.

'Hold on to the handle above the door, Jack, and when I swing, shoot the tires of the closest vehicle!' Louis shouted.

Frantically cranking down the window, I grabbed the handle with my left hand and rested my right on the side-view mirror to steady the gun.

The bald, pale guy hanging out of the Peugeot was in our headlights now, aiming the shotgun left-handed. He touched one off, blowing out one of our headlights and cracking my side of the windshield into spiderwebs.

Louis didn't flinch; instead, he spun the wheel and swung the rear end of the van around into that spur road we'd walked to get deeper into the project. As he did, the Renault floated into my pistol sights at twenty-five yards. I dropped my aim below the passenger-side front fender and squeezed.

The Glock bucked, and the bullet threw sparks off the lower fender. The second shot, however, was on target, and blew out the tire. The Renault swerved right toward the Peugeot, and I tapped the trigger a third time. The driver's-side tire destructed. The front end of the car came down hard on the pavement, peeling strips of smoking rubber that spun crazily through the air.

The Peugeot's rear end struck the Renault's flank, and I was sure the pale shooter was going to sling off like a daredevil from a cannon. But the guy must have had uncanny reflexes and strength, because he managed to hang on.

Louis hit the brakes. We came to a bouncing, screeching halt in front of some of those gang members we'd passed earlier on foot. The whole lot of them were jumping up and down and cheering as if we were the best thing to happen in Les Bosquets in months, maybe years.

One of them yelled something in French that I didn't catch, but Louis did, and he started laughing as he threw the little van into forward again, and pinned the accelerator to the floor. We passed other groups of immigrants who were now screaming those same words at us.

'What are they saying?' I yelled as we shot back out onto Avenue Clichy-sous-Bois, heading opposite the way we'd come in.

'Bad-Ass Plumbers!' Louis said, grinning, a little mania in his eyes.

I started laughing a little myself. Warm, good, crazy – the mix of emotions surging in me felt familiar, as if I was back on a mission in Afghanistan, mainlining on adrenaline, about to land my helicopter and a squad of marines in range of Taliban snipers and rocket grenades. Sometimes it was all about the risk.

Then I realized that I hadn't checked on Kim and that she'd stopped whimpering. Fearing the worst, I twisted around fast and saw that she'd left her seat and gone back into the small cargo area to look out the rear door.

'Are you okay?' I yelled.

There was a flash of headlights behind us.

'Kim?'

She jerked her head around, mascara running down her cheeks, and said, 'They're coming.'

I undid my seat buckle and jumped into the back just as Louis took a hard left. It threw me off my feet and I crashed hard into the wall of the van, briefly stunned, until I saw Kim crawling toward me.

'Are you okay?' she asked, fighting back tears.

Over her shoulder, headlights glared through the rear window. There was a sharp cracking noise and the window blew out, showering us with little chunks of shatterproof glass.

'Get them off of us, Jack!' Louis yelled. 'Before they take our tires!'

That jerked me back fully alert. Scrambling by Kim, I got to the back door. Crouched below the window frame, I reached up and pushed the Glock out the hole the shotgun had made. I tilted the pistol toward the headlights and pulled the trigger twice.

There was a screeching of tires and the headlights retreated.

I can't give you every detail of the chase that ensued in the next few minutes because I haven't the foggiest idea what roads we took or when we turned or where. For me there was only those headlights and trying to shoot them out every time they got close, while Louis tried to shake them.

'Merde!' Louis shouted at one point. 'Hold on!'

Cars skidded and honked all around us.

Cars crashed all around us.

Chapter 8

Louis ran a red light, and we shot up onto National Route 3 south of the town of Sevran. I got up to peer out the hole in the rear window and saw five demolished vehicles in the two hundred yards of road leading to the highway ramp. The Peugeot and the bald guy with the rotary-mag shotgun had somehow gotten through the pileup unscathed. We had put distance between us, but they were still coming, and coming hard.

'You got to go faster!' I yelled.

'I'm going as fast as a Mia goes!' Louis shouted. 'Sixty-eight top speed.'

We were screwed. I didn't know the top speed of the Peugeot, but it was a safe bet it was a whole lot more than sixty-eight. Kim must have been thinking much the same thing, because she shouted, 'How far can we go?'

'Fifty-two more miles,' Louis said. 'Plenty of power.'

I stood in the back of the van now, left hand pressed against the roof, and punched out the rest of the glass with the butt of the Glock. The Peugeot was back there less than a quarter of a mile, weaving through traffic.

Louis managed to stay ahead of them through the interchange onto autoroute 4, a three-lane freeway heading south. But the additional lane thinned traffic and the Peugeot took advantage of it, charging after us at eighty, ninety miles an hour. The crazy pale guy hanging out the window didn't seem to care when I shot at him and missed.

He raised the shotgun with one hand. I dropped just in time. Buckshot clanked and pinged off the rear door. I was going to jump up and return fire but then noticed that the Glock's slide was locked open. The pistol was empty.

I pivoted, stayed low, and duckwalked past Kim, who was on the floor of the van, holding tight to the legs of the jump seat with her eyes closed. Louis was hunched over the wheel like some pinball wizard. Grabbing the backs of the two front seats to stabilize myself, I said, 'I'm out of ammo. I need your–'

'No time,' Louis barked as he cut the Mia hard left into the fast lane before the Peugeot could get up alongside us again.

In the next moment, everything seemed to move slower, and I was hyperaware of everything around us. There was a blood-red BMW coupe in our lane, three car lengths in front of us, just beyond the nose of a blue flatbed truck to our

44

immediate right. Beyond the truck, in the far right lane and two car lengths ahead, a woman in a silver Mercedes sedan was singing with her radio. To our left the guardrail flickered in the headlights of the Peugeot, which was closing in fast.

We started up a rise. The flatbed downshifted and slowed. The BMW sped up, opening space. In the rearview, the bald, pale guy was aiming for our tires, and I held on tight, figuring we might be crashing in the next few seconds.

Without warning, Louis wrenched the wheel to his right. The bald guy shot and missed us, hitting the BMWs tires instead. Our right rear quarter panel brushed the front bumper of the flatbed, which sent us careering into a clockwise 360-degree slide across the freeway.

It was surreal and blurred, almost like being in a helicopter when it's going down. I held on for dear life, sure we were going to roll or collide hard with that Mercedes in the far right lane.

But Louis made a quick cut with the wheel and we missed broadsiding the Mercedes by inches. The van straightened out and we shot up the exit ramp for the D34 highway heading east.

I was shaking head to toe as we merged into Paris-bound traffic. In all my life I'd never seen a gutsier move than that one. Boxed inside the fast lane by the slower flatbed and the crippled BMW the guys in the Peugeot never had a chance of following us.

Louis clenched his fist and smiled his wild smile at me again.

'That, Jack,' he said proudly, 'is how a plumber drives in Paris.'

I laughed, but then heard Kim Kopchinski say in a strained voice, 'They knew I was there. How did they know? How could they?'

'Don't worry, Mademoiselle Kopchinski,' Louis said. 'I'll call some friends at La Crim. Get you protection that–'

'No!' Kim shouted. 'You call in the police and you might as well shoot me right here, right now.'

Chapter 9

8TH ARRONDISSEMENT
8:30 P.M.

Louis Langlois pulled us over on the Rue du Boccador. A man wearing a white chef's shirt and apron smoked a cigarette to one side of an open door, and a petite woman in a neat gray suit waited on the other side. Louis waved to her, and she made a small beckoning motion.

'Her name is Elodie,' Louis said. 'She takes care of everything, Jack.'

'What is this place?' Wilkerson's granddaughter asked before I slid back the Mia's side door.

'Kitchen entrance to Alain Ducasse's restaurant at the Plaza Athénée,' Louis said. 'That door gives us access to the room service elevator. No one will know you are here. It's how the famous and the infamous go in and out.'

Kim hesitated and then nodded to me. I opened the door and we moved quickly toward the hotel's rear entrance. I'd stripped off the plumber's coverall and retrieved my blue blazer so I fit in somewhat at the ritzy address in the heart of Paris's fashion center. But Kim looked as though she'd been sleeping in her old clothes for days.

Elodie didn't seem to care. 'Bonsoir, Monsieur Morgan,' she said brightly, and then bowed to Kim. 'Madame.'

The chef, a lean, handsome guy in his thirties, stubbed out his cigarette, smiled, and gestured toward the open door and the sounds of pans and dishes rattling. 'Please,' he said.

Elodie led the way inside, and within seconds we were weaving through a state-of-the-art kitchen and a feverish pack of young men and women in white toques cleaning up after the evening service. Several of the kitchen staff glanced our way, but then saw the chef coming behind us and returned to their jobs with renewed vigor.

Elodie took us to a service elevator and punched the button for the eighth floor.

'At Monsieur Langlois's request, Monsieur Morgan, we have moved your things to a new suite with two bedrooms and a generous sitting area,' she said. 'You're lucky we had it available. Several Saudi princesses are arriving with their entourage tomorrow and will take over the entire seventh floor.'

'That work?' I asked Kim.

Hugging her chest as if suddenly cold, she nodded, but it was with little enthusiasm. We got out on eight and trailed Elodie to a door.

'A beautiful suite,' Elodie said, sliding an

electronic key card.

She pushed open the door and we entered a spacious living area with black-and-white art deco furniture and French doors that opened onto a small balcony.

'You have a view of the Eiffel Tower from the balcony and your bedroom,' Elodie told Kim.

'Storybook,' I said.

Kim said, 'This looks like the room Carrie stayed in during the last few episodes of *Sex and the City.*'

The concierge laughed. 'No, that's down on seven, and almost always reserved, I'm afraid. The Saudi women love staying there.'

Elodie quickly showed us the suite's features, and left us with assurances that we could call her anytime during the night, and that room service was available twenty-four hours a day. After she left, I went through the place again, checking the windows and doors, including a locked one that Elodie said led to a third bedroom, should we need it.

Kim, meanwhile, had gone to the minibar and opened two splits of Stolichnaya vodka. She poured them both in a glass, took a long draw, shuddered, and carried it and her knapsack out onto the balcony.

I used the toilet, picked up a menu, and heard a knock at the door. Louis lumbered in, scratching at his salt-and-pepper beard, looking as though he'd just been roused from sleep instead of jacked up after a high-speed car chase.

'She say anything yet?' he asked quietly.

'Just giving her a little space,' I replied.

We went to the open doors to the balcony, finding Kim looking at the Eiffel Tower and putting an unlit cigarette to her lips. She unsnapped that silver rectangular jewelry piece from the chain around her neck and pressed at it with her thumb. A lid shot back, revealing the workings of a lighter.

She thumbed it to a flame and took two deep drags off the cigarette before Louis said, 'You want to tell us about it?'

Kim turned and looked at us with that glassy, faraway stare I'd seen on marines I was airlifting out of combat.

'I'd rather not tonight,' she said. 'I just need to sleep.'

I said, 'If you don't tell us what's going on, we can't protect you.'

She drained the vodka and said, 'In the end, no one can protect me, and if I tell you, no one will be able to protect you either.'

'But no one knows where you are now,' Louis said.

'It doesn't matter,' Kim said, pushing by us. She got both splits of Glenlivet scotch this time.

'You made it sound as if police are involved in your problem.'

'If you get them involved, I'll have another problem.'

I sighed in exasperation. 'You're not looking out for yourself.'

Her laugh was hard and short. 'That's where you're wrong, Jack. I most definitely *am* looking out for myself. Now, if you don't mind, I'm going to go enjoy my view of the Eiffel Tower, take a

49

shower, and get some sleep.'

She went into her bedroom and shut the doors behind her.

Chapter 10

For several moments I thought about barging in on her and demanding that she tell us what was going on. We'd damn near died coming to her rescue. We had a right to know.

I saw Louis's frustration and said, 'Why don't you go home, my friend? I'll take the night shift.'

'I have a man outside, and I'll be back first thing in the morning,' he said, handing me a new loaded magazine for the Glock and then leaving.

The shower was still running on Kim's end of the suite when I ordered a strip steak and *pommes frites* from room service. I'd no sooner hung up than my cell phone rang. Sherman Wilkerson was calling.

'Do you have her?' he asked, sounding anxious.

'I do. She's fine. Taking a shower.'

'She's terrified, Jack. Am I wrong?'

'No, you're right.'

'Did she say why?'

'Not yet.'

'Can you protect her?'

I chewed the inside of my cheek, and considered informing him of the gun battle and car chase that had ensued after we took Kim from Les Bosquets housing project, but I knew it would only worry him.

'We can, but how long are we talking about?'

'As long as it takes,' Wilkerson said. 'In Paris, and back here in Malibu.'

'Sherman, with all due respect, that could get very expensive.'

'I don't care what it costs,' he shot back. 'For that I'll pay anything.'

'Okay, Sherman,' I said. 'I just needed to understand the ground rules.'

'Is there anything I can do on this end to help?'

'I'll call tomorrow once I've had a chance to talk to her.'

'Don't worry about the time difference. And tell her I love her, Jack.'

'I'll do that, Sherman,' I said, and heard the line click.

I checked my watch. It was 10:30 p.m., which was 1:30 p.m. back in Los Angeles. I hesitated, punched in Justine Smith's number, and waited.

Justine used to work as a psychologist on contract with the criminal justice system in L.A. But a few years back she came to work at Private, where she has become one of our best investigators. And once upon a time, before I screwed it all up, we were lovers. Now she was seeing Emilio Cruz, another of my operators in Los Angeles. It had been awkward between the three of us for nearly six months now, and the second I heard Justine's voice I realized nothing had changed since I'd been overseas.

'Jack?' Justine said.

Even over the static on the international connection, her voice filled me with a sense of regret, of things that could have been if I hadn't been such a stubborn idiot and let her walk out of that part of my life.

'Hey,' I said. 'You holding down the fort?'

'No barbarians at the gate, if that's what you mean,' Justine replied. 'I finished up the Dawson case. And Del Rio is handling the CTI thing.'

Rick Del Rio was my closest friend. We'd crash-landed together in the marines and he'd been with me from the day I launched Private. Del Rio broke his back the previous fall, and had only just returned to work.

'How's he doing?' I asked.

'You can see he's still in some pain, but damned if he'll tell anyone,' Justine replied.

'Cruz?'

There was a moment of silence before she said, 'He's in Phoenix. His mother has breast cancer.'

'Tell him my prayers are with him and his mother.'

'I'll do that,' she said. 'Thanks.'

I told her about Sherman Wilkerson and his granddaughter.

'Sounds like she's been through something traumatic,' she said.

'Yeah, I wish you were here, to see if you could get her to open up.'

'You telling me to pack my trousseau and fly to Paris?'

'Sorry,' I said. 'I need you there to work the L.A. end of this. I want you to take a team to Sherman's home and office. Look for signs he could be under surveillance.'

'By who? French drug dealers?'

'Honestly, Justine, I'm still trying to figure that out.'

When I hung up, the shower was still running at Kim's end of the suite. She'd been in there almost thirty minutes. But then again, I could see her wanting a long hot shower before crashing.

A knock came at the door. Room service. The attendant wheeled in a cart, and made a racket lifting the metal covers over the plates, showing me a prime steak with béarnaise sauce, fresh asparagus, and crisp shoestring fries.

I noticed the shower was off when I settled down to my meal. The meat was tender, and the fries were out of this world: crunchy outside and soft inside, not even the hint of oil. So when I finished every last bit of it, and washed the meal down with a cold Coca-Cola, I was evidently a rare man in Paris: a truly happy camper.

And then I wasn't.

Over the street sounds echoing through the open balcony doors, I caught poor Kim Kopchinski's muffled sobs. They were coming from deep in her gut, and made me feel horrible, made me wonder what in God's name had happened to her and who the pale psycho with the shotgun was.

I went to the door and raised my hand to knock, to comfort her if I could.

But her sobbing ebbed to painful moans that reminded me of my mother's when she'd locked herself in her bedroom after fights with my drunken father.

I dropped my hand and did what I'd done for my mother back when I was a boy. I stood guard at the door until the moaning died out altogether.

PART TWO

AB-16

Chapter 11

9TH ARRONDISSEMENT
APRIL 7, 1:45 A.M.

Émile Sauvage left the Chaussée d'Antin Métro station. The major had changed from his army uniform and now wore a dark brown fedora, a thigh-length black leather jacket, and dark pants, gloves, and rubber-soled shoes. He noted to his satisfaction that the lens of the CCTV cameras inside and outside had been sprayed with fresh black paint.

Well done, Epée.

Walking briskly west on Boulevard Haussmann, Sauvage felt jittery, like a junkie in need of a fix. The major had spent most of his career in reconnaissance. For years he had led an elite NATO scout squad that probed the enemy's front lines. The job was not only to find and document Taliban or Al-Qaeda positions but also to draw fire from their defenses.

It took nerves of titanium and a love of *la pagaille,* a French military slang word that means 'chaos in battle.' Sauvage had both traits, and in spades.

The major had been in thirteen full-on gun battles in Afghanistan. Other officers, lesser officers, had withered when bullets flew or they saw men dying around them. But Sauvage thrived

57

under such pressure, excelled because he had almost instantly become addicted to the sensations of war.

Man against man. Kill or be killed. It was all primal and pure, and he loved it. Especially when the fight was over something that he believed in or opposed.

Like tonight.

Sauvage kept to the shadows thrown by the triangular-shaped Société Générale building to his immediate left and by the massive Galeries Lafayette shopping center on the other side of the boulevard. The sidewalks on both sides of the boulevard were largely empty, save for the lone pedestrian or two. And the few cars that passed all seemed in a rush to be somewhere else.

At the west end of the block, where the boulevard gave way to a traffic roundabout, Captain Mfune was coming in his direction, dressed in civilian clothes. As they walked past each other, the captain said, 'They went in twenty minutes ago. I'll give you three.'

'All I need,' Sauvage said, and kept on.

At the west end of the Société building, Sauvage affected a drunken manner and wove to his left, toward the back of the Palais Garnier, the older and more famous of the two opera houses in Paris. The front of the opera house, which faced the Avenue de l'Opéra, was famously ornate and opulent in the beaux arts style. But the architecture at the rear of the building was drabber, almost plain.

Still, Sauvage took it all in as he crossed the Rue Gluck toward the back gate to the palace. The palace was set well back from the street, and the roof of the main hall dropped away almost six stories to the roof of the backstage area, which had two wings jutting off it, one to each side. On the walls of the wings, long banners promoted upcoming performances of Handel's *Giulio Cesare*. Between the wings there was a courtyard protected by a tall curving wall interrupted by three iron gates.

The first gate was closed, as was the middle one, which was the largest of the three. The far gate, however – the one closest to the Rue Scribe – was open. Only a narrow traffic control arm blocked the way.

Sauvage had the hood of his raincoat up and sang a drunken song as he walked past the gate, aware of the security guard sitting in a booth there, but not paying him a bit of attention.

The major had taken five strides past the gate when there was a soft thud somewhere behind him. He slowed, glanced over his shoulder, and saw the first flames rising off the roof of the Galeries Lafayette.

Chapter 12

Sauvage pivoted and stood there, watching the flames grow taller and wider. Seconds later, the opera security guard was running across the island in the rotary toward the shopping center, his cell phone pressed to his ear.

The major dodged into the gate and vaulted the

traffic control arm. He used a tiny can of hair spray to coat the lens of the security camera mounted on the security booth and kept moving. Sauvage ran toward the rear wall of the opera house's backstage area.

The major dashed upstairs, hearing the first sirens in the distance, and sprayed the camera above a door. It opened. He slipped inside and softly shut the door behind him. Immediately, the sirens were gone, silenced by the opera house's thick acoustical walls.

Sauvage heard only the clicking of a woman's high heels now. He turned and saw Haja Hamid in the security lights. Her hair was dyed red and pinned up. She wore stiletto heels and a tight, black sleeveless dress that showed off the iron worker's powerful muscles. Haja glanced back over her shoulder at the major, revealing ruby lips and eyes that were no longer ice gray, but as brilliantly blue as tanzanite.

Sauvage got out a folding pocketknife with a razor-sharp blade and nodded to her. Gesturing onward with her chin, she led Sauvage through several turns in dark hallways before halting when a man's voice echoed from just ahead.

'Mariama?' he called. 'Are you there?'

'Coming, Henri,' Haja called.

She held her hand behind her, signaling to Sauvage to creep along, even as she sped up, her heels cracking off the wood floor until he could no longer see her. The major slipped off his shoes, leaving him in a pair of thin neoprene socks. He locked the knife's blade open, and then went on as a dog might, pausing to listen for sound, sniffing the air, feeling his way forward until he reached the wings off the stage, where only apron lights glowed.

'My God,' Henri said. 'Look at you. You're a goddess.'

Haja laughed and said, 'You're sure we won't be bothered here?'

'By who?' He chuckled. 'The guards? They wouldn't dare.'

The major eased up to one of the curtains. His left gloved hand found the ropes that controlled it before he peeked around the curtain. Haja stood about ten feet away at the head of an Egyptian-looking couch. She faced a tall, patrician man coming toward her in an expensive suit, no tie. He carried a bottle of champagne and two glasses.

'Pour me some, *chéri*,' Haja said.

'With pleasure, my dear,' he replied.

Sauvage took that as his cue. Slipping fully behind the curtain, he reached up and, with the blade, cut the curtain rope just above his hand. Holding that end, he crouched and cut the rope again where it passed through a floor pulley, giving him about three feet in total.

He heard the cork pop and champagne pouring.

'Come,' Haja said. 'Sit by me.'

Henri made a murmur of approval. The divan creaked under his added weight. 'What shall we drink to?' he asked.

'The future,' she said.

'The future,' he said, and glasses clinked. 'You are my muse, you know.'

'So you said.'

Hearing them sip, the major dared not move, and fought to slow his breath and heart as he unlocked the blade and slid it back in his pocket. Then he wrapped the rope around both of his gloved hands with fourteen inches of slack between, and waited.

'I've thought about nothing but you all week,' Henri said. 'It's been maddening we couldn't meet, and ... you know.'

'We needed a break,' Haja replied. 'Kiss me?'

'With the greatest pleasure.'

Haja made a purr of contentment. There was a rustle of fabric, and Sauvage made his move, sliding out from behind the curtain. He spotted Henri on the couch, back turned in Haja's embrace.

Stealthy and supple, the major took four silent steps up behind him.

Haja broke the kiss, laughed throatily, and pushed Henri back several inches. It was all Sauvage needed. He flipped the rope over the man's head and wrenched it tight beneath his chin.

Henri began to struggle, his hands flying to the rope as he let out a squeal of disbelief and fear. The choked man kicked over the champagne bottle and one of the glasses. The major ruthlessly wrenched him off the divan and onto the stage floor.

'No,' Henri wheezed. 'Please.'

Sauvage realized he was saying this to Haja.

But Haja only had eyes for the major as she rose from the couch and the older man's struggles subsided into quivers and then death.

'You are a revolutionary, Émile,' she said as he lowered the dead man until he lay on his side. 'A man on the right side of history.'

Twenty minutes later, they shut down the apron lights and made their way to the rear door of the backstage area. Sauvage opened it a crack and saw the security post still empty and cops, the guard, and other bystanders across the traffic circle watching firemen up on ladders, spraying down the smoking roof of the Galeries Lafayette.

No one gave them a second glance when he and Haja slipped out the gate and strolled up the Rue Scribe, arm in arm and heads tilted inward, like lovers heading home after a nice late night on the town.

Chapter 13

Several sharp knocks woke me.

Sweat poured off my head and I looked around wildly, realizing I was on the couch in the living room of my suite at the Plaza.

The knock came again. I glanced at my watch. Two minutes to seven.

'Coming,' I grunted, and got up to pad across the carpet to the door. I heard the shower start up again in Kim Kopchinski's end of the suite.

I looked through the peek hole. Louis Langlois was out in the hallway behind a room service cart laden with baskets of croissants and delicate pastries, and two carafes of coffee that immediately piqued my interest.

'I didn't know room service was part of your

job description,' I said after opening the door to let him in.

'It's not,' Louis said. 'But I adore the croissants here, so perfectly buttery and flaky, you know? I just could not wait for you to make the order.'

When we returned to the living area, Louis began pouring us coffee. 'She talk?'

'Never left her bedroom,' I said.

'What's she been doing?'

'Showering, crying, sleeping, and now showering again.'

'Perhaps she is a compulsive obsessive?' Louis asked before taking a big bite of the croissant that melted his face into pure contentment.

'You ask her that,' I said before tearing off a piece of croissant and popping it in my mouth. The taste was simply incredible, not like the stuff you get back in the States, even in the best of bakeries.

'You like these, yes?'

'Extraordinary.' I said, chewing and then taking a long sip of perfect café au lait. 'God, how is it possible that the French eat like this every day and don't weigh three hundred pounds?'

'That is a cultural secret I am bound to keep,' Langlois said. He laughed and then sobered after glancing at the door to Kim's room. 'I suspect she has been abused.'

'Why would you think that?'

Louis drank more coffee and then said, 'Many times when I have interviewed poor victims of such abuse, I have found that we could not collect evidence from their bodies because they had scrubbed them so clean.'

I looked at the closed door, wondered if that

was the case. It would certainly explain why she'd been so reluctant to talk to us.

'Maybe we should bring in one of the women in your office,' I said. 'Make her more comfortable.'

Louis shook half a croissant at me and said, 'A good idea. I'll see to it at once.'

He finished the pastry, drank down more coffee, got out his cell, and punched in the number for Private Paris. Interested to see what was going on back in the States on CNN, I turned on the television, getting instead a commercial for cheese on TF1, a French station. I was about to change the channel when the commercial ended and the screen switched to a Paris street scene at night. A crowd watched firemen spraying the roof of a smoking building.

'Garde will be here in half an hour,' Louis said. 'She's excellent.'

'What's going on here?' I said, gesturing at the television.

He stepped up beside me, listened, and then said, 'A fire last night at the Galeries Lafayette. No one was injured. Must be a slow news day.'

I looked from the television back to the closed doors to Kim's bedroom. The shower was still going.

Walking to the doors, I knocked lightly and called, 'Kim?'

I waited and then knocked louder, and called, 'Kim, we have breakfast out here for you. Could you come out?'

Hearing nothing in return, I glanced at Langlois, who squinted and then made a twisting motion with his right hand. I found the door locked, so I knocked loud enough to be heard easily over the falling water. Nothing again.

'God help me if she's cut her wrists in there,' I said, pulling out my electronic key card and jimmying the lock.

It took me less than fifteen seconds to pry back the hasp and push open the door to find a rumpled bed, an open window, and a closed bathroom door. I almost went to the door to knock again, but I noticed a note on a piece of hotel stationery sitting on the dresser.

Scrawled in big letters, it said, 'Tell my grandfather I'm sorry to have bothered him in troubles of my own making. I'm sorry to everyone.'

Chapter 14

'Son-of-a-bitch,' I groaned, sure that she'd gone and done it – committed suicide on me.

I wrenched open the bathroom door and was enveloped in steam. The bathtub was empty. So was the shower.

'She's running,' Louis said behind me.

'Impossible,' I said, rushing out. 'How could she have gotten out of here?'

'The window?' He was already heading that way.

But we were eighty feet up. She'd have to be a human fly.

What about that locked door to that other bedroom? I ran to it, tried the knob, but found it still locked and no sign that the lock had been picked.

Then I noticed the chair in the closet. It faced shelves and drawers and, high on the closet wall, an air duct, which was missing its grate. The hole would have been impossible for me or Louis to squeeze through. But Kim Kopchinski was certainly small enough.

But could she get out? Or was she still in the ductwork somewhere?

Jumping up on the chair, I peered into the duct and saw, ten or twelve feet away, a thick beam of light shining in where another grate had been.

'Damn it,' I snapped, and jumped off the chair, finding Louis searching the bedroom. 'She used the air system to get next door. But I heard her turn on the shower right before you knocked. She can't be ten minutes ahead of us.'

Louis yanked out his phone again, punched in a number, and began barking questions in French. I went out into the living area, grabbed my shoes, and laced them quickly.

Louis stuck his phone in his pocket and started moving fast toward the suite door, saying, 'My man outside, Farad, saw a woman matching Kim's description leave the hotel ten minutes ago and head north. If she has not taken a taxi, we can catch her.'

We bolted from the suite, ran to the stairs, and took them two at a time, emerging in the wide hallway between the hotel lobby and the dining room. A maître d' holding breakfast menus smiled and then frowned when we sprinted by him toward the lobby.

But an absolutely huge man in a $5,000 blue suit got in our way. He was at least six foot five and

230 pounds of solid muscle, with a thin beard and mustache, and there was a twisting coil of tubing running up his neck to the back of his ear.

'I'm sorry. You can't enter the lobby just yet,' he said in a Texas twang.

'We have to get outside!' Louis cried. 'What is this?'

'We have members of the Saudi royal family checking in. I'm sorry, sir. As I understand it, you may exit through the Dior spa downstairs.'

Rather than argue, we turned and bolted, with Louis telling our ride where to meet us. We emerged from the spa a few moments later, and a BMW sedan skidded up in front of the hotel. We jumped in.

Louis yelled, 'Go. Head for George V Métro.'

The driver, whom I'd met only the day before, was Ali Farad, a former investigator with the French National Police based in Marseille. In addition to speaking six languages, Farad had been trained in anti-terror and drove like it. He wove us through the streets toward the George V Métro station, which Louis said lay in the direction Kim Kopchinski had gone in.

We almost caught her.

Her hair and clothes were still dusty from the ductwork when I spotted her crossing the Avenue George V toward the Champs-Élysees and the Métro entrance. Jumping from the moving car, I raced after her.

Cars skidded and horns blared at me as I dodged out into heavy morning traffic. Kim heard the commotion, looked over her shoulder, saw me, and started running as well, but in the other direction.

Crossing the southbound lane on the Avenue George V, a work truck appeared out of nowhere and damn near clipped me. I was forced to halt, gasping and angry. 'Kim!' I shouted.

She never broke stride and disappeared into the Métro station. I got there less than thirty seconds later, vaulted the turnstiles, and sprinted toward the sounds of screeching metal and pneumatic doors whooshing open.

I hit an intersection in the tunnel where I had to decide on northbound or southbound platforms.

I chose south.

It was the correct platform.

But by the time I pounded down the stairs and reached it, the train doors were shutting on Kim who waved at me sadly and mouthed the words, 'Good-bye, Jack.'

'C'mon!' I shouted. 'Really?'

When I ran back out the exit, breathing hard, I found Louis standing there, his cell phone pressed to his ear. He looked pale when he spotted me, held up a finger, and said, 'Yes, of course, Evangeline. I'll go there right now.'

He hung up. 'You catch her?'

Pissed off, I said, 'She went southbound. Maybe we can still find her.'

Louis shook his head. 'We don't know where she is going. And Private Paris has just been called in on a delicate case.'

'Louis,' I began, 'Sherman Wilkerson is one of our biggest clients, and–'

'Jack, you are the boss. I know this. But it is clear

to me that Kim Kopchinski is a grown woman who does not want our protection,' Langlois said firmly. 'So for the time, while *you* may go on a silly goose chase after her, I am going to the Palais Garnier. Henri Richard, the director of the Paris Opera and an esteemed member of L'Académie Française, has been found there, murdered. We have been hired to help the police find out why.'

Trying to slow my breath and still pissed off about losing Kim, I said, 'By who? His wife?'

'Come, Jack,' Louis said wearily. 'This is Paris. That was Richard's mistress, Evangeline, who just phoned me.'

Chapter 15

6TH ARRONDISSEMENT
9A.M.

Gasping for air and sweating, Sauvage rolled off Haja for the second time since they'd returned from the opera house to the small flat where he lived.

Haja propped herself up on one elbow. 'Satisfied?'

'More than satisfied,' Sauvage said, lying on his back. 'You're a genius.'

'I pleased you,' she said. 'I'm glad. It pleases me.'

The major glanced over at her. Her hair was still red from the evening before, but she'd taken out the contact lenses that had turned her eyes so electrically blue. Now they were back to that ice-gray color, which made her look even more striking. She was smiling, but he caught the envy in her expression.

'Is it ever satisfying for you?' he asked.

'In a way,' she said, tightening and looking away.

'I'm sorry.'

'Don't be,' Haja replied. 'You had nothing to do with it.'

Sauvage hugged her and said, 'You'll get your revenge.'

'It's so close I can taste it like salt.'

The major looked down at her again, and he felt that thing about her that had attracted him almost immediately, that thing that excited him every time he was with her. Haja gave off the sense that she was a true nomad, unfettered by rules, laws, and convention, as if she were limitless, as if there were no boundaries to what she'd say, and no telling what she might do at any given moment. In many ways, she was the most alluring woman he'd ever known.

Haja moved away from him, rose naked from the bed. He watched her cross the room toward the bathroom, her back and arms as powerful as a swimmer's, her legs and bum as firm as a sprinter's.

'Where are you going?' he asked.

'To meet Epée. And you have class in forty minutes.'

The major groaned, looked at his watch, realized she was right. Getting up from the bed a few minutes later, he padded past the bathroom, where she was already rinsing. He joined her, seeing that her hair was no longer red at all and significantly darker, almost back to that deep mahogany color he loved.

'No one would ever recognize you,' Sauvage said.

'Funny that something so superficial as color blinds people.'

'It will be on the news soon.'

'I know.'

'You're ready?'

'I was ready when I turned twelve.'

'Where will I find you later?'

'At the factory. Working on the beast.'

'Have you figured out how to make it burn?'

She smiled. 'Yes, I think so.'

'See?' the major said, taking her in his arms. 'I said you were a genius.'

Chapter 16

9TH ARRONDISSEMENT
9:30 A.M.

The street in front of the Galeries Lafayette remained cordoned off. The air still stank of smoke, and there were firemen still working up on the roof. Then I saw the yellow sawhorse and tape across the rear gate of the opera house, which made me wonder how we were going to get inside the crime scene.

'Make nothing of it, Jack,' Louis said when I asked. 'There is only one investigator with La Crim who might try to keep me out. The others I've known and worked with for years. They trust Private and they trust me.'

At the barrier, a police officer stopped us, but then Louis and I showed him identification. He got on his radio. A few minutes later, the officer shook his head.

'What?' Louis said, acting offended. 'Who is the *investigateur* in charge?'

'Hoskins,' the officer replied.

'*Merde,*' Louis said.

'Don't tell me,' I said. 'The one detective?'

'The one,' Louis said, his face twisting in annoyance.

'What's he got against you?'

'She,' Louis corrected. 'And hell has no fury like the woman scorned.'

'You scorned her?'

'No, of course not,' he replied testily. 'But we had an affair shortly after she came to Paris, an affair that didn't turn out as she wished, and she does not let me forget it.'

'So what do we do?'

'What any man in my position would do,' Louis said. 'I will – how do you say? – gravel.'

'Grovel,' I said.

'That one,' Louis said, digging out his phone again.

He turned and walked away from me, going to stand against the Société Générale building, hunched over as if preparing for blows to his upper back. He listened and then put his palm to

73

his forehead just before my cell rang.

'This is Jack,' I said.

The line crackled before Justine said, 'I'm at Sherman Wilkerson's place in Malibu. Someone broke in and trashed the place. Sherman must have walked in on them. It's bad, Jack. They beat him. He's unconscious, bleeding from his ears and nose. Del Rio called in Life Flight. They'll be here in five minutes. He'll be with the neurologists at UCLA Medical in twelve.'

'Jesus Christ,' I groaned.

'What do you want us to do?'

I paused, trying to collect my thoughts.

'Jack?' Justine said.

'I'm here,' I said. 'Once he's in the air, and before you call the sheriff, go through the place, very low impact. Try to figure out what's missing without screwing up the scene. I figure you've got an hour before you absolutely have to put in the call. Use it well, and look for anything to do with France.'

'We can do that.'

'Keep me posted,' I said, and hung up, hating the fact that I was eight thousand miles from Los Angeles and unable to help, and wondering if the break-in and assault were connected to Kim. Had to be.

Louis tapped me on the back and, with a weary smile, said, 'We're in.'

'You grovel well,' I said.

'One of my many talents,' Louis agreed. 'But it was your name that did the trick. She wants your take on the murder scene.'

Before I could ask why that could possibly be,

74

the officer at the barrier pulled a sawhorse aside for us. We walked to a rear door, where crime scene techs were working and a woman in her early forties was waiting.

Fit and attractive, Hoskins had spiked, frosted hair and wore jeans, a pink blouse, and a brown leather jacket. Her Paris Prefecture badge hung on a chain around her neck. She shot Louis a look that could melt ice, and then smiled at me.

She shook my hand firmly, saying, 'Sharen Hoskins. Nice to meet you, Mr. Morgan. I've read and heard a lot about you and your company.'

To my surprise, Hoskins's accent was not French. In fact, I swore it sounded like the Bronx. But before I could ask about that unlikelihood, she turned to Louis.

'You don't touch a thing inside. Are we clear on that, Louis?'

'It will be as if I have leprosy. No fingers to speak of.'

'Nice image,' Hoskins said sourly. She handed us booties and latex gloves, saying, 'Nothing of what you are about to see gets out. Understood?'

'I guarantee it,' I replied. 'But I'm a little confused as to why we're being allowed in here in the first place.'

'You are said to be a smart, observant guy, Mr. Morgan,' she replied before leading us inside. 'And I don't believe in turf wars. Long as I put the handcuffs on whoever did this, I'll be a happy girl.'

We followed her down a long series of hallways before exiting a door into a stunning foyer, with a dramatic vaulted ceiling, huge mirrors, and gold paint that shimmered in the light of what looked like gas lamps. A grand marble staircase rose to a landing before splitting and climbing again.

Hoskins started up the first flight, and I followed, saying, 'Why does this seem so familiar to me?'

'*Phantom of the Opera?*' Hoskins said.

'That's it,' I said, looking around in some awe. My late mother had taken my brother and me to see the play when we were boys.

'Where was the body found?' Louis asked. 'Richard's office?'

'Not so lucky,' the *investigateur* said, and crossed the landing between statues that supported a marble slab inscribed 'Amphitheater.'

We went through double doors and emerged in a horseshoe-shaped and lofty space decorated in gold and deep reds. A giant chandelier glowed overhead, revealing the incredible design and sheer opulence of the theater.

'Where's the body?' I asked.

'I wanted you to see him just as he was discovered,' she said, and barked a command into a radio.

The curtains began to open. The area behind it was shadowed until a spotlight went on above and behind us, throwing a beam aimed into the air ten feet above the center of the stage.

'You don't see that every day,' I said softly.

'Exactly,' Hoskins replied.

Chapter 17

Henri Richard's corpse hung upside down from a rope tied about his ankles. His white dress shirt had come free of his suit pants and hung bunched up around his lower rib cage. A length of rope dangled from his neck.

Other ropes were lashed to his wrists and held his arms directly out to the sides. All the blood in his body had responded to gravity and had rushed to the opera director's head. His face was bug-eyed and dark purple.

'Who found him and when?' I asked.

'A security guard shortly after the shift change at six a.m.,' Investigateur Hoskins replied. 'The guards on duty last night said Richard arrived on foot at the rear gate at around twelve thirty with an exotic redhead half his age.'

'Why do so many Parisian tales begin with a younger woman?' Louis asked.

Hoskins ignored him and said, 'Because she was with Richard, the guards didn't ask for her identification, and she managed to keep her face turned from the security tapes we've reviewed.'

'So she's your killer?' I asked skeptically. 'That's a big man. It would take a woman of Amazonian proportions to hoist him up like that.'

Hoskins tilted her head as if reappraising me before saying, 'Yes, and it would take an Amazon to strangle *monsieur le directeur* with a length of rope cut from one of the curtains. It appears she had one or more accomplices.'

'Is that fact or conjecture?' Louis asked.

The investigator directed her answer to me. 'After the fire broke out across the street, the security guard forgot all about Monsieur Richard and his mystery date. But the tapes from the security cameras at the gate and above that stage door we came through indicate that someone sprayed the lenses with a gel of some kind shortly after the fire started.'

'So the fire was a diversion?' I said.

'That's what I'm thinking.'

'Motive?'

'None that we understand at the moment.'

'Meaning what?' Louis asked.

'Meaning there's more to this scene than you can see from back here,' Hoskins said curtly before marching down the aisle.

We followed her past plush red orchestra seats to stairs that climbed the left side of the stage. I could see high above us that the other end of the rope tied to Richard's ankles had been lashed to a catwalk that gave access to scrims and over-head lights. The ropes that held the opera direc-tor's arms at ninety degrees to the body were tied to light poles at the left and right of the stage.

Hoskins halted just shy of the corpse.

'There's your motivation,' she said, gesturing to the stage floor.

I came around her with Louis trailing and stopped, seeing for the first time the looping, bloodred graffiti that would torment Paris in the coming days.

AB-16

Chapter 18

I studied the tag, then looked almost straight up at the opera director's corpse. Henri Richard's eyes seemed to stare directly down at the graffiti.

'What does it mean?' I asked. 'AB-16? Some French thing?'

'We have no idea,' Hoskins said. 'Or at least *I* have no idea. Yet. But tell me, Mr. Morgan, what does it all suggest to *you?* This mystery woman Henri was with. The fire diversion across the street so her accomplice could enter. The weapon. The setting. The position of the body post-mortem. And this graffiti.'

Louis cleared his throat and said, 'I'll tell you what I think.'

'I didn't ask for your opinion, Louis,' Hoskins said brusquely. 'I'm interested in an L.A. perspective for the moment.'

Langlois puffed up in irritation but bit his tongue when I gave him an almost imperceptible shake of my chin and said, 'From an L.A. perspective, the position of the corpse and the tag is meant to cause shock, attract attention, provoke interest, and perhaps invite speculation. Through a West Hollywood lens, it could be interpreted as fetishistic, the killers acting out some kind of

79

perversity, real or imagined.'

'The weapon?'

After considering that, I went with my instincts and said, 'The curtain rope is part of Richard's world, so it could be symbolic or it could be ironic. The setting could be interpreted in either way as well, depending on the killers' intent.'

The investigator wrapped her arms together and pursed her lips.

'And this graffiti?'

'In L.A., graffiti can mean a lot of things,' I replied. 'But here it strikes me like gang graffiti, meant to define turf in some way.'

Hoskins walked around the tag, considering it, glancing up at the body, and then halting. She looked at Louis. 'And you, Monsieur Langlois?'

Louis's eyelids went heavy. 'Jack has said it all.'

She stared at him with her jaw moving slightly, but then smiled at me and extended her hand. 'Well, then, I appreciate you coming in, Mr. Morgan. At the moment, we need to clear the theater so the criminalists can do their job.'

I shook her hand, took her card, and gave her mine.

As we turned to leave, she said, 'And Louis, I know you said Private Paris has been hired by Richard's mistress, but that gives you no legal standing to get in the way of my murder investigation. We're clear on that?'

His eyelids still heavy, Louis said, '*Très clair, madame l'investigateur.*'

The streets outside the Palais Garnier had been turned into a media circus by the time we exited the opera house. Word of Richard's death was out. There were white television vans parked beyond the cordoned area. Several reporters recognized Louis and started peppering him with questions in French.

He begged off, telling them that Investigateur Hoskins was the person to find. When we'd finally broken free of them, Louis lit a cigarette and puffed on it violently while using his iPhone to summon a ride through Uber, an app and company that provide on demand private cars and drivers.

'Two minutes,' he said. 'This Uber thing really works, you know.'

I nodded. 'I've used it in L.A. when I've wanted to go out, have a few drinks. On another note, Hoskins really does not like you.'

'Oh, really?' Louis said, drawing it out and dripping with sarcasm. Then he flicked his ash and added, with a tinge of regret, 'It is a pity, actually, because I do admire her, and in the art of love she was truly magnificent.'

The Uber car turned up before I could reply. We climbed in and Louis gave the driver the address of our new client, the opera director's mistress.

When we were rolling, I said, 'You did see something in the opera house that I missed, right?'

'Perhaps,' Louis said.

'Want to enlighten me?'

'There is a friend of mine I wish to consult before I draw any conclusions or make any claims.'

'Former cop?'

'A professor of art,' he said. 'And an expert on graffiti.'

Chapter 19

16TH ARRONDISSEMENT
11:35A.M.

Louis and I pulled up in front of a beautiful old building in a chic neighborhood north of Place du Trocadéro. The mistress's maid, a tiny Vietnamese woman, opened the apartment door before Louis could knock.

She led us into a well-appointed living area where two women sat on a couch, holding hands and struggling not to weep. The younger and larger of the two women was in her late forties, with dark, Mediterranean features. The older woman, a petite platinum blonde with a dancer's posture, might have been sixty, but if so she'd aged incredibly well.

The younger woman said, 'Louis, we are so glad you've come.'

'How could I not for an old and dear friend?' Louis said, taking her in his arms for a brief bear hug. Then he turned and said, 'This is Jack Morgan, the head of all Private. Jack, this is Evangeline Soleil.'

She greeted me with a sad smile and said, 'I wish it were under different circumstances, Monsieur Morgan. And may I introduce Valerie Richard?'

Before the name could register with me, Louis

went straight to the woman and clasped her hand in his great paws, and said, 'Madame Richard, I am so very sorry for your loss. If Private Paris can do anything, please ask.'

For a second there I admit I was kind of floored to find the widow and the mistress comforting each other in their hour of grief, but then I chalked it up to one more thing that confused me about the French. I shook Madame Richard's hand and she, too, thanked me for taking an interest.

After the maid brought us coffee, the women sat side by side again, holding hands, looking expectantly at Louis.

'What have you found out?' Evangeline Soleil said.

'La Crim will tell us nothing,' Valerie Richard said.

'How did you know your husband was dead?' I asked.

The opera director's wife said, 'One of the guards called me, and I immediately called Evangeline.'

'And I called La Crim,' the mistress said. 'And all they said was that someone would be along to talk with us in due time.'

'Have either of you heard Henri mention the phrase "AB-16"?' I asked.

Both women shook their heads.

'What does it mean?' Valerie Richard said.

'We don't know,' Louis said, and then masterfully recounted what we'd learned without telling them what we'd seen, as I'd guaranteed Hoskins.

Rather than express shock or outrage that

Richard had been with a young redhead, the two women looked at each other as if in vindication.

'We were right,' the mistress said. 'He was up to his old tricks.'

'The foolish old goat,' the wife said. 'It got him killed after all.'

Both women said that Richard was ordinarily given to melancholy, but he had been acting strangely happy in the past few weeks, disappearing at night for mysterious meetings and telling neither of them where he'd been.

Richard's wife said she had confronted her husband finally, and he had said there was no new love interest, that he'd been holing up in a studio flat in Popincourt that he'd inherited from his mother to work on the libretto of a new opera. He had told his mistress the same thing.

'Devious, wasn't he?' Evangeline Soleil said to Valerie Richard.

The wife sighed in anguish and said, 'There are things we cannot change about some men no matter how hard we try.'

'Some men?' the mistress said. 'All men.'

This vein of discussion made me shift in my seat and try to change course. 'Did he have any enemies?'

Valerie Richard shot me a look as if I were mentally challenged. 'What man in a position like his does not have enemies?'

I hadn't thought of opera house director as being a particularly dangerous or controversial job before. 'Anyone specific?'

Evangeline Soleil let out a long, slow breath and said, 'Anyone in the opera community you might think of, Mr. Morgan. I mean, they all acted nice to Henri, but you know how it is when someone is successful in Paris.'

'Uh, actually, I don't,' I said.

Louis said, 'The people in the same field, they hate you for your success. They think something must be wrong, that you're corrupt in some way.'

'Of course,' Richard's wife said. 'They plot against you.'

I said, 'Was there anyone actively plotting against him lately?'

'The redhead, obviously,' his mistress sniffed.

'Focus on her,' the wife agreed. 'A woman will be at the center of it all.'

Chapter 20

18TH ARRONDISSEMENT
NOON

Haja Hamid exited the women's toilet and went to the fountain in the lobby of the mosque. She performed the ritual of ablution – washing her hands and feet – with practiced ease. When she stepped into the women's prayer hall, there were already fifty or sixty women inside. Like Haja, they all wore brown or black robes and matching scarves. Some, like Haja, also wore veils.

She knelt at the back, listening to the clicking of worry beads and the voices murmuring sur-render to Allah. The sounds brought back so many memories that she was filled once again with strength and resolve.

Facing east, Haja started the physical motions of Islamic prayer, bowing to put her forehead flat on the carpet and then rising with a stiff posture. She wasn't silently reciting lines from the Koran, however. Her lips curled around vows she'd made long ago.

She waited until Imam Ibrahim Al-Moustapha went to the front of the prayer hall to lead the service. The second his back was turned, Haja got up and returned to the anteroom, searching for her sandals amid all the other shoes.

The Imam began his talk just as she snatched up her sandals and went out the door, into the street. Head down, Haja kicked into the sandals and moved past three men trying to paint over the AB-16 tag on the mosque's outer wall.

Satisfied that the bloodred tag was still bleeding through, she walked by a man sweeping the sidewalk in front of FEZ Couriers, a messenger service next door to the mosque, and then a tailor shop that sold robes.

'*Ay, pétasse!*'

The call – 'Hey, bitch!' – came from the other side of the street.

Haja glanced left and saw him: late teens, pale skin, and brown curly hair. Carrying a camera slung across his chest, he was pointing at her in a rage.

'Can't wear the veil in public, Muslim bitch!' he yelled.

Haja tore down the veil, turned her head from him, and broke into a trot. When she glanced

86

again, he was angling across the street at her.

That kicked her into an all-out sprint down the sidewalk toward an old green Peugeot sedan. She got there half a block ahead of her pursuer, jumped in the backseat, and said, 'Get us out of here. Now.'

Epée already had the Peugeot running. He threw it in gear and squealed out, heading back toward the mosque. The teen stepped from between two cars, trying to aim his camera.

Haja pulled up the veil. In the front passenger seat, Mfune, who was dressed in the green jumpsuit of a Paris sanitation worker, turned his head. Epée jerked the wheel toward the kid as if to run him down.

The photographer jumped back between the parked cars and they were past him.

'What was that all about?' Epée asked.

'My fault,' she said. 'When I came out of the mosque, I still had the veil up and he started shouting at me that I was a Muslim bitch.'

'Why the camera?' Epée demanded, turning off the boulevard heading toward the train tracks.

'I have no idea,' she said, taking deeper and slower breaths. 'None.'

'Did you get the job done?' Mfune asked.

The tension fell from Haja's shoulders. She wiped at the sweat on her brow, saying, 'Just as we planned. You?'

The captain held up a green translucent plastic bag filled with trash and said, 'What do you think?'

Chapter 21

We left Evangeline Soleil's flat, having received permission from Valerie Richard to search her home. She'd offered to take us there straight-away, but Louis said he wanted to go take a look at her husband's opera-writing hideaway first.

The Uber car was waiting, and Louis gave the driver the address.

'So is that the norm in Paris?' I asked. 'To have a mistress and a wife who are friends?'

'No,' Louis said. 'And even to have a mistress now, it is not so common among men younger than fifty.'

'Why's that?'

'Changing times,' he said with a note of wistful-ness. 'Now, the young are all in relationships, except when they are – how do you say? – exchanging.'

'Exchanging what?'

'Each other,' he said.

'You mean swinging?'

'That's the word,' Louis said. 'There are clubs, even, for these things.'

As we pulled out into traffic, I stared out the window at people and wondered how many had mistresses, or were mistresses, or were swingers. I live in L.A., and I am hardly a prude, but I found Paris behind closed doors oddly fascin-ating.

'Are they right?' I asked. 'About the redhead being at the center of it?'

'She's part of it. But the center? I don't think so.'

'Reason?'

He brooded for several moments before saying, 'Just my instinct, Jack. Still nothing hard that I can hold on to yet.'

That seemed to remind Louis of something because he got out his iPhone and started punching in numbers. Before he finished and hit send, my own cell rang. It was Justine calling from L.A.

'How's Sherman?' I asked.

She sounded exhausted and upset. 'He's in surgery, Jack. They're removing a piece of his skull to relieve the pressure from brain swelling.'

'That's awful,' I said, frustrated again that we didn't have his granddaughter in a safe place. 'What's his prognosis?'

'The doctors won't tell me,' she said. 'I'm not next of kin. But a nurse in the ICU said he'll probably be held in an artificial coma for the next couple of days. Is the granddaughter on the way home?'

'She ran. We don't have her.'

'This is bad, Jack,' she said. 'There's no one here to make decisions.'

'Find out who he named as the executor of his living will.'

'After I get a few hours' sleep,' she promised. 'It's four a.m. here and – Del Rio just came in. He wants to tell you something.'

'Jack?' Del Rio growled.

'You're up early.'

89

'Late,' he replied. 'One of the great perks of the job.'

Del Rio told me that he'd gone through Wilkerson's home before alerting the L.A. sheriff about the assault and break-in. The deputies and detectives who arrived weren't very happy about the delay in notification, but they'd live.

'You figure out what they were looking for?' I asked.

'No,' Del Rio replied. 'At least nothing that jumped right out at me. But I did find something you might find useful. Wilkerson still keeps paper bank statements around, and some involve her trust.'

'You've got an account number?'

'I do. She uses a debit card and makes cash withdrawals from ATM machines. No checking account.'

'You have records of the withdrawals?'

'Not for this month yet, if that's what you mean.'

'It is what I mean,' I said. 'Even though Sherman's old-school when it comes to keeping his financial records, his bank won't be. You should be able to get an up-to-the-minute electronic record of all withdrawals she's made.'

'It's a private account.'

'Use your imagination.'

'That's never been one of my long suits, but I'll let you know.'

'Get some sleep. The both of you.'

'Nah, we'll stick around until he comes out of surgery, and charge you double time while we're doing it.'

'Nice of you.'

'I'm a saint. Didn't you know?' Del Rio said, and hung up.

Louis ended his call as well and said, 'My friend the graffiti expert will see us once classes are over for the day. Around four.'

I brought him up to date on Sherman's condition and on Del Rio's discovery of Kim's trust account.

'If you can get some kind of alert every time she uses her ATM card, we should be able to track her down,' Louis said.

'Exactly,' I said. 'I'd still like to know what they were after – the guys who beat Sherman, I mean.'

'Maybe the same thing,' he grunted. 'Some way to track Kim.'

It made sense, and it made me anxious. Even though she'd run on us, I didn't want to see her end up like her grandfather, with surgeons sawing off part of her skull to relieve the swelling.

The driver pulled over a few minutes later in front of a pharmacy on the Rue Popincourt, a narrow street of trendy boutiques. Louis led the way to the high arched double doors next to the pharmacy and was ringing the bell when I happened to glance at the lower wall. I tapped Louis on the shoulder and gestured at the small red letters.

AB-16

'Looks like we came to the right place,' Louis said.

91

Chapter 22

I got out my phone and took a picture of the tag before the door opened and the concierge, an older woman in a smock and apron, looked out at us suspiciously, and barked at us in a French patois that completely lost me.

Louis showed her his identification and spoke to her. She argued for a bit, but then reluctantly allowed us in. We entered a nice courtyard, and Louis spoke again to the old woman, who scolded him in return.

'Okay,' he said. 'Richard's mother's place is on the top floor.'

As we climbed a steep set of switchback staircases, I said, 'I didn't understand a thing that came out of that old woman's mouth.'

'Because she's from Portugal,' he said. 'Most concierges are.'

'What were you arguing about? The apartment?'

'No, no,' he said. 'About the woman. She says she never saw a redhead come to see Richard here. Plenty of other women, but no redhead.'

'She here all the time?'

'Pretty much.'

'When was the last time she saw him?'

'Four days ago.'

We reached the upper floor. The ceiling of the garret was quite low and we had to stoop beneath a beam to get to Richard's studio flat. We put on latex gloves. Louis got out a pick set and fiddled with the lock until it clicked.

When we pushed open the wooden door there was a rush of wind. Shredded paper and several pigeons flew everywhere. The windows were wide open. Once we'd shooed out the birds and closed the windows, I could see that the place was less than five hundred square feet and completely in shambles.

Bookcases turned over. Desk drawers pulled out. Files dumped. A laptop computer lay smashed beside them. The kitchen cabinets were open. So was the small refrigerator, which smelled of rotted meat and curdled milk.

Paper was strewn across the floor and on the bed, which had been stripped of linen and blankets save a blue pillowcase. And on the wall above the headboard there was the tag again: AB-16.

Louis picked up a handful of papers and files and started going through them.

I went to the head of the bed, leaned over, and sniffed the graffiti paint.

'New,' I said, pulling back and crinkling my nose. 'Past day or so.'

Louis said, 'And it looks like he *was* working on an opera libretto.'

Then he looked confused and went back to reading.

I got down on my knees to look under the bed, hearing Louis grab up more files and more paper. At first glance, I saw nothing. But as I drew my head back to get up, I noticed that a section of floorboard about eighteen inches long was sticking up a half inch or so over by the wall.

I got up and moved the bed to get at that floorboard. I was able to use my fingernails to pry up the board, revealing a plastic Tupperware-style container.

I lifted it out, unsnapped the lid, and looked inside.

As I did, Louis slapped the files in his hand and said, 'I sensed at the murder scene that Monsieur Richard had been playing with fire. This proves it. No wonder he got burned.'

That didn't register for several seconds while I studied the shocking contents of the box. Finally, I looked up and said, 'Come again?'

'The libretto of his opera, Jack,' he said. 'It is the tale of a doomed love affair between a Catholic priest and a Muslim woman.'

I glanced back in the box, squinted one eye, and said, 'Then I'll bet this is what they were in here looking for.'

Coming over to look, Louis said, 'What have you got?'

'The gas Henri Richard played with when he was playing with fire.'

Chapter 23

Inside the box were condoms, lubricant, and sex toys. There were also raunchy porno photos of Richard in a priest's collar having sex with a woman.

In some of the pictures she wore a flowing black robe hitched up over her hips. In others, she was naked from the neck down. But in every picture we found, she wore a black hijab and veil that hid her face except for deep-brown eyes that seemed to stare defiantly into the camera lens.

I took the pictures out, one by one, and set them on the lid, where Louis could see and make his own judgments. When I did, I realized there was something else zipped inside the kind of clear plastic case my mother used to use to protect her sweaters.

'I've got the priest's collar and the hijab here,' I said. 'Those could be different women in the pictures using the outfit to fulfill his fucked-up fantasies.'

Louis shook his head and said, 'It is the same woman. *Sans doute.*'

I looked at him skeptically and then he pointed out the evidence in the pictures, and I was horrified and sickened. Setting the pictures back on the box top, my mind whirled with questions and speculations.

Was the veiled woman in the photographs also the redhead Henri Richard was seen with last night? Were these disturbing photos behind the opera director's murder? Someone in the woman's Muslim family seeking vengeance?

Something Louis said came back to me, and I looked over at him. 'What was that you said earlier about the murder scene being more than it seemed?'

His jaw stiffened. 'With these photos, I cannot see it another way now. The whole thing looked highly symbolic to me, Jack.'

'Okay.'

Louis hesitated and then said, 'Remember how Richard was hanging?'

I nodded and said, 'Inverted, arms out to his side, looking down at the graffiti.'

'Yes, now put a narrow beam of wood behind him from above his toes to below his head, and a second one holding his arms out at right angles.'

I saw it, and my eyes flew open. 'An upside-down cross?'

'The cross of the apostle Saint Peter,' Louis said. 'Do you know this story?'

Though lapsed, I'd been raised a Catholic by my staunch mother, and vaguely remembered the story. 'When the apostle Peter was condemned to death for spreading Christ's word, he asked his executioners to crucify him upside down because he thought he was unworthy of dying as Jesus had died.'

'This is correct,' Louis said.

'But what does that have—'

96

He held up his hands and said, 'Over the centuries, Saint Peter's upside-down cross also became an anti-Christian symbol, one that suggested the religion's ultimate demise, especially among Islamists and during the Crusades.'

'Crusades?' I groaned. 'I hope you're not telling me this is one of those hokey stories that link a killing to some secret Christian society and a valuable ancient whatever belonging to Saint whomever.'

'No, no,' he snorted. 'No evidence of that, thank God. I'm just saying that you can interpret Richard's body position as anti-Christian, and perhaps pro-Islamist. That's how it struck me at first view, but I had no other link. Now, with pictures of Richard role-playing a priest having sex with a Muslim woman, and Richard writing an opera about a torrid affair between a Catholic priest and a Muslim woman, I'd say we have the link.'

'So who killed Richard? Father? Brothers? And who was the redhead?'

'I don't–'

The door blew open behind us and the little flat became crowded with men aiming pistols at us.

Chapter 24

Sharen Hoskins came in behind her men. Her face contorted and red, she snapped, 'You are both under arrest.'

'On what charges?' Louis demanded.

'Obstruction of justice!' the homicide investigator shouted. 'Evidence tampering! And I can probably come up with six more!'

'We were given permission by the widow to be here,' I said. '*And* we followed Interpol search procedures. This place was tossed before we got here.'

Hoskins's expression soured, and she said, 'You have absolutely no say in any of this, Monsieur Morgan.'

Louis said, 'Can we help it if La Crim moves at a snail's pace, while Private Paris makes discoveries missed by whoever searched this place first?'

Hoskins narrowed her left eye and said, 'What discoveries?'

Langlois told her about Richard's opera libretto. I showed her the hijab and veil, and the pictures. She studied them coldly while Louis explained his belief that the women were all one and the same, and that the opera director's body position was meant as an anti-Christian statement.

'Do you see?' he asked. 'Now imagine if we are under arrest and we explain this to every jour-

98

nalist we can get interested in our case.'

Hoskins set the photographs down, thought for several moments, and then said, 'For finding this evidence you are no longer under arrest.'

'It was just a mix-up,' Louis said in a magnanimous tone.

'Yes,' I said. 'And in a gesture of goodwill, I can offer you Private Paris's forensics team to work this room. They are fully certified.'

'I'm sure,' she said, cool. 'But we can take care of it.'

The *investigateur* stepped toward Louis, hardened, and shook a finger in his face, saying, 'But so help me God, Louis, if you or your boss breathe one word of what you've seen in here, or if you pursue anything having to do with what you've seen in here, Monsieur Morgan will be deported immediately, and you, Louis, will be held incommunicado for as long as I see fit.'

'You don't have that authority,' he said in a soft growl.

'But I know people who do,' Hoskins said. 'Now, gentlemen, I need you to get far, far out of my way.'

Langlois looked ready to argue further, but I said, 'Louis, don't we have that other appointment anyway? The art lady?

'What art lady?' the *investigateur* asked.

'Another case,' Louis said, brightening and moving toward the door. 'On my honor, we will not breathe a word of what we have seen here.'

'Louis, you have no honor,' she said.

'You wound me,' he said, opening the door, and we left.

Outside on the street, I said, 'So what do we tell the wife and mistress?'

'Officially, we say that we cannot continue under orders from La Crim,' he said. 'Unofficially is another story. As you have just heard, I have no honor.'

'I, for one, disagree.'

'You have not known me long enough,' Langlois grunted, and laughed.

He lit a cigarette, and we walked along the Rue Popincourt.

Recalling that Del Rio was trying to track Kim Kopchinski through her finances, I suggested we do the same for the opera director. Louis said that it was certain Hoskins had frozen access to the accounts.

'Even his wife couldn't get at them now,' he said, and then smiled and blew smoke rings. 'Ah, but I bet a dog I know could get to them.'

Chapter 25

20TH ARRONDISSEMENT
3 P.M.

Louis said we still had almost an hour and a half before we were due to meet with his friend the graffiti expert, so we took a short Métro ride and came aboveground at the Philippe Auguste station.

We headed north along the Boulevard de

Ménilmontant until we reached the Rue de la Roquette, where we headed west to number 173. Louis rang the bell of an apartment on the second floor of the small building, but no answer.

'No problem,' he said to me. 'I know where Le Chien will be.'

'Why are we looking for a dog?' I asked as he lit another cigarette.

'Not *a* dog, Jack. *The* Dog. And if he is not home, he is usually sniffing around gravestones.'

We crossed the boulevard and entered Père-Lachaise cemetery.

'This place is huge,' I said. 'How are we going to find him?'

'He usually orbits between the tomb of Héloïse and Abelard and the grave of Jim Morrison.'

I'd never been in the famous cemetery before, and as we walked the paths I had to hand it to the Parisians. They knew how to commemorate their dead. Each headstone or tomb face was carved in some bas-relief or fitted with the statues of angels, or children, sleeping men, or women whose bronze faces were streaked with green patinas so they seemed to be weeping.

We passed tourists gathered by the tomb of the ill-fated twelfth-century lovers Héloïse and Abelard, but spotted no one who fit Louis's description of Le Chien. For several minutes I thought we were on a wild dog chase, but then we looped toward a crowd around Morrison's grave.

Many of the pilgrims wore pictures of the dead singer on their shirts. Others were lighting

101

candles. A speaker cabled to an MP3 player was blasting 'Peace Frog,' which caught my attention because the song had played a part in a bizarre series of crimes in Los Angeles the year before. In any case, Jim Morrison was chanting about ghosts crowding the child's fragile eggshell mind when Louis said, 'And there he is.'

Mouthing along with the lyrics and carrying a filthy green book bag, the Dog moved outside the perimeter of the crowd, seeming to know which monuments he could step up on to get a better look at the people in front of the rock singer's grave. There he'd pause a second, make a slight sideways twitch of his head, pop the tips of the fingers on both hands together, and then move on a few feet and repeat the ritual.

Louis cut him off. 'Chien?' he said.

The Dog stopped and looked afraid, but then relaxed a bit and said, 'Louis?'

'Right here, my friend, as always,' Louis said, and held out his fist.

The Dog hesitated, scratched at his scraggly reddish beard, and contemplated Louis's hand for a long beat before reluctantly bumping it.

'I have a job for you,' Louis said. 'If you feel like working.'

'Who's *he?*' he asked.

'Jack,' Louis said. 'He's my boss.'

'Boss is from fantastic L.A.,' the Dog said, as if remembering the fact.

'That's right,' I said. 'I live in Los Angeles.'

He seemed to tune us out then, and started to sing with Morrison, 'Blood in my love in the terrible–'

Louis snapped his fingers in front of the Dog's eyes and said, 'Work?'

The Dog tilted his head sideways, and I noticed a thick white scar high on the left side of his head, not quite hidden by his hair.

'How much?' he asked.

'Sensitive job,' Louis said. 'Two thousand euros.'

'Make it twenty-five hundred, and the Dog starts right now.'

'Deal,' Louis said.

'Need somewhere quiet,' he said, and then started walking away from us.

We followed as the Dog strolled on, tilting his head, popping his fingertips together, and never looking back. He finally took a seat on the marble stairs to the right of Frédéric Chopin's grave, which featured a muse with a lyre sitting in grief.

The Dog took off his knapsack and pulled out a MacBook Pro. He set it in his lap and opened it. When he did, he seemed to change – become calmer, certainly. The facial tics did not stop, but they subsided as he stared at the screen, and his language became more fluid and connected.

'What do you need, Louis?' he asked.

Louis handed him a piece of paper he'd scribbled on during the Metro ride and said, 'I need this man's financials. Past three months.'

The Dog looked at it and said, 'He's the opera director.'

'Yes.'

'He's dead.'

'That's right.'

'So the accounts will be frozen.'

'You're right again.'

'This will take a while,' he said. 'Later today?'

'That will be fine.'

'Cash on delivery.'

'Same as always.'

And then it was as if we'd been dismissed. The Dog gazed at the screen as if it were a doorway into another world, and he started to type.

Louis tugged on my sleeve. We left him, heading back toward the cemetery's front gate. When we'd gotten out of earshot, I said, 'Okay, so what's his story? What's that scar on his head?'

'The scar and his story are one and the same,' Louis replied sadly.

The Dog's real name was Pierre Moulton. Louis had been best man at the Dog's parents' wedding. The boy was born soon after and proved to be a prodigy. He could speak with fluency at fourteen months and learned algebra at five years old. His true genius surfaced at age eight, when his parents gave him a computer and he taught himself how to write code.

'They lived there on the Rue de la Roquette, where we rang the bell,' Louis said. 'Pierre was, as I said, a genius. But he was not very coordinated and possessed very little common sense. When he was fourteen he went out riding his bike without a helmet.'

A motorcyclist clipped him, sending him flying. His head collided with a curb and caused a massive injury to his skull and brain.

'A tragedy,' Louis said. 'It is only because of his incredible natural intelligence that he can do what he can now. He's still a brilliant hacker.'

'What's with the name?'

He shrugged as we left the cemetery. 'It was something he just came up with one day. He liked that it made him sound tough.'

'Parents?'

Louis dipped his head and said, 'Both dead. His mom to cancer, and his dad to a heart attack. In the will, I was named his guardian and the trustee of the insurance money he got from the accident, which was not much when you consider he'll probably live a long time.'

'But you give him work when you can?'

'Of course,' Louis said. 'He's a genius and I'm all the Dog has left.'

Chapter 26

6TH ARRONDISSEMENT
4:35 P.M.

We climbed from a cab on the Rue Bonaparte and went to the security gate at L'Académie des Beaux-Arts.

Langlois asked for Professor Herbert and was given directions to a studio in a large building across the cut-stone courtyard. Classes were letting out. Scores of young hipsters poured out into the courtyard carrying sketchbooks as they bustled toward the street.

'This is *the* school for artists in France, correct?' I asked.

'The students are less French these days. You get kids from the States, or Japan, or wherever, and they want to study art. Their rich parents have heard of this place, which was, at one time, the very center of the art world. Now not so much. The art world has passed by this place, except for my friend Professor Herbert, who is a ground-breaker, as you will see.'

Louis led the way to a high-ceilinged room, where an older man with gray frizzed-out hair was talking to a lean woman in jeans and a starched white shirt with the collar turned up against her bobbed hairdo. He stood in three-quarter profile. She had her back to us.

They were studying a huge collage that featured iconic Parisian street scenes as a backdrop. Over the top of the backdrop were images from France's past, both good times and bad. There were bright blue graffiti tags as well. They featured arrows and question marks linking the images in a way that suggested the city's vast history and commented on it.

'Professor?' Langlois called.

I don't know why, but I expected the older guy to reply.

Instead, the woman smiled and cried, 'Louis Langlois, it has been much too long!'

To say that Professor Herbert was good-looking would be like saying Usain Bolt jogged or Adele sang a few songs in her spare time. She had a flawless complexion; high, pronounced cheek-bones; and a delicate jaw that ran out from lush dark hair to a dimpled chin that featured a tiny mole on the left side.

Her eyes were soft, aquamarine, and turned up ever so slightly at the outer corners, as if fashioned after teardrops. Her nose looked wind-carved, with a narrow bridge and flaring nostrils. Her lips were thinner and more alluring than the Botox pout you see on so many models and actresses back in L.A., and her smile, though brilliantly white, wasn't perfect. Like the actress Lauren Hutton, she had a small gap between her upper two front teeth.

'This is my boss, Jack Morgan,' Langlois said after embracing her and blowing Euro kisses. 'Jack, may I present Professor Michele Herbert.'

Her smile broadened, and she pressed her tongue into the back of that gap between her teeth. She held out her hand and said in lightly accented English, 'Enchanted to meet you, monsieur. I have read of Private's exploitations. That is the word, yes?'

I was frankly mesmerized, but managed to say, 'Close enough. And I am the one who is enchanted.'

Her eyes and hand lingered on me before she pressed her tongue again to that gap in her teeth and turned, gesturing to the old guy with the frizzy hair.

'Louis?' she said. 'Do you know François? My representative?'

François took Louis's hand and then mine in that weird little three-quarter thing the French call a handshake.

'Michele has made a miracle, yes?' he said, pointing at the collage.

Louis nodded and said, 'Something that the

French can ponder and argue about for years to come.'

'And Monsieur Morgan? It pleases you?'

'It intrigues me,' I said.

'"Intrigue" is good, yes?' said Michele Herbert, who smiled impishly.

'I've made a good living out of intrigue.'

'And Michele will do this as well,' her rep said. 'I have galleries all over the world clamoring to represent her.'

Herbert blushed and said, 'François, you make too much of me.'

'I must be going, to make much of you everywhere I can,' he replied. He blew kisses past her cheeks and then sort of shook our hands again before leaving.

'So, how may I help you?' the art professor asked.

'I told Jack that you are an expert on graffiti,' Louis said.

Herbert turned the smile on me again and said, 'He also makes too much of me. Graffiti is my interest as a historian, and it has become a part of my own work over the years.'

Digging out my iPhone, I showed her the photograph we'd taken of the AB-16 tag outside Henri Richard's pied-a-terre.

She said, 'I have never seen this before. What does it mean?'

'We don't know,' Louis said.

Herbert looked at it again, a frown appearing as she said, *'C'est bizarre.'*

Chapter 27

'What's bizarre?' Louis asked.

'Can you e-mail this photo to me?' she asked. 'So I can see it better?'

I did, and she blew it up on a computer screen in a corner of the studio. She made a little puffing noise and then gestured at the loops and shadow work on the *A* and the *B* of the tag. 'You see how these come together to create that – how do you say? – pop?'

'The three-dimensionality?' I asked.

'This too,' Herbert said. 'But you see the letters, how they seem to hover? It is one of the signature methods of a Parisian graffiti artist who called himself Zee Pac-Man.'

'Where can we find him?' I asked.

'He was murdered late last year, just after Christmas. Found dead in the 9th beneath his last tag. Stabbed several times in the back.'

Louis said, 'So what? This could be a follower of Zee Pac-Man?'

'Or simply a thief,' Herbert replied, and then looked to me to explain. 'Artists steal what we like and admire, you know this?'

'Makes sense,' I said.

'Do you still have all those followers?' Louis asked.

'Yes,' she said.

'Think you could ask them if they've seen this

tag elsewhere?'

'*Bien sûr,*' she replied. 'What do I say it is about?'

'Just say you're interested,' Louis replied, and then explained to me that Herbert had a Facebook page where people from all over the world posted shots of interesting graffiti. The page had been 'liked' by more than half a million people.

'She has thousands of Parisians who follow her. Isn't that right?'

Herbert blushed again. 'They follow the graffiti. I just help others see it.'

I liked her. A lot. In the past I've met a few successful artists, and had several as clients. The majority are quirky egocentrics quick to turn the lights on themselves, a trait that inevitably leads to self-destructive behaviors. But Herbert seemed normal as well as self-deprecating, smart, and, well, just gorgeous.

'Any help would be much appreciated,' I said.

'Of course,' she said. 'You are in Paris long, Monsieur Morgan?'

I glanced at Louis, thought about all that had happened since my arrival, and said, 'That's unclear. But a few more days, anyway.'

'Well, then, I will put the request on the Facebook page *rapidement.*'

'Excellent,' I said. 'And it was an honor to meet you.'

Herbert touched her neck, laughed, looked at Louis, and said, 'An honor?'

'The man has a way with words.'

Herbert smiled and said, 'And it is ... sorry, it

was wonderful to meet you.'

Louis's eyes bounced between us a few times before he said, 'Michele, would you care to have a glass of wine with us?'

Her head cocked left, and then right, before she laughed again and said, 'Why not? I have been working much too hard lately.'

'Come, then,' Louis said. 'Where should we go?'

Before she could answer, my cell phone rang. It was Rick Del Rio.

'How's Paris?' he asked.

I glanced at Michele Herbert, held up a finger, walked away, and said, 'Looking up all of a sudden.'

'Well, then let me make your day even sunnier.'

Del Rio had managed to get hold of Kim Kopchinski's most recent cash withdrawals and credit card charges.

'Anything today?' I asked.

'Oh, yeah,' he said. 'I'll e-mail you the particulars. I also arranged it so we'll both get alerts of any future transactions sent automatically to our phones.'

'You're a machine.'

'Bionic man,' he said, and hung up.

I hurried to catch up with Louis and Michele Herbert. My phone dinged to alert me to an e-mail. I opened it and showed it to Louis as we left the building.

He slowed and scanned the addresses of the ATM withdrawals and debit charges. 'These are all in the Marais.'

'One of my favorite areas in Paris,' Herbert

111

said. 'We could go there for drinks, and maybe something to eat?'

'Perfect,' I said.

Chapter 28

4TH ARRONDISSEMENT
5:20 P.M.

Louis took us to a café on the Rue des Archives.

The art professor looked around and said, 'Louis, there are much more sympathetic places to entertain Jack in the Marais.'

'This is true, Michele,' the big bear of a man said, taking a seat outdoors. 'But we are mixing business with pleasure.'

'Does it have to do with the tag?' she asked.

'It's a missing persons case,' I said.

'Well, sort of,' Louis said. 'This person wants to be missing.'

'Who is this person?' Herbert asked.

'The granddaughter of a client of mine back in Los Angeles,' I said.

'So, she is a runaway?'

'Not like a teen runaway. But she's trying to escape something or someone and we don't know why, other than knowing that drugs are involved.'

'And you think she's here somewhere?' the artist asked, looking around.

Louis pointed across the street and said, 'At eleven o'clock this morning, she withdrew five

112

hundred euros from an ATM machine in that pharmacy. Twenty minutes later, she used a debit card to pay for a haircut in that salon. She also bought wine at that shop over there. And forty minutes ago, she returned to get more money from the pharmacy ATM.'

The artist grew excited and said, 'We are on the stakeout, yes?'

'Something like that,' Louis said.

'I feel like I am in a film noir,' she said, beaming at the idea.

'Nothing that thrilling,' I said, flashing on the car chase and shoot-out from the night before and wondering just how much we should tell her.

A waitress came. Louis ordered a bottle of Pouilly-Fuissé. It soon arrived and was chilled perfectly. There was a warm breeze as Michele described the neighborhood. First settled in the 1200s, Le Marais – the marsh – was one of the oldest districts in the city. During the Renaissance, it was the preferred neighborhood of noblemen. Jews had lived there for centuries. The Chinese came after World War I, and the gays more recently.

'Many galleries in Paris are here,' she said. 'Nice restaurants too.'

'Do you have pieces in them? The galleries?'

'I do,' she said. 'I can show you some later.'

The conversation drifted to discussions of Paris and Los Angeles. Time seemed to disappear as we chatted and laughed. The artist had a semi-humorous take on nearly everything, and after a while I became less flabbergasted by her looks than I was by her mind, which could be cutting

113

or playful. Again and again, I heard this voice in my head saying that I'd never met a woman like Michele Herbert.

'So,' she said at one point. 'Are you in love, Jack?'

I startled and glanced over at Louis, but was surprised to find him not there. I'd been so engrossed in my conversation that I hadn't heard or seen him get up.

'Jack?'

'I'm in love with life,' I said.

'But there is not someone special?'

'Not at the moment,' I said, feeling my cheeks burn slightly. 'You?'

'Just my art,' Michele said, doing that tongue-in-the-teeth thing before draining her glass. 'More?'

I finished my glass and poured us both another. Louis returned and said, 'Henri Richard's murder is the talk of the café.'

'A terrible thing,' the artist said. 'Have they got a suspect?'

'Not yet,' Louis said, and eyed the bottle. 'Shall we order another?'

'Why not?' Michele said.

I was about to agree when I felt my phone buzz with an incoming text. I read it, looked up at Louis, and said, 'She just bought something at Open Café.'

He jumped up and said, 'It's two blocks. One of the big gay clubs.'

We both looked at Michele, who started laughing and making shooing gestures. 'Go, go!' she said. 'I'll pay and then come to find you.'

Louis was already moving. I had to run hard to

catch up with him.

'Why would she be in a gay bar?' Louis grunted.

'Good place for a woman to hide?' I said.

We ran to the Rue Sainte-Croix-de-la-Breton-nerie. Open Café was on the southwest corner. A crowd of men had spilled from the club onto the sidewalk, blocking our view of the tables inside and out.

Rather than go straight into the bar, however, Louis kept us on the opposite side of the inter-section, walking north across the Rue Sainte-Croix and then west across the Rue des Archives. In front of the Agora bookstore, I panned the crowd and looked right past Kim Kopchinski at first and second glance.

Then she turned and I caught her in profile, sitting at a table by the club entrance. Her shoulder-length brown hair was gone in favor of short spikes dyed the color of straw. She wore no makeup, a black T-shirt, and pants. If I hadn't just spent time with her, I might have thought she was an effeminate-looking guy.

'You see her?' Louis said, still searching.

'Yes,' I said. 'Let me do the talking.'

Crossing the street, I felt many eyes in the crowd turn toward me, sizing me up. I'm over six feet with a football player's build. The men ogling me looked as though they'd never seen a gym, but one came at me straightaway and started propositioning me.

I told him I was flattered, but straight, and on my way to meet a friend. He said something unflattering that I didn't catch and turned his shoulder.

Kim lit a cigarette with that lighter she kept on a chain around her neck. She was chatting with a man in a white tennis sweater who had his back to me. I was trying to close the last few feet to her table when an older Brit got in my way.

'Don't you even think of not talking to me, cowboy,' he said loudly.

'I'm straight,' I said again, trying to get around him, only to bump into a waiter, who dropped a tray.

The sound of breaking glass was enough to split the crowd and draw Kim's attention. She took one look at me and got to her feet fast.

Her wineglass exploded.

Hit by flying glass, she panicked and pivoted right to get inside the club, but another waiter holding a tray at shoulder height blocked her path.

She ducked as if to go under his arm. The waiter jerked, dropped his tray. A plume of bright blood appeared on his white shirt, and he collapsed.

'Shooter, Jack!' Louis shouted.

I dove to the ground, twisted, and saw that pale, gaunt guy from the night before crouched in a combat shooting stance and aiming a suppressed pistol from twenty-five feet away.

Kaboom!

That shot was Louis's. He roared, 'Everyone down!'

The crowd threw themselves to the street and sidewalk, leaving Louis to my right leveling his Glock at the pale guy who still faced me.

The gunman must have caught sight of Louis in his peripheral vision, and his reflexes had to have been astounding, because in a move that was as quick as a cobra strike he dropped to his knees, pivoted the gun, and fired, hitting Louis square in the chest and blowing the big man off his feet.

Chapter 29

The gunman swung his weapon back my way, and then looked past me into the club. A split second later, he took off west on the Rue Sainte-Croix.

My marine training kicked in.

Lurching to my feet, I charged toward Louis, who sprawled in the gutter. Sirens wailed in the distance when I crouched beside him, expecting the worst.

'Get him,' Louis croaked.

'You're hit,' I said. 'I'm staying right here.'

'Armor,' he croaked. 'I'm fine.'

I stared a second at the hole in his loose shirt and the blue ballistic vest showing beneath it before I jumped back up to start after the gunman. But he was gone. And after I searched the nightclub, I knew that so was Wilkerson's granddaughter.

Michele Herbert came running to me when I exited.

'*Mon Dieu*,' she cried, looking at Louis still lying there, trying to get his breath back. 'I heard the shot. Is he...?'

'He's good,' I said. 'Just had the wind knocked

out of him.'

The same could not be said of the waiter who'd taken the second bullet. He died before the ambulances got there. The police were on the scene quicker and soon cordoned off the area until La Crim could arrive.

To our chagrin, Investigateur Hoskins was the first to arrive. She took one look at us and groaned.

'All of it!' she shouted. 'I want all of it. Right now!'

It took us twenty minutes to tell her everything – the phone call from Sherman Wilkerson, the trip to Les Bosquets, the car chase and gun battle the evening before, Kim's escape and the way we tracked her.

I said, 'Because of the break-in at Sherman's house back in Malibu, I think the pale guy must have had access to the same bank and credit card accounts that we had. When she paid for those drinks, she brought him in as well as us.'

The investigator chewed on that for a few moments, and then said, 'A shoot-out last night on the A5 and you don't report it?'

'Discretion is often the better part of valor,' Louis replied.

That seemed to annoy her, because she said, 'Your license to carry is still up to date?'

'Of course,' he said wearily

'Why are you hassling him?' I said. 'If it wasn't for Louis standing up and taking the hit, who knows how many people that guy might have killed?'

Hoskins appeared to struggle with that, but

then let it out in a sharp exhalation. 'You're right, Monsieur Morgan. I apologize, Louis.'

'Accepted,' Louis grunted, and rubbed at his chest.

The investigator turned her attention to Michele Herbert. 'You are the art expert they went to see?'

'Yes,' she said.

'So where's the art in all this?' Hoskins asked.

'No, no,' Louis said a little too quickly. 'A different case entirely. Michele had merely joined us for a drink.'

I hated to think what would happen if Michele mentioned that her expertise was in graffiti art. Me deported. Louis tossed in some dungeon.

'True?' Hoskins asked the artist.

Michele nodded. 'Just as they said.'

Clearly exasperated, the investigator said, 'And you have no idea why the pale guy wants to kill her?'

'None,' Louis said.

'What about the man she was sitting with? The one with the curly brown hair and the white tennis sweater?'

'I didn't get a good look at him,' I replied. 'And I haven't seen him since. Believe me, I looked.'

'I saw him,' Michele said. 'He ran right by me after the shooting stopped.'

'Which way was he going?' Hoskins asked.

'South on Rue des Archives.'

We were kept on the scene for another two hours and then brought to La Crim, where we made formal statements. Because he had discharged his weapon in the city, Louis was still giving his statement when Michele and I were released.

We were both hungry, so she took me to a bistro near her flat in the 8th Arrondissement.

'The best *frites* you have ever had,' she said on the way in, and she was right. They were shoe-string, hot, salted, and crispy.

'These could be addicting,' I said.

Michele smiled. 'I try to stay away, but I can't. I must have them at least once a week.'

'If I lived in Paris, I think I'd be here every other day.'

'Your job,' she said after we'd finished and were drinking coffee. 'It is always dangerous like to-day?'

'No,' I said. 'Well, sometimes.'

She made a throwaway gesture with her hand. 'It makes me think that what I do is – how do you say? – trivial.'

'Oh, I don't think that at all. Artists help us explain the world to ourselves.'

'I like that,' she said later, when I was walking her back to her apartment.

'What?'

'What you said about artists,' she replied.

'I think I read it somewhere, but it makes sense.'

We got to her building. 'Thank you for the most exciting day I think I have ever had,' Michele said.

I smiled and said, 'My pleasure.'

She walked up the stoop, used her keys to open the front door, stepped inside, and turned to me with that impish expression on her face.

'You have nice eyes, Jack Morgan,' Michele said, and shut the door.

Walking away, I'd rarely been happier.

Chapter 30

9TH ARRONDISSEMENT
APRIL 8, 1 A.M.

Wearing soiled clothes, his face smeared with grime, Émile Sauvage acted the drunken bum and lay sprawled in an alleyway upwind of a Dumpster and downwind of some of the most amazing odors he'd ever smelled. The scents boiled out of a steel door that was ajar about fifty feet away, and made the major realize he should have eaten more. Then the breeze stilled and he could smell the beer he'd poured on his pant legs.

Sauvage glanced around, saw no one, and pressed his hand to the tiny transceiver in his ear. 'How many left?' he murmured, knowing that the throat microphone would pick it up loud and clear.

'Two,' Epée said. 'Maître d' and the sommelier.'

'Stay patient,' Sauvage cautioned. 'You know his rep. Every day the same way. Like clock–'

The steel door pushed open. The maître d', a plump, intense-looking man in his late thirties, exited and immediately lit a cigarette. The sommelier, a younger woman, came after him, turned, and called back inside, '*À demain*, René.'

Then she closed the door, locked it, and followed the maître d' toward Sauvage's position.

'He works too hard,' the wine steward was saying.

'It's his passion,' the maître d' said.

'His heart will just break one of these days.'

Glancing in disgust at Sauvage lying in the filth, the maître d' replied, 'The price of greatness.'

'I just wish he'd pause to look around, relax, enjoy what he's built.'

The man said something Sauvage did not catch, and then they were gone.

'Fifteen minutes,' the major said, and rolled to his feet, putting on gloves.

Down the alley, Captain Mfune was already up and moving toward the door. The captain picked the lock and they were quickly inside a small entry area with work clogs on the floor and white jackets in a large hamper.

The major took two careful steps and peeked around the corner of a doorway, seeing a large, softly lit commercial kitchen with a high ceiling. A cluster of red enamel ovens and stovetops dominated the room, with gleaming copper pots of all sizes hanging from an overhead beam.

Sauvage knew at a glance that the kitchen was immaculate. This was a restaurant run with discipline. The major admired it, and almost changed his mind about the target. But when it came to impact, this was the man they wanted.

They padded through the kitchen. Sauvage glanced through the porthole into the dining area. Pitch-dark. Near the refrigerators and a freezer, they reached a door that Mfune opened, revealing a steep wooden staircase and an exposed stone wall. Light glowed in the cellar below them.

Keeping their feet to the outside of each step, right above the riser support, they made it to the basement with nary a creak. The light came through an open oak door down a narrow hallway.

The major led the way, quiet as possible, until they'd reached the doorway. Sauvage drew a pistol and stepped around and through the passage.

Wine bottles filled floor-to-ceiling racks on all sides of a room about forty feet long and fifteen feet wide. A silver-haired, barrel-shaped man in a white blouse and apron sat at a table with an open bottle of red wine, an almost empty glass, and a plate holding a baguette, cheese, chocolate, and fruit.

'Chef Pincus,' Sauvage said as Mfune came in behind him.

The chef startled, saw the gun, and jumped up, knocking the table. The bottle fell over. Wine spilled across the tabletop, dripped on the floor.

'Who the hell are you?' Pincus demanded.

'The future,' the major said. 'We need you to help us set things right.'

'Right about what?' the chef asked, stepping back, looking around, seeing that he was cornered. 'Is this about the Bocuse d'Or?'

'We're about so much more than the quality of French food,' Mfune said.

'What do you want, then? If it's money, I'll take you upstairs, give you tonight's till.'

'That's a start,' Sauvage said, and waved the gun. 'You first.'

Chef Pincus hesitated, rubbed his hands on his apron, and walked by them. Sauvage and Mfune stayed close to the chef as they navigated the hall and climbed the narrow stairs back to the kitchen.

When Pincus tried to exit out into the dining area, the major stopped him and said, 'I read in *Bon Appétit* that you make chicken stock once a week.'

Pincus stiffened, nodded. 'It's the last thing I do on Saturdays before having my wine and going home.'

'Can we see it?' the captain asked, joining them.

'That is what this is about, isn't it? The Bocuse? Stealing my secrets?'

'Believe what you want to believe. Just show us the soup.'

Sullenly, Pincus jerked his chin at one of the refrigerators. Mfune opened it. On the middle shelf stood a forty-quart stockpot with a lid. The captain grabbed the handles, lifted the pot with a grunt, and carried it to one of the prep tables.

'Go over there,' Sauvage said to the chef. 'Stand right in front of it.'

Reluctantly, Pincus followed his orders and stood before the stockpot, with Mfune at his left. The captain lifted the lid, set it aside. The major came around to the chef's right and looked in at fat starting to congeal on top of the liquid.

'Smells good,' Mfune said.

'Of course it does,' Pincus snapped.

'Take a smell. Lean right in there and sniff your masterpiece.'

The chef frowned and glanced at Sauvage, who said, 'Do it.'

Pincus looked uncertain but stepped closer,

and brought his nose over the top of ten gallons of cooling gourmet chicken stock. He sniffed, started to raise his chin, and then squealed with fear and alarm when the officers grabbed the back of his skull and plunged his face into the cooling liquid.

Terrified screams bubbled up out of the broth.

Then the chef started to fight, squirming side to side against their grip and throwing his fists wildly. Sauvage took a blow to the ribs and another to his hip before he flipped the pistol in his hand and chopped below the collar of Pincus's white blouse.

The flailing stopped. The squirming subsided and then halted altogether when the major hit the chef a second time.

'There,' Sauvage said, his breathing shallow, rapid. 'Not a bad recipe, really.'

Chapter 31

8TH ARRONDISSEMENT
6 A.M.

My dreams whirled with visions of the blood blooming on the waiter's shirt, Louis blown off his feet, and the pale gunman tracking the pistol muzzle over me.

In every vision, in every dream, I kept catching glimpses of Michele Herbert standing at the periphery of the action, and watching it all unfold as if through a glass, darkly. But when I awoke in my bed at the Plaza, my first thoughts were of the art professor laughing at the café the night before, and then climbing her stoop, smiling as if we were already sharing secrets, and telling me I had nice eyes.

Had any woman ever told me that?

If they had, I didn't remember.

Who cared? Michele thought my eyes were nice and that's all that mattered. My God, she was beyond belief good-looking and off-the-charts smart and creative. And yet she didn't seem to take herself too seriously.

She seemed relaxed, good in her own skin, free of issues, someone you wanted to spend time with. In the darkness of my room at the Plaza Athénée, I grinned like a fool, sat up in bed, and turned on the lights.

There was no chance I'd sleep any more, and given my embarrassing teenage giddiness, I knew I'd just sit there thinking about her unless I gave myself a task that could be taken care of at this early hour. Nothing came to mind until I realized it was only 9 p.m. back home.

Grabbing my phone, I punched in Justine's contact. I listened to her cell ring twice before she answered, 'I was just thinking about you, Jack.'

'That right?'

'I don't know exactly why, but you've been on my mind,' she said. 'So, anyway, how are you? Any luck with Kim Kopchinski? Del Rio told me there was a charge to a café in Paris.'

I told her about my entire crazy day, from losing Kim, to seeing the opera director's corpse, to

126

finding the secrets of his pied- à-terre, to Michele Herbert's collage. I took care not to make much of the artist beyond her smarts. I certainly wasn't going to babble on about Herbert's beauty and wit.

Instead, I emphasized her thoughts, her legions of followers, and her belief that someone who'd studied under or emulated a famous dead graffiti artist had painted the AB-16 tag.

Then I described the scene at Open Café, how we'd closed in on Kim Kopchinski, the gunplay that had ensued, and her escape. I didn't say a thing about dinner or the world's greatest fries or the fact that the artist liked my eyes.

'Sounds like you've got your hands full,' she said. 'And this Michele Herbert sounds like quite a woman.'

'Oh,' I said. 'Yeah, she's nice.'

'Uh-huh,' Justine said.

'You can't resist analyzing every word, can you?' I said hotly. 'It's like you can take the therapist out of the therapy room but you can't keep the therapy room out of the therapist.'

'Uh-huh,' she said.

'How's Sherman?' I asked.

'They've got him in a deep medical coma,' Justine said. 'They said it could take a few days for the swelling to subside enough to bring him out of it. I plan on stopping by there in the morning.'

'Sounds like you're all carrying on well without me.'

'You've assembled a strong team,' she said. 'You should be happy.'

'Oh, I'm a happy guy,' I said. 'April. Paris. Mysteries up the wazoo.'

'Hobnobbing with famous French artists,' she added.

'That too,' I replied. 'I've got to go. I'll call tomorrow.'

'Uh-huh.'

I clicked off, wondering what I'd said or tone I'd used to cause Justine to home in so quickly on Michele Herbert. It was as if she had an emotional radar or something, an innate sensitivity that had made her so effective as a psychologist for the L.A. district attorney and as an investigator with Private.

I took a shower, flashing on Michele and finding it nice that she hadn't spent the night scrutinizing me, trying to figure out what made me tick, or what old wounds I was trying to work out. Instead, she was interested, fun, and easy to be with, and I vowed I would not leave Paris without seeing her again.

Chapter 32

I went downstairs for breakfast.

The second the elevator opened, the big, shaved-headed Saudi royal bodyguard with the Texas accent was looking at me.

He nodded. 'Mr. Morgan.'

'You know my name?'

'We know everyone who's staying here.'

128

'What's your name?'

'Randall Peaks.'

'Need a job, Randall Peaks?'

'I don't think you could afford me.'

'Probably not. Can I go have breakfast?'

'Just don't get near the princesses, and you'll be fine.'

'So the royals don't use Saudi bodyguards?'

'A few,' he said. 'The rest of us are contracted.'

'How long have you been working there?'

'Seven years,' Peaks said as the elevator pinged behind me. 'Have a good day, Mr. Morgan.'

I left him and went into the dining area, spotting a large table of Middle Eastern women who looked ready for fashion week. Every one of them was wearing a couture dress. Every one of them had flawless makeup, a dramatic hairdo, and stunning jewelry.

Laughing, chatting, and generally having a good time, they paid no attention to me. But the guards positioned discreetly around the room watched me all the way to my seat.

I read the *International Herald Tribune* and had an exceptional breakfast of poached eggs, asparagus, and a dill sauce that I wanted to eat with a spoon.

The princesses left before I had finished. Only one of them looked even remotely my way as they exited the room. She was the youngest, probably in her mid to late teens, and by my estimation the most beautiful of them all. It took me a moment to realize that she wasn't looking at me, but studying a painting over my right shoulder.

Brought back to earth, stuffed and caffeinated,

I was at the offices of Private Paris by seven fifteen and not surprised to find Louis already at his desk drinking an espresso.

'Do you ever sleep?' I asked.

'Five hours, every night,' he said, and snapped his fingers. 'Five hours and I am ready to go. I have only just heard from Le Chien.'

'Yeah?' I said, taking a seat. 'He find anything on Richard?'

'Many things,' Louis said. 'Including the fact that several times in the last week he ate at a very famous restaurant in Paris, Chez Pincus. By the amount of money he spent, it suggests that he was entertaining a woman. Perhaps the woman in the—'

Ali Farad, Private Paris's newest hire, came in. 'You wanted to see me?'

'Yes,' Louis said, leaning over a desktop computer and typing in a command. When he finished, he peered over the screen at Farad and said, 'Ali, what you're about to see you aren't going to like, and you are to keep what you are about to see completely to yourself.'

'Okay...' Farad said.

'Okay, what?'

'Okay, okay.'

Louis pivoted the screen to show the hijab and veil that I'd photographed with my phone when we were inside the opera director's love shack. Farad looked at them with little expression, and then shrugged. 'Why are these important?'

'Because of these,' Louis said, and gave the computer another command.

The screen blinked, divided into quadrants,

and up popped four photographs of the opera director in the Catholic priest's collar having sex with the fierce-eyed woman in the hijab and veil.

Farad's lips thinned. 'That's Henri Richard.'

'Correct,' Louis said. 'He seemed to have a fetish about priests and Muslim girls. He was writing an opera about it.'

'We think he might have been killed because he was also living out his fantasies,' I said. 'Are we off base on that? Could you see a Muslim father, or brother, or uncle finding out about the affair and deciding to kill Richard?'

Farad nodded without hesitation. 'Sure, I could see it. I mean, this is just the rankest porn imaginable. Among radical sects, it would be just cause for revenge on Richard, and perhaps her death as well.'

'Richard was with a woman last night, before his death. A redhead,' I said. 'Maybe this woman.'

'Any idea how we'd find her?' Louis asked.

Farad stayed quiet and scratched at his chin while my thoughts tracked to the hijab and veil, and I thumbed through the pictures I'd taken of them on my phone.

When I found what I was looking for, I sent it to Louis's e-mail address and said, 'Pull this picture up when you get it on e-mail, and blow it up on the screen.'

The file went through almost immediately, and quickly Louis had the picture up on his screen, where we could all see it well. The hijab and veil were turned inside out, exposing labels in Arabic.

'What's that say?' I asked Farad.

The investigator scooted forward, studied the

image, and said, 'Al-Jumaa Custom Tailor and Embroidery. I know this place. It's around the corner from my mosque.'

Chapter 33

18TH ARRONDISSEMENT
12:35 P.M.

Haja Hamid slipped in among the other women retrieving their shoes and sandals. She fell in behind three women leaving the mosque, and followed their lead, removing her veil before she passed through the door. She wanted none of the attention she'd received the day before.

But when she stepped down onto the sidewalk, she noticed that same young man – he couldn't have been more than seventeen – standing across the street, holding his camera. He spotted her, came her way. She tried to duck behind some other women, but he was relentless and came right up beside her.

'You are so beautiful,' he said.

Haja said nothing, increased her pace.

'Please. My name is Alain Du Champs, and I am doing a project where I am taking pictures of Muslim women without their veil on, showing the world what it and they have been missing. Can I take your picture, please?'

'No. Never,' she said, and hurried on.

Hurrying up beside her, the photographer

began to sing to the tune of Billy Joel's 'Only the Good Die Young.'

'Wake up, Fatima, don't let me wait. You Muslim girls start much too late. Aw, but sooner or later it comes down to fate. I might as well be the one!'

Haja picked up her pace, trying to get away, but he kept after her, still singing. Three men were coming at her down the sidewalk: an older one with longish iron-gray hair, smoking a cigarette; a younger, athletic, blond, hazel-eyed guy; and an even younger Arab man wearing a black leather jacket and jeans.

Something about the trio triggered fear in Haja. For a moment she thought they were police. But then they stood aside. The Arab guy said, 'Accept my apologies, mademoiselle. Not all Frenchmen are assholes like the kid with the camera and the voice of an ass.'

Haja smiled, nodded at the men uncertainly, and then hurried on toward Epée and the car.

Chapter 34

We watched her hurry away with her head down. The kid who'd been singing to her held tight to his camera as he tried to get around us.

Ali Farad stopped him and said, 'That's enough. Leave her alone.'

The photographer scowled and said, 'Makmood, in case you hadn't noticed, France is still a free country. We don't do Sharia law here.'

'It *is* a free country, and she has the right not to be harassed.'

'You a cop?'

'No.'

'Then fuck yourself, and eat pork while you're doing it,' the kid said. But he did not pursue the woman, instead crossing the street and walking away from us.

'He was right about something,' Louis said when we moved on.

'What's that?' Farad said, clearly still pissed at the kid.

'She was beautiful. Did you see her face? And those eyes? In my opinion, it is a waste of the feminine mystique to have her covered up like that.'

Farad seemed unimpressed and said, 'People have a right to their culture.'

'*Sans doute,*' Louis replied. 'As long as it does not infringe on my right to my culture, and men of my culture enjoy the female form.'

We walked on past several young men putting a coat of paint on top of a coat of paint on top of an AB-16 tag, which had bled through. An older man in a long white tunic was watching with his arms crossed.

'Imam,' Farad said, his face falling. 'They've defaced the mosque.'

The imam nodded grimly. 'Do you know what this means? AB-16?'

'No,' Farad said, and then introduced us.

Imam Ibrahim Al-Moustapha was one of those men who beam with kindness. He shook our hands, looked deeply into our eyes, repeated our names, and said how happy he was to meet us.

'When was this done?' I asked, gesturing to the tag.

'Two nights ago,' Al-Moustapha replied. 'The police chased him but he caused two police cars to collide up the street as he made his escape.'

'Imam?' one of the painters said.

Al-Moustapha excused himself and went over to him.

We continued on, and Farad said, 'The imam is a great man. He stands for a moderate, progressive, and inclusive Islam. And he speaks up for it, and against the radicals.'

'A rare man, then,' Louis said.

With heat in his voice, Farad replied, 'With all due respect, Louis, no, he's not. There are many of us who think this way, who want to build communities, not destroy them.'

He gestured to a storefront just beyond the mosque.

The FEZ Couriers sign in the window featured a large Moroccan hat with a gold tassel hanging off the top. There were several men smoking out front and wearing jackets featuring the FEZ logo as well.

'Firmus Massi built this business from nothing,' Farad said. 'His parents came from Algiers, as mine did. He saw a need for a messenger service and started it on a credit card. Now he employs twenty messengers in Paris. A builder. Not a destroyer.'

'An entrepreneur in France,' Louis said, impressed. 'A rarer thing than a moderate Muslim.'

Farad ignored him and gestured to the store next to the messenger service. 'This is where the hijab and veil were made.'

'Al-Jumaa Custom Tailor and Embroidery' was written above the door in French and Arabic. Farad went in first and we followed. The interior was crowded with bolts of fabric stacked in cubbies, several women working on sewing machines, and racks of robes, tunics, and veils on the far wall.

Farad was soon talking to Monsieur Al-Jumaa, a gaunt man in a white tunic and black pants. His wife, who stood beside him, was dressed the same as the woman we'd seen running from the kid with the camera: long dark robes and a hijab that surrounded her face like a frame. For some reason she had been staring hostilely at me from the get-go. Maybe she didn't like blonds.

Farad did the talking in Arabic, and then in French, with Louis translating for me. We showed the tailor our Private badges. He seemed unimpressed. His wife, a pudgy-faced woman with the constant threat of a snarl on her upper lip, looked at the badges, flung her hands in the air, and chattered something in Arabic. Her husband chattered back.

'She thinks we're here to persecute them,' Farad said. 'He agrees.'

'Tell them Private doesn't do persecution,' I said. 'We just ask questions. They're under no obligation to answer, but we could use their help.'

Farad rattled that off, and we got grudging harrumphs in return.

'Show them the picture, Jack,' Louis said.

I did, and the Al-Jumaa studied it. Immediately

the tailor turned suspicious and said, 'Why do you have this picture to show me?'

'It's part of a murder investigation,' Louis said. 'I'm sure the police will be by at some point to talk to you about it. We're looking into it for the victim's wife.'

'We know nothing about a murder,' the tailor's wife said, on the defensive now. 'We are good people. We work hard.'

'I'm sure you do,' I said. 'And you keep records, yes?'

'What kind of records?' Al-Jumaa asked, the suspicion returning.

'Orders,' Louis said. 'Measurements. Addresses. Phone numbers. Who bought that hijab and that veil and when.'

Madame Al-Jumaa clucked sharply at her husband in Arabic and threw her hands up in surrender. Al-Jumaa shrugged and asked to see the picture again.

The tailor enlarged the photo and stared at the label for a moment, and then shook his head and said, 'Ready-to-wear. No records of this.'

'Explain that,' Farad said.

Al-Jumaa pointed to two short, thin, black lines in the corner of the label and then gestured at the racks along the far wall.

'All the premades carry these two lines,' he said. 'The custom hijabs and robes carry a crescent.'

'So you don't keep a record of who bought ready-to-wear?' Louis asked.

'Just that a robe was sold. No names. No addresses. We are not required to keep them.'

'How's business?' I asked.

The tailor studied me, nodded, and said, 'Business is good. Every year it gets better. The future is bright for us.'

That surprised me. 'Even with the laws on wearing the hijab and veil?'

His wife heard that and started clucking in amusement this time.

'She says those laws will be repealed eventually,' Farad interpreted.

'What makes her think that?' Louis asked.

Her husband said, 'The population of old France is aging and dying, while the immigrant population is young and growing. The birthrate in old France is less than two children per marriage. The birthrate among immigrants is in the fours. We have five children. Sooner than later, we will simply outnumber the old French, and then the law will fall, just as I will grow rich.'

His wife added, 'It is simple mathematics. Like Allah's will: indisputable and inevitable.'

I couldn't argue with the tailor's logic. The numbers were the numbers.

'How long until you see it happening?' I asked Farad and Louis once we were back out on the sidewalk.

'It already is happening,' Louis said. 'You can see it in places like Les Bosquets. There they are, bulging at the seams.'

'Twenty years?' Farad said. 'Twenty-five until the law changes?'

'Something like that,' Louis agreed. 'But by then I shall be too old to care.'

'But by then, won't the immigrants have assimilated more into French culture?' I asked.

'Not if we isolate them,' Louis said. His cell phone rang and he answered.

'What do you think?' I asked Farad.

He shrugged. 'I am not much interested in politics.'

'Pincus?' Louis gasped. 'Yes, of course. We'll be right there.'

Shaken, Louis shut his phone, looked at me, and said, 'That was Sharen Hoskins. She has been ordered to accept your offer of a forensics team. La Crim's criminalists are backlogged and AB-16 has struck again.'

'Jesus,' I said. 'Who's the victim?'

'René Pincus. Arguably the greatest chef in all of France.'

PART THREE

LES IMMORTELS

Chapter 35

9TH ARRONDISSEMENT
1:20 P.M.

The greatest chef in all of France hung upside down from a rope tied to his ankles and lashed to a steel beam that ran down the center of the kitchen ceiling. René Pincus's swollen head hovered a few feet over the stovetops, and his arms were spread to the sides, tied with cooking twine.

'Same general position as Henri Richard,' Sharen Hoskins observed. 'But the graffiti is much more visible this time. We won't be able to contain it.'

The tag was painted three times inside the restaurant: once on the stovetop below Pincus, once on the dining room wall, and a third time across the front window. Word of the great chef's death had leaked and a mob of media types gathered out front, training their cameras on the tag on the front window.

'Was he strangled?' I asked.

'No,' the *investigateur* said. 'Drowned in his own chicken stock.'

'So the method of killing is different, almost ironic,' I said.

Hoskins nodded. 'And it changes things, don't you think? With those pictures you discovered, Henri Richard's murder was easily attributed to

143

revenge. Now I think we must look for a link between Henri Richard and René Pincus, some reason they were targeted for death.'

'There is one link,' Louis said.

'What's that?'

'Henri Richard ate dinner here several times in the last six weeks.'

Hoskins squinted, crossed her arms, and said, 'And how do you know that?'

Louis realized he'd set a trap for himself, but he smiled and said, 'Private Paris never reveals its confidential sources, but I can assure you it's true.'

'Louis,' she began.

'*Chéri,*' he said. 'Are we here to follow every nuance of the law? Or are we here to catch a killer who grows more prolific?'

Hoskins stuck out her jaw. 'Don't call me *chéri.*'

'Ah,' Louis said, acting chagrined. 'A slip of the tongue, no? I promise never to address you this way again.'

Claudia Vans, Private Paris's chief forensics tech, came up to Louis. She showed him several plastic evidence bags containing cigarette butts and said, 'What's the chance the staff has a habit of flicking cigarette butts around this place?'

'Seems unlikely, but we'll ask,' Hoskins said.

Out in the dining area, other Private Paris forensics techs were photographing and taking samples from the AB-16 graffiti on the wall. Hoskins went to speak with them. When she was satisfied that they were covering every angle, she went to the front door and started letting in the staff to be questioned.

Louis provided a running translation.

The maître d', a plump, nervous man named Remy Fontaine, said, 'Is it true? He is dead?'

'I'm afraid so,' the *investigateur* said.

Fontaine and the other four employees broke down crying and hugged each other. The sommelier, a stocky blonde named Adelaide St. Michel, stopped crying long enough to say, 'Does it have to do with the Bocuse d'Or?'

'What makes you say that?' Louis asked.

'The other chefs in France hated Chef Pincus,' she said. 'Three times he wins the Bocuse d'Or, and every time you hear the vicious rumors right away, the terrible things they said about him. It was all envy, and I think it was strong enough for people to want him dead. How did he die?'

Hoskins hesitated.

'How *did* he die?' asked Fontaine, the maître d'.

'He was drowned in his chicken stock,' I said.

The sommelier snapped her fingers at me, and then at Hoskins, who was glaring my way. 'There you go, then,' Adelaide St. Michel said. 'Chef Pincus was world famous for his stock. This is a statement.'

I had to agree. Killing him in his own soup was designed to send a message. But what, exactly?

Chapter 36

It certainly didn't appear to me that any of the staff were involved. All of them appeared genuinely heartbroken. To a person they seemed to have loved René Pincus. He was demanding. He was precise. He could be a withering critic of their work. But he was also extraordinarily generous.

'It was a side of René that no one outside of us knew, really,' said the maître d'. 'To the staff, he was like a demanding uncle. In public, he was the French chef of iron.'

He'd said this last in English, so I corrected him. 'Iron chef.'

'Yes?' Fontaine said. 'René was the iron chef of the world, and now he is no more.' The grief-stricken man broke down sobbing again. 'What is to become of us? Who will carry on with the restaurant?'

'Who would be the natural person to step forward?' I asked. 'There must be a senior chef working beneath Chef Pincus.'

'That would be me,' said Peter Bonaventure. He looked about forty but had the build of a marathoner. 'But I can't even think this way. I did not want his throne. I loved my job. René was a genius who made our work a passion. And he paid us well, gave us profit shares that were equal to his own.'

'Equal?' I asked.

They nodded. With every one of them making the same amount of euros as Pincus, the idea of financial gain as motive seemed to be diminishing rapidly.

'How many of you smoke?' Louis asked.

Four of the staff members, including the maître d', raised their hands.

'How many of you would discard a cigarette on the kitchen floor or in the wine cellar?'

All four hands dropped. To a person they looked horrified.

'That would be grounds for termination,' the sommelier said. 'No smoking in the restaurant. René would have a fit.'

Louis, Hoskins, and I exchanged glances. Someone with no fear of Pincus had tossed the cigarettes. Probably his killers.

Louis got out his iPhone and called up a picture of Henri Richard. He showed it to them. 'Did you see him in the restaurant in the past six weeks or so?'

Remy Fontaine, the maître d', took one look and said, *'Bien sûr.* He is the dead opera director. Monsieur Richard. He came here often.'

'Alone?' Hoskins asked.

'Never alone,' Fontaine said. 'Always with a woman.'

'Same woman?' I asked.

The maître d' and the sommelier glanced at each other before she said, 'The last two or three times we think it was the same woman. Exotically beautiful, with perfect caramel-colored skin and big cat eyes. But she was different every time she

147

came in. Hair color and cut.'

'And eye color,' the maître d' said. 'Twice they were dark brown, but the last time they were in, her hair had been hennaed red, and her eyes were, I don't know, like a cat's eyes?'

'So she's wearing different-colored contacts,' I said.

'And more than that,' the maître d' said. 'She had – how do you say? – extensions in her hair, and her cheeks, the thickness, they seemed to change.'

Louis said, 'Probably putting cotton high in her mouth.'

'You ever hear him use her name?'

'Mariama,' the headwaiter said. 'No idea on her last name.'

'You're positive?' Hoskins said.

'Definitely,' he replied. 'I heard him call her Mariama several times.'

The name could be useful, I thought. But then again, this is a woman who changes her hair and eye color and used cotton to alter her looks. It wasn't a stretch to see her using an alias.

'Did Chef Pincus know Henri Richard?'

The maître d' nodded. 'They were not close friends, but they knew each other. In fact, the last time Richard was in with Mariama, René came to their table and talked.'

'About what?' Hoskins asked.

Fontaine shrugged. 'I don't know, but the chef shook his hand and seemed very happy returning to the kitchen.'

The wine steward agreed. 'He was whistling.'

'And when was this?' I asked.

'Last week.'

'Are there security cameras here?'

Investigateur Hoskins sobered, shook her head. 'There are very few outside of government buildings. The French see it as an invasion of privacy.'

'Who was the last to see Chef Pincus alive?' Louis asked.

The maître d' and the wine steward raised their hands. They gave us the timetable, and then described leaving the restaurant shortly after 1 a.m., and seeing a drunk passed out in the alley by the Dumpster.

'You rarely see that in this neighborhood,' Fontaine remarked. 'But you could smell the alcohol all over him, even over the garbage.'

'What does it mean?' the steward asked. 'The graffiti?'

'When we figure it out, we'll let you know,' Hoskins said. 'For now, I want to clear the restaurant and let the forensics team complete its work.'

Louis and I didn't argue. We went back through the kitchen, where Chef Pincus's body had been cut down and covered with a sheet. Out in the alley, we crossed to the Dumpster, finding a broken bottle of beer sitting upright beneath it. There was still two inches of booze in the intact bottom.

'Why didn't he drink it?' Louis asked.

'What, from the broken part? There are glass shards in there. He'd have swallowed them.'

'A clever wino would strain them out with his shirt,' Louis said. 'Maybe this bum just wanted to smell drunk.'

Chapter 37

8TH ARRONDISSEMENT
6:12 P.M.

I got out of a taxi in the twilight, and felt vindicated and excited as I bid good evening to the doorman at the Plaza Athénée. Earlier, Louis and I left Investigateur Hoskins to deal with the media mob gathered around Chez Pincus, and went back to the offices of Private Paris. We put together a priority list for the evidence our techs had gathered at the scene.

It was a big deal for a Private forensics team to be called in by a local police department, and especially by a renowned investigative operation like La Crim. The decision spoke to the level of training and adherence to state-of-the-art forensics methods that I'd insisted on after deciding to get my company into the crime analysis business. Our labs were certified in fifteen states in the U.S. We maintain Interpol standards throughout the rest of the world, and police agencies were starting to recognize us for our efforts.

That alone had put a positive spin on my day. But around 2 p.m., I'd gotten a call that put me in an even rosier state of mind. Michele Herbert asked if I would like to have dinner with her. Though I'd felt like doing a back handspring in response, I kept my cool, and we made a date for nine.

I moved through the lobby and through an arch. I glanced to my right and saw a gathering happy hour crowd milling in an interior loggia that abutted the dining room and the courtyard. Along the walls of the high, narrow space, groups of the beautiful, the wealthy, and the famous sat in fine furniture, sipped from thirty dollar cocktails, and nibbled at plates of foie gras and caviar tureens.

About halfway down, I spotted Randall Peaks by that gaggle of Saudi princesses, all of whom appeared to have changed dresses since the morning. Peaks looked at me and nodded. I nodded back, and then got on the elevator. As I did, my phone rang.

'Jack Morgan,' I answered.

'It's me,' Justine said. 'The swelling on Sherman Wilkerson's brain has started to subside. The doctors think they'll be able to bring him out of the coma tomorrow, or the day after at the latest.'

'Long-term prognosis?' I asked.

'Could take a year of therapy, but good, I think,' she replied.

'That's excellent,' I said, and breathed a sigh of relief. Not only was Sherman Wilkerson one of my oldest clients, but he was a truly good man, someone who most certainly did not deserve to live out his days in a vegetative state.

'Anything on the granddaughter to report?' Justine asked. 'I'm sure she'll be the first thing on Sherman's mind.'

'She's gone to ground. I haven't seen any new alerts that she's used her card.'

'How's Paris otherwise?'

'Still the most beautiful city in the world.'

'The most romantic too, I hear,' she said.

'I wouldn't know about that,' I said. 'Things are all business here.'

'Uh-huh,' she said as the elevator dinged open and I got out at the eighth floor. 'That's not what Louis just told me.'

'Don't know what you're talking about,' I said, digging for my key card.

'Gorgeous famous artist and graffiti expert?'

I used the key card and pushed the suite door open, saying, 'Oh, her.'

'Yes, her,' Justine said. 'Louis says you're smitten.'

'Take that with a grain of salt. The man is smitten himself about six times a day.' I walked the short hallway into the suite's living area and set the key card on the table.

'Jack, it's okay to be smitten.'

'I'm well aware of that,' I replied. I entered the bedroom and headed toward the walk-in closet.

Before she could reply, I heard a squeak behind me before something hit me hard right between the shoulder blades, stunned me, blew the wind out of me, and drove me to my knees.

Chapter 38

The second blow between the shoulder blades caused me to drop the phone, and threw me forward on my stomach, grunting, trying to get my breath.

A black tactical boot appeared in my peripheral vision and crushed the phone while someone grabbed my wrists, pulled them behind my back, and locked them together with zip ties. Still gasping for air, I saw a gloved hand come forward, take my chin, and wrench it down. Another gloved hand stuffed fabric so far into my mouth that I gagged and choked.

I was hauled to my feet and tossed on my back on the bed. Two men wearing jeans, black jackets, and panty hose over their heads to smear their features stood there. The dark-haired guy had a big nose. He also had a suppressed SIG Sauer pistol aimed at me.

The other, a blond guy with pale skin, held a ball-peen hammer in his right hand. In a thick accent, he said, 'Here's how it works, Monsieur Morgan. I take the gag out and you tell me where to find Kim. If you try to yell or if you lie, I will break your kneecap. Understand?'

My breath had come back, and already my senses were searching for a possible counter-attack. I found it in attitude. Relaxing my face and softening my eyes, I acted as if I somehow had the upper hand in this negotiation.

'*Vous comprenez?*' the pale guy demanded.

I bobbed my head. The one with the gun reached over and yanked the gag from my mouth.

'Where is she?'

'Don't know,' I croaked.

He raised the hammer.

'No, really,' I said. 'Last time I saw her, she was running from your terrible shooting skills.'

'Fuck you.'

'If I'd been behind the gun, she would have hit the ground, not some waiter,' I said. 'What do I call you, anyway? Since the first time I saw you, I kept thinking of you as 'Pale Guy.' So what name do you want? Pale Guy or Whitey?'

Pale Guy stiffened. But the one with the gun snorted, and under his breath he murmured something I barely caught before Whitey said in a reasonable voice, 'My name is of no consequence to you, Monsieur Morgan. However, the things I can do, my expertise, in fact, is of total consequence to you.'

He slapped the hammer into his gloved palm. 'Do you enjoy walking?'

'One of my favorite pastimes, but as I said, Whitey, I don't know where Kim Kopchinski is. In case you hadn't noticed, she's been trying to avoid me as much as get the fuck away from you. Other than that, go ahead and turn my legs into oatmeal. It's not going to change my tune. What did she do to you, by the way, that's got you shooting up Paris?'

Whitey said to the one with the gun, 'I believe him.'

154

'Yeah?'

'*Oui*,' he said, and then lowered the hammer and came closer to me. 'Did you hear? I believe you, Monsieur Morgan.'

'Great. Just a little misunderstanding.'

'Exactly,' Whitey said, again in that reasonable tone. 'Tell me. In the time when you were with Kim, was she still smoking and using that lighter she has on a chain around her neck?'

What did that have to do with the price of a croissant?

'She smoked like a chimney,' I said. 'The pack of Gauloises was never far from her hand, and she still had the lighter.'

Before Whitey could respond to that, someone began banging loudly on the outer door to the suite.

Chapter 39

'Jack!' I heard Louis yell. 'Jack, open up!'

Big Nose pivoted and moved out fast. Before following him into the outer room, however, Whitey threw his hammer from close range, hitting me hard and high on the flank of my left leg.

The effect was electric and painful, but I gritted my teeth and rolled off the bed and to my feet, barely able to feel my left butt cheek and thigh. No more than ten seconds had elapsed since Whitey and Big Nose had left the bedroom, but already the suite's living area was empty. The doors to the balcony were open. Even in the dim light I could tell that it, too, was empty.

What the hell had they done? Jumped seventy feet to the sidewalk?

I limped fast to the door, where Louis was still pounding. Turning my back to the latch arm, I hooked the zip tie on it and pressed down.

Louis almost knocked me over, shoving his way inward.

'Justine was right!' he cried, pulling me back to my feet. 'Who did this?'

'Our friend Whitey, and his pal, a guy with a big nose and dark hair,' I said. 'You spooked them.'

'Where'd they go?' Louis asked, and I felt a blade slip between my wrists and sever the tie.

'They either jumped or they climbed to the roof,' I said, rubbing my wrists.

'The roof! Come, Jack. With luck we can cut them off!'

'They'll be long gone,' I said, limping after him.

'Maybe not,' he said. 'The footing up there is treacherous when it's wet.'

Several months before, the Plaza Athénée hired Private Paris to do a complete rethinking of its security system as part of a remodeling of the current hotel and an expansion into three adjoining buildings. Louis had inspected the four structures, cataloging all ways in and out of the future hotel, and in the process developed the new system.

My leg was no longer numb but threatened to charley horse now. But I managed to keep several steps back from Louis as he wound his way through the hallways to a stairwell. He stopped on the landing and looked up at a hatch in the ceiling. It was locked. There was a red plastic tag on the lock hasp.

'That's my seal,' Louis said. 'They didn't get in this way.'

'How many other ways to the roof are there?'

'One other in the hotel. But six others among the three buildings the hotel bought for the expansion. They're all empty, ready for interior demolition.'

He started up the ladder, got out his knife, cut the seal, and then dialed in the combination he said was the same on all eight hatches. When he pushed the hatch door open, I heard a whoosh. Wind and light rain blasted down on us.

By the time I got out on the roof, Louis was ahead of me in the low light, moving gingerly across the roof, which was copper, ghostly green, slick, and steeply pitched. To the left, it was an eighty-foot fall to the hotel's power plant, and to the right, a drop of the same distance into the hotel's famous courtyard. The windows of the rooms overlooking the courtyard were glowing, giving enough light that when I happened to glance back toward the Avenue Montaigne, I spotted two figures moving around air-conditioning compressors.

'Louis. There they are,' I hissed.

'I know where they're going,' he said, scrambling over to me. 'Back into the hotel through that second hatch.'

We scuttled back to the near hatch, climbed back down the steep ladder, and started to run through the hallways again.

'Call hotel security,' I grunted. The pain in my leg had died to a throb.

'And risk a shoot-out in here?' Louis said. '*Excusez-moi*, but that's a bad idea that would probably cost us our lucrative contract with the Plaza. Best thing we can do is let them think they're home free, and follow them wherever they go.'

It made sense, so I didn't argue. But by the time we'd reached the second hatch, it was open, and the rain was blowing hard into the stairway. We heard the slap of footsteps several floors below us.

We ran to the elevator. It came up from two floors below. We climbed in and hit the lobby button.

'There are only a few exits and all are on the first floor,' Louis gasped.

The elevator dropped, and then opened, and we spilled out into the loggia, which was even more packed than it had been thirty-five minutes before. I spotted Randall Peaks still at his post. Beyond the Saudi entourage some people moved, revealing Whitey and his companion strolling with their backs to us as if they had not a care in the world.

'They're going to the crystal bar,' Louis said.

He'd no sooner said that than the two men took a right toward open doors. Just before they disappeared into the bar, Whitey happened to look back and saw us staring right at him from fifty yards away.

Chapter 40

The next few seconds seemed to unfold in slow motion.

Even as Louis and I started to move toward them, Whitey reached under his leather jacket and said something to his comrade, and they both twisted our way, pistols rising amid the happy cocktail hour din.

They each touched off two rounds. I'd expected the sound suppressors to still be on, but they weren't, and the four loud shots shattered a mirror behind us and a large vase to our left.

Beautiful, rich, and powerful people started screaming and diving for the floor. Whitey and his buddy disappeared into the crystal bar. Louis yanked out his Glock and we started to run forward, jumping over patrons crawling for cover.

Before we could get even close to the bar, Randall Peaks and three other Saudi royal bodyguards blocked the way. They were set up in a defensive semicircle, backs to the terrified princesses. Their guns looked a heck of a lot bigger than Louis's.

'Drop it or I will shoot,' Peaks roared in French, and then English.

'They were shooting at us!' I yelled. 'We're the good guys, Peaks!'

'Drop the gun now, or I will kill you.'

'Screw you,' Louis said. He turned and began

running back the other way.

'Don't shoot him!' I shouted. 'We're going to the street.'

When I spun around and headed after Louis, however, there was an unmistakable prickle at the back of my neck, a sensation that only happens when there's a gun aimed my way. Ignoring it, I followed Louis through the lobby and out into the street.

I heard screams down the block. Whitey and the Nose jumped an iron fence that surrounded an outdoor seating area off the bar and were sprinting away from us.

We chased them down the Avenue Montaigne, up the Rue François 1er, and then north on the Rue de Marignan. But my hip was killing me, and they were far younger than Louis. By the time we hit the crowded sidewalks of the Champs-Élysées, we'd lost them.

We trudged back to the Plaza Athénée to find six police cars out front with their lights flashing, and a crowd growing on the sidewalk across from the hotel. At first the police tried to keep us out, but when Louis explained that we were not only witnesses to the shooting but the targets, we were allowed entry.

There were ten, maybe fifteen uniformed officers already inside, and four detectives from La Crim, including Investigateur Hoskins, who took one look at Louis and me and said, 'Really? The second night in a row you're involved in a shootout? Really?'

'Calm down, Sharen ... *investigateur*,' Louis said. 'They came after Jack. One of these men

160

was the same pale guy who shot up Open Café.'

'That true?' Hoskins asked.

'He wore a pair of panty hose over his head, but I'd put money on it,' I said. 'They were looking for the same woman they tried to kill last night.'

'Do we know why they're after her?'

'Something to do with drugs,' I said.

'They didn't say anything else to you?'

'Uh, no ... wait. Yes. They asked if she was still smoking, and I said like a chimney, and then Louis started banging on the door.'

'Well, just so you know, you've both caused an international incident,' Hoskins said. 'There were Saudi royals in there when the shooting started.'

'We noticed,' I said.

'If they and their bodyguards weren't there, I might have caught them,' Louis said. 'They blocked us. Threatened to shoot me.'

'What about *royal family* don't you understand?' Hoskins asked.

'Last time I looked, France was a European country,' Louis snapped.

'And last time I looked, the Saudis were vital allies of France,' she retorted. 'I guarantee I'm going to be hearing all sorts of flak over this.'

'My condolences,' Louis said. 'What about Pincus?'

'Nothing more than you knew this morning,' she replied. 'You'll need to come into La Crim in the morning to make a statement. Both of you.'

'First thing,' I promised. 'Can I go back to my room?'

'They were wearing gloves?' she asked.

'They were, and, like I said, panty hose over

their heads. So I don't think they left much evidence other than the hammer Whitey threw at me.'

'I'll send an officer up to collect it,' she said, and then turned away.

It was almost eight when I left Louis. Despite all that had happened, I was going to make my date with Michele Herbert. When I reentered the suite, it felt unprotected, strange, and violated. I double-locked the balcony doors, took a shower, changed clothes, and went back out in less than fifteen minutes.

The police had begun letting witnesses leave, and the loggia was emptying out. The staff was clearly out of sorts, and several of them, including fair Elodie, the concierge, glared at me as I walked through the lobby. I guess word had gotten around that the bad guys had been trying to kill me, and somehow I'd become a villain for aiding in a breach of the Plaza's legendary decorum.

When I got in the taxi and gave the driver the address and name of the restaurant Michele Herbert had suggested, I tried to compartment-alize and clear my mind, tried to look forward to the artist's company and several glasses of wine.

But something came back to me, something Whitey had said when they had me semi-hog-tied on the bed. He hadn't just asked about her smoking: he'd specifically mentioned the lighter on the chain around her neck.

What the hell was that all about?

Chapter 41

11TH ARRONDISSEMENT
10:30 P.M.

A line snaked down the sidewalk outside Le Chanticleer Rouge. Most of the patrons trying to get into the Red Rooster club were well dressed and attractive couples, plus a few single women.

'Unaccompanied males are not allowed in the club tonight,' called a bouncer who was walking along the line with a short, severe brunette carrying a clipboard and studying everyone they passed.

'You,' she said to a woman with a plunging bust. 'You four behind her.'

The bouncer stood back to let the woman and two attractive and now happier couples go forward. He ignored the people complaining that they'd been in line longer. It didn't matter. The Red Rooster was not a first come, first served kind of place. Like at Studio 54 in Manhattan back in the hero days of disco, you had to be selected to enter.

The bouncer and the 'hostess' continued to move along the line, dismissing at least twenty people before stopping in front of a brunette with skin the color of fresh crème and a big black guy.

He wore sunglasses despite the hour and a sharp suit with an open-neck white shirt, and thin black driving gloves. When he smiled, a gold cap glowed on one of his top front teeth. He could have been anything from a rap mogul to a movie producer to a gangsta on holiday, and he certainly looked nothing like Captain Mfune of the French Army, currently assigned to École de Guerre.

The brunette's attire only added to the couple's mystery and allure. She wore green cat-eye contacts and carried a black snakeskin purse. Her sleek gray dress was sleeveless, and she wore black elbow-length gloves, black pumps, black hose, and a black pillbox hat with a modest lace veil.

'You two are in,' the hostess said, and the bouncer directed them forward.

'Told you I knew what it takes to get in here,' she said out of the corner of her mouth as they walked along the line, giving scant attention to the envy and resentment in the faces of those who'd been passed by.

'You called it, Amé,' the captain agreed.

A bouncer pulled open the door, and they were hit by a wave of electronic dance music. They entered an opulent lobby, bypassed a coat check, and went to a cashier's counter, where Mfune paid the forty euro cover charge.

'You have been here before?' the cashier asked. 'Or do you need a tour?'

'I've been,' Amé said. 'I'll show my friend the ropes.'

'You'll find those in the dungeon,' the cashier reminded her, and then looked at the captain. 'And please, no cell phones. Not even texting when you are inside. This is to protect your anonymity as well as that of the others who enjoy this refuge from the real world.'

'No cell phones,' Mfune said. 'Got it.'

The cashier put neon bands on their wrists and said, 'We close at four a.m. tonight, but last call is at three.'

'Good crowd?' Amé asked.

'Very sexy,' the cashier said. 'Have fun, and please, no means no.'

'Always.'

Amé led the way through plush red curtains and into a vast space decorated as if it were a fantasy harem encampment in the desert, with palm trees and murals of sand dunes and oases on the high walls. Below them stood arabesque tents, all gold and black, some with their curtains open to reveal beds, and others already closed to wandering eyes.

Two large gilt birdcages hung from the ceiling. In them women writhed against each other, oblivious, it seemed, to the crowded floor below them, where fifty or sixty provocatively dressed people danced and pulsed with the techno music.

To the left there was a long bar crowded with hard drinkers and lascivious friends. Within moments of Mfune and Amé entering Le Chanticleer Rouge, couples and single women began offering to buy them drinks and teasing them about what could be enjoyed inside the tents.

Amé turned them all down, saying, 'We're voyeurs for now.'

The truth was that they were looking for some-one. Ten minutes later, they spotted her at the satellite bar upstairs, drinking a salt-and-pepper martini. In her forties, with short silver hair and a long, lithe body clad in a pearl-colored pant-suit, she was watching a writhing group of people in a room with glass walls.

'Ready?' Amé asked.

Mfune nodded. 'Let's do this.'

They sidled up next to her and ordered drinks. It didn't take long for the woman to take her eyes off the orgy and glance their way. The instant she did, she turned fully toward them as Amé had suspected she would. Based on her surveillance, she knew that the woman liked black men and bisexual white women.

'My, my,' the woman said. 'And who might you two be?'

Amé pursed lips glossed ruby red and smiled. 'Lynette and Nico. And you?'

'Lourdes,' she said. 'I've never seen you here before. First time?'

'First time for Nico,' Amé said, squeezing Mfune's hand. 'Not for me. I used to come here regularly with my lipstick girlfriends.'

'I've done that too,' Lourdes said softly as she raised one eyebrow. 'So fun.'

The captain said, 'You're quite beautiful, Lourdes.'

'And you, Nico, are the definition of a man's man.'

'You have no idea,' Amé said mischievously.

Lourdes's eyebrow went up again. *'C'est vrai?'*

'Shockingly true,' Amé said, and pressed back languidly against Mfune, who beamed to expose that gold tooth.

'I must say, you two have made me rather

breathless,' Lourdes said, setting her drink down and fanning her face. 'And my skin – look. It's gooseflesh.'

'We could solve that,' Amé said, 'and any other problem you have.'

'And I yours,' Lourdes said, beaming. 'Shall we go some place private?'

Chapter 42

Lourdes tried to lead them into the dungeon, but Mfune said he'd feel better in one of the tents. Amé found an empty one at the back of the club.

She let Lourdes and the captain enter the tent first. Glancing about, she saw no one else in the immediate vicinity – at least not in the visible vicinity. As Amé let down the flaps and tied them shut, she heard the smack of a paddle on flesh from the tent to the left, and cries of orgasm to their right.

She turned and saw the king-size bed with fresh sheets, and the sex swing above it hanging from a cable that ran down through a hole in the tent peak. Lourdes was finishing the last of her drink and eyeing Mfune hungrily.

'Do you like textures, Lourdes?' Amé asked, sinuously stroking her black gloves one against the other.

'I like everything,' Lourdes said. 'Engage my body. Engage my mind.'

'I guess that's a yes.'

'It's a definite yes,' Lourdes purred. 'What did you have in mind?'

'We want to worship you,' Amé said.

'You're our goddess tonight,' Mfune said.

'You don't know how right you are,' Lourdes said huskily, as the captain moved behind her and pressed his hips against her back. She trailed her hand along the side of his leg.

Amé sandwiched the woman. She and Mfune caressed Lourdes through her clothes until she was trembling with desire.

'Show us how beautiful the goddess is,' Amé said, standing back.

Lourdes did a provocative striptease that left her naked except for her backstrap high heels.

'You *are* a goddess,' Mfune said.

'I want to see you too,' Lourdes said.

'Not yet,' Amé said. 'Lie back, Lourdes. Lose yourself in pleasure.'

The woman hesitated, but only for a moment before scooting onto the bed and looking at them saucily. 'I have to admit, being naked like this and you both in your clothes is a total turn-on.'

'Just you wait,' Amé said.

Mfune walked around to Lourdes's feet and began stroking them with the gloves, moving his hands slowly up her calves and pressing her knees apart.

'God. Kiss me there,' Lourdes whispered.

'Not yet,' Amé said, climbing onto the bed behind her. Reaching over Lourdes's shoulders, she caressed the woman's breasts. 'Lie back now and shut your eyes. It will heighten your senses, make your climax more powerful.'

The captain's gloved hands were massaging Lourdes's inner thighs now, and she gave in completely, sliding back off her elbows so that her head came naturally into Amé's lap, where she sighed with contentment and closed her eyes.

'You don't know how much I've needed this,' Lourdes said.

'We see that,' Amé said, looking at Mfune as he moved his gloves higher.

Amé waited until Lourdes's hips began a slow, sensuous squirm of anticipation, then reached over for one of the pillows.

With the naked woman's eyes still closed and her mouth slightly parted in pleasure, Amé brought the pillow smashing down on the woman's face even as Mfune pinned her legs and hips to the bed. Lourdes almost immediately began to fight and writhe. Her arms shot up, grabbing for Amé.

Her hands wrapped around the fabric of the black gloves covering Amé's forearms and tried to tear them apart. She was strong, but Amé was stronger and threw her full weight onto the pillow even as Lourdes began to scream and whine. Muffled by the pillow, however, the noises sounded no different than other cries of ecstasy and spasm echoing from the tents all around them.

A little more than a minute later, Lourdes's struggles lessened, and then she collapsed. They held her there long after the tension and the spirit had left her.

'Check her heart,' Amé whispered as the people in the tent to their left started paddling again.

Mfune reached up, rested his hand on her chest

a moment, and whispered, 'She's finished.'

Only then did Amé allow herself a long exhale. She lifted the pillow to find Lourdes's mouth slack and her open eyes dull and still.

'You're a martyr to the cause,' Amé whispered. 'You're a hero, Lourdes.'

'Let's get busy,' Mfune said. 'We've got a lot to do.'

Twenty minutes later, after peering out a slit in the tent flap and making sure there was no one wandering this part of the swingers' club, they exited quickly. Mfune carried the sheets in a bundle under his arm. Amé drew the flaps of the tent shut, with the Do Not Disturb sign still up. They walked away knowing that under the rules that governed the Red Rooster, no one would enter the tent before closing, and that was hours away.

They carried the sheets to the other side of the club and buried them in a hamper. Amé went into the women's toilet, stripped off her gloves, and put them in her purse before washing her hands with scented soap to mask the odor of bleach. Only then did they head for the exit to Le Chanticleer Rouge.

'Going so soon?' the cashier said. 'The party's just getting started.'

'We've had our fun,' Amé said without turning back. 'And we both have to work in the morning.'

Chapter 43

6TH ARRONDISSEMENT
APRIL 9, 12:20 A.M.

When the waitress cleared her throat, I startled.

Looking around, I realized that Michele Herbert and I were the only patrons left in the restaurant. It seemed like minutes since we'd walked in the door, but we'd been talking for nearly three hours.

At first our conversation had been directed at the death of René Pincus and the tag. The graffiti expert had been getting pictures of the tag in various places in and around Paris. As of early that evening, she'd received pictures of sixty-two different iterations of the tag, but no explanation of its meaning.

I told her about the men who'd shot up the Plaza Athénée, and their interest in the cigarette lighter that Kim Kopchinski kept on a chain around her neck. Michele agreed that it was an odd thing to ask about.

'There's a lot of danger in your life, I think,' she said

'At times,' I said.

'Tell me about your life, Jack.'

Usually I play things close to the vest, but Michele looked so radiant, and acted so, well, empathetic, that I started opening up to her. I told her about my fucked-up childhood and my dysfunctional family, especially my dad, who'd been a cop, a private investigator, a swindler, and a crook before dying as an inmate in a California penitentiary.

I told her about my mom's death, and about my borderline-psycho twin brother, Tommy, and some of the stuff he'd pulled in the past. I even told her about the marines, my time in Afghanistan, and the helicopter crash that still haunted me.

'How terrible it must have been for you and your friend Del Rio to walk away from it when so many others died,' she'd said.

'It was the worst thing that has ever happened to me,' I admitted. 'In some ways I don't think I'll ever get over it.'

'We all have such moments in our lives,' Michele said. 'These are the times that define us, no?'

'In some ways, I guess how we handle tragedy defines us,' I replied. 'Have you had such moments?'

She got sad then, and nodded. 'I saw my parents die when I was nine.'

'Jesus. How awful. What happened?'

'A train accident in Italy on their twelfth anniversary,' she said.

Michele was sent to her only living relative, her mother's older sister, who was divorced and had two children of her own. Her aunt squandered Michele's inheritance and treated her horribly.

'I found art in school and retreated into it,' she said. 'Out of that loss and that mistreatment came my life and my life's work.'

That's when the waitress cleared her throat.

'We should go,' I said.

We apologized and left a generous tip. Outside I was more than pleased when Michele put her arm through mine. We walked and talked for another hour. Around two, we were strolling across the Pont Saint-Louis.

'I could talk like this all night with you, but I must go home,' Michele said as we crossed the bridge. 'I have an eleven o'clock class.'

A cab pulled onto the bridge and I hailed it. Opening the rear door, I said, 'Thanks for the fine company and conversation.'

'I had a wonderful evening.'

'I'll call tomorrow, see if you've gotten any more pictures of the tag.'

'Or I can call you.'

'Either way,' I said, and closed the door, thinking she was a remarkable woman. Gorgeous, yes, but a whole lot more.

After watching the taxi drive off, I headed east, hoping to find another cab on the Boulevard Henri IV. Halfway there, my cell phone rang.

I dug the phone out of my pants, looked at caller ID, frowned.

'Up late, Louis?'

'I was just awoken by Investigateur Hoskins, who needs our forensics help again,' he growled. 'AB-16 has struck a third time, and once more they didn't pull any punches.'

'Who was the victim?'

'Lourdes Latrelle,' he said. 'One of France's foremost intellectuals and best-known writers.'

Chapter 44

6TH ARRONDISSEMENT
2:58 A.M.

Wearing gloves, rock-climbing shoes, and dark clothes, Epée adjusted the straps on his knapsack as he walked along the Rue Mazarine. His heart was beating wildly because he believed that the greatest act of his life was at hand.

It was audacious. It was daring. It was absolutely in-your-face, and Epée was beside himself with excitement. He hung a right onto the narrow sidewalk that ran between the Rue de Seine and a huge, five-story limestone building. The road ahead curved left. The wall of the building traveled a deeper arc, which created a larger, triangular space between it and the road.

Motorcyclists often parked there during the day, when it was in use almost constantly by pedestrians. But at that hour, the Rue de Seine and the sidewalks that bordered it were empty. Epée broke into a jog toward an arched passage, seeing through it to the bright lights of the Quai de Conti.

Instead of entering the passageway, he looked around one last time before taking two steps to a stout metal downspout that dropped straight down from the eaves and roof high overhead. Hefty metal brackets every thirty inches held the

174

drainpipe solidly to the wall. Epée grabbed hold of the second bracket and then stepped up onto the first, finding that the gummy soft soles of the climbing shoes easily clung to the protruding half inch of metal.

In seconds, Epée clambered up the pipe and onto the narrow second floor ledge, where he paused to take in the scene below him. Still empty. He did the same at the third floor, and was near the top of the drain when he heard voices.

He had to freeze in an awkward position when a couple came through the arched walkway from the Quai de Conti, lingered, and kissed before finally continuing south on the Rue de Seine. Epée's fingers were cramping before the couple was gone, and for the first time he thought about the long fall to the pavement.

No way. Not when he was this close to becoming a legend.

Epée had rehearsed this climb dozens of times. He'd taken photographs of the route from every angle and pored over them, studying every inch of the building's face, eaves, and roofline until he believed he could climb it blindfolded.

He shinnied up against the eaves where the downspout disappeared. He got his right foot up onto a ledge about three inches wide.

Epée rotated his body over into a three-point bridge, with his left foot free. His core trembled as he pushed hard against his right hand and right toe before he stabbed up and over the eaves with his left hand, catching the bottom of the roof. He took a strained breath and then transferred his weight entirely to his left hand, and dangled there for a split second before throwing up his right hand and grabbing the roof.

Grunting with effort, he pulled his head, shoulders, and ribs up onto the roof. He scooted sideways into a valley where several rooflines came together and squirmed his hips and legs up into it.

Epée lay there, soaking wet and panting with effort, but also knowing that the worst of it had been conquered. When he'd regained some of his strength, he got up on all fours and used opposing pressure to ascend the roof as a climber would a chimney opening in a rock. He made the ridge a few moments later and sat there, straddling it.

Before *la crise*, with the spotlights shining on the front of the building, he'd have been easy to spot up there. But the recession had forced Paris to shut off the lights on its famous buildings and monuments after midnight. In the dark like this, he might as well have been a phantom.

Twisting around, Epée quickly surveyed the avenue and the pedestrian bridge that crossed the Seine to the Louvre Museum, which was also dark. There was no one on the bridge that he could see, and very few cars on the avenue. He got up on the curving peak of the roof and followed it toward a giant domed tower that rose fifty feet above the main building.

To his relief, he found the safety line, a three-quarter-inch cable discreetly mounted up the side of the tower, exactly where he'd spotted it the month before. Men cleaning the walls of grime, restoring the pale limestone color, had put the line up, and Epée used it now. Unzipping his jacket, he felt for the mechanical devices known as Jumars that were attached to a harness he wore and favored by rock climbers. The cams of these devices ran only in one direction: up. When pressure was applied downward, they locked.

Epée unclipped one of the ascenders. He attached it and the one still tied to the harness to the safety line, and then frogged up the side of the tower, taking rests at the various articulations in the dome.

The last ledge was underhung, and Epée had to make another contortionist move to get up onto it, right next to the base of the cupola. In daylight or under lights, the mosaics were a deep, cerulean blue. But now they were black as coal, which suited Epee's purposes perfectly.

He got in position in line with the Louvre and the Pont des Arts bridge, looking straight down on the plaza in front of the building and the Quai de Conti. He paused a moment to reflect on the sheer magnitude of the moment.

Then he got out the spray paint and set to work.

Chapter 45

11TH ARRONDISSEMENT
3:40 A.M.

According to Louis, Le Chanticleer Rouge was the greatest of Parisian clubs for *les échangistes,* the swingers of France. Like most things French when it came to sex, the practice of going to places like the Red Rooster to engage in anonymous physical relations was accepted with a shrug.

Politicians and their wives did it. So did the big bankers and their girlfriends. That infamous chairman of the International Monetary Fund practically lived in one of these clubs. So did well-known painters, musicians, and television personalities, and, of course, writers.

That last category included Lourdes Latrelle, the famous French author, novelist, and television personality, who, ironically enough, was best known for being an expert on the politics of gender and sex. I say 'ironically' not only because her corpse was found in a swingers' club, but because she'd been hung upside down and naked from a sex swing.

Black parachute cord tied to her wrists ran out to the tent supports and held her arms in that upside-down-cross position. As with the other victims, her face was bloated by the blood rushing to her head. A crude version of the AB-16 tag had been drawn on the victim's belly with lipstick.

'That's a first,' I said. 'Defacement of the corpse.'

Investigateur Hoskins said nothing. For the first time since I'd met her, I saw indecision and uncertainty on her face. Claudia Vans, Private Paris's chief forensics tech, was on the bed, examining the body.

'I've got something,' Vans said, holding up a pair of tweezers. 'Pubic hairs. Three of them. And obviously, because of the wax job, not Ms. Latrelle's.'

'That helps,' Hoskins said. 'Nothing like DNA. Let me know if you find anything else organic.'

Vans nodded. Hoskins suggested that we leave the tent.

Out in the hall, the *investigateur* said, 'Louis, I believe you're right.'

'*C'est vrai?*' he said, arching his eyebrows in a way that suggested she rarely admitted he was on the right side of anything.

Hoskins nodded uncomfortably. 'The position of the body *is* symbolic. And because the victim is Lourdes Latrelle, it takes AB-16 to a whole other level.'

Louis paused with muted delight before looking to me. 'It would be like a high-profile movie or television star being murdered in the States.'

'I thought you said she was an intellectual author,' I said.

'The French idolize the brilliant person,' Hoskins explained. 'The person who is above the fray, living the life of the mind while facing none

179

of reality's consequences. Latrelle is a cultural icon, a member of L'Académie Française, for God's sake.'

Louis said, 'The news of this murder will strike deep. Mark my words.'

Behind us a man said, 'I *am* marking them. And unfortunately I couldn't agree with you more.'

We all turned to find a short, older, painfully stooped man in a gray suit. He was balanced on a cane and had to twist his head to peer up at us through thick, round, wire-rimmed glasses. 'Which is why we are going to keep all information about this crime scene from the press,' he added.

He pointed the cane at Louis, then at me, and said, 'You two shouldn't even be here, but I'll allow it because of Private's proven forensics work. That does not, however, excuse you from my gag order. Are we clear?'

'Crystal clear, Juge Fromme,' Louis said.

The older man came closer. Every movement seemed to cause him great discomfort, and he had to will himself beyond it to crane his head up at me.

'I am Guillaume Fromme, *le juge*,' he said in perfect English, offering his hand. 'I've heard a lot about you and your company, Monsieur Morgan.'

'That's nice of you to say so, sir,' I replied, taking his hand, which was surprisingly large, leather-palmed, and strong. 'What exactly is your role here?'

'In the French legal system, a *juge* is brought in on all major cases, especially those involving murder,' he said. 'I am not a judge in the U.S. sense – more an investigative magistrate. Someone who will oversee the case from a legal perspective until a defendant is brought to court.'

He looked at Hoskins and Louis. 'Do I speak correctly?'

They nodded, Hoskins unhappily.

Fromme must have seen it because he lifted his cane toward the detective and said, 'It is unusual to see someone like me at a crime scene so early in an investigation, which has made Investigateur Hoskins here nervous. But I am under orders. And based on my review of the case files to date, I agree with them. The position of the bodies and the photographs found in Monsieur Henri Richard's pied-à-terre suggest that AB-16 poses a clear and present danger to Paris and to France.'

Chapter 46

Fromme moved as if he was walking on nails before stopping in front of the tent where Lourdes Latrelle hung. He stood there several seconds before turning back to us, his face gone grave.

'Who found her?' he asked. 'Who's seen her like this?'

'An employee of the club opened the drapes after someone complained that they had been closed for hours,' Hoskins replied. 'She had the good sense not to scream, and got the manager, who called us.'

'So two people besides those present at this moment?' *le juge* demanded.

'Yes, I think that's right, sir,' Hoskins said.

'I wish to speak with the manager and the employee,' Fromme said. 'Any leads on who was with her in the club before she entered the tent?'

'Yes,' Hoskins said. 'Several patrons and the bartender said Madame Latrelle was watching an orgy when she was approached by a large francophone African male with a gold upper front tooth and a pale, brunette Caucasian woman with green catlike eyes.'

This was the first Louis and I had heard of the couple, but I remembered that someone at Chez Pincus had mentioned that the woman Henri Richard had brought to the restaurant once wore cat-eye contacts.

I said, 'You catch them on tape?'

'God no,' Louis said. 'A place like this, Jack, is based on anonymity, and a belief in personal space. The French do not like security cameras.'

'Especially in their sex clubs?'

'Now you understand,' Louis said.

'Sketch artists?'

Hoskins said, 'That we can take care of.'

When the investigator and magistrate moved off to discuss matters off-limits to Private Paris, I checked my watch. It was nearly five in the morning, and I was running on fumes.

I was about to tell Louis that I was going back to the hotel for a few hours of sleep when something he'd said earlier came back to me.

'Wasn't Henri Richard a member of L'Académie Française?' I asked.

'Oui,' Louis said. 'But if you think there is a connection, it stops with Lourdes. Chef Pincus, as highly regarded as he was, was not a member.'

'That shoots that.'

Then Louis stared off into the distance and muttered, 'Unless...'

'Unless what?' I asked.

'Come, Jack,' he said, hurrying toward the exit. 'We must go talk to the only other Parisian I know who gets up and goes to work as early as I do.'

Chapter 47

6TH ARRONDISSEMENT
5:15 A.M.

Louis and I climbed from a taxi on the Quai de Conti across the Seine from the Louvre. In the glow of streetlamps, I could make out the massive curved bulwark of a building and the silhouette of a domed tower that loomed above it.

'What is this place?' I asked, feeling irritable after dozing off in the cab.

'The Institut de France,' he said. 'The epicenter of French culture.'

'What does it do?' I said, following him across a courtyard in front of the grand building.

'On a practical level, the institute oversees about ten thousand different foundations concerned with everything from French historical sites to museums and castles,' Louis said. 'The five academies within the institute were formed back in the days of Louis XIV, and designed to preserve and celebrate the French culture, language, arts, sciences, and our systems of law and politics. The members represent the best of France, and must be voted in.'

'There's a nomination process?'

He bobbed his head. 'Anyone can be nominated. You can even nominate yourself. But then you must run a quiet campaign, almost like a political race, in which you prove that you are one of *les immortels*, the best of France.'

Louis stopped before a door. 'Hold on a second.'

He punched in a number on his cell phone, waited, and laughed. 'It's Louis. I knew you were up. Listen, I'm out front. Can you buzz us in? It's a matter of great importance, and potentially involves the institute.' Louis listened and said, 'We shall meet you there.'

The door buzzed and we entered a dimly lit hallway that led us to staircases and other hallways that Louis seemed to know intimately.

'So who are we meeting?' I asked.

'The director,' he said.

'And how do you know this person?'

'The director is an old, discreet, and dear friend,' Louis said.

He went to some double doors and opened them, revealing a breathtaking room composed of four large and dramatic alcoves that met at a central amphitheater. The massive arches that defined the alcoves also supported a cupola that soared above the amphitheater to a dome built of stone buttresses and stained glass. The glass was starting to glow blue and gold with the dawn.

A woman in a red pantsuit with a blue and white scarf about her neck stood below the cupola on an oval rug in the dead center of the amphitheater. She was talking to a younger man in a crisp white shirt and red tie. She was in her fifties and strikingly handsome, with silver-blond hair.

'This is where all members of Les Académies meet,' Louis said quietly. 'You could say that there is no place more French than this one room.'

Before I could reply, the younger man turned and headed up the far set of stairs. The woman spotted us, grinned, and came over quickly to embrace Louis and buss his cheeks. 'How are you, old friend?' she said in French.

'I am magnificent as always, *chéri*,' Louis said in English, before gesturing to me. 'Allow me to introduce Monsieur Jack Morgan.'

She reached out to shake my hand and began speaking to me in perfect British English. 'Pricilla Meeks, director of the institute. Very nice to meet you, Mr. Morgan. Louis has spoken highly of you in the past.'

I shook her hand, wondering how she could speak both languages with such perfect accents. But before I could dope that out, the spotlights went on outside. They hit high on the cupola, illuminating the interior of the tower while Louis went straight to the matter at hand.

'Was René Pincus up for a vote on admission to Les Académies?' he asked.

Pricilla Meeks sobered and said, 'You know I can't discuss things like that.'

'Pincus is dead,' Louis grumbled. 'So is Henri Richard, a member of the academy. And now, I

185

hate to say it, Lourdes Latrelle.'

Meeks gasped. 'Lourdes! My God, Louis. How?'

'I can't get into the particulars under orders from a magistrate. But she's dead. I saw her body myself.'

Meeks sank into one of the plush blue seats, shaking her head. 'What a tragedy. Why would anyone target–'

'Pricilla!' the man with the red tie cried from the far staircase. 'Someone has defaced the cupola!'

The director jumped up and we had a hard time keeping up with her as she ran through the hallways and outside. The sun was just rising. It was difficult to see from the front courtyard, but when we retreated across the street and onto the Pont des Arts, the pedestrian bridge that spans the Seine, we got the full effect.

High on the curved front face of the cupola's dome, someone had painted a huge version of the AB-16 tag and an inverted cross in three parallel colors: red, black, and fluorescent green.

'My God,' Meeks said, clearly horrified at the way the graffiti seemed to glow in an otherworldly way against the dark blue skin of the dome. 'Why are they doing this?'

'AB-16 is declaring war,' Louis said, as grim as I've ever seen him.

'On what?' I asked. 'The institute?'

'Think of the symbolism and the placement,' Louis said. 'AB-16 is making war on the entire French culture.'

Chapter 48

I thought about that, and maybe Louis was right. Paris was his city and France his country. He would know the symbolism and the meaning of this sort of thing. And yet I wondered if there was more to it than that.

'Do you have any current or former disgruntled employees at the institute?' I asked.

'Everyone in France is disgruntled to some extent these days,' Meeks said dourly. 'But actually, people who work at the institute are by and large happy. Unless they really screw up, the job is for life, and it is a life of and for the culture, which they love, or they wouldn't get hired in the first place.'

'No one has screwed up lately?'

Meeks said, 'In answer to your question, Mr. Morgan, no. It's been some time since we've had a major screw up. I run a tight ship.'

'Okay, are there any current or former campaigners, people trying to be elected into one of the academies, who are embittered by their exclusion?'

Meeks hesitated and said, 'Many great Frenchmen and -women were never elected to Les Académies, including Victor Hugo and Marie Curie.'

I picked up on the hesitation and said, 'Since they're both dead, we'll put them out of consideration. I'm talking the last year or two.'

Meeks glanced at Louis before sighing. 'There is one who has been giving us – uh, me – many headaches.'

'A name?'

She seemed to struggle inside.

I said, 'AB-16 is targeting your members, Madame Meeks. I should think you'd want to protect them.'

That got to her. 'Of course I wish to protect them!'

News vehicles pulled up in front of the institute. Cameramen got out and filmed the tag up on the cupola.

'Who is it, Pricilla?' Louis grumbled.

'Jacques Noulan,' she said, and filled us in.

Noulan, a noted Paris fashion designer, was evidently infuriated when he lost an open seat in the academy of fine arts to Millie Fleurs, a more famous member of the fashion world. Meeks said that Noulan, who was more an expert marketer than an innovator, had organized a smear campaign after the election, trying to get Fleurs unseated. He was unsuccessful.

'He made threats to me at a party recently,' Meeks said. 'He was quite drunk, and belligerent.'

'He unstable enough to start killing academy members?' I asked.

'I don't know how to answer that,' she said, playing with an earring.

'You just did,' Louis said.

'Pricilla!' cried a female television news reporter who'd come out onto the bridge to get a better angle on the cupola and the tag. 'Have you heard about Lourdes Latrelle?'

Meeks turned toward the reporter, and the klieg lights went on.

Squinting, I took a step back as Meeks replied, 'I have heard, and it's a tragedy. France has lost another of her immortals.'

Investigateur Hoskins and Juge Fromme climbed from a police car and were swarmed by reporters. The tag's placement and the murders had struck a deep nerve. No doubt about it now.

'I still think we want to talk to Monsieur Noulan, and sooner than later,' I said, backing away from Meeks and the journalists grilling her.

'Why?' Louis said, unconvinced.

'From an L.A. point of view, this is starting to feel like a well-organized marketing campaign with the tag as a brand,' I said as I headed toward the west bank and the Louvre. 'Noulan is supposedly strong at this kind of thing, right?'

Louis stopped, looked back over his shoulder at the tag, and said, 'With the coordination and the brutal precision of the murders, it feels more militant to me.'

Chapter 49

PANTIN, NORTHEASTERN SUBURBS OF PARIS
8:35 A.M.

Haja lifted the welding mask to study the latest muscle group she'd been working on, deciding that it suggested the beast's raw power but didn't overstate it, at least up close. She'd have to climb down and get a different perspective to tell for sure.

But when the sculptor reached the floor of the old linen factory, Émile Sauvage opened the door that led to the war room and called out to her, 'Haja, you need to see this.'

She took one more look at her work in progress, sighed, and hurried through the steel door. At twenty-five by fifteen, the room was windowless. The wall to Haja's left was covered in whiteboards. Across the top it said, 'AB-16.'

Underneath there was an appointment calendar of sorts with dates on a long horizontal axis, hours in military time stacked on the vertical axis, and cryptic notations in the boxes.

The wall opposite the door featured fifty black AK-47 7.62mm assault rifles standing upright in an improvised gun rack. Boxes of ammunition stamped 'For disposal' were stacked below the rifles, along with empty magazines and a thick, rolled-up Oriental rug.

Captain Mfune sat beside the rug, oiling the action and barrel shroud of one of the rifles. Epée lay on a couch watching a television screen that showed a close-up of the AB-16 tag up on the cupola.

'There it is again!' he cried. 'They keep showing it over and over!'

'I knew putting it there would do the trick,' Amé said.

'A brilliant idea, brilliantly executed,' said Mfune, returning the now gleaming rifle to its spot on the rack.

The screen cut away to show the entrance to the Red Rooster, along with an author photo of Lourdes Latrelle.

Epée said, 'Your execution was brilliant too, Captain. The great minds are under fire. That's all they're talking about besides the tag.'

'And we got out clean,' Amé said. 'The mystery of AB-16 intact.'

'Perhaps too intact,' Sauvage said. 'They think this is solely about Les Académies.'

'The slow burn is critical to mass awareness,' Amé insisted. 'You have to let them chew on the mystery of it, employ their imagination to suggest answers, so that when the true scenario is revealed, it comes as even more of a shock to the population.'

'A call to action,' Mfune said.

'Exactly,' Amé said, snapping her fingers. 'If we make the next few moves well, AB-16 will be bigger than the Dreyfus Affair.'

The screen jumped away from coverage of

Lourdes Latrelle's murder to an interview with Pricilla Meeks, the Institut de France's director, who was out on the bridge with the tagged cupola visible behind her.

Haja spotted two men behind Meeks. They looked familiar.

Did she know them?

The screen cut to an exterior shot of La Crim and a shaken Investigateur Hoskins, who was vowing to track down AB-16 at all costs.

'I have been authorized to bring in as many detectives as is necessary to solve these murders,' Hoskins said. 'We have even brought in the world-famous Private agency to work forensics and as consultants on the case.'

That provoked silence in the room until Mfune looked at Sauvage and said, 'Private has a strong reputation, Major. A first-class operation.'

Sauvage said nothing, just twisted his head as if adjusting his collar.

'Can you rewind that?' Haja asked. 'Back to when Meeks was talking?'

'Sure,' Amé said, and backed the feed up.

'Stop there,' Haja said, and then stepped closer to study the men behind the institute's director. 'I know these two. I saw them outside the mosque the other day.'

'Are you sure?' Sauvage asked, engaged again.

'Positive,' she said. 'I never forget a face, Émile. The older one is French, but I think the other one is American.'

'Then we have a problem,' said Epée, who'd lost color. 'The old one is Louis Langlois. He used to be a top investigator with La Crim.'

192

'How do you know that?' Haja demanded.

'He arrested my father for burglary when I was a kid,' the tagger said. 'I think he runs Private's Paris office now.'

'I'll check,' Amé said, grabbing a laptop. A moment later, she said, 'It's Langlois. And the American is Jack Morgan, the owner of Private and the guy who found the Harlows last year.'

Haja knew exactly what she was talking about. Who didn't? Thom and Jennifer Harlow, Hollywood's most famous couple, had been kidnapped along with their three children. Morgan and Private L.A. had found and rescued the family in Mexico.

She felt minor panic ripple through her. Why had Morgan and Langlois been at the mosque that day?

Mfune and Epée were upset as well.

'Those Private guys,' the tagger complained. 'I read about them in *Paris Match* last year. They cut corners, break laws. They're not like normal cops. They never give up once they get on something, especially Morgan.'

Though his arms were crossed, Sauvage smiled. 'No, they're not like normal cops,' he said. 'And Morgan and Langlois would appear to be formidable foes. But with a little creativity, I think Private Paris can be neutralized without much change in our original plans.'

'How?' Mfune demanded.

'We'll put a pincer move on them, and squash them like bugs.'

Chapter 50

8TH ARRONDISSEMENT
10 A.M.

The design studio and haute couture showroom of Jacques Noulan was on the Rue Clément Marot, only a couple of blocks from the Plaza Athénée – a plus given the fact that I hadn't slept in thirty hours. I planned on talking to the designer and then getting some much needed sack time.

But when Louis and I reached the reception desk, we were told that Noulan had come down with the flu several days before and was convalescing at his country home in Nance. When we asked for a phone number and address, we were politely told that it was impossible to disturb him. Louis left his card and asked that Noulan call as soon as he returned to work.

'Convenient that he's out of touch,' I said outside.

'I grant you that, Jack.'

I was about to tell Louis that I was going to the hotel to get some sleep when he gestured down the street and said, 'That must feel like a thorn in Noulan's ass. Maybe this is about jealousy and revenge after all.'

Yawning, I said, 'I'm not following you.'

'Millie Fleurs,' he replied. 'That's her shop not a block away, Jack.'

Flashing on my bed at the Plaza, I sighed and said, 'Maybe *she* can shed light on the situation.'

We crossed the street and went down the block to the shop. The shop lights were on, but the door was locked. It was one of those places where you had to buzz to get in. A tall, thin man in an impeccably tailored mouse-gray suit was working behind the counter. We must not have struck him as impressive because he glanced at us on a computer screen, grimaced, and went back to ignoring us.

Louis buzzed a second time and held up his Private badge to the camera. The man studied it, curled his upper lip against a pencil-thin mustache, and then buzzed us in. Surprisingly, the shop had very few actual clothes, but it had many life-size black-and-white photos of models wearing Millie Fleurs's gowns and evening wear. Samples of the designer's famous purses occupied translucent pedestals around the room, but otherwise the place was empty and white save for the fitting mirrors and counter workstation.

'Yes? Can I help you?' the man behind the counter asked in a voice that suggested he had zero interest whatsoever in helping us. 'This is the haute couture shop. Perhaps you'd be more interested in the ready-to-wear line? It's a few blocks from–'

'We're not here to buy,' Louis grumbled. 'We're here to talk to Madame Fleurs.'

'Yes, well, wouldn't we all like to?' he sniffed. 'I'm afraid that's out of the question. You'll have to call for an appointment, and the soonest time she has is three months out.'

'What's your name?' I asked.

He hesitated, twitched his mustache, and said, 'Laurent Alexandre.'

'Mr. Alexandre, is Millie Fleurs here?'

'No,' he said, and turned away. 'I am the only one–'

Then a woman called out, 'Laurent, are you down there?'

Unfazed at being caught fibbing, he hurried toward a curtain at the rear of the shop, calling, 'I'll be right up. No need to–'

The curtain parted. A woman who reminded me of Shirley MacLaine appeared. Wearing black tights, gold slippers, and a crème tunic, she had a dancer's posture. Her hair was pulled back in a girlish ponytail. She shook a black fabric sample at Alexandre.

'This is not the fabric I ordered for the princess's cocktail dress.'

'Of course it is, Millie,' Alexandre said wearily.

'It looks wrong.'

'It's what you ordered. I checked myself.'

'It's not good enough for the princess!' she protested.

'It will have to be,' her assistant said. 'She's coming tomorrow morning.'

When Millie Fleurs looked ready to continue her argument, Alexandre gestured at us. 'Besides, these men would like to speak with you about ... what is it about? And who are you?'

'We are with Private,' Louis said, walking toward Fleurs with his badge and ID visible. 'And we are here to talk about Jacques Noulan and murder.'

Millie Fleurs's eyes went wide. 'Noulan has been killed?'

'No, no,' I said. 'But as you probably know by now, Lourdes Latrelle has been murdered, and–'

'Lourdes is dead?' she cried, her hand covering her heart. 'And you think Noulan did it!'

'Madame Fleurs, please,' Louis said. 'If you would just let us–'

'You were right about those e-mails,' Fleurs said to her assistant. 'The great Noulan has lost his mind and gone homicidal.'

It took us a few minutes to get them up to speed on the developments of the past twenty-four hours, including the fresh graffiti tag on the cupola of the Institut de France.

This all seemed to dumbfound her. 'So you think Noulan is targeting the academy for letting me in and not him? And what does this "AB-16" mean?'

'We don't know,' Louis said. 'Has he threatened *you?* Noulan?'

She made a throwaway gesture with the black fabric swatch and said, 'Jacques has been threatening me since I would not sleep with him thirty-five years ago.'

Fleurs explained that she had worked as a designer for Noulan early in her career, but after he tried to make his bed part of the work arrangement, she quit and started her own company. For nearly three decades, he had gone out of his way to make disparaging remarks about her designs, and when she was elected to the academy, he went ballistic and started sending her threatening e-mails.

'Can you print them out, Laurent?' she asked. 'Bring them to the studio?'

'Of course, Millie,' her assistant said, and went behind the counter.

'I'm sorry, messieurs, but you'll have to come along if you wish to speak further,' she said, heading toward the curtain. 'One of my most important customers is coming tomorrow for a fitting, and I'm still the cocktail dress short. I'll probably be up all night finishing.'

We followed her. I happened to glance at Alexandre as I passed, and saw beside the computer a sketch pad with a drawing of a dramatic black cocktail dress on it – probably what he'd been working on when we rang the shop bell.

Fleurs led us behind the curtain and up a steep staircase to a workshop with two cutting tables, three industrial sewing machines, and four mannequins, three of which sported dresses: one maroon, another white, and the third crème-colored. On the wall behind them hung sketches of those same dresses with notations regarding fabric choices, color, and stitching instructions.

The designer gestured to the dresses. 'What do you think?'

'Stunning,' Louis said. 'Never have I seen such beauty.'

Fleurs raised an eyebrow at him, and then at me.

'Remarkable enough for a princess,' I said.

The designer smiled. 'I hope so.'

'A Saudi princess?' Louis asked.

'Who else can afford haute couture these days?' Fleurs said. 'There are fewer than two hundred customers in the world for one-of-a-kind Parisian dresses, and ninety percent of them are Saudi royalty.'

'This is true?' Louis said, astonished. 'Where do they wear them?'

The designer laughed. 'At women-only parties in Riyadh, where even their husbands don't get to see their hundred thousand dollar dresses. And they wear them when they visit Paris. They wear their robes and veil until they clear Saudi airspace, and then poof! The veils and robes come off and—'

'I have them here, Millie,' said Alexandre, who held a sheaf of paper.

'Let them look,' she said.

The assistant handed Louis the papers, and he scanned them and said, 'Have you shown these to the police?'

Fleurs looked uncomfortable. 'I didn't because the rumor is that Noulan is sick, perhaps with early dementia. I figured these e-mails were due to that.'

'She's too kind in some ways,' Alexandre told me.

That made the designer harden. 'He was my mentor once, Laurent. I still admire his genius. Maybe he deserves it, but I thought it would be a crime to run his reputation through the mud if all that was going on was senility and spite.'

'Three people dead,' her assistant replied, and then looked at us in alarm, as if he had just realized something. 'Do you think Millie is in danger?'

'You are still a member of Les Académies?' Louis asked.

'Election is for life,' Fleurs replied.

'Then I suggest you take every precaution,' I said. 'At least until the police have a suspect in hand.'

'Perhaps you should finish the last dress at home,' Alexandre said.

'Nonsense,' the designer snapped. 'This is *my* atelier. No one is scaring me away from it, at least until the princess is pleased and a check has been written. There's too much riding on this. You of all people should know that.'

Her assistant nodded, but he wasn't happy. 'You are the boss, Millie. As you wish.'

Chapter 51

My cell phone rang me awake after a much needed nap back in my suite at the Plaza. Groping for the phone on the nightstand, I knocked it to the floor and had to turn on the light. By the time I had the phone in hand, the ringing had stopped. When I checked caller ID, it said, 'Michele Herbert.'

Before calling her back, I went into the bathroom and splashed cold water on my face. My cell rang again, and I answered, 'How's my favorite art professor?'

'I wouldn't know, Jack,' Justine said.

'Oh,' I said. 'I didn't realize it was you.'

'I got that,' Justine said coolly. 'Anyway, I'm just leaving UCLA Medical Center. Sherman

Wilkerson has come out of the coma.'

'Thank God,' I replied. 'How is he?'

'The doctors say he could be a lot worse.'

That made my heart sink. 'That bad?'

'He's disoriented and had no idea who I was, even after I identified myself for the fourth time,' Justine replied. 'But he knows who you are, and he remembers that you are protecting his grand-daughter.'

'You didn't tell him we lost her, did you?'

'No, I figured it'd upset him too much,' she replied, and then paused. 'The problem is he thinks Kim is twenty, and taking a junior year in Paris.'

'Oh, that's sad.'

'Heartbreaking, actually,' Justine said. 'He kept talking about how she loved hot chocolate, and how her favorite place in Paris served the best hot chocolate in the world.'

'Okay...'

'I'm just giving you a report. Nothing on your end?'

'Kim's vanished. And honestly, we haven't had a minute to look for her.'

'Who has the beef with Les Académies?' she asked.

'Jacques Noulan, for one.'

'Noulan,' she said, impressed. 'I owned one of his dresses once. Made me look glamorous.'

'You always look glamorous.'

'Sweet,' she said, softening. 'And you almost always look dashing.'

'How's Cruz's mother?'

'Fading,' she said. 'Going into congestive heart failure.'

'Sucks.'

'It does. I'll be back to talk with Sherman in the morning, and I'll call you afterward with an update.'

'That works,' I said, and hung up.

After a deliciously hot shower and a shave, I tried Michele Herbert and got her machine. I left a message that I was sorry to have missed her call. I dressed and ordered a croque monsieur sandwich and a salad. The melted ham and cheese on a fresh baguette was fantastic, and I was thinking I should order another when something dawned on me, and I picked up my phone again.

'You awake?' I asked Louis Langlois.

'I never went to sleep,' he said.

'Are you some kind of freak of nature?'

'You hadn't noticed before?' Louis laughed.

'Can you come get me?'

'Of course,' he said. 'Where are we going?'

'To search for the best hot chocolate in Paris.'

'A much debated subject, Jack,' he grunted. 'Liable to start a fight. Or a squabble, anyway.'

Chapter 52

According to Louis, every Parisian has his or her own idea of where the best foods can be found in the city, from croissants and baguettes to cassoulet and goat cheese.

'But with hot chocolate, the argument verges on impossible,' Louis said as we stood outside the Plaza waiting for an Uber car.

'C'mon,' I said.

He shrugged and walked over to several other patrons of the hotel who were waiting for cars or taxis.

'*Mon ami,*' Louis said loudly to the doorman. 'Where is the best hot chocolate in Paris served?'

'Angelina,' the doorman said without hesitation. 'Rue de Rivoli.'

'For tourists!' cried a young woman smoking a cigarette. 'Jean-Paul Hévin on Rue Saint-Honoré, no doubt. The blend they serve is heaven. An aphrodisiac.'

'Ah,' scoffed her friend, a sallow man in a suit and a thin tie. 'I have nothing against aphrodisiacs, but the hot chocolate at Les Deux Magots is sublime.'

A fourth person chimed in to nominate the Café Martini, and a fifth said Carette in the Trocadéro was without a doubt the best purveyor of hot chocolate in the world.

The Uber car pulled up. Louis was roaring with laughter when we pulled away, and they were all still arguing the point. 'I love Paris,' he said. 'I really do.'

We went to Angelina first. The staff at the Viennese-style tearoom did not recognize Kim Kopchinski from the pictures we showed them. Neither did the various waiters and waitresses we talked to at Jean-Paul Hévin, Les Deux Magots, the Café Martini, and Carette.

It was almost 4 p.m. by then, and I'd all but decided that this was nothing but a wild-goose chase. When we climbed back into the Uber car outside Carette, I was going to declare surrender and suggest that we return to Private Paris. But then something occurred to me.

'Where was the best hot chocolate in Paris seven or eight years ago?'

Louis looked perplexed, but the driver said, 'That's simple. Besides Angelina, in those days it was definitely the Hôtel Lancaster on the Rue de Bern. Best hot chocolate of the new millennium.'

I shrugged. 'Can't hurt.'

'And it's not that far,' Louis said. 'We go.'

About ten minutes later, we pulled up in front of the Hôtel Lancaster, another of Paris's famed five-star hotels. The entrance was far more understated than the Plaza's, and we had to search for the front desk, where we asked about the hot chocolate.

We were directed to a tearoom overlooking a courtyard, and soon found an older waitress named Yvette, who took one look at the photograph and smiled.

'*C'est Kim*,' she said. 'She's been coming here off and on for years.'

'Lately?' I asked.

She nodded and said, 'Yesterday, about this time. And the day before that.'

We thanked her, and she walked away.

'She's not a celeb or a high roller,' Louis said. 'She'll be coming in the main entrance.'

We crossed through a lobby to a short hallway that led to double glass doors, where the valet and doorman were posted. I'd taken two steps when I saw Kim Kopchinski sprinting diagonally across the street, heading for the opposite sidewalk with Whitey in close pursuit and carrying a pistol.

Chapter 53

By the time Louis and I burst out of the Hôtel Lancaster, they were well down the block, heading south and west. I took off after them, with Louis bringing up the rear.

I was closing the gap when I realized that Big Nose was running ahead of me on the opposite sidewalk, paralleling them. Just shy of the Champs-Élysees, he cut across the street.

Kim and Whitey reached the corner.

A blue van screeched to a halt in front of them.

Whitey grabbed Sherman's granddaughter, and she screamed, 'I don't have it anymore! I threw it—'

The pale man pushed her inside. The van squealed away, leaving the Nose, who had slowed to a walk. I hadn't. He saw me coming just before I tackled him and knocked him to the street.

'What is this?' he yelled, and began to struggle beneath me. 'Police!'

'You like hitting people with hammers?' I shouted, and was about to pop him low and in the back so he'd stop squirming.

But out of the corner of my eye, I saw something white and brown launch at me from between the parked cars. On instinct, I ducked a second before it landed on me and started viciously biting at my ear and neck.

Surprised by the pain, I rolled off the guy below

me, and tried to defend myself. But the dog was in a frenzy, making these satanic throat noises that had me convinced a pit bull or something like it was attacking me.

'Napoleon!' a man shouted. 'Napoleon, no!'

As soon as he yelled, the biting stopped, and I sat up, feeling blood drip from my ear and from wounds to my neck. The Nose was gone, and a twenty-two-pound wirehaired Jack Russell terrier sat about two feet from me, tongue hanging from his bloody muzzle as he panted through what looked like a smile.

A tanned man in jeans and a black leather jacket was running across the street, looking mortified. 'Napoleon, what have you done?'

The dog was wagging its tail but barked when Louis pulled up, gasping and looking at my wounds in disbelief.

'I am so sorry, monsieur,' the man said. He was in his early forties, carried a leash, and was built robustly for a Parisian. 'I've never seen him do anything remotely like that! Bad dog, Napoleon! You are a little terrorist!'

The dog cringed and lay flat on the sidewalk.

'Are you all right?' the man asked me.

'Does he look all right?' Louis asked, handing me a handkerchief.

'My God, you'll need stitches,' the man said.

'And a rabies shot,' Louis said.

'Napoleon is up to date on all his shots,' his owner said.

'It's all right,' I said. 'I just need to see a doctor.'

'Of course,' the man said. 'There's one nearby, I'm sure.'

'We'll take you to Private Paris's contracted doctor, Jack,' Louis said.

'Private Paris?' the man said, sounding surprised.

'We both work for the company,' I said, gingerly touching my ear.

'This makes it all the worse, then,' the man said. 'Again, I am so sorry for my little terrorist's activities, and...'

'You have a name, sir?' Louis asked. 'Somewhere we can contact you with the bill?'

He hesitated, but then reached into his coat and handed Louis a business card. 'My name is Rivier, Phillipe Rivier. I'm just up here from Nice on business.'

Louis glanced at the card as I got up, and the dog came up off its belly and growled. Rivier took a quick step toward the dog and it lay down fast.

'Be quiet now,' he growled. 'You're in big trouble when you get home.'

'How about you put the emperor on his leash?' Louis said.

'Oh,' Rivier said, looking chagrined. 'It's just that he's usually spot-on with his voice commands and–'

'The leash,' Louis said.

'Right,' Rivier said, and clipped the lead on the little dog's collar.

Louis's cell rang, and he turned to answer it.

Rivier smiled weakly at me. 'Again, I couldn't be more sorry. And please, I'm more than happy to pay for all medical expenses – and dinner. Let me buy you dinner, Monsieur...?'

'Morgan. Jack Morgan,' I said.

'Please. We are here for another day or two. Call me if you think of it. You have the number there.'

Louis turned, the cell pressed tight to his ear and his eyes squinting.

'I can't promise anything,' I said, glancing at the dog, which had not taken its attention from me.

Rivier smiled weakly, and went off, scolding the dog, which skulked along beside him.

My ear was throbbing, and I was berating myself for letting Big Nose get away, when Louis said, 'No one else sees it until we get there, Ali. And get the concierge doctor on duty to meet us at the offices. Jack's suffered a dog bite and requires stitches.'

He hung up, looking shaken.

'That was Farad. AB-16 just sent Private Paris a letter, Jack, and he says the contents are beyond explosive.'

Chapter 54

15TH ARRONDISSEMENT
6:20 P.M.

'Why you, Louis?' Sharen Hoskins demanded the second she barged through the doors into the lobby of Private Paris's offices, which were situated in a newer building near the Porte de Versailles.

'It was not addressed to me, but to our newest associate,' Louis said. 'Ali Farad, a recruit from the narcotics bureau in Marseille. The second Farad saw what it was, he acted to protect it, and the envelope, then called me immediately. Then I called you immediately, *non?*'

'Where is it?' said Juge Fromme, who limped in behind the *investigateur.* 'What does it say?'

'It's in the lab being analyzed by our best people, and we only just got here,' I said. 'We haven't read it.'

'Stop all tests until we've seen it,' Fromme insisted.

'As you wish, *juge,*' Louis said. 'We are on your side here.'

'That remains to be seen,' Fromme replied curtly. 'Take us to it.'

Louis went to a bulletproof door below a security camera and put his hand on a fingerprint reader, his eye to a retina scanner. The door whooshed open.

'You expecting terrorists?' Fromme demanded.

'We always prepare for the worst-case scenario,' I said.

Louis led us into a large open area where the agents worked, and then down a staircase to the lab, which was virtually identical to our state-of-the-art facility in Los Angeles. Dr. Seymour Kloppenberg, who ran the L.A. lab and was better known to us as Sci, also oversaw all forensics for Private, and he insisted that every lab be as well equipped as his.

It had cost me a small fortune, but the results were convincing. Outside of the FBI's labs at Quantico, and Scotland Yard's facilities in London, Private's forensics were the finest in the world.

We passed techs working on evidence from the two AB-16 crime scenes on our way to an anteroom, where we were issued clean white paper jumpsuits, latex gloves, and operating room caps and shoe covers. After passing through an air lock, we entered a clean room where Ali Farad was watching Marc Petitjean, Private Paris's head of forensics. Petitjean was peering through a ten-inch magnifying glass mounted in a frame above a plastic evidence sleeve containing a piece of paper and an envelope.

'Move away from the evidence, please,' Fromme said.

Petitjean, who had a strong French ego, looked insulted and almost started to protest, but Louis and I both made cutting signs across our necks.

'Juge Fromme and Investigateur Hoskins wish to read the letter, Marc,' Louis said.

'There is much here besides the letter,' Petitjean said, openly peeved as he stepped aside so the magistrate could limp to the workbench and pick up the evidence sleeve.

He and Hoskins studied it for several moments, growing graver and paler by the second, which made me wonder what in the hell the letter said.

'Who has seen this?' Fromme demanded.

'Just myself and Marc,' Ali Farad said.

'It will remain that way,' the magistrate said. 'This comes with me.'

'Wait. What?' Louis said. 'Our lab meets–'

'I don't care,' the magistrate said. 'French national security is at stake, and under our censorship law, I forbid these two from disseminating this message in any way whatsoever. Are we clear?'

Neither Farad nor Petitjean seemed happy about it, but they nodded.

'How did the letter arrive?' Hoskins asked. 'There's no stamp.'

'It was there at the front desk, waiting,' said Farad. 'Juliette, the receptionist, went to the toilette, returned, and it was there.'

'Did we pick up the drop-off on security tapes?' I asked.

Farad hesitated. 'I hadn't looked.'

'We need to,' Louis said, nodding to Petitjean.

The scientist picked up an iPad and asked Farad, 'About what time?'

He shrugged. 'An hour ago?'

Petitjean gave the iPad some instructions, and a flat-screen hanging above the examination table blinked on, showing the lobby with a running time stamp. Farad had the envelope in hand and was talking to Juliette. The scientist sped the tape in reverse, and we saw images of Farad walking backward through the bulletproof glass door, and then the receptionist returning to find the letter.

'There he is,' Louis said when the squiggly image of a man went by. 'Take us to when he comes in.'

Petitjean rewound further and hit play. A man with swarthy skin, a scruffy black beard, and sunglasses entered the lobby carrying a motorcycle helmet with the FEZ Couriers logo clearly visible. He dug in a messenger bag with gloved hands, came up with a manila envelope, and left it, turned, and exited the lobby.

'You don't get a very good look at him, do you?' Hoskins asked.

It was true. Other than the suggestion of Arab features and the color of his neck and cheek, he gave us no clear view of his face.

'There'll be a record at FEZ of who the messenger was and where the letter came from,' Louis said.

'I can call Firmus Massi,' Farad said. 'We attend the same mosque.'

'You'll do nothing of the sort,' Fromme said, eyeing him before turning to Petitjean. 'You indicated there was more here than the letter.'

'Physical evidence,' Petitjean confirmed. 'Under fluorescent light you can see several stains on the page. And there were hair fragments in the envelope and in the glue. Three of them. And what looked like fabric lint.'

'They're here?' Fromme said, shaking the evidence sleeve.

'Here,' Petitjean said, holding out four small sealed sleeves that carried stickers and numbers indicating that they'd already been logged into our system.

Fromme took these as well, and had Hoskins take note of the time of day and the names of the witnesses to the evidence exchange.

'Monsieur Farad?' the magistrate said.

'Yes?'

'You will need to come with us.'

'Why?'

'We want to know why you received the letter.'

'I can tell you right here. I have no idea.'

'And the fact that it came from a messenger

212

from a friend's service?'

'Massi is more an acquaintance than a friend,' Farad said. 'We attend the same mosque. Beyond that, it's a coincidence.'

'Perhaps,' Fromme said. 'But we would like you to come with us, or I can have Investigateur Hoskins arrest you and bring you in for questioning.'

'*Juge*,' Louis sputtered. 'What you're insinuating here is... Farad was a decorated officer with the Sûreté, and Private Paris is–'

'Out of this investigation,' the magistrate said strongly. 'This has gone to a whole different level, Langlois, and the government's probe cannot be compromised in any way. I'm sorry, but that is the way it must be. Monsieur Farad must be looked at vigorously, and Private Paris will sit on the sidelines.'

Louis looked at Farad. 'Go with them. I will call our attorney.'

'I don't need one.'

'It's a federal investigation now,' Louis insisted. 'You need a lawyer.'

Farad looked beyond angry, and I couldn't blame him. He'd done exactly the right things and was now under suspicion for God knows what.

When Fromme, Hoskins, and Farad had exited the air lock and were out of earshot, Louis looked at the forensics expert and said, 'Feel like ignoring the magistrate's order?'

'And break a federal law for a colleague?' Petitjean said. 'But of course.'

He went over to the keyboard and gave it a command.

A screen quickly showed a blown-up image of

the letter and the envelope.

It was written in French in letters cut from various newspapers and magazines. I got the gist of it, and my stomach yawned open into a deep, cold pit.

Chapter 55

8TH ARRONDISSEMENT
8:10 P.M.

'You'll find an attorney for Farad?' I said, climbing out of an Uber car in front of the Plaza Athénée.

'First thing,' Louis promised. 'Get some sleep.'

In a mild daze, I entered the lobby, imagining a hot, hot shower and long, long uninterrupted sleep in my big empty suite. That's all I wanted.

'Monsieur Morgan?' called a woman's sweet voice.

I blinked, fought back a yawn, and spotted Elodie rushing out from behind the concierge desk. She danced over and said quietly, 'I wanted you to know that we took care of Mademoiselle Kim for you.'

It took a moment to penetrate my exhausted brain. 'Kim is here?'

'In your suite. We gave her a key. That's what you wanted, yes?'

'Uh, yes,' I said, flashing on that image of Kim being thrown into the van outside the Hôtel Lan-

214

caster and wondering how she'd escaped.

'When did she arrive?'

Elodie thought about that and said, 'Two?'

That was right after I left the hotel and two and a half hours *before* we saw her taken.

'When did she leave?' I asked.

'She didn't. At least not through the lobby while I've been on duty.'

I smiled. 'She got by you or ducked out a side door because I saw Kim later, around four thirty. Could you check and see when the door to the suite was opened after she went in?'

Elodie appeared miffed but went behind the concierge counter and worked on a computer. She looked up at me, chagrined. 'Fifteen minutes later.'

'Perfect, really. Thank you for your graciousness.'

The concierge beamed. *'Je vous en prie, monsieur.'*

When I entered the suite, the lights came on, and I stood there in the living area, thinking. Why had Kim come here, and for only fifteen minutes? Her time of entry – roughly 2 p.m. – was less than twenty minutes after Louis and I got in an Uber car in front of the Plaza, leaving a heated discussion about hot chocolate in our wake.

Was that a coincidence? Had she come to us for protection, and found me missing? Or had she been watching, waiting to see us leave?

But why would she?

In my befuddled state, I couldn't come up with an explanation until I thought of what I'd heard her scream as Whitey threw her into the van.

'I don't have it anymore!'

She had hid something in here.

A good part of me wanted to sack out and look for it in the morning, but as I moved through the living area toward my bedroom, I kept thinking of how brazen and violent the men after Kim had been again and again.

They were willing to kill. Would they be willing to torture?

I had to imagine they would. And I had to imagine that, unless there were dimensions to Kim Kopchinski that I did not understand, she would break. And then they would come for whatever was hidden in my suite. Whitey and his pal had broken in once. They'd no doubt try a second time.

Realizing I would not sleep worth a damn there now, I went to the toilet, turned on the cold water in the basin, and stuck my head under it until the cobwebs cleared. Then I set about searching the place.

I went through my bedroom, my closet, and my bathroom from top to bottom. I checked under the mattress, in the drawers, and under my clothes, and even rifled through my suitcase. Nothing.

I began to doubt myself. Why would she bring it *here* in the first place?

For safekeeping, I supposed. It was the simplest answer.

I checked the safe in my closet: still locked. I typed in the six-digit code I'd given it, and found my passport and extra currency untouched. After hurrying into the room Kim had used, however,

I entered the closet, took one look at the safe, and knew she'd locked something inside.

Elodie knocked at my door fifteen minutes later with a workman carrying a red toolbox.

'I must have slipped putting in my code,' I said. 'I've tried twice and I know it will lock up for an hour if I try a third time.'

'No problem,' Elodie said. 'It happens.'

But when I led her toward the room Kim had used, she balked.

'This isn't your room,' she said.

'My suite.'

'Yes, but...'

I pulled her aside and murmured, 'Remember the guys who shot up the place a few days ago?'

She nodded sourly.

'They've got Mademoiselle Kopchinski, and I have no doubt that eventually they're coming back to the Plaza because of what is in that safe,' I said. 'Now, Kim is my client. I was hired to protect her by her grandfather, who was beaten into a coma, I believe because of what is in that safe. So, to get the Plaza out of the line of fire and help Kim, I need that safe opened. What's it going to be?'

The concierge hesitated, but then said, 'You'll remove this thing from the premises?'

'Immediately,' I promised.

Elodie nodded to the workman and we followed him into the closet. He attached a digital override device to the safe with coaxial cables and gave it several instructions before typing in a six-digit number. The safe made a whirring sound and then a click.

Before I could tell the workman not to open the door, he did and shined a flashlight inside. The beam picked up the glimmering object inside.

'What is it?' Elodie asked.

'A cigarette lighter,' I said.

Chapter 56

16TH ARRONDISSEMENT
11:20 P.M.

On the Avenue de Montespan, Guy LaFont carried a briefcase as he climbed from the back of his car. A tall, elegant man in his late fifties, LaFont bid his driver adieu in front of the doors to the courtyard of his building. He used a key to flip the dead bolt, stepped inside, and closed and locked the door behind him.

Two soft lights cast the courtyard in warm shadows. He could clearly see his neighbor's new Mercedes parked there, and the beautiful boxed flower garden his neighbor's wife tended. It already bloomed with tulips and daffodils.

LaFont almost couldn't bear to turn away from the box garden and walk to his door past another box garden that lay fallow and weedy. He did his best to avoid looking at it, and went inside. Locking the door behind him, LaFont took a deep, familiar, and agonizing sniff of home, and wondered at the chest-buckling pressure of his grief and loneliness.

When would it go away? Would it ever ... go away?

LaFont recalled what his psychiatrist had told him: that grief was a process, a tearing down and a rebuilding. He didn't often feel this crippling melancholy at work. His job still consumed him, drove him, and he believed he had fulfilled his responsibilities and stayed true to his principles in the past fourteen months with admirable strength and courage.

Without question, he thought forcefully. Without question.

But here in the home LaFont had shared with his beloved wife of twenty-six years, duty could not compensate for loss. He walked past Evelyn's kitchen without stopping. He crossed through the salon she'd designed with such care. In the study where they'd watched television, he looked at pictures on the bookshelves: that snapshot from their honeymoon in Sardinia, their sons playing soccer and skiing at Chamonix, and Evelyn sitting in his lap at their favorite spot in Barcelona.

'We were so young,' he muttered.

LaFont stared at his reflection in the mirror, wondered when he'd gotten so old. He wondered if he should go back to the office, get something done, and then sleep on the couch.

Maybe his sons were right. Maybe it was this place that was keeping him from moving on. They were urging him to sell, but he hadn't had the heart to call a realtor to put it on the market.

This was Evelyn's home and he simply wasn't ready to part with it or the ghosts of their life together. Turning on the television, he flipped the channels until he found a newscast. It led, as all newscasts had that day, with images of the AB-16 graffiti tag high on the cupola of the Institut de France.

The image filled LaFont with outrage!

He'd known Henri Richard and Lourdes Latrelle and had admired René Pincus. Attacking the French culture by murdering the best and brightest? LaFont wanted to pick something up and hurl it at the screen. Who the hell were they to do such a thing? What the hell did they want?

It all gave him a headache, and he hit the mute button before going to a cabinet and finding a bottle of Armagnac. He popped the cork, poured himself twice the usual amount, and drank until a fire exploded in his belly.

LaFont poured himself another generous amount, and took the glass with him after shutting off the news. He'd probably wake up with a scorcher of a headache, but at least he'd have slept, and the last time he'd looked, his agenda was thin in the mor–

He reached the landing at the top of the stairs and halted. The door to Evelyn's art studio was ajar and there was light flowing from it into the hallway by their bedroom.

Who would have been in there? The maid? Wasn't it her day?

Believing it was, LaFont marched down the hall, meaning to reach inside the room, flip down the light switch just inside the door, and seal the studio again.

Standing there, however, smelling the faint odor of paint and turpentine, LaFont decided

220

that maybe it *was* time for a visit, and maybe a good cry. He hadn't allowed himself one of those in at least a month.

He guzzled the rest of the Armagnac, pushed the door open, and stepped inside an L-shaped airy space with large skylights, windows, and banks of adjustable lights.

LaFont's eyes welled and spilled, and he looked around, hoping to find solace in her paintings. There were dozens of them around the studio in various stages of completion. But through his tears, all he could see of his late wife's imagined and real landscapes were the vivid colors she was known–

He sniffed. Was that fresh paint? He took off his glasses and wiped at his eyes with the sleeve of his suit. Putting the glasses back on, he froze.

On a long oak table, LaFont spotted a section of loose canvas that had been spray-painted with 'AB-16.'

What the–

His disbelief was replaced by surprise when he picked up movement in the shadows at the rear of his late wife's studio. His killer stepped into the light with a suppressed pistol, aiming in a way that spoke of honed skill.

An assassin.

Exactly the way Evelyn had always feared it would end for me.

LaFont did not run or cry out for mercy.

He looked at the death messenger, bowed his head in relief, and said, 'Please.'

Chapter 57

8TH ARRONDISSEMENT
APRIL 10, 1:45 A.M.

In her workshop on the Rue Clement Marot, the fashion designer Millie Fleurs sipped a glass of Fumé Blanc, studied the dramatic black cocktail dress on the mannequin, and compared it to the drawing on the table beside her.

An off-the-shoulder sheath, the dress was more tailored than flowing, meant to hug the wearer, and it featured a daring geometric cutout at the navel. The edging of the cutout was embossed silver. So were the tips of the black leather strap that hugged the low belly and hung provocatively off the left hip.

Fleurs walked around the dress, analyzing it from every angle. My God, it *was* stunning, certainly one of the best dresses to come out of her workshop in years.

The designer knew it was exactly what her client wanted: classical enough to be worn at a gala, but hip enough for hitting a nightclub afterward. This dress fit the bill in every respect. No one who saw her in it would ever forget it.

Which was both good and bad. As an haute couture creation, it was supposed to be one of a kind. But Fleurs already knew in her gut that she was going to introduce a replica with only the slightest of modifications at the July shows.

The dress would be the showstopper that she needed to turn things around. The last few seasons had seen a drop-off in her company's growth rate, and she saw the frock as a return to wider acclaim and bigger profits.

Fleurs figured there were only a few things standing in the way of putting the dress on the runway. The client's m–

The designer thought she heard something behind her in the hallway off the workshop that led to stairs and the rear exit. She was alone. She'd been alone for hours tinkering with the more subtle aspects of the dress.

It had to be the cat. Where had she gotten to?

Fleurs set her wineglass down and headed toward the rear hallway, calling, 'Madeline?' and making kissing noises. 'Come here, little puss.'

She flipped on the hallway light and managed a short shriek of surprise and terror before a six-inch leather awl was driven straight into her heart.

'What?' Fleurs coughed. She stared blankly down at the tool handle sticking out of her chest and then up at her killer. 'I was going to...'

She coughed again and reached for the handle.

Then she staggered backward into her workshop, careened off the cutting table, and died on the floor, facing the mannequin and her final creation.

Chapter 58

5 A.M.

'Jack?'

I startled awake at the whisper, pistol up reflexively, wondering where I was before realizing that I was back in the suite at the Plaza Athénée, sitting in an overstuffed chair by the bed, and Louis Langlois was standing in the open doors to my bedroom.

Louis murmured, 'If Kim's friends are coming, it will be soon.'

'Okay, I'm up,' I said. 'Petitjean?'

'Still working on the lighter,' Louis replied. 'But the letter? AB-16 sent it to ten different news services.'

Louis handed me an iPad. The screen showed the France 4 television website and a photograph of the letter in a hodgepodge of font sizes and styles clipped from various newspapers. In that respect, it looked different from the one Ali Farad had received at Private Paris, but the text was the same as I remembered it, word for word.

'AB-16 is trying to light that powder keg you were talking about last night,' I said to Louis, handing him back the iPad.

'Most definitely,' Louis replied grimly. 'And Fromme is petrified of that happening. I would not be surprised if–'

The doorbell to the suite dinged.

I glanced at my watch: 5:15 a.m.

'Here we go, Jack,' he murmured, drawing a Glock, which carried a stubby sound suppressor. 'Back-to-back.'

In our stocking feet, we crept out into the living area. Louis followed me into the entry hall, walking backward and watching the balcony, which we'd left lit.

I smeared myself into the wall on the hinge side of the door. Knowing that someone as ruthless as Whitey might shoot through the peephole the second they saw a shadow appear, I held up the room key card in front of it.

Nothing.

I glanced at Louis, eased over, and peered out into the hallway.

Randall Peaks, the Saudis' security guy, was staring back at me, looking as though he'd recently developed an ulcer.

What the hell was he doing here? And at this hour?

Peaks reached over impatiently and rang the bell again.

'We're good,' I murmured to Louis. I stuck the gun in my waistband and opened the door.

'How many men can I hire through you?' Peaks asked.

'When?' Louis said.

'Now,' he replied. 'Can we speak inside?'

I let him in and closed the door behind him.

'What's going on?' I asked.

'I'm missing a princess,' Peaks grunted.

'Never a good thing,' Louis said.

225

The Saudi security chief glared at Louis. 'This is bad, Mr. Langlois, and I need Private Paris's help finding her as soon as possible.'

'Of course,' I said. 'Whatever you need. Which princess?'

Peaks hesitated and said, 'This has to be handled discreetly.'

'I gather you're the client?'

He nodded. 'I don't want the other princesses knowing. No one can know.'

'And heaven forbid the dad back in Riyadh,' Louis said. 'Which princess?'

'Mayameen,' he said, showing us his cell phone and a picture of the young princess I saw in the Plaza's breakfast room a few days before. 'She's just turned sixteen.'

'When did she disappear?' I asked.

'Shortly after midnight she snuck out of her room while one of my men was using the john. We didn't pick up on it until twenty minutes ago, when we checked our security tapes.'

'How was she dressed when she left?' Louis asked.

'For a club,' Peaks said sourly. 'Stiletto heels. Black leather pants. White top. Too much skin between the two.'

'She went out alone to a club?' I asked.

Peaks cocked his jaw. 'She has a history of this sort of behavior.'

'So she'll come back eventually?'

'I can't afford "eventually",' the security chief insisted. 'If she's not at Millie Fleurs's for a fitting at nine with her mother, I'll be terminated.'

'Then we start now,' Louis said. 'Ten thousand

dollars and I'll send investigators to every club in the city still open.'

It sounded like highway robbery to me, but Peaks said, 'Done.'

Louis said, '*Bon*. Most of the late-night clubs are in the 11th and 17th, but the two closest are Showcase and Le Baron. I will go there myself.'

'I'll go with him,' I promised.

'You'll text me the moment you find her?' Peaks asked.

'Immediately,' Louis promised. 'And in the meantime, if her mother and sisters ask after her, say that she's got the terrible twenty-four-hour stomach virus that's been going around Paris.'

Peaks brightened. 'Is there one going around Paris?'

'Not that I know of. But it should buy you some time.'

Peaks texted us the photograph of the princess and a picture of her passport. We promised to be in touch.

Though the air exiting the elevator spoke of croissants baking and espresso brewing, the area outside the breakfast room and the lobby were dead.

Even Elodie was struggling to remain awake until she saw me approaching. She stiffened enough to complain quietly, '*S'il vous plaît*, Monsieur Morgan, can it wait? I'm off duty in just five minutes, and—'

I showed her the photograph. 'Did she come through here after midnight?'

The concierge studied the picture and then said, 'She looked much older than in the picture.

Who is she?'

'You don't want to know. Leave it for the shift change.'

Elodie tried to hide her worry with a professional smile. 'When will you be leaving us, Mr. Morgan?'

'Believe me, Elodie,' I said, 'as soon as I can.'

I found Louis out front, trying to hail a cab. But the Avenue Montaigne was as quiet as the lobby of the Plaza.

Louis gestured up the street two blocks toward the Rue François 1er, where a taxi crossed, and then another. 'We have better luck there.'

He began to jog, with me following. We were crossing the Rue Clément Marot when a woman's bloodcurdling screaming stopped us in our tracks. Louis ran toward the screams, which had turned into hysterical crying.

Racing after him, I realized that she wasn't on the street. Her weeping was coming from overhead, through an open, lit window on the floor above the haute couture shop of Millie Fleurs.

Louis tried the front door. Locked.

He hesitated, but only for a moment, before he drew the suppressed Glock, stepped back, and put three rounds through the glass, which turned to spiderwebs above the door handle. He flipped the gun over and used the butt of the pistol like a hammer to break out enough glass to reach inside.

'Gonna have an alarm,' I said.

'Good,' Louis said. He flipped the dead bolt and turned the handle. The door swung open silently.

The shop did have a security system. I remembered that from our visit. Why no alarm?

But I had no time to think about that because as we hurried across the darkened space, the crying stopped and we heard the sound of someone running overhead. Louis threw back the curtain and charged up the steep staircase toward the light and Millie Fleurs's workshop.

We both got to the top of the staircase and came to a dead halt.

Millie Fleurs hung upside down by her ankles, which were bound with fabric twisted into a rope that was thrown over a rafter. The designer's arms and hair hung limply. Blood from a chest wound had soaked her blouse, drained across her face, and dripped to the floor.

The pool of blood below the dress designer had reached but only partially obscured a variation of the AB-16 symbol, depicted not in red spray paint but with black and red silk fabric.

'Hoskins and Fromme are going to–'

Louis held up his index finger and then pressed it to his ear. I stopped, listened, and heard the whimpering.

It came from behind a door beyond the only bare mannequin in the studio. Louis gestured to a bloody footprint on the floor, and stepped around it.

He looked over his shoulder at me. I squared up, aiming at the door. He reached over and opened it.

'No! Don't shoot!'

She was slurring and blubbering, a pretty young teenager with long black, braided hair, pressed to the back of the shallow closet, terrified and holding her hands up as if to block a bullet. Blood slicked her exposed palms, stained her white blouse, and gelled on the thighs of her black leather pants.

Smelling the strong scent of alcohol and cigarettes coming off her, I lowered the gun and said, 'Princess Mayameen?'

She nodded feebly before sliding down the wall into a sobbing heap. 'My mother is going to kill me this time, isn't she?'

Chapter 59

We talked with Maya, as she preferred to be called, for a good ten minutes before we put in a call to Sharen Hoskins, and for another ten minutes before calling Randall Peaks.

The Saudi security chief and the La Crim *investigateur* showed up at almost the same time, with Peaks following Hoskins up the stairs. The detective's eyes were puffy and her demeanor on edge. She glanced at me and Louis, shook her head, mumbled something under her breath, and then shifted her attention to Millie Fleurs's corpse.

Peaks reached the workshop, saw the teenager passed out on a daybed in the corner and the blood on her hands and shirt, and said, 'Princess Mayameen will be leaving. Now.'

'Not a chance,' Hoskins said. 'She's explaining

herself to me before she goes anywhere.'

'That young lady is Saudi royalty and has complete diplomatic immunity,' Peaks insisted. 'She cannot be held against her will.'

'Who's holding her?' Hoskins asked. 'She looks to be a drunken adolescent to me, and as such is a danger to herself. I'm going to talk to her, make sure she's fit to travel.'

'No lawyer, no talking,' Peaks said.

'She'll talk and you'll shut up, or I'll have you arrested because I know *you* do not have diplomatic immunity,' said Juge Fromme, disheveled and in pain as he came up the stairs, leaning hard on his cane.

Looking as though he was having a root canal, no Novocain, Peaks said, 'The Saudi family and government will take this as an affront to—

'I don't care,' Fromme said. 'My country and countrymen are under direct attack, and that takes precedence over any foreign concerns. Period.'

Louis said, '*Juge?* For the record?'

The magistrate glowered. 'You two are like flies to shit in this, aren't you?'

Louis smiled weakly. 'In a manner of speaking, I suppose. But for the record, the princess may be guilty of reckless judgment, of drinking too much liquor, and of deciding to pay Millie Fleurs an impromptu visit on her way home from clubbing. But she is not remotely connected to the murder.'

Peaks's eyebrows rose, and he said, 'Exactly.'

'She's covered in her blood,' Hoskins said.

'Because she was trying to help her,' I said.

'I'd rather hear this from the princess,' Fromme said.

'I'm sure,' Louis said, glancing at the princess, who was curled up fetal and sucking her thumb. 'But from the looks of it, you might wait hours before she is in any condition to talk again.'

The magistrate fumed, but Hoskins said, 'Out with it.'

Louis and I recounted the story we'd gotten out of the princess. On her way home from the night-club Le Baron, she saw the light on in the work-shop above Millie's shop, knew she was going there with her mother in a few hours anyway, and, on impulse, wanted to take a sneak peek at her new dresses. She knew the location of the rear entrance from an earlier visit, hit the buzzer, and got no reply. She tried the door and found it unlocked.

'When she came into the workshop, she saw Millie hanging upside down, with her back to her,' Louis said. 'She ran to Millie, and tried to lift her body, which explains the blood on her hands and blouse. Then she started screaming, which is when Jack and I heard her.'

Fromme squinted. 'Why would she try to lift her?'

'Millie was special to the princess,' I said. 'Her favorite designer. Drunk as she was, she was just trying to help a friend in need.'

'There,' Peaks said. 'You have it, then. Now can we avoid an international incident here? I'm sure the princess's father will be more than grateful if we can keep her name out of the press. Please: that would smear her reputation at home for years, and home is Riyadh, not Paris. She doesn't deserve what would happen to her there.'

Hoskins and Fromme exchanged glances. The *investigateur* said, 'I'll need some kind of statement from her.'

Louis waved his iPhone. 'You'll have it. I videoed our conversation and her physical condition *with* her consent.'

'Wait. What?' Peaks protested. 'She can't consent. She's a drunk minor. Whatever she told you is inadmissible.'

'What do you care?' I asked. 'She's on the record, but the record stays private because she's a minor. Correct?'

Juge Fromme said, 'I can live with that.'

'I can too,' Hoskins said, sighing. 'Clean her up. Take her back to her mother.'

Peaks looked at Louis and me with an expression that said, I owe you both in a big way. We nodded, and he went to the princess's side and tried to wake her. She groaned and threw an arm over her head.

There was a commotion downstairs, and I could hear Laurent Alexandre arguing with the police officers securing the crime scene.

'That's Millie's personal assistant,' Louis told Hoskins.

The *investigateur* leaned over the railing and called down to the officers, telling them to allow Alexandre to come up. He did a few moments later, dressed in a bespoke blue suit with highwater pants and yellow socks that matched his tie. The outfit was totally at odds with the expression on his face as he climbed up from the shop: he looked like a scared little kid being forced into a haunted house at a carnival.

'She's dead?' he asked in a quavering voice full of disbelief.

Louis gestured in the direction of the designer's corpse, which still hung from the rafter. Alexandre didn't seem able to turn that way.

Instead, he said, 'Noulan? Did he kill her?'

'Doesn't look that way,' Hoskins said. 'AB-16.'

'What?' he whined before pivoting to face the workshop.

His trembling right hand came arthritically to his mouth, which gaped in horror. 'Oh, dear God, Millie,' he whispered. 'What have they done to you?'

Then his knees buckled, and he fainted dead away.

Chapter 60

Dawn was coming on while Randall Peaks cleaned Princess Mayameen with water and paper towels, and Hoskins revived Alexandre, who came around choking and weeping as he answered questions.

The designer's assistant said he had left the workshop at around eight the previous evening. Millie had still been working feverishly on the princess's dresses.

'She said she would sleep here on the daybed,' he said. 'She did it all the time when she had clients coming, and wanted me here at six fifteen sharp to wake her. If the princess hadn't ... I would have...'

Peaks got the princess to her feet, but she

234

didn't like it.

'I want to sleep, Randy,' she groaned.

'Back at the Plaza,' Peaks said.

'No,' Maya grumbled. 'I want to sleep here.'

The bodyguard hesitated, and then hauled off and slapped her hard across the rear.

'You're going to the hotel, Maya,' he said. 'Now.'

That got her wide awake, and she shouted, 'You'll lose your job for that! I'll make sure of it!'

Peaks grabbed her tightly about the wrist and dragged her toward the rear hallway, saying, 'I figure I've already lost the job because of you, but I will get you to your mother's room safe and sound whether you like my methods or not. You're a princess, for Allah's sake! Start acting like it!'

When they'd gone, Alexandre's lower lip quivered, and he said to Hoskins, 'Can I go downstairs, please? I can't stand seeing her this way.'

'Of course,' the *investigateur* said.

Strong lights bathed the window.

Louis went over and looked out. 'Television cameras. Four of them.'

The designer's assistant went to the stairs, wiping his eyes with his suit sleeve. 'Am I free to inform her family and friends?'

Fromme said, 'Yes, but don't talk about the crime scene.'

'No, I couldn't.'

As Alexandre trudged down the stairs, I studied the room again.

'Why is the body positioned differently?' I asked. 'Her arms, I mean. They're not spread to the side like with the others.'

Louis said, 'Maybe someone from AB-16 was in

here about to do that when the princess opened the door downstairs.'

'We can't suppose that until we get a time of death,' Hoskins said.

'Where is our forensics team?' the magistrate asked.

'They're wrapping up another scene.'

'Once again, I offer Private Paris's aid,' Louis said.

Fromme shook his head. 'We will wait for our people, and the both of you should leave. Now.'

He stated this all flatly, without the rancor and innuendo he'd shown after he'd seen the letter sent to Ali Farad.

'*Juge?*' I said. 'Has our associate, Mr. Farad, been released?'

The magistrate stiffened and said, 'He has not.'

'What?' Louis said. 'Why not?'

'As I indicated last night, Monsieur Langlois, AB-16 is a direct threat to our national security, and–'

'So Farad is a suspect because AB-16 sent him a letter?' I asked, incredulous. 'Are you going to arrest people at all the news outlets that received copies of the letter?'

Fromme glanced at Hoskins, who was stone-faced.

At last the magistrate cleared his throat and said, 'There is more to it than just the letter, Monsieur Morgan, I assure you. Beyond that, I–'

Phones buzzed, alerting Fromme and Hoskins to incoming texts. They got out their cells and read them. The detective's breath caught in her throat. Fromme went deathly pale for several beats, and then pointed his cane at us.

'You two: out. Now,' he growled. 'Back door. And no talking to the media under promise of arrest. Are we clear?'

Louis's eyebrows knitted in anger. 'You'll arrest us if we—'

'Without hesitation,' Fromme said. 'Now out and silent.'

'You act as if there's been another AB-16 murder,' Louis said.

'An assassination,' Hoskins said, shock in her tone.

'Investigateur Hoskins,' Fromme said in warning.

'Who's the victim?' I asked.

'*Madame investigateur*,' Fromme said.

The detective ignored the magistrate and said, 'Guy LaFont. Minister of culture.'

Chapter 61

Louis was not himself as we circled through the streets from Millie Fleurs's shop to the Plaza. A light drizzle fell and people were already heading to work, heads down and balancing their umbrellas.

'I fear for France, Jack,' he said grimly. 'AB-16 assassinated not only a sitting member of the president's cabinet, but one of the staunchest opponents of letting Muslims from our former colonies continue to immigrate here. There will be

237

repercussions, I'm sure. This could easily spin out of control.'

On that disturbing note, we entered the hotel lobby, which was crowded now. Another member of Peaks's security team stood watch outside the breakfast room. He nodded to us, giving us a one-finger salute.

Upstairs, we walked in heavy silence to the suite door. I was going to take a shower and Louis was going to order breakfast before we called our attorneys to work on getting Ali Farad released from custody.

'They seem to think they have evidence implicating him,' I said, passing the key before the lock.

'I don't believe it,' Louis said. 'Not for a minute. I vetted Farad myself. Ali is – how do you say? – squeaky-clean.'

I pushed the door open and knew something was wrong. The drawer to a desk in the suite's hallway had been tugged open. I got out my gun and motioned to Louis to do the same.

We snuck into the living area, seeing that the French doors to the balcony were ajar and that the suite had been tossed in our absence.

Every drawer was open or on the floor. The mattresses had been thrown aside and my personal belongings searched and strewn about. Both safes were unlocked and empty, as I'd left them. When I'd taken the lighter to Petitjean for examination, I'd also brought along my cash and passport and left it all in a safe at Private Paris.

'I'll call housekeeping,' I said, and headed toward the phone by my bed.

Louis grunted in reply, and then his cell phone rang. He answered, listened, and cried, *'Merde!* We are coming!'

He stabbed off the phone and shook it at me. 'Hoskins and Fromme – they had to have known! And they say nothing to us!'

'Calm down. What's going on?'

'It's bad, Jack. Government agents are searching our offices, taking our computers, and seizing all evidence in the lab.'

Chapter 62

15TH ARRONDISSEMENT
10:40 A.M.

When we climbed from the Uber car, there were black vans parked in front of our building and plainclothesmen wearing body armor and carrying submachine guns standing guard.

'Shit,' Louis said. 'They're carrying MP5Ks. Those guys are anti-terror.'

This was bad – very bad for Private Paris, and for me. The suggestion that Private was tied to terrorism was probably the worst thing that could ever happen. Clients would flee us like rats off a sinking ship.

Louis walked up to the nearest officer, his identification out.

'May I inspect the warrant?' he asked.

The officer played it professional and retrieved

the document. While Louis studied it, Marc Petitjean and Claudia Vans were shown out the door by two more anti-terrorists.

Petitjean was enraged. 'Thrown out of my own lab!'

Vans said, 'You act like we're criminals.'

'Maybe you are,' one of the officers said laconically. 'That's what we're here to find out. If so, you will most definitely be hearing from us.'

'This is slanderous,' the scientist said.

'But legal,' Louis said with a sigh, handing back the warrant. 'When can we reenter?'

'Couple of hours?'

'Please lock it when you leave,' he said, and turned to me. 'We should go, Jack. The press will get word of this, and it does not help us to be photographed in connection with a terrorism investigation.'

The four of us walked away.

When we were well down the street, Petitjean said, 'Given the letter and the initial reports we sent to La Crim yesterday, it didn't surprise me that we were raided.'

'What reports?' Louis asked.

Vans frowned and said, 'We ran DNA on the cigarette butts left at Chez Pincus and the pubic hairs we found at the sex club, and got enough to know that we are dealing with seven different people: five male, two female, and all of Middle Eastern or North African descent.'

'Farad?' I asked. 'Is he a match?'

'He's from the same general gene pool,' Petit- jean said. 'I could know more definitively in a couple of days, but they took the samples.'

Vans said, 'We did get a match on the newsprint used to compose the letter. They were all cut from Algerian and Tunisian newspapers.'

'You can tell something like that?' Louis asked.

'It's technical,' Petitjean said. 'But yes.'

We rounded the corner, and I realized something else and groaned.

'What is it?' Louis asked.

'Kim's lighter was in the lab. My passport and my money too.'

'No,' Vans said. 'I've got your passport and cash.'

'And I have the lighter here with my cigarettes,' the scientist said, patting his breast pocket and smiling. 'By the way, I know what it really is.'

After making sure we weren't under surveillance, we found a café, went inside, and ordered double espressos and croissants that were good, but they didn't splinter like the Plaza's.

'So, what is it?' Louis said after the waitress had left. 'The lighter?'

Private Paris's head scientist dug in his breast pocket and came up with a blue box of Gitanes cigarettes and the stainless steel lighter that had caused havoc all over the city in the past few days. He held the lighter, admiring it.

'Quite a piece of technology,' Petitjean said. 'Must have cost a small fortune to engineer. Very James Bond. Took a bit to figure it out, but I did.'

He turned the lighter upside down. He used a paper clip to press against the bleeder valve at the center of the flame control dial.

'There was actually butane in it the first time I tried,' the scientist said. 'And that kind of threw

241

me, until I...'

He used his thumbnail to turn the dial clockwise. Setting the paper clip aside, Petitjean took the lighter by both ends and tugged. It separated into two pieces, and revealed, sticking out of the bottom piece, a USB micro-B connector similar to the one that attaches a charger to my camera.

'It's a data storage device,' Vans said.

'And heavily encrypted,' said Petitjean, who looked irritated that she'd spilled the beans. 'I tried to hack my way in, but it was beyond my skills.'

'And mine,' Vans said.

I looked at Louis. 'Le Chien?'

He smiled and said, 'Excellent idea. We'll put the Dog on it.'

Chapter 63

11TH ARRONDISSEMENT
11:35 A.M.

The brain-injured hacker cradled an iPad connected to the memory stick and went into slow orbit around the perimeter of his apartment, completely ignoring Louis and me as he probed the method of encryption.

Louis shifted gears and put in a call to our French legal team regarding Ali Farad. I got on the phone with a Palo Alto, California, company that provides twenty-four-hour data backup services for Private offices around the globe, and authorized it to move a copy of all of Private Paris's files to a secure virtual office where we could access them.

I called Justine, too. It was 2:35 in the morning, L.A. time, but she picked right up. The Dog orbited past me while I got her up to date on Kim Kopchinski's kidnapping, the lighter, and the raiding of Private Paris.

'Private the focus of an anti-terror investigation,' Justine said. 'A disaster.'

'Tell me about it,' I said.

'What about Farad?'

'Louis swears by him. And his record is immaculate. Not even a rumor of Islamic radicalism.'

'But you said the police hinted that they had more than a rumor?'

'Yes.'

'What is it?'

'I honestly have no idea,' I said, glancing at Louis, who was in the Dog's kitchen intently listening to his cell phone.

'Has news of the raid gotten out?' Justine asked.

'Not that I know of,' I said.

'Could be time to hire a publicist who specializes in crisis management,' Justine said. 'Have something ready in case it does come out.'

'Maybe,' I said. 'How's Sherman?'

'Slightly better,' she said. Wilkerson had remembered her when she visited the night before. He also remembered that three men wearing masks had assaulted him in his house. They had wanted to know where Kim was.

'Sherman kept asking me if you had her safe,' Justine said. 'I told him you were working on it, and that seemed to undo his progress. He got very agitated and angry with me – shouting, even – and the nurses asked me to leave.'

'Great,' I said, watching the Dog leave the cluttered living area and orbit into a back hallway.

Shaking his head, Louis hurried from the kitchen, glanced at me in deep distress, and said, 'The lawyers, Jack. They say to watch the news. Life is getting worse for us and for Farad.'

Before I could reply, he snatched the remote off a coffee table.

I told Justine I had to go, and hung up in time to see the flat-screen on the wall blink and then jump to a Parisian street scene I recognized immediately.

'That's Barbès,' I said. 'The mosque. FEZ Couriers.'

'And Al-Jumaa tailors,' Louis said as the camera angle shifted to show officers wearing bulletproof vests and carrying MAT-49s as they led the tailor out of his shop in handcuffs.

Other anti-terrorists stood guard at the doors of the mosque and the courier service. A perimeter had been formed, blocking off a growing crowd of onlookers that burst into angry shouts when the police brought out Firmus Massi in cuffs. The owner of FEZ Couriers looked shaken and bewildered.

'Killers!' some began to chant. 'Assassins!'

I recognized one of the protesters as that kid who'd chased the robed woman down the sidewalk, trying to get her picture. He still had the camera hanging around his neck, and shook his fist at the camera, yelling, 'These immigrant AB-16 bastards want to destroy France, but France will destroy them!'

The mob's fury built when the feed cut to the mosque doors, where anti-terrorists were hauling out Imam Ibrahim Al-Moustapha, who held his head high despite the wrist restraints and the hysterical crying of his wife and three children behind him.

Immigrants in the crowd began to shout, protesting the arrest.

'They think Farad's involved because that's his mosque,' I said. 'And he knows that guy Massi, right?'

Louis nodded, transfixed by the imam, who looked right into the camera as he went past it, saying forcefully, 'We are innocent. We have nothing to do with AB-16 or these killings. France is our home. We would never–'

The anti-terrorists pushed the imam into the back of a black van along with the head of the courier service and the tailor. The doors slammed shut and the van drove off.

Several men wearing FEZ jackets appeared, shouting angrily in French.

'I'm not getting what they're saying,' I said.

Louis replied, 'They say that the imam is a man of peace, and that this is a travesty of justice and a mockery of France's tolerance. They say Massi was targeted because he's a Muslim immigrant who has built a big business during the economic crisis, and the old French hate him for it. They don't agree with the AB-16 killings, but they

245

understand the reasons.'

On-screen, a bottle sailed through the air. It struck one of the men on the side of the head, and he staggered, bleeding. A piece of brick followed. Within moments the street all around the reporter erupted into chaos and fighting before the feed cut and the screen went to black for several seconds. Then it jumped to a pair of rattled French news announcers apologizing for the break in coverage.

Louis looked over at me gravely.

'I fear we are entering a dark and dangerous time in Paris,' Louis said. 'We may be seeing the end of Private in France, and perhaps Europe.'

My stomach plummeted. This sort of thing could easily snowball, destroy the reputation of an investigative firm I had nurtured over years.

'Unless Farad and the imam are telling the truth,' I said. 'But if they're not?'

Before I could answer, the television feed cut to, of all people, Laurent Alexandre, who was on the sidewalk across from Millie Fleurs's shop, fighting back tears as he publicly mourned her death and denounced AB-16.

'French culture is not going anywhere,' Alexandre vowed. 'Paris is the number one tourist destination in the world because we are so fierce about our culture. Millie was fiercely passionate about Paris and France, and I know she would want us to fight for it, to show her killers that her spirit and our culture go on. I have spoken with several of Millie's friends, and instead of a funeral or memorial, we are going to put on a celebration of her life, a runway show in her honor. We're hoping it will be televised to the nation.'

Before I could begin to wrap my fatigued brain around that, the Dog orbited back into the room.

'Louis,' he said before someone knocked sharply at the apartment door.

The hacker moved straight down the short hallway and looked through the peephole. Still cradling the iPad and the memory stick, he started to unlock the dead bolts.

'Who is it?' Louis asked.

'Maria,' he said.

'The concierge,' Louis told me.

Our attention shot back to the television screen, where the feed had cut from Laurent to Barbès. Tear gas was being fired at the rioters.

The Dog made a weird noise. I turned to see the hacker crouched and moving backward, and the old concierge shaking from head to toe.

Whitey was behind her. He had a gun to her head.

Chapter 64

'Weapons on the ground and back away, or she dies, and the retard's next,' Whitey said, leering at us with yellow teeth.

Louis grimaced but unholstered his pistol and set it down. I did the same.

Whitey pushed the old woman inside, and his buddy, the Nose, appeared, also armed. He followed Whitey, shutting the door.

Still pressing his gun to the concierge's head,

Whitey said, 'Where's the lighter? Start talking or she dies.'

'You're out of luck,' Louis said. 'Government took it along with everything else when they raided our offices last night. It's true – you can check.'

'Is that what you've been after all this time?' I asked. 'A lighter?'

Whitey ignored me, but he was looking conflicted.

His partner said, 'What do we do, Le Blanc? Call–'

'Shut up,' Whitey said, and I thought for a moment that he was going to cut his losses and bolt.

But then the Dog said, 'I'm not retarded.'

'Yeah, whatever,' Whitey said, and then did a double take at the hacker.

He threw the old woman aside. In two bounds, he was in front of the Dog, who shrank in terror. Whitey snatched the iPad from him, held it up so his partner could see the memory stick jutting out the bottom, and said in triumph, 'Bonus coming! We got it!'

The Nose grinned, then sobered and said, 'They get in?'

Whitey slid his finger across the screen, studied it, and said, 'Negative. We're good.'

He pulled the memory stick and stuck it in his pocket. He tucked the iPad under one arm and said, 'Just in case.'

'Whatever's on that stick, you've got what you were after,' I said. 'Let Kim Kopchinski go.'

The Nose snorted, 'That's not exactly up to us.'

'Zip 'em up, and we're gone,' Whitey said.

They used zip ties to bind our ankles and wrists behind our backs. They shoved rags in our mouths and forced the four of us onto the floor.

'The shit you've caused us, we should shoot the both of you,' Whitey said, waving his pistol at me and Louis. 'But we're not sore winners.'

Then he kicked me hard, in the stomach. And the Nose did the same to Louis, low in the back. It took several painful minutes after they'd left for the two of us to recover enough to try to free ourselves.

The Dog was way ahead of us. He'd gotten to his feet somehow, hopped into his kitchen, and soon returned holding a pair of scissors behind him. Several contortions and a careful snip later, Louis's hands were free. Louis took the scissors and cut off Maria's binding first and made sure she was okay before removing the Dog's restraints and then mine.

I was feeling exhausted and low. We'd lost the memory stick, and whatever leverage we might have had to get Kim Kopchinski back. What was I going to say to Sherman? What could I say?

The hacker, meanwhile, went over to the concierge, and said something to her in Portuguese. She nodded, rubbed her wrists.

The Dog looked at us and said, 'I am not retarded.'

'Absolutely not,' Louis said.

The hacker took several steps away with that vacant expression, and I thought he was going off into orbit again. He stopped, however, and said, 'I'm smarter than they are, Louis.'

'I have no doubt, my—'

'No,' the Dog insisted. 'I am smarter, Louis. Before I went to the door, I quit out. But I'd already cracked the security and copied most of the stick wirelessly to my iCloud account.'

PART FOUR

IS PARIS BURNING?

Chapter 65

PANTIN, NORTHEASTERN SUBURBS OF PARIS
4:48 P.M.

Serge Mfune drove a stolen delivery van out of the condemned linen factory on the Canal de l'Ourcq. The sliding doors quickly slammed behind them, blocking any view of the sculpture inside.

In the passenger seat, Émile Sauvage looked over his shoulder at the thick, rolled Oriental rug on top of a painter's tarp that covered the heavy load of two large wooden crates.

The major turned his attention to the side-view mirror and appraised his disguise: thick black eyebrows, a dense black beard, and a wig. With a healthy dose of instant tan to turn his already bronze skin darker, a worn and faded gray workman's jumpsuit, and a black-and-white checked scarf, he looked infinitely more North African than French.

Mfune was similarly dressed. Satisfied that they would pass muster, Sauvage turned his attention to the portable police scanner in his lap. It crackled with reports of building protests over the arrests. They mentioned disturbances in Sevran, like Pantin a suburb of Paris with a high concentration of immigrants.

'Building protests,' the captain said. 'That's good.'

'Predictable,' Sauvage said, nodding. 'Sevran is always up for a riot.'

He got out a piece of paper with three phone numbers on it, and entered them into the burn phone's memory.

Mfune glanced over. 'Where'd you get them?'

'From someone who thinks like we do,' Sauvage said, and left it at that.

Fifteen minutes later, they came upon a burning vehicle being doused by a fire crew. A police officer stopped them and said, 'Where are you headed?'

'Les Bosquets,' Mfune said.

'Not the best place to be after dark tonight.'

'We just deliver a rug and go,' Sauvage said in a thick accent.

The cop shrugged and waved them forward.

Mfune found a place to park the van on the Avenue Clichy-sous-Bois, next to the Bondy Forest and across the street from Les Bosquets housing project. Several groups of young immigrants milled about on the other side of the street. A few eyed the van suspiciously,

Sauvage and Mfune pulled on workmen's gloves and climbed out, leaving the keys in the ignition and ignoring the watchful eyes. They went to the rear of the vehicle, opened it, and pulled out the rug, leaving the tarp and cargo in place.

After the doors were closed, they hoisted the rug onto their right shoulders, blocking a good look at their faces, and walked diagonally left across the boulevard. Rather than veer right onto one of the streets that veined the housing project, however, they walked on past the nearest high-rise apartment building, hearing music and voices pouring out the open windows.

They went around to the rear entrance, where several young men were standing about and smoking.

'Who's that for?' one boy asked.

'Madame Lao,' Mfune said.

'That nosy old bitch?' he replied with a chuckle, and even opened the outer door for them.

They moved to a stairwell where they could not be seen from outside. Sauvage slid forward to take the complete weight of the rug.

Captain Mfune split off and started down the stairs. The major began to climb. He encountered no one, and reached the fifth floor quickly.

At the top of the stairwell, Sauvage peered through the window in the door and down the hall. A woman and two children were walking the other way. The major waited until the trio had entered an apartment at the far end of the hall before opening the stairwell door and hurrying forward, noticing once again how loud and disjointed life was inside places like this. At best it was controlled chaos, which helped his chances a great deal.

Sauvage stopped in front of a dinged and scratched metal apartment door with the remnants of yellow crime tape on the hinges. He set the rug down and got out a key that Haja had stolen from the landlord when she had come through the week before, acting like a new refugee in need of shelter.

Haja had said a woman and her mother had

been knifed inside the apartment two months before, and no one wanted to rent it. Haja also said that when he opened the apartment door, he'd get immediate attention. Sure enough, the second he threw the dead bolt, he heard a door over his left shoulder open.

Sauvage turned his head enough for nosy Madame Lao to see the beard, the eyebrows, and the hair before he pushed the door open and pulled the rug in after him. The door closed, and he locked it, sniffing at the lingering odor of powerful disinfectants. Leaving the lights off, he dragged the rug through the vacant apartment over to a window that faced the boulevard.

The major unwrapped the black-and-white checked scarf from around his neck and shoulders, revealing a headset with a jawbone microphone. Putting it on, he flipped the tiny power switch and said, 'In.'

'Same,' Mfune whispered.

'Same,' Epée said.

Chapter 66

Sauvage got out the burn phone, highlighted the only three numbers in its memory, and pressed text. A blank box appeared, and the major felt his pulse quicken. His words had to be well chosen now.

He thumbed in: **If you condemn the Barbes arrests, back us up tonight.**

Sauvage hit send and waited.

A few seconds later, much faster than he'd expected, a reply came back from one of the phone numbers.

–Who is this?

Your ally, Sauvage typed.

–Who is this?

That question had come from one of the other numbers. Sauvage again texted all three: **See crate contents of blue work van opposite Bosquets on Clichy-sous-Bois. Take enough to defend yourselves. Distribute rest to other believers.**

–Who is this?

The third phone number had checked in. They were all waiting. He gave it twenty seconds, then replied: **The Prophet's warhorse.**

Sauvage did not wait for a reply. He took off the back of the phone, pulled the battery and SIM card, and broke the unit in two. The pieces went in the baggy pocket of his coverall for later disposal.

The major stood in the shadows by the window, watching. Given his recon background, he was a patient, disciplined man. He would have stood there all night not moving a muscle if the job required it.

But it didn't take more than ten minutes for the first two to emerge out of the bowels of the project. Both were male, under twenty-five, and dressed in loose drab green cotton pants and tunics. One looked African. The other was clearly of Arab descent.

They crossed the street and circled the van warily. The African peered in through the

257

passenger window. He had to have seen the keys, had to have realized that the door was unlocked. But instead of going around to the driver's side and getting in, he went to the back doors.

After a moment's discussion with his partner, he opened them, and the Arab climbed inside. The African shut the doors and stood there. His partner wasn't in the van more than a minute. When he jumped out, he was lit up, agitated. Both men got out cell phones and began pushing buttons.

Three other men came out of the project. They were in their late teens, early twenties: a Vietnamese, another African with beefy shoulders, and a big, big guy who looked French Polynesian to Sauvage.

They went straight to the rear of the van, and an argument began among the five men. There was some pushing and shoving by the Polynesian, and shouting among all of them when a third group appeared: two men this time, and both far better dressed than the others. This duo joined the fray for several tense moments before the first African guy began to play peacemaker.

He gestured at the van. He gestured at Les Bosquets. There seemed to be enough agreement with his argument that he was allowed to get in. He started the vehicle. With the six other men following closely on foot, he drove the van slowly across the boulevard and into the housing project, where Sauvage could no longer see it.

No matter, the major thought, and pressed the transmit button on the headset. He whispered, 'We have a take.'

'Understood,' Mfune said.

'And ready,' Epée said.

'Sit tight,' Sauvage said, very pleased.

The crates in the back of the van contained fifty cleaned and oiled AK-47 assault rifles and seven thousand rounds of 7.62mm ammunition.

It was only a matter of time now.

Chapter 67

8TH ARRONDISSEMENT
6:25 P.M.

When I woke up, dusk was falling over Paris, and beyond my bedroom door I could hear voices out in the suite's living area.

How long had I been out?

I checked the clock on the nightstand. Four hours? We'd gotten back from the Dog's place at around two that afternoon, and despite the fact that we had the contents of the memory stick to examine, I had been so tired and dizzy that I'd gone into my room, fallen into bed, and passed out cold.

After shaving and showering, I dressed and went out the bedroom door, finding several room service carts in the living area, and Louis, Petitjean, and Vans eating and working on laptop computers.

'Jack, you have arisen!' Louis cried, and gestured to the food. 'Eat. Drink. Get your strength back.'

'Have you slept?' I asked.

'Why would I do that when there is so much to

be done?' he replied.

'I'm beginning to think you're a meth addict,' I said, moving to the service carts, which were loaded with delicacies from the Plaza's kitchen. 'You find anything yet?'

'Of course we did,' Petitjean said.

As I piled my plate and gorged, they got me up to speed on what they'd learned while I slept.

The memory stick contained thousands of files in various formats. Some were textual and contained random notes in French and English that referred to various people using initials. Other files contained diary entries and mentioned places by name, including several in the south of France. But again, no names used – just initials. And still others – the majority of the files, as a matter of fact – were copies of Microsoft Excel spreadsheet files that documented a large and very lucrative trading and distribution company.

'What company?' I asked.

'We don't know yet,' Petitjean said, sighing. 'And we don't know what kind of business they're involved in, or who they're doing business with, because they're using an alphanumeric code that we haven't been able to crack.'

'Drugs,' Louis said. 'Has to be.'

'If so, they're highly disciplined drug dealers,' Petitjean said.

I poured a cup of coffee and said, 'Give me a copy of the memory stick. I want to lend a hand.'

'We can do better than that,' Vans said. 'Louis's canine friend uploaded it all into our virtual office. Files that have already been examined are flagged.'

After getting my laptop from the bedroom, I

took a seat on the sofa and followed Vans's instructions to get access to the memory stick files.

I opened a few of the spreadsheets and studied them enough to see that the code made it a waste of time to search them further. I found several Microsoft Word documents that hadn't been flagged and started opening them. Some did seem like random notes, ideas jotted down, but others were lists of orders to be given to certain initials along with various snippets of that code.

Because I wasn't sure of my French-to-English translating skills with even the noncoded stuff, I exited those documents as well and did not flag them. Feeling kind of useless, I wondered how Sci would handle this kind of situation. I was about to give him a call, ask him for advice, when it dawned on me that he might try to take an inventory first.

'Can you get me a list of files filtered by type?' I asked. 'A directory?'

'Sure. By format or extension?' Vans asked.

'I don't know. What's easier?'

She took my computer, gave it a few instructions, and then nodded and returned it to me.

I scrolled down the list, scanning past all Microsoft Excel and Word files, finding more than twenty files in a format – RCP – that neither I nor my computer seemed to recognize.

I dragged the RCP files into a new folder that I intended to e-mail over to Sci, and continued on with my scroll.

Five minutes later, I saw another three of the RCP-type files, but my attention shot below them on the list to two JPEG files. They'd been flagged as examined, but for some reason I highlighted both and double-clicked.

My laptop seemed to grind a moment before two pictures popped up, splitting the screen. I studied them, both offhand shots, and felt confused by the odd sense that the subjects of the photographs were familiar to me, but I didn't know how. Then it struck me, and I stared at the pictures long enough to consider alternatives before the unarguable meaning of them became clear.

'I'll be a son-of-a-bitch,' I said.

'What?' Louis said.

'The guy behind all this – the lighter, Kim, everything. He was right under our nose, Louis, and we let him walk away.'

Chapter 68

14TH ARRONDISSEMENT
7:40 P.M.

A cold drizzle fell over Paris as Louis and I left the taxi and hurried toward a blue gate in the dark stone fortress walls of La Santé prison.

For decades, and through the turn of this century, La Santé regularly made the list of the world's worst places to be incarcerated.

'A hellhole, Jack,' Louis said angrily. 'It's supposed to be closed now, which makes the fact that they're keeping Farad and the others in here an absolute outrage as far as I'm concerned.'

At the gate, Louis called someone on his cell phone. Ten minutes later, the gate was unlocked by a uniformed police captain, Alain Grande, a burly guy with pocked skin. He scowled and said, 'You owe me on this one, Louis. He's not supposed to have visitors beyond counsel.'

'We are working on his behalf and his counsel's behalf,' Louis said.

'Ten minutes,' Grande said begrudgingly, and let us pass through.

Erected in the 1860s, La Santé was built like spokes on a wheel, with a central hub and four multistory wings jutting off it. A modern maximum-security wing was added later, and it was there that Grande led us.

'I can't believe they have them in here,' Louis said.

The police captain shrugged. 'It's still the highest-security facility in Paris, and intelligence and anti-terror wanted quick and easy access to them.'

We passed construction debris and supplies for the prison renovations and at least twenty officers wearing bulletproof vests and carrying submachine guns.

'They think AB-16 is going to attack the prison? Free their leaders?'

'They killed a cabinet minister, didn't they, Louis?' Grande snapped. 'What makes you think they wouldn't try?'

That shut Louis up, and we walked the rest of the way in silence. Captain Grande brought us into a room with two doors, a steel table bolted to the bare cement floor, and four metal folding chairs.

A few minutes later, the other door opened, and Farad was brought in wearing the same clothes from the other night, and leg-irons and shackles. His eyes were sunken and bloodshot. His hair was greasy, and he had two days' growth of beard on his face.

He glared at us and at Captain Grande as officers ran a chain from his handcuffs through a steel eyebolt welded to the table. When they were done, Farad said in a hostile tone, 'Nice of you to visit, Louis. Jack.'

'They wouldn't let us see you before,' Louis explained. 'It is only this past hour that we even knew where they were holding you.'

'It's true, Ali,' I said.

Farad set his jaw before looking to Grande. 'Can we have some privacy?'

'No,' the captain said.

'Ali was a decorated officer of the *judiciaire*,' Louis complained.

'I don't care,' the captain replied. 'I'm not moving.'

Looking as though he was on the edge of a meltdown, Farad said, 'They think I'm part of the AB-16 conspiracy because I attend the imam's mosque. They have him here too, and Firmus Massi. Both men are like me: moderate, and absolutely opposed to radicalism. We are being framed.'

'If so, we'll prove it,' Louis said. 'I promise you that, Ali. But right now we need your help on the Kopchinski case. It now involves, we believe, certain people you might know.'

Farad shook his head in weary disbelief. 'You

264

think I'm involved on the wrong side of this case too?'

'No,' I said. 'Nothing like that.'

He puffed out his lips and blew out. 'What can I do for you?'

Louis slid his cell phone across the table and showed him the two pictures I'd found on the memory stick. He tapped the face of the only person in either photograph. 'Recognize him?'

Farad leaned over and studied the picture, and his head retreated. 'Really? You've got actual evidence that *he's* involved?'

Before I could reply, we heard a man and a woman shouting outside, demanding to know where we were, and how the hell we'd gotten inside.

Chapter 69

Captain Grande lost several shades of color. 'Time's up, Louis.'

Louis ignored him and said, 'Tell us what you know about—'

'I said enough!' Grande roared just before the door flew open, and Investigateur Hoskins and Juge Fromme stormed in.

The crippled magistrate pointed his cane at Farad and said, 'Take that man back to his cell. Now. And put these two under arrest for obstruction.'

'Obstruction?' I said, getting to my feet. 'We're

265

part of his defense team. We have the right to–'

'What do you know of rights in France?' Fromme thundered. 'You, Monsieur Morgan, have no rights here. And I'm going to make sure you're deported in the morning.'

'You let them in here?' Hoskins asked Grande.

'They said they were working on another case,' the captain sputtered. 'Nothing to do with AB-16.'

I expected Louis to jump in, but then I glanced back and saw him talking fast and low to Farad, and I knew I had to stall.

'That is one hundred percent true,' I said. 'It's a missing persons case involving the granddaughter of one of my oldest clients back in California.'

Completely unconvinced, Fromme said, 'Her name?'

'Kim Kopchinski,' Louis said, standing up from the table with a nod to Farad. 'She's a U.S. citizen, and we believe she is being held by someone involved in a murder here in Paris a few days ago – someone who is also of great interest to the judicial police in the south of France. Isn't that right, Ali?'

Farad nodded. 'You can call my former partner, Christoph Le Clerc, if you don't believe me. He's been working to put this guy away for years. It would be a great coup if he were taken down.'

The magistrate looked as though he wanted to break his cane over his knee, but then said, 'Out with it. Everything.'

It took us about fifteen minutes to explain to the judge about Kopchinski, the lighter, the memory stick, and the connection to Marseille. When we were done, you could tell he didn't like it, but he said, 'You have this memory stick?'

'We have the data on it,' Louis said.

'We just want to make sure Ms. Kopchinski is returned safe and sound to her grandfather,' I said. 'That's all this discussion was about.'

The magistrate glanced at Hoskins, who shrugged.

'Fine,' Fromme said. 'You are not under arrest. But you are leaving, right now, and Monsieur Farad is going back to his cell.'

'Keep the faith,' I said to Farad as officers led him out. 'Private Paris is behind you one hundred percent.'

'This is a miscarriage of justice,' Louis told Fromme and Hoskins after Farad had gone. 'There is nothing concrete that I know of that links Farad or the imam or Firmus Massi to the AB-16 murders.'

'You don't know what you're talking about, Louis,' Hoskins said sadly. 'We do have such evidence.'

Fromme nodded grimly. 'When we searched the mosque we found crucifixes taken from Henri Richard, René Pincus, and Lourdes Latrelle.'

I said, 'How can you be sure that – '

'They've all been positively identified by next of kin, Monsieur Morgan,' Hoskins said firmly. 'There is also preliminary DNA evidence that puts the imam and Firmus Massi at the scene of Guy LaFont's murder last night, and other DNA material that puts your employee, Monsieur Farad, inside the restaurant the night Chef Pincus was murdered.'

Chapter 70

MONTFERMEIL, EASTERN
SUBURBS OF PARIS
10 P.M.

Monitoring a Paris news station and the police scanner, Émile Sauvage remained in disguise and waited patiently in the dark apartment, looking out the window and monitoring the street and sidewalks around Les Bosquets.

In the past two hours, the bands of immigrant youth roaming the area had been getting larger and angrier. The stolen van was brought out and lit on fire in the middle of the boulevard. When police arrived, rocks and bottles had flown in their direction.

That had prompted the cops to retreat two blocks from the housing project and call for reinforcements. Satellite news trucks were already on the scene, and the major was pleased when several rioters responded by spray-painting a crude version of the AB-16 symbol on the road near the burning van.

Based on radio reports and the scanner, in response to the arrests and riots in Barbès, similar mobs were forming and causing destruction in other Parisian suburbs with large immigrant populations. Surprisingly, there had been no reports of shots fired.

That's about to change, the major thought coldly as the scanner lit up with word of riot police heading toward the housing project.

Sauvage got out a pocketknife and cut the strings that bound the rug. Grasping the fringe, he unrolled the cheap Oriental slowly, until he saw the edge of a five-by-seven-foot silver fire blanket wrapped inside.

He kept on unrolling the rug until he'd freed the fire blanket and a loaded Swedish-made AT4 shoulder-mount rocket grenade launcher.

'Alert,' Epée said into his earbud's microphone.

'Confirmed,' Mfune said.

'Confirmed,' Sauvage said, and picked up the fire blanket, which he draped over his head and about his shoulders like a hooded robe.

At sixty inches long and eighty-four inches wide, the blanket more than covered him from the back when he took a knee so he could see further down the boulevard.

Two white Mercedes-Benz Unimog police trucks pulled behind the patrol cars. The Unimogs were equipped with antiriot gear, including water cannons and a front blade used as a battering ram. Riot police poured out the backs of the trucks. Wearing helmets, visors, body armor, and carrying Plexiglas shields, they quickly assembled in a tight line that spanned the boulevard.

An officer used a bullhorn to tell the rioters to disperse and return to their homes or face arrest. That only seemed to incense the mob. Molotov cocktails spun through the air, burst, and burned on the street.

Sauvage smiled when some in the crowd of

immigrant youth began to chant, 'AB-16! AB-16!'

On a shouted order, the riot police raised their shields and began to advance down the boulevard. The major waited until they were half a block closer before he pushed up the window and reached for the rocket launcher.

The AT4 was green, forty inches long, and fourteen pounds when loaded. A single-shot, recoilless weapon, it featured a hollow fiberglass barrel that was open at both ends. Sauvage pulled out a cotter pin, which unblocked the firing rod. Then he pushed the cocking mechanism up and over the barrel, locking it on safe with a red lever.

The major put silicone plugs in his ears before shouldering the weapon and settling in behind the simple iron sights, gloved left hand resting on the red safety lever, and gloved right thumb on the button trigger. Watching the police march steadily forward, he noted that the antiriot trucks were trailing them closely.

Thud. Thud.

Canisters of tear gas flew from behind the shields and burst in the street.

'On my mark,' he muttered into the mic.

When he was positive that the police and armored trucks were well within the launcher's three-hundred-yard effective range, he whispered, 'Now.'

Mfune cut all power to the apartment building.

Shouts and curses echoed out the windows of the housing project. Sauvage released the rocket launcher's safety lever, swung the sights over the heads of the advancing police, and steadied his aim.

He punched the trigger.

There was an initial thumping sound like a bass drum being struck. The rocket blew a plume of intense pressure and fire out the rear of the launcher. The flames and blast waves bounced off the apartment walls and pummeled the blanket and Sauvage from behind like a crashing wave of fire.

Despite the heat and force of the backblast, the major never lost sight of the contrail of the 86-millimeter rocket, the warhead of which contained 440 grams of Octol, a substance so volatile that it's also called HEAT, for high-explosive anti-tank.

Many of the riot police threw themselves to the ground just before the HEAT rocket struck the blade of one of the antiriot trucks and detonated in a thunderclap that spawned a brilliant red mushroom cloud.

Chapter 71

Sauvage dropped the spent rocket launcher on the floor and threw off the singed fire blanket. He tried to stand but felt unbalanced by the backblast that had ruptured the air pressure in the apartment and upset his equilibrium.

On this second try, however, the major was up and yanking out the ear protectors in time to hear chaos in the streets below as the riot police shouted to one another, and bands of immigrant

271

youth cheered the attack.

Sauvage did not pause to savor the havoc he'd caused. Instead, he pocketed the police scanner, threw the rolled rug over his shoulder, and went to the door, ignoring the charred and smoking apartment walls.

He pulled open the door. The dark hallway was filled with people panicking at the explosions and trying to get out of the building. Stepping into the hallway, he got out a pen flashlight and turned it on, saying into the jaw mic, 'Joiners?'

'Not yet,' Epée said.

'Encourage them,' Sauvage said, head down, focused on the light beam, moving fast and straight toward the stairwell, using the rug as a soft battering ram to push people aside.

Through the open door by the stairway, the major heard Epée squeeze off three short bursts of automatic rifle fire. That caused pandemonium and shrieking in the hallway, which the major used to his advantage.

While most of the immigrants went to the ground, Sauvage went over the top of them, and shouldered his way through the staircase door. Holding tight to the rug, he started leaping down the stairs, taking them two or three at a time.

Behind and above him, Sauvage heard more shots, quick and erratic – not the disciplined bursts of fire that Epée employed.

Amateurs!

They had the AK-47 assault rifles and 7.62mm ammunition!

And they were fighting for AB-16!

The major barreled down the stairs like a wild

man now, using the rug to knock the people below him aside and roaring out, *'Allahu akbar! God is great!'*

When he reached the first floor and burst out the rear entrance, Mfune was waiting. The captain took the rug, and they hurried with a knot of people fleeing pistol shots and submachine gun fire.

It wasn't until they were well south of the housing project and crossing the Rue du Général de Gaulle that Sauvage felt comfortable enough to get out his real phone and call Amé, who answered on the first ring.

'It's live!' she cried. 'They've broken into programming!'

'Claim it,' he said, and hung up.

On the Avenue des Rossignols, Epée was waiting with the car. They put the rug in the trunk and got in. The tagger pulled out and drove away at an untroubled speed.

Feeling safe behind the tinted glass, Sauvage stripped off the beard, wig, and fake eyebrows before rolling the window down.

When they stopped at an intersection, he heard police sirens wailing north toward Les Bosquets. To his ears, it sounded like a triumphant symphony.

Chapter 72

INTERNATIONAL WATERS OFF THE
COAST OF MONACO
APRIL 11, 4:10 A.M.

I pulled on a black wet suit top and balaclava-style neoprene hood. The night sky was overcast. There was nothing visible anywhere around us except for faint lights a mile or more off the bow of our Zodiac raft, which floated silently.

Louis was already in his wet suit, lashing shut a rubber dry bag with the equipment we'd need. Randall Peaks was futzing around back by the engine, and I was amazed and pleased at what a Saudi prince could do when he's grateful to someone for keeping his sixteen-year-old daughter out of the headlines.

Need a raft? No problem. Need weapons? No problem – whatever you need, Mr. Morgan. We'll move heaven and earth to help Private in whatever–

'Ready?' Peaks asked.

'*Oui*,' Louis said.

'Yes,' I said, and felt myself slip toward a mind-set I was taught in the marine corps and have continued to cultivate over the years: the cold, alert, and harsh way of thinking that seems to take over whenever I'm anticipating violence.

'Hand signals from here on out,' I said.

Peaks started the electric trolling motor mounted next to the outboard, and we started slowly toward the lights. He cut the motor when we were less than five hundred yards from the 120-foot triple-deck motor cruiser. She was sleek and midnight blue, and if it weren't for the running lights, I think we would have had trouble finding her even with the GPS coordinates we'd been given.

Peaks lowered an anchor to slow the raft's drift while Louis and I put on swim fins, masks, and snorkels before picking up the small dry bags. We slipped over the side and breaststroked through the swells, constantly scanning the yacht's three decks. Nothing moved until we were right on the edge of the glow cast by the running lights.

Then Whitey lit a cigarette and walked forward along the rail of the main deck. The second he disappeared around the front of the yacht, we pulled the neoprene up over our lower faces and swam cautiously toward the stern and a wooden swimming platform to which a small speedboat was tied.

We hung off the rear of the smaller craft, stripped off the snorkeling gear, and opened the dry bags. I dog-paddled around the motorboat clenching a Glock 19 between my teeth to keep it out of the salt water. I placed it on the swimming platform. Louis came up beside me.

He climbed onto the platform first and rolled over tight against the hull, just below the painted name of the yacht, which read *'Predator.'*

I ignored the threat and followed Louis. Barely on the platform, I smelled cigarette smoke and caught sight of Whitey coming around the port side, still on the rear lower deck, moving as if he were on leisurely patrol.

I couldn't move without being seen. Instead, I drew up the neoprene over my face and smeared myself against the wooden platform, gripping the Glock, pressuring the trigger safety, prepared to fire.

Whitey's footsteps came closer, and then stopped. I held my breath, listening for the sound of a gun squeaking free of a holster, or worse, a shout of alarm. Instead, he walked on.

I gave Whitey two seconds before pushing up to my bare feet. Without a word or gesture to Louis, I oozed over the stern and onto the mahogany deck, as smooth and quiet as a snake. Whitey was twenty feet away, ambling and smoking with his back to me. I stalked him.

When I had closed the gap between us to less than five feet, I coiled to strike. Whitey seemed to sense something and began to turn, the cigarette glowing in his mouth. By the time he saw me, the butt of my Glock was already chopping toward his skull.

Whitey managed a cough before I hit him just above his right eye. He dropped dumbly to his knees, probably already out cold. But I wasn't taking any chances. I hammered him again, and he pitched sideways onto the deck. I got zip ties from the dry bag, bound him to the rail, and gagged him while Louis stood guard.

It was ten minutes to five. The first hint of dawn showed on the horizon. We had to move.

Louis led the way off the rear deck, through a

sliding glass door, and into a plush living and dining area. We padded forward, pistols leading, and I thought we were being quieter than your average ninja.

Then the dog started barking.

Chapter 73

'Shut the fuck up!' a muffled and frustrated man yelled in French from somewhere on the deck above us. 'Goddamn, it's just Le Blanc getting coffee!'

But the dog wasn't listening. He was still barking, and we could hear him bounding toward the gangway, which gave us little time to prepare. I looked around, wanting an alternative to killing the dog, and saw none.

Louis, however, grabbed a cushion and a cotton throw from a love seat.

Before I could reach for another cushion, the Jack Russell terrier exploded from the gangway, back bristled, teeth as big as a Doberman's. He took two surprisingly long jumps, ducked his head, and leaped at my throat.

I ducked, and he sailed over me. Louis swatted him out of the air with the cushion, jumped on him when he hit the floor, and wrapped up the dazed pooch nice and snug and safe in the cotton throw. We used zip ties to keep him that way, though we could not control his shrill, panicked. whines, which must have been relatively normal sounds for the dog to make because the man now coming down the gangway seemed irritated but unalarmed.

'If you take a dump before I can let you out, you are a dead little terrorist,' he called in warning as he exited the gangway. 'Napoleon, I swear–'

Wearing nothing but red athletic shorts and the silver lighter on a thin chain around his neck, Phillipe Rivier halted at the sight of us aiming pistols at him from less than twenty feet away.

The man who'd ordered his Jack Russell terrier to attack me near the Hôtel Lancaster didn't yelp, or shrink, or show any outward sign of fear. He just glanced at the open sliding glass door before raising his hands and calmly said, 'What do you want? Money? I keep very little aboard, and–'

'We want Kim Kopchinski,' Louis said.

Rivier acted bewildered and said, 'Wrong yacht. There is no–'

'We've got the right boat,' Louis said. 'Now, where is Kim? Or should I put a hole in your kneecap to make you remember?'

Rivier's calm demeanor vanished. He snarled softly, 'Do you have any idea who you're fucking with here?'

'You're Phillipe Rivier,' I said, pulling off my hood. 'You pose as an import-export entrepreneur. But behind the cover you're a middleman and silent financier in everything from illegal arms deals to heroin smuggling and human trafficking. It seems there's nothing you won't do for an illegal buck, which is why you spend most of your time in international waters

278

with bodyguards, and a vicious little dog for your only real companion.'

Rivier hardened. 'You should have kept the hood on, Morgan, because now that I know who *you* are, I'm going to make sure that you and Private–'

Louis snapped, 'You're doing nothing to him or to Private. We've got a copy of that memory stick you use to track your black businesses. That's how we figured out you have Kim. You were disciplined and careful with the codes and initials and all, but you couldn't help putting a couple of pictures of your dog on the drive, and one with your brother in the background.'

'Luckily, I recognized the little terrorist,' I said. 'And Investigateur Le Clerc of the French National Police in Marseille recognized your brother, Benoit, who, it turns out, is gay, lives in Le Marais, loves Kim, and hates your guts. He told us exactly where to find you. So do the world a favor: shut the fuck up, Mr. Rivier, and go facedown on the floor, hands behind your head.'

Rivier remained furious, but he dropped to one knee and made to put his hands on the ground. That's when I caught a flicker of motion through the window behind Louis.

The Nose was out there on deck with some other guy. Both men were crouching to aim through the window.

Chapter 74

Throwing up the Glock, I shouted 'Down!' at Louis and shot two wild rounds at the window. They sounded like cannon fire inside the cabin. Neither bullet connected, but they were close enough to make the two men dive for cover and hesitate to return fire.

'Kill them!' Rivier bellowed.

Louis grabbed the middleman and hauled him up in front of us as a shield.

I put my gun to Rivier's head and said, 'Wrong suggestion, Phillipe. Tell your boys to come in here, or *we* will do the world a favor and kill *you*. You've got five seconds to decide. Five, four, three...'

Rivier looked as if he'd eaten something rancid, but finally shouted, 'Nez! Captain! Lower your weapons and come in here.'

The Nose appeared first, his pistol still up, looking for a clear shot at us, but finding none. We, however, had him dead to rights, and he knew it.

'Drop the weapon, and kick it away,' Louis said.

Rivier's goon looked at his boss, who nodded. The Nose let the gun slip from his hand. It fell to the carpet and he toed it away.

'*Bien*,' Louis said. 'Now, on your belly, hands behind your head, feet wide. You, same thing.'

The captain, a weathered man in his forties, put

the shotgun aside before he even stepped inside the cabin and went face down on his own. Louis had both men's ankles and wrists in zip restraints before I did the same to Rivier.

'What do you mean to do to me?' Rivier asked after I'd shoved him down beside the others.

'Depends on you,' I said. 'You can continue to stonewall us as to Kim's whereabouts, which will force us to search the yacht, a time-consuming process that will truly piss us off and force us to take desperate measures with the memory stick, like sending a copy to the police. Or you can tell us where she is, we get her, and we leave you to your sorry-ass life, keeping several copies of your records in various locations as insurance that you will never, ever try to contact Kim again or try to take revenge against us.'

'Sums it up,' Louis said.

'How can I trust you?' Rivier asked.

'We told you the deal,' Louis said harshly. 'Take it or leave it.'

Rivier hesitated, and then said, 'She's up one deck and forward. Master stateroom at the end of the hall.'

Relieved that she wasn't dead, I said, 'I'll get her.'

'I'll wait here and call our friend,' Louis said.

I suppose I expected to find Kim in handcuffs or tied down. But when I pushed open the door to the stateroom, it was worse than I could have expected.

Rivier had stripped her to her underwear and attached leather straps and bonds to her wrists and legs that held her loosely spread eagle on a bed with black sheets. She was blindfolded, and when she heard me enter, she started to beg in a thick, slurred voice, 'Please, Phillipe. Just kill me. I can't go on like—'

'You're safe now, Kim,' I said, crossing to her. 'It's Jack Morgan. You're safe and going home to your grandfather.'

I pulled off the blindfold so she could see it was true, and she dissolved into soft weeping as I pulled my knife from the diving sheath strapped to my calf. I cut free her wrists. When I did, I saw the livid tracks on the insides of her arms. There were syringes in the wastebasket.

'What has he drugged you with?' I demanded.

'Heroin,' she managed. 'Trying to get me hooked again.'

I wanted to ask her how in God's name she'd gotten involved with a guy like Phillipe Rivier, but I figured it could wait. The sooner we were off the yacht, the better. I found a blanket and covered her with it.

'Can you walk?' I asked.

She nodded groggily, and I helped her up. She was wobbly and leaned on me as we left her prison cell and made our way back to the living area. When she saw Rivier, she came out of her stupor and shrieked at him, 'I hope you rot in hell for what you've done to me.'

'What I did to you?' Rivier said, amused. 'You asked for it, Kimmy. You always asked for it.'

She pushed away from me, tried to go for a knife in the galley, but I caught her and said, 'That only hurts you. It's over now. He can't hurt you anymore.'

'I'll always hurt her,' Rivier said. 'She'll never get away from that, no matter how hard she tries to escape it.'

Kim stared at him, and then broke down sobbing in my arms.

'Get her out of here, Jack,' Louis said. 'Our ride's out there already.'

'Take care of the rest of it,' I said.

'What "rest"?' Rivier asked.

As I led Kim toward the rear deck, Louis said, 'I'm going to raise your anchor, start your motors, and set a course on your autopilot. In about an hour, an hour and a half, you'll enter French waters. And when you do, you'll quickly be boarded by Investigateur Christoph Le Clerc of the Marseille office of the French National Police. He'll take evidence on an obvious incidence of piracy on the high seas, and the first thing he's going to collect is that fancy lighter around your neck.'

'What?' Rivier shouted. 'We had a deal!'

'Jack, what is this phrase from *Animal House* again?' Louis asked.

Over my shoulder, I said, 'You fucked up. You trusted us.'

Chapter 75

NICE, FRANCE
7:22 A.M.

We boarded Private's Gulfstream at the airport.

Kim had been quiet for most of the ride in on the Zodiac, nodding off at times. But on the drive from Monaco to Nice, she'd started to shake from withdrawal. We'd anticipated her having some physical issues and had brought along a concierge doctor and nurse. They immediately took Kim to the back of the cabin and shut the divider.

We were soon in the air, heading back to Paris.

'This your normal duty at Private?' Peaks asked from across the aisle. 'You know, rescues? That sort of thing.'

'They come up,' I admitted, and yawned. 'Why?'

'The prince is happy Maya's safe, and grateful to you and Langlois,' Peaks said. 'I don't think the same can be said about me.'

'Looking for a job?' I asked.

'If it comes to that,' Peaks said.

'If it comes to that, I'd love to talk,' I said.

Louis, to my surprise, was already snoring in the seat in front of me. I put in earbuds and called up a white noise app for the sounds of waves softly crashing on a beach. It was as if I were home, and that noise was coming in my window I fell hard and deep.

When I felt someone shaking my shoulder what seemed like a few minutes later, I jerked awake in a foul mood, pulled out the earbuds, and stared angrily at the doctor.

'I didn't want to disturb you, but you've been sleeping an hour,' she said. 'And Kim keeps asking for you.'

'Okay,' I said, forcing open my eyes. 'I'll be right there. How is she?'

'Considering what she's been through, the heroin and all, she's good,' the doctor said. 'We gave her a slight dose of morphine to stay her withdrawal for a more suitable time and place, and a smaller dose of amphetamine salts to keep her heart rate up in the meantime.'

'She stable enough to make the trip to L.A.?' I asked.

'I think so.'

I thanked her and went aft, knocked, and went through the divider. Kim lay under blankets, propped up against pillows. She had an IV in her arm and looked wrung out and pale.

The nurse left and shut the divider behind her.

'You don't give up, do you, Jack Morgan?' she asked in a hoarse whisper.

'Not as a rule,' I said. 'The doc said you wanted to talk to me.'

Kim looked at her lap, bit the corner of her lip, and nodded weakly.

'I owe you an explanation,' she said. 'After what you've done, you deserve it. But please, I'd appreciate it if my grandfather hears none of this. He's ... he's one of the few people in my life who always believed the best of me.'

I leaned up against the cabin wall and said, 'You don't owe me an explanation. But whatever you feel comfortable telling me stays with me.'

Chapter 76

Over the course of the next forty minutes, Kim gave me the CliffsNotes version of her story. After her parents died in the boating accident, she felt compelled to return to France, where she ended up working in Cannes as part of the film festival staff. She ran with a young, wild Euro crowd. There were drugs, and she got a taste for them, heroin in particular.

Kim met Phillipe Rivier the night of her twenty-fifth birthday at a nightclub in Cannes. He was fifteen years her senior, but he was handsome, sophisticated, mysterious, and by all appearances fabulously wealthy.

'There was also this...' Kim started playing with the blanket. 'He was very, very sexy. And it was like in that book, you know?'

'Book?'

'*Fifty Shades of* you know?' she said. 'Except it all took place on the boat.'

'Oh,' I said.

'Yeah,' she said, and fell silent for several beats. 'It was good for a while, an escape from everything, I guess. And then it wasn't. I realized he was keeping me isolated on the yacht, and when I complained, he either punished me or gave me a little heroin, which kept me in line.'

Kim said she lived aboard Rivier's yacht for more than two years. During that time, she became a junkie, using the heroin to deaden herself to her predicament.

Then one night, four months before Louis and I got the call from her grandfather, Kim said she overheard Rivier tell Whitey and the Nose that it was time to get rid of her, that the drugs had made her a liability. They were moored in the harbor at Marseille, one of the few times the yacht was so close to land.

'They were going to kill me once we were back out to sea,' Kim said. 'Phillipe seemed to get aroused by that because later that evening he came to my cabin for the first time in weeks. I thought he might, so I had prepared.'

Instead of shooting up the powdered heroin he had given her earlier in the day, she'd saved it. When he gave her more, she heated both batches and pretended to shoot it while he stripped off his clothes. She lay back, acting as though she was in a heroin-induced stupor, and when he came to her she stabbed him with the hypodermic needle and drove the drugs into him.

Whitey and the Nose were ashore. And Rivier enjoyed S and M, so the captain never came to check when his boss yelled. Rivier punched Kim a few times before he passed out. Kim got dressed and decided she was owed something for the years he'd kept her prisoner. She knew the combination to his safe, and took one hundred thousand euros, and the only thing Rivier never let out of his sight: the lighter.

'You had no idea that it disguised a digital memory stick?' I asked.

'Is that what it was?' she said. 'He always told me it was a present from his mother. I took it for spite.'

Kim got the keys to the speedboat. The captain saw her, tried to stop her, but it was too late. She made it to a dock in Marseille, and then to a church. She told the priest she was addicted to heroin and in trouble, but also that she had money to pay for her own rehabilitation.

For a twenty-five-thousand euro contribution to his church, the priest got her out of the city and to a private detoxification and addiction recovery center near Aix-en-Provence. Kim gave the center the rest of the money – seventy-five thousand euros – and spent three and a half months cleaning up there before Rivier's men somehow found her.

'They asked for me at the gate, but the doctors refused to say whether I was there or not,' she said. 'I took off that night and made my way to Paris, to a friend's place in Les Bosquets. I had an ATM card from my trust, but no passport. I didn't know what to do, so I called my grandfather, and he called you.'

I stood there, digesting it, until Kim said, 'You think I'm a bad person.'

'I think you've got a few issues,' I said. 'But I also think you got caught up in something that was way beyond your ability to either anticipate or control, and ultimately I have to commend you for escaping like that. It was gutsy.'

Kim smiled wanly. 'Thank you.'

'One thing. Why didn't you go to the police?'

'Because Phillipe always said he had the French police in his back pocket,' she said. 'Especially in Marseille.'

I wondered about that, wondered whether Ali Farad knew cops in Marseille that he suspected were corrupted by Rivier. But before I could come up with reasons for or against the possibility, the doctor returned.

'The pilot wants us to take our seats for landing,' she said.

'Okay,' I said, and buckled myself into the jump seat next to her bed. 'Rivier's brother, Benoit. He cares about you.'

'He was in Cannes when I first met Phillipe,' she said softly. 'He always cared about me. A true friend.'

'Did he know his brother was mistreating you?'

Kim shook her head. 'Benoit lived in Paris, and never visited the yacht while I was there. He was shocked when I showed up at his door and told him.'

'So you were staying with him in the Marais the night of the shoot-out in the club?'

'Yes,' she said, and we banked in and landed.

When we'd pulled into a private jet hangar, I left my seat and held out my hand to shake hers. 'They'll refuel, take you to Los Angeles. The doctor will be with you the whole way, and I know your granddad will be thrilled to see you.'

Kim gripped my hand, tears in her eyes, and said, 'Thank you for saving me even when I didn't seem to want saving.'

'You're welcome,' I said, and moved toward

289

the divider.

'Jack?' she called after me.

She had this pitiful expression on her face when she asked, 'Can people change for good? Someone like me?'

I flashed on my brother, Tommy, and felt torn, but said, 'I hear it happens all the time if you just have faith and accept help from the people who love you.'

Chapter 77

CHARLES DE GAULLE AIRPORT
10:40 A.M.

We waited until the jet had lifted off before taking a car back into Paris. From the highway we could see fingers of black smoke rising above the eastern suburbs. We'd been gone less than nine hours, but we entered a city that had fundamentally changed.

The rocket grenade attack and gunfight in Les Bosquets was all over the French media. Three police officers had been killed and nine wounded in the HEAT explosion and ensuing gun battle.

Six immigrant youths had died. Two had been weaponless. Four had been armed with AK-47 assault rifles. The footage of the AB-16 battle had gone viral, and more violence had erupted in public housing areas throughout the suburbs.

Cars were seized, sprayed with the tag of AB-

16, and then set afire. Police who'd rushed to the scenes had been met with automatic weapons fire and forced to withdraw

In the front seat, Peaks seemed to have had enough. He pulled out his phone, punched in a number, listened, and then said, 'Your highness, I'm thinking that today might be a good time for the princesses to be leaving Paris.'

He listened and said, 'If you can make that call, I will arrange everything.'

Peaks hung up and said, 'He's calling his wife to pull the plug on the shopping spree, and it sounds as if I have a job for at least another day.'

'My loss,' I said.

Peaks began making arrangements for three bulletproof limos to be brought to the Plaza Athénée in three hours' time. That was followed by a call to the prince's pilot. An estimated departure was set for four that afternoon.

I called Justine, who, it turned out, was visiting Sherman Wilkerson.

'Put him on,' I said.

'Jack?' he said in an airy voice. 'Do you have her?'

'She's on her way to L.A. as we speak,' I said. 'She's a little beat up and will need first-class medical attention, but I think she's going to be all right.'

'And the danger she was in?'

'That's been taken care of, sir,' I said.

For several moments I listened to Sherman's labored breathing, and then he said, 'You are one of the good ones, Jack Morgan. Everyone at Private.'

'We aim to please,' I said, and asked that Justine be put back on.

'You want me to meet her at LAX?' she asked.

'Yes. White-glove treatment,' I said, and then explained how Rivier had been trying to get Kim addicted again.

'I'll get her to Betty Ford,' she said.

'But not until Sherman has seen her,' I said.

'Sure,' Justine said. 'How's the art professor?'

'I haven't seen her in several days,' I replied. 'Kidnappings, murders, and general insurrection have a way of killing the whole romance thing.'

'So there was a "romance thing"?'

'I'll admit to a crush and nothing more.'

There was silence.

'What?' I said.

'Nothing,' she replied. 'When should I tell people you're coming back to L.A.?'

'What people?'

'Your brother, for one,' she said. 'He keeps calling.'

'His trial is coming up,' I said. 'Maybe I'll stay in Paris until it's over.'

'Really?'

'No,' I said, sighing. 'Thanks for your work with Sherman. Job well done.'

'I've just been a regular in the ICU, but thanks.'

I hung up, feeling weirdly disconnected from my 'normal' life back in L.A.

How long had I been in Paris? Five, six days?

It seemed longer. It seemed like–

'I have seen twenty-nine AB-16 tags just since we left the airport,' Louis said. 'A week ago, there were none.'

'Okay...' I said, yawning.

'I think this is a tipping point,' he said at last. 'With the rocket grenade and the AK-47 assault rifles, the government won't have a choice now. They'll declare martial law.'

Chapter 78

7TH ARRONDISSEMENT
NOON

Inside the War School, Major Sauvage and Captain Mfune stood at attention with four of their classmates. They had only just been summoned to the office of Brigadier General Anton Georges, commander of École de Guerre.

General Georges was a tall, laconic man, proud of his bureaucratic skills. Sauvage, however, thought him a fraud and a jackass because he had risen to his rank and station in life without ever once experiencing combat.

'Gentlemen,' General Georges began. 'Paris and *les banlieues* will be subject to martial law as of nineteen hundred hours, and to curfew between twenty-three hundred hours and oh six hundred hours. All French students of the War School are needed, especially the six of you, who speak Arabic. You will be deployed in command positions this evening throughout the eastern suburbs.'

General Georges said they'd be issued weapons

and combat gear, and he handed out their assignments.

Sauvage wanted to pump his fist in the air when he saw where they were putting him. Mfune was also pleased.

'Go home and take care of your personal affairs,' the general said. 'Rendezvous at seventeen hundred hours. Dismissed.'

'General?' one officer said. 'Any idea how long we will be in the field?'

'Unclear, Captain,' General Georges said. 'Depends on how quickly the AB-16 movement can be brought under control.'

The officer groaned softly. Sauvage understood and glanced at him scornfully. War School was a necessary stop on the way to high command. The officer was asking what would become of his career if he didn't get to check the 'War School' box on his résumé.

Another jackass, thought the major. *Can't he see the possibilities? No, of course not. He's like the general: incapable of it.*

Sauvage, however, saw all the possibilities, and he was almost beside himself with excitement. The army was putting them inside the flash points!

As the general was dismissing them, an audacious idea popped into Sauvage's head. It bloomed and became part of the plot in an instant.

Outside, Sauvage told Mfune what he had in mind, and they split up with promises to stay in close touch. The major took the train to Pantin, and went straight to the Canal de l'Ourcq, where he entered the condemned linen factory through the footpath door.

The back room had been stripped of the whiteboards, the television screen, the table, chairs, and couch. Out in the cavernous space he found Haja and Amé finishing up beneath the sculpture.

Sauvage told them about the martial law decision and a change of plans.

'Wait,' Haja said. 'You've already built this thing?'

'Months ago,' the major replied. 'Just to see if I could do it. But it's there, and it *will* work.'

Doubtful, Amé said, 'But the curfew.'

'You'll be long gone before curfew,' he assured her.

'What about afterward?' Haja asked.

'I've removed everything identifiable.'

For a moment, both women were hesitant.

'Haven't we done enough?' Amé asked. 'Hasn't a tipping point been reached already with the riots and gunfights last night?'

'Do you want to risk them containing things?'

Haja stewed for a beat. 'Where do you want it to happen?'

The major thought about his assignment, and then said, 'Sevran.'

Chapter 79

8TH ARRONDISSEMENT
3:45 P.M.

Waking up after a solid five hours of rest, I realized I was becoming a creature of the night in Paris. The television was on in the outer room, and after showering and shaving, I found Louis drinking coffee in there.

'Predicted it, didn't I?' he said, gesturing at the screen. 'Martial law.'

'No kidding,' I said, moving around behind him.

'They're putting army units in the eastern suburbs. Curfew at eleven.'

The screen split then to show Laurent Alexandre, who was talking about the various designers he'd gotten to agree to put their work on at the upcoming Millie Fleurs memorial in defiance of AB-16, but I didn't have a chance to hear the names because my cell phone rang.

I saw the caller ID, smiled, and answered.

'Michele Herbert,' I said. 'How are you?'

'I was beginning to think you were avoiding me, Jack,' said the artist and graffiti expert in a teasing tone.

'I've just been a little busy the past few days.'

'Make nothing of it, but I might have something for you on that tag.'

I put her on speaker so Louis could listen. Herbert explained that she'd been receiving hundreds of photographs of the AB-16 tag from all around Paris. She'd been comparing them to the one up on the cupola at the Institut de France, and found that only one in ten tags matched the one on the cupola. The rest were copies, even the ones at the crime scenes.

'They didn't use paint at Millie Fleurs's,' Louis said. 'It was done in fabric.'

Herbert said, 'I hadn't heard that.'

'It's true,' I said. 'Saw it myself.'

'Well, that doesn't fit, but I don't suppose it matters,' she replied. 'Anyway, an old student of mine who is also obsessed with graffiti art examined the ones that were definitely done by the cupola tagger, and he agreed that the technique reminded him of Zee Pac-Man's work.'

'The tagger murdered before Christmas?' I asked.

'Correct,' she said. 'Which is what he found intriguing.'

'How's that?' Louis asked.

'Taggers are like most artists. They start out copying others. Once they've mastered their techniques, they start introducing their own methods,' she said.

'So your old student remembered someone who copied Zee Pac-Man?'

'Someone who was once a suspect in his murder.'

'Pac-Man's?' Louis asked.

'Correct,' she said.

'Name?' I asked.

'Piggott,' she said. 'Paul Piggott, but he calls himself Epée, like the dueling sword. Besides graffiti, he's obsessed with parkour.'

Louis scribbled on a pad of paper and showed it to me.

'I know Epée,' his note read. 'Arrested his father once.'

'Does that help?' Michele asked over the speaker.

'Most definitely,' I said. 'In fact, I owe you dinner before I leave Paris.'

'I'd like that, Jack,' she said. 'Very much.'

Chapter 80

20TH ARRONDISSEMENT
5:15 P.M.

Louis and I slid into seats outside a café on the Rue de Bagnolet, where we could see the front door of an apartment building that had seen much better days. Louis had pulled strings in France's motor vehicles department and gotten the address for twenty-eight-year-old Paul Piggott, a.k.a. Epée.

We also had a three-year-old driver's license photograph and Epee's rap sheet, which featured multiple counts of destruction of property for putting up graffiti art. The only felony Piggott had ever been convicted of was assault and battery five years before. He had spent eight months in jail for the offense, and had been clean ever since.

We had Petitjean and Vans digging into his background while we staked out his apartment.

'He doesn't look like your average Islamic militant,' I said, studying the driver's license photo.

'They come in many shapes, shades, and sizes,' Louis said. 'But you know, come to think of it, his father was ... *merde!* There he is!'

I twisted in my chair and saw Piggott turn away from the door to his apartment building. Long, lean, and athletic, he wore a black warm-up suit, gym shoes, and a black-and-white checked scarf around his neck. A black messenger bag was slung across his chest, and he snugged it to his hip as he walked east.

'Let's get to it,' Louis said.

We bolted from the café. Louis crossed the street. I paralleled him on my side. When Louis was less than twenty feet from Piggott, he called, 'Hey, Paul. How's your old man doing?'

Still moving, Epée glanced over his shoulder.

'Remember me?' Louis said.

Piggott seemed to remember Louis all right. He swiveled and took off like a four-hundred-meter sprinter, long legs and arms pumping as he accelerated, with Louis and me in pursuit.

True to his nickname, Epée had uncanny reflexes and remarkable evasive instincts. He parried and cut through the late-day crowd as if he'd memorized every move, and we almost immediately started to lose ground. Then I jumped out into the street and ran between the parked cars and oncoming traffic.

With no one to avoid, I was catching up to him when he took a hard left onto Cité Aubry, where he left the sidewalk and ran up the middle of the residential street. Where the paved way veered left, he continued straight ahead on a cobblestone street called Villa Riberolle.

Piggott was not only quick and evasive but insanely fit. Or at least he was fitter than me, because he kept putting distance between us, never once looking back. I did, however, and saw Louis several blocks behind, limping and hobbling slowly after me.

Louis bellowed, 'I tore my knee! Get him!'

That filled my gas tanks. I put my head down and ran harder. If he *was* the one who had tagged the Institut de France, he was part of AB-16, knew the leaders. We could not afford to lose him.

At the end of the cobblestone road, Piggott took another hard left. When I got to the turn, he was forty yards ahead of me, climbing a tall, ivy-covered wall as if he were part monkey. In three quick moves he was up and over the top – again, never once looking back.

I got to the wall seconds later, and almost started up after him. Then I realized that if Epée was as clever as I thought he was, he wouldn't look back until he'd cleared the wall. He'd get well out from under it and watch for half a minute or so before moving on.

So I forced myself to rest, taking in big, slow breaths while I watched the second hand of my watch. At thirty-five seconds, I began to climb. Reaching the top, I kicked up my right leg to straddle the top of the wall, and felt something slip from my pocket. My iPhone shattered on the cobblestones. I cursed and then hauled myself up and over.

Chapter 81

The hilly terrain on the other side of the wall was covered in dense rows of stained grave markers, ornate mausoleums, and marble and limestone statues set amid leafy hardwood trees that made it difficult to see far. So I jumped.

I landed in a crouch inside Père-Lachaise cemetery and scanned all around me. I didn't see him at first. But then I caught sight of his head and shoulders about a hundred yards ahead. He was weaving through the tombs, heading northwest at an angle away from me. Had he seen me?

I ran forward to the nearest large crypt and peeked around the corner. Piggott hurried on, but no longer sprinted. He hadn't seen me come over the wall.

Had he seen me back there? He'd definitely seen Louis, but me? Once he had committed to fleeing Louis, I never saw him look back. He'd never hesitated because he'd scouted his escape route, and knew that the wall to Père-Lachaise cemetery would be a barrier to most pursuers.

Epée had not gotten a good look at me, I decided. But I couldn't take any chances. I had to change my look and I had to do it fast. Stripping off my jacket, I tossed it on a grave, leaving me in jeans and a pressed white dress shirt as I hustled to keep him in sight.

I soon spotted him again, continuing northwest. He kept checking his back trail, but I'd gone off it by fifty yards or so, paralleling him through the gigantic graveyard for ten minutes, maybe more.

Then he stopped to take a sweeping look around. I had no place to hide, so I just went to my knee and acted grief-stricken before the nearest gravestone.

Epée turned and walked on. He had to have seen me there, but to my relief, he had not bolted. Still, with the white shirt, I was sure he'd recognize me the next time he checked for followers.

I wasn't wearing an undershirt, so stripping a layer was not an answer. I'd almost surrendered to the idea that he was going to spot me at some point when he led me to the answer.

Epée skirted a large group of people gathered at a grave I remembered. I kept the crowd between us as I hustled toward the mourners, already hearing the music of the Doors playing.

Fifty pilgrims of all ages, sexes, and sizes surrounded Jim Morrison's grave this time, so I had my pick of disguises. I chose a beefy guy with an Irish pie face who looked fairly drunk on his bottle of Jim Beam.

'Son of Fenway?' I asked, whipping out my wallet. 'I'll give you a hundred euros for your Sox hat and sweatshirt.'

'Nah, man. We're talking Boston Strong here.'

'Three hundred euros,' I said, pulling out a wad of bills.

He shrugged, took the money, and handed me

the red hat and matching hoodie. I had to jog to catch up this time, tugging the sweatshirt on over my shirt and pulling the cap down tight over my blond hair.

For several nerve-racking minutes I thought I'd blown it, that Epée had doubled back or used some other technique to shake me. Then I spotted him far ahead, moving northeast.

Using that parallel trailing technique, I followed him to a gate that opened out onto Rue des Rondeaux. He crossed the street and continued on the Avenue du Père-Lachaise, with me hanging well back in pedestrian traffic until I saw him enter the Place Gambetta and circle toward the Métro stop.

I sprinted after Epée and was less than twenty yards behind him when he went through the turnstiles. I waited until he was well down the stairs to jump the stiles and race after him, a Métro worker ranting behind me.

I got on the subway car behind the tagger, heading east on the 3 train, and then managed to loosely trail him through the Père-Lachaise Métro station to the 2 train northbound. I got into a car in front of him. He got off five stations later, at Jaurès, which also serves the S line.

Jaurès was a small station, but I'd bought a dark blue windbreaker from a college kid on the train and wore it as I exited after Epée, and got on the same car going in the direction of Bobigny.

I stood with my back to Epée, and never looked his way.

Epée got off at the fifth stop, Église de Pantin. I waited until the last second to toss away the Red

Sox hat and get out the door. There were no more than seven people leaving the train, so I wasn't going to hide easily. I improvised, picking up a discarded newspaper and putting it under my arm.

Exiting the station, I spotted a clear public trash bag, went to it, and fished out a plastic bag filled with the remains of a meal. The light was fading now, and I hoped I'd be able to avoid detection if I just kept switching up the things I carried or wore, and stayed back.

Epée turned left out of the station and then left again onto a pedestrian mall that wandered north. Trees made the mall a place of shadows and a surprisingly popular hangout for the youth of Pantin.

Using the shadows and the thirty or forty teenagers smoking and posturing in the area, I was able to stay in visual contact with Piggott until he reached the far end of the mall and took a right onto a footpath.

The footpath ran along a canal. There were many joggers on the path. Still, I felt uneasy as I followed Epée past construction sites toward abandoned factories and warehouses along the canal's south side.

Light was fading. We were a solid eighty yards apart, but I didn't think I could remain below his radar if he led me to a less frequented spot. Piggott neared a bend in the path and an old building covered in brilliant graffiti. The tagger didn't give the art a second glance.

He did, however, stop to look back along the footpath, and there weren't enough joggers in the way to shield me. He saw me ambling along for sure.

But I didn't seem to pose a threat because he calmly pivoted and strolled on beneath a pedestrian bridge that spanned the canal. The closer I got to the bridge, the more I thought about the fact that he had ignored the graffiti on the building. Even in the streetlight, the colors were impressive.

Then it hit me. He knows this place. He comes here often enough that he wouldn't give the artwork a second glance. Epée was close to his destination.

A jogger went by me, and up the stairs to the pedestrian bridge. I followed him. The bridge had high steel-mesh walls to keep people from jumping off into the canal, which stank.

I walked out onto the bridge and casually glanced back along the footpath. Piggott had turned toward a large four-story building. It was old, perhaps the oldest of all the abandoned buildings in the area, and the only one that seemed to have been constructed entirely out of wood.

The roof had once been tin like the others, but it looked as though the metal had been stripped for salvage. There were stacks of it leaning up against the front of the building, partially covering faded white paint and the word *linen*.

Walking on across the bridge toward the north bank of the canal, I saw Epée go to a door that had a condemnation notice on it and knock. A moment later, the door opened and he disappeared inside.

Chapter 82

PANTIN, NORTHEASTERN SUBURBS OF PARIS
6:15 P.M.

Haja closed the door behind Epée, saying angrily, 'You're not supposed to be here. We're just about to leave.'

He noticed that she and Amé were wearing robes.

'What's going on?'

'What's going on is you're not supposed to be here.'

'Why are you wearing robes?'

'Forget the robes,' Amé said. 'Why are you here?'

The tagger said nothing for several beats before blurting out, 'Louis Langlois – the head of Private Paris – he came after me as I was leaving my flat.'

Haja's expression soured. 'What do you mean, came after you?'

'He was just there all of a sudden, saying something about my father. But why would he be there, you know?'

'So what happened?' Amé demanded. 'What did he say? More importantly, what did you say?'

'I didn't say a goddamned word,' he replied fiercely. 'I took one look at him, figured it couldn't be a good thing, and took off. He's, like, in his fifties. Didn't stand a chance. I climbed the back wall of Père-Lachaise, and it was over.'

'You're sure you weren't followed?' Haja asked.

'Like I said, it was over at the wall.'

'But now he thinks you've got something to run about,' Amé said.

'I do have something to run about. We all do.'

'Have you told Sauvage?' Haja asked.

'I don't have his new burn cell number, or Mfune's.'

'I'll call him,' Haja said. She punched in the number, handed the phone to Epée.

He told the story again. Sauvage said nothing until the end.

'You're positive you were clean after the cemetery wall?'

'Yes.'

'I want you out of Paris immediately,' the major said. 'Haja will give you money and the address of a safe house in the south. Let me speak to her.'

Epée handed Haja the phone.

Haja took the phone, listened, and nodded. 'I'll get both taken care of.'

She hung up and said, 'We'll give you ten thousand euros, and the address. Move in disguise. Use burn phones.'

'Okay,' the tagger said.

'It's out in the factory with the creature,' Haja said, and went through another door into the cavernous space that held her sculpture.

The place was only dimly lit, but the beast loomed above them, looking otherworldly and fantastic. Epée tripped over electric cables on the floor.

'It's all hitched up?' he asked.

'Yes,' Haja said curtly as she went to the table where she kept her tools.

Epée peered at the creature and thought he saw where the electrical cables attached to the lower legs of the beast. He pivoted to ask her if he was–

Haja's powerful arms and shoulders were already swinging a piece of rebar. It cracked against the side of the tagger's head. Fire and pain seized his brain, and he crashed to the ground.

Haja stepped over Epée's quivering body and hit him again, so hard she heard and felt his skull cave in.

'God. What did you do that for?' Amé whined.

'He became a liability,' Haja replied coldly. 'Émile said we had to martyr him for the cause.'

Chapter 83

Darkness fell. The number of joggers running along the canal dwindled to stragglers, and all of them were on the better-lit south bank, which was a problem.

In the twenty minutes that had passed since Epée went into the old building, I'd wanted to call Louis and tell him roughly where I was. But the two or three runners who came by either laughed at my pitiful efforts at French – one of them said that I spoke the language like a Spanish cow – or shook their heads at my request to use their cell phones, and carried on.

I decided to go back across the bridge and was a quarter of the way across when the door that Epée had used opened, and two Muslim women wearing dark brown robes and head scarves exited and headed west carrying large shopping bags with a logo on them that I couldn't make out. One of them glanced up at me as I continued to cross toward them. She craned her head around and did it again after they'd walked beneath the south end of the bridge.

I continued on, as if I hadn't a care in the world. When I started down the stairs, I meant to find a cell and wait for Louis before entering the building in search of Piggott. But when I looked after the retreating figures of the Muslim women, there was something about the way they were walking, as if there was something heavy in their shopping bags.

Blame it on my time in Afghanistan, because there was nothing rational or logical about it, but at the bottom of the stairs I decided to go with my instincts, abandon Piggott, and follow the women. They seemed even warier than Epée. It took all of my skills to stay below their radar. They turned left into that pedestrian mall. I stripped the Windbreaker, leaving the red hoodie exposed, and ran to catch up.

Fewer than half the teens were still hanging out in the area, but there were still enough of them that I didn't seem to arouse the attention of the two women as they headed toward the main drag.

Instead of turning right toward the Métro station, however, they hung a hard left past a bar called the Pause, which was bustling with a happy hour crowd. I drifted toward a group of men and women chatting merrily, but stayed focused on the two women hurrying down the sidewalk.

I had a moment of doubt, thinking that I should go back and sit on Piggott, but then the women veered toward a small blue Suzuki two-door SUV. They opened the driver's and passenger doors and popped forward the front seats so they could put the bags in the back.

They climbed in and started the car.

I didn't know what to do. They pulled out of their parking spot and up to a red traffic light. I went to the curb as if I meant to cross the street. I memorized the license plate but could tell little about the women because they had their visors down.

The light changed. The engine revved and the vehicle drifted forward. For an instant a streetlamp lit up the interior enough that I could see the shopping bags.

The driver must have slipped her foot off the clutch pedal because the Suzuki suddenly bucked. Several pieces of what looked like white gravel fell off the rear bumper into the gutter. The car caught gear and roared off.

Stepping down off the curb, I picked up a piece of the gravel and saw that it was actually a powdery blue color. I smelled it, tasted it, spit it out, and felt my suspicions become hard convictions.

Spinning around, I jumped out into the street in front of an oncoming maroon and black Citroën, waving my hands wildly. The old car skidded to a stop inches from my knees, and I could see that the elderly woman driving was wide-eyed and scared.

I came around, opened the door, and climbed in. She was hunched over and gray, easily in her late seventies, but she began to hit me backhand with her fist and scream, *'Non! Non! Police! Police!'*

'Je suis avec police!' I said, fending off the blows, trying to dig out my ID. *'Privé Paris police. Suivez la voiture bleu là! Le Suzuki! C'est les defaceurs de l'Institut de France! AB-16. Vous comprenez?'*

I was butchering the language, but she must have gotten the gist of what I was trying to say, because she stopped hitting me and looked down the street, where the Suzuki was making a U-turn to go east on the N3 highway, before crying in an angry voice, *'Ah bon!'*

Then she pegged the gas, popped the clutch, and we squealed out of there with the tires smoking.

Chapter 84

She spoke no English and suffered badly from scoliosis, but that old lady was sharp as a tack and could have given Danica Patrick a run for her money.

Weaving in and out of traffic with deft shifting of the gears and an easy touch at the wheel, she Tokyo-drifted us through the U-turn, and quickly brought us to within two cars of the Suzuki in moderate traffic. She chattered almost nonstop, as if she hadn't had a listener in a while, and even though I was definitely missing the nuances of her monologue, I learned that her name was Eloise La Bruyere. Madame La Bruyere was a retired librarian. She had learned to drive from her husband, who had been involved in rally car racing and was now deceased.

At seventy-nine, Madame La Bruyere lived alone and rather liked it that way. Her children – two sons and a daughter – did not visit enough. She had six grandchildren, one of whom had purple hair. Best of all, she took great pride in France and her culture, and therefore hated AB-16, which she knew all about from the newspapers.

'We have to fight them,' she declared more than once, shaking her bony fist. 'France cannot be destroyed. We must throw them all out!'

When I finally got a word in edgewise, I managed to ask her if she had a cell phone, and she shook her head and muttered something dismissive about them that I didn't get.

The Suzuki stayed on the N3 for five or six miles before taking the N370 north. Madame La Bruyere trailed them like a pro, keeping three, four, and sometimes five cars between us, and all the while fuming about the 'Muslims and immigrants' out to destroy her beloved country. Indeed, when she saw the two women get off at the Sevran exit and head east, Eloise went into a minor tirade about the area and the immigrants who lived there.

She drove us down the Boulevard de Stalingrad, past shabby shopping malls and drab clusters of high-rise public housing projects. Judging by the broken shop windows and charred cars along the route, Sevran had been a hub of violence the night before.

The people on the sidewalks seemed tense, in a hurry to be home and off the streets as armed French soldiers prepared for curfew. I thought about having Madame La Bruyere stop so I could tell one of the soldiers what was going on, but feared losing track of the two women.

The Suzuki took a left and headed north on a side street. We lost them several minutes later, when an ambulance blocked us from following them onto the narrow, windy Rue de Rougemont.

'Où sont-elles?' Madame La Bruyere kept saying, meaning, 'Where are they?'

I was peering anxiously down every alley and side street and didn't see the women anywhere. I feared we'd been spotted. A sinking sensation was drilling through my lower belly when the road bent hard left. Going around that tight curve, I got a good look down a lane that led to an old church.

The Muslim women had parked, back bumper facing the wall of the church. They were out of the vehicle, toting those heavy shopping bags, and heading from right to left and out of my vision.

For a beat I couldn't remember the word for stop, but then sputtered, *'Arrêtez! Arrêtez!'*

Madame La Bruyere screeched the old Citroën to a stop. I kissed her on the cheek, jumped out of the car, and said, *'Merci,* madame!'

Chapter 85

SEVRAN, NORTHEASTERN
SUBURBS OF PARIS
7:10 P.M.

Tearing the red hoodie off so that I was again down to that white dress shirt, I ran down the lane into the churchyard, where several other cars were parked as well. The Suzuki was next to a closed green gate that blocked access to a larger parking lot and a brick building immediately north of the Saint Martin Church.

Two police cars were parked in that lot, along with two small white sedans. I could see a well-traveled route beyond them. A bus sighed, caught gear, and then roared past the mouth of the bigger parking lot.

Figuring the women had gone to the main route, I jumped the gate and ran through the lot to a large traffic rotary with a park at the center.

The bus stop was to my left, along with an Asian grocery store and a clothing shop, both closed, and a pharmacy, still open. When I looked right, I was surprised to see another police car, and more surprised to realize that I was right in front of the Sevran police station.

Had they gone in there? Did I have this all wrong?

I hurried inside to check. The officer behind a

pane of bulletproof glass was on the phone but lowered it when I adopted a prayer pose. When I asked in halting French if two Muslim women had come inside, she looked down her nose, shook her head, and immediately lifted the phone to her ear again.

I tried to talk again, but she held up her finger and turned away from me.

Frustrated, I went out onto the sidewalk. Where the hell had they gone?

There were three people at the bus stop now: an elderly man wearing a turban, a young Vietnamese girl, and a woman with long, braided reddish hair. She wore a laborer's clothes, leather boots, tan canvas pants, and a denim shirt. She had her back to me and was smoking.

A heavyset blond woman wearing heavy make-up, a white pantsuit, and carrying a large black purse was coming down the sidewalk toward me. A mother and child exited the pharmacy, and I headed their way. As I walked by the bus stop, the woman with the reddish braids flicked her cigarette into the gutter, and squatted to rummage in a stonemason's bag at her feet.

I kept going. The blonde in the pantsuit passed, giving me a quick, bright smile. Sweet perfume lingered in her wake. The lights in the pharmacy went dark. A bus approached. I wanted to punch something.

Had they circled me? Gone back to the car? I could go there and sit on it, or just go back to the police station and make the officer understand the situation.

Changing direction, I followed the bus to the

stop, seeing the four people board and wondering if the Muslim women had gotten on the first bus I'd seen leaving the area.

I thought about the pale blue gravel that had fallen off the Suzuki's bumper. It was definitely ammonium nitrate fertilizer. I'd tasted and smelled remnants of the stuff in the air after IED explosions back in Kandahar.

But if they'd left the area with the bags...

Oh, Jesus. I had it wrong.

I took off toward the police station. The bus doors closed. As I came abreast of the bus, it began to pull away. I happened to glance at the windows.

The woman in the work clothes, the one with the reddish braids, was sitting in the third row from the front, looking out the window at me. She was exotically beautiful, with haunting nickel-gray eyes and high cheekbones across which stretched burnished, dusky skin.

As the bus drove off, I was puzzled by the sense that I had seen her somewhere before...

I began to sprint after the bus, trying to get a better look at her. But crossing the mouth of the narrow parking lot next to the Sevran police station, I understood that I was too late. I'd never catch up.

I staggered to a stop just beyond the entrance to the parking lot, right in front of the station, and was sucking wind, cursing, and watching the bus disappear into the dusk when the car bomb erupted.

Chapter 86

The blast threw me off my feet and to the pavement. Shock waves pounded through my back, deafened me, and rattled my brain for several minutes. And I took some body shots from falling debris.

But thanks to the northwest corner of the Sevran police station, which stood between me and the parking lot and the Catholic churchyard where the robed women had left the Suzuki, I was otherwise uninjured.

There was dust and debris everywhere, and that acidic fertilizer smell permeated the air like humidity on a stiflingly hot day.

Struggling to my feet, I saw that all traffic on the roundabout had come to a halt. People were outside their cars, covering their mouths, or stretching them wide to scream. But I could barely hear them. Their voices were drowned out by a high-pitched ringing in my ears.

Still in a daze, I stumbled a few steps and looked into the parking lot. Through the thick cloud of dust, I could see that the entire front of the church had been blown inward, collapsing the roof. A large jagged hole had been opened in the rear sidewall of the police station.

A policeman staggered from it, covered head to boots in dust and plaster. His face showed blood from a nasty scalp gash.

I went to him, tried to talk to him. But he looked at me as if I were a creature in a nightmare, and walked dumbly past me. I looked into the hole, into the dark hull of the police station, seeing human silhouettes amid the wreckage.

I threw my sleeve across my chest and fought my way in across the debris, finding an officer dead at his desk and the pieces of a dead man in a holding cell. Then I spotted the desk officer who'd ignored me minutes before.

She was trying feebly to get up from the floor. I went to her, got her in a fireman's sling, and got her outside. Her face was a mess. Blood soaked her right leg and I could see the bulge of bone sticking from her thigh.

I took off my belt and cinched it tight around her upper thigh. If I was right, the blast had broken her femur and probably nicked her femoral artery. Had the bone fully cut the blood vessel, she would have been dead where I had found her.

I was acting on autopilot at that point, focused on saving the officer and nothing else. Surging with adrenaline, I scooped her up again and moved back toward the roundabout, where red and blue lights were flashing.

Reaching the sidewalk, I saw cops, firemen, and paramedics racing to the scene. I set her down amid the rubble in front of the station.

A team was working on her in seconds. I stood there and watched numbly. One of the new officers on the scene began talking to me, but I still couldn't hear for the ringing.

I said, *'J'ai vu les saboteurs.'*

I saw the bombers.

Chapter 87

That statement got me a lot of attention in the next couple of hours. The cop went and returned with a captain. The ringing in my ears began to fade and I repeated what I'd said, showed them my Private identification, and told him to contact Louis Langlois at Private Paris, or Investigateur Sharen Hoskins from La Crim, or even Juge Fromme. They would all vouch for me.

Klieg lights shone from the park across the street, where a gathering horde of media was encamping. The police captain was caught in the glare of indecision, looking at my identification card and then at me. Finally he dug in his pocket for his phone, and hurried off.

He returned about an hour later, but not with Hoskins or Fromme or Louis. A French Army officer in full battle gear and helmet trailed him, his eyes going everywhere until they settled on me.

'I am Major Émile Sauvage,' he said in flawless English. 'French Army. I am in charge of this area under martial law.'

'Lucky you,' I said.

'What can you tell us?' he asked, studying me from under his helmet brim.

Sauvage listened attentively and wordlessly during my summary of events. I gave it to him, all of it, from following Epée to a condemned linen factory in Pantin to the moment when I lost sight of the two robed women after they'd parked the Suzuki in front of the church.

'I think they changed out of the robes,' I said. 'And left on a bus that pulled away shortly before the bomb went off.'

'What bus?' he demanded tersely. 'What route?'

'I don't know.'

'What makes you think they were aboard?'

'Because I think I recognized one of them.'

That seemed to dumbfound the major. 'You knew one of the women?'

'No, not like that,' I said. 'It was just a feeling. The redhead. Her face. Like I'd seen it before somewhere.'

'Where?'

Shaking my head slowly, I said, 'I don't know. As I said, it was a feeling. The shape of her face. Her eyes. The way it all came together.'

'But nothing more specific, sir?' Major Sauvage asked.

'No,' I said. 'At least right now. My bell got rung in the explosion.'

'Take care of that,' the major advised. 'I speak from experience. Concussions can make you feel stupid or nuts.'

Another French Army officer, a big dark-skinned captain, hurried up and signaled the major for his attention.

'You are not to leave France without notifying me, Monsieur Morgan,' the major said. 'I'm sure there will be others who make the same demands on you.'

'I'll help any way I can, Major,' I said.

With a stiff nod and a limp handshake, he

320

pivoted and went to the captain. They spoke and moved off.

Louis hobbled up with Sharen Hoskins and Juge Fromme, and I had to repeat my story all over again.

'You don't know where you saw that woman before?' Fromme asked.

'Only that she reminded me of someone.'

'Could she be the same redhead the opera director was seen with the night he was murdered?' Louis asked.

'Again,' I said, 'I'm clueless. Maybe it will come to me.'

Hoskins said, 'We can't do a thing here. Military intelligence and anti-terror will be all over it. Think you can find that linen factory again?'

Knitting my eyebrows, I thought back, still fuzzy, but said, 'I think so.'

Chapter 88

10:20 P.M.

Hoskins drove. She and Fromme got us past the blockades near the blast site. Louis and I sat in the back and studied Google Maps on an iPad that the magistrate had produced from his briefcase.

Gesturing at the screen and the roof of a building close to a narrow bridge over a canal, I said, 'That's it, I think.'

321

'You have an address?' Hoskins asked.

Louis tapped on the satellite image and an address popped up. He gave it to her and she called it in while driving toward Pantin.

I said, 'You'll want to take a look from the other side of the canal before you go kicking down the door.'

Hoskins looked ready to argue, but the magistrate said, 'He's right. We must consider them heavily armed.'

The *investigateur* sighed, nodded, and altered her route. Someone called Hoskins a few minutes later to inform her that the address she'd called in was a condemned property that had been seized for taxes and was due to be razed to make way for a vacant lot sale in the coming weeks.

'Perfect safe house,' Louis said.

'Again I agree with you,' Hoskins said. 'These *are* miraculous days.'

She pulled over fifteen minutes later on a deserted industrial street and said, 'We're two blocks off the canal here, close to the north side of that bridge.'

We set off in that direction slowly, having to wait for the magistrate and Louis to limp along behind us. A block closer to the canal, headlights appeared. A news van shot by and skidded to a halt by a construction site beside two other news vans.

'What the hell is going on?' Hoskins cried, and ran toward the canal.

I did my best to stay with her, but she reached a small crowd gathered just east of the pedestrian bridge before I did. The reporters had their backs

322

to the canal and the condemned factory, and were barking at the cameras.

When I caught up, Hoskins looked at her watch and said, 'AB-16 sent out a message calling the media to be here at ten thirty p.m. In less than a minute they're supposedly going to deliver a message to France.'

Juge Fromme and Louis hobbled up to us, gasping.

A series of thumping booms like mortar fire echoed across the canal. Fire fountained high inside the condemned factory. Plumes of it billowed out the broken windows and set the whole structure ablaze.

In minutes it was a runaway, throwing shimmering heat and fire that blew through the roof and licked at the Paris skyline like so many snake tongues. Hoskins was calling for fire and police backup, but the rest of us were transfixed by the growing inferno.

Was this the message AB-16 wanted to send in the wake of the bombing? That Paris was burning?

I got my answer a second later, when many of the reporters gasped.

Deep inside the factory something else had ignited, blue and then white and silver hot, almost blinding in its intensity. That brilliant new fire within a fire expanded and took shape at a blistering pace, two bent columns rising from the floor of the factory to a massive curve that soon became the powerful haunches of a giant prehistoric-looking horse reared up on its back legs, pawing at the flames and the sky.

As the roof fell in, there was a third ignition. The horse had wings that burned so hot it was as if the creature actually had molten silver feathers that fluttered in the greater inferno, as if the beast was poised to take flight.

'It's Al-Buraq,' Louis said.

I nodded in grim awe. 'The Prophet's war-horse.'

PART FIVE

WARHORSE

Chapter 89

8TH ARRONDISSEMENT
APRIL 12, 7:20 A.M.

Brothers and Sisters,

We the warriors of AB-16 fight in the name of Al-Buraq, warhorse of the Prophet Mohammed, blessings be upon his name. Flying into battle on the back of the winged Lightning, AB-16 calls to all immigrants and immigrant youth:

Look at the way France has treated you.

No job. No future. No hope.

And brutal oppression when you protest.

This will be your useless life unless you join our fight now. Take up the sword of divine justice. Wage holy war for your children's lives.

Help us drive out the decadent French culture now, and replace it with one that will make the Prophet proud.

Lightning has taken flight over Paris. The warhorse soars over all of France in 2016.

Hear his battle cry. Spread the message. Join our ranks.

Al-Buraq in 2016!

AB-16!

Sitting in the living area in the suite, with the television on and my breakfast eaten, I set the letter aside. It was the fifth time I'd read it since Ali Farad first received a copy three days before, but it was the first since I'd watched the sculpture of the Prophet's warhorse ignite and burn so furiously hours before.

The two together – image and call to jihad – felt greater than the sum of their parts. The letter alone was incendiary, a call to treason and revolution. But footage of the factory fire and the statue was dominating the news in ways the letter could not.

Every station I turned to, even the ones out of Japan and China, was showing images of the Prophet's warhorse engulfed in flames. CNN kept broadcasting a clip with firemen arriving on the scene. When they had turned the hoses on the still-glowing sculpture, it had hissed and thrown steam, which made it seem otherworldly and threatening all over again.

The BBC was reporting that in response to the bombing in Sevran and the factory fire in Pantin, the riots had spread. The feed cut to a knot of youths, their faces wrapped in head scarves, defying the curfew and chanting, 'AB-16! AB-16!'

In voice-over, the British reporter said that police and army officers, firemen and ambulance workers, had been shot at repeatedly during the night, and dozens of vehicles had been set ablaze and used to block streets.

I changed to a French station and was reaching for the pot to pour myself more coffee when the screen jumped to someone I recognized.

It was Major Sauvage, the French Army officer from the night before. He was giving the press a

328

briefing. He looked hard and focused, not tired at all.

'It has been a violent night,' Major Sauvage began. 'While trying to stop a van of immigrant men from breaking curfew and attempting to leave Les Bosquets at around three a.m., my men came under intense fire. Three men in the van were killed. The other two are in custody.

'All five men were carrying AK-47 assault rifles and a considerable amount of ammunition,' he went on. 'As of now, we consider all members and supporters of AB-16 to be armed and dangerous.

'Despite this brazen show of force, my soldiers remain committed to preventing outside forces from destroying France and its culture. *That,* I can tell you, will not happen on our watch.'

The screen jumped to Barbès, where the imam's mosque had been firebombed, and several white French teenagers had been beaten by immigrant gangs.

A picture appeared, showing one of the boys and identifying him as Alain Du Champs, an aspiring photojournalist who had been hospitalized in serious condition. To my surprise, I recognized him. He was the same kid who'd sung that funny version of the Billy Joel song to the Muslim—

The room phone rang. It was Louis.

'Hoskins wants you to work with a sketch artist on that redhead you saw on the bus,' Louis said.

I thought of her, saw her clearly in my mind, and somehow it all clicked.

'I know where I saw her before,' I said with growing conviction. 'You've seen her too, Louis. Remember the day we went to Al-Jumaa tailors and there was a white kid with a camera singing to a beautiful Muslim woman?'

'I remember. It's her?'

'Her eyes were a different color, but I think so,' I said.

Louis said in a leaden voice, 'She was coming from that mosque then, Jack, so the imam has to be involved with AB-16. And by extension Ali Farad.'

I didn't know what to say to that, and then I did.

'We'll deal with whoever is involved later,' I said. 'Right now we need to find out what hospital the rioters in Barbès were taken to last night.'

Chapter 90

12TH ARRONDISSEMENT
8:30 A.M.

In the bedroom of Haja Hamid's small apartment, she and Amé watched the television footage of the linen factory collapsing upon itself and the giant winged warhorse surrounded by burning timbers, smoke, and ash. The beast was so hot that the feathers and some of the skin were going molten and falling away, revealing the skeleton.

'It's brilliant!' Amé cried. 'My God, what a statement, Haja! That image will never be forgotten in France – ever.'

As an artist, Haja was pleased with the overall effect: sculpture and fire as performance art. The whole had been better than she'd hoped, and iconic as well – a symbol of her adopted nation's inner, hidden turmoil.

But at the same time, Haja's satisfaction was tempered by the memory of Jack Morgan staring at her from outside the bus in Sevran. Had there been a flash of recognition in his expression?

She wasn't sure.

But if so, Morgan had probably followed them to Sevran after he'd followed Epée to the linen factory. Haja had not told Amé of her suspicions and certainly not Émile Sauvage. As much as the major craved her, she knew his unwavering commitment to the cause. If he ever thought that she had become a liability, he would sacrifice her the same way he'd sacrificed Epée. She wondered whether it was time for her to slip off, and leave the country until things had shaken out.

'How did you do it, Haja?' Amé asked. 'Make it burn like that?'

'Math, thermodynamics, and magnesium,' Haja said.

'Translation?'

'A wood fire can burn up to four hundred degrees,' Haja said. 'Throw gasoline in, and a wood fire can create temperatures well over five hundred. Magnesium ignites at roughly four hundred and seventy-three degrees, and can then burn as hot as four thousand degrees. I made the horse's skin with sheets of magnesium, which caught when the first fire was at its hottest.'

Amé shook her head. 'How in God's name did you figure that all out?'

'God had nothing to do with it. I looked it all

up on the Internet.'

Her burn phone rang.

Sauvage.

'Your art,' he said. 'It's all they're talking about. Your masterpiece is raising a revolt, *chéri*. I'm seeing it with my own eyes.'

Haja smiled at last. 'I'm glad you're pleased.'

'Beyond pleased,' he said, and paused. 'Did you see Jack Morgan there?'

'The Private guy?' she said. 'No.'

'He told me he saw you through the bus window, but didn't recognize you.'

Haja had gone from a state of relative calm to desperate alertness.

'Why would he?' she asked. 'That one time I walked by him I was wearing a robe, head scarf, and contact lenses – a totally different woman than the one on the bus.'

Sauvage paused and then said, 'Destroy your burn phone and lay low for a while. It'll be a few days before I can come see you.'

'Done,' Haja said simply, and hung up.

She went to the bedroom window, breaking the phone and removing the SIM card. There was scaffolding outside the window. The building's owners were having the exterior plaster replaced and painted.

Haja opened the window and looked down through the scaffolding, past a flower box on a lower floor, to a Dumpster in the alley below. She tossed the phone parts, watched them fall, all the while wondering whether she should be in a hurry to be long gone from Paris.

Chapter 91

18TH ARRONDISSEMENT
10 A.M.

'We are here to see my nephew,' Louis said when we reached the nurses' station outside the intensive care unit at Bretonneau Hospital. 'Alain Du Champs?'

The nurse on duty grimaced bitterly and said, 'Doubt they'll let you in to see him. He's got a police guard. They think he firebombed the mosque before he was beaten by people trying to save it.'

'A horrible thing,' Louis said. 'I don't know how he came to this. But perhaps I should talk with the police officer? I used to work for La Crim.'

She shrugged and then gestured with her chin down the hall. 'Down the hall, left, then first door on your right.'

I hung back while Louis spoke with the officer sitting outside Du Champs's room. At first I thought he was going to turn us down, but then Louis gestured to me. The officer had changed his mind.

'*Merci,*' he said, nodding at me as we went by him toward the door.

'What'd you tell him?' I whispered to Louis in English.

'The truth,' Louis said. 'You saved that police

officer in Sevran last night. It was enough to get us a few minutes.'

We went through hospital curtains and found Alain Du Champs lying in a bed, looking as though he'd been everyone's favorite punching bag. His face was swollen almost beyond recognition. A few of his front teeth were missing, and his arm had six or seven pins jutting out of it.

'Detectives?' he slurred. 'I'm not saying nothing 'til I talk to my attorney.'

'We work for Private Paris,' Louis said. 'You've heard of us?'

Through the swelling, Du Champs's eyes moved to study us.

'I've heard,' he said.

'Speak English?' I asked.

'Little,' he said.

'How long have you been a photographer?' I asked.

'Not about the mosque?' he said.

'No,' Louis said.

'Ten years,' Du Champs said, running his tongue along the gums where his teeth had been. 'Since I got my first camera, when I was nine. Loved it.'

'Take a lot of photographs?' I asked.

'Can always throw the bad ones out.'

'Remember the girl you sang to last week near the mosque?' Louis said.

'I don't sing.'

'Really?' I said, and then sang, '"Wake up, Fatima, don't let me wait. You Muslim girls start much too late"?'

The kid broke into a painful smile and laughed

as if his ribs were broken. 'I remember now. She was hot.'

'Any chance you took a picture of her?'

'Who is she?'

I said, 'She may have been involved in the Sevran bombing last night.'

'Yes?' he said, the gears of his brain meshing and spinning. 'So a pic of her could be a get-out-of-jail-free card? 'Cause I did not set that mosque on fire. I was in the area taking pictures and got attacked.'

'*Did* you get a picture of her?' Louis demanded.

'Had to,' he replied, grinning painfully. 'That sweet Fatima was one of a kind.'

Chapter 92

17TH ARRONDISSEMENT
11:15 A.M.

Outside a café near the headquarters of La Crim, we found Investigateur Hoskins and Juge Fromme drowning their sorrows in a bottle of wine.

'Kind of early to be drinking on the job,' Louis said.

'We're off the job,' Juge Fromme said miserably.

Hoskins nodded. 'Counter-terror and the military are taking over.'

'Guess you're not the people we want to show this to then,' Louis said, sliding his iPhone across the table.

'It's her,' I said. 'The woman on the bus.'

Fromme set his wine down and fumbled for his reading glasses. Hoskins peered at the photograph, and then used her fingers to blow it up.

Du Champs had caught her from an odd angle: looking up and in three-quarter profile, from the chest of her brown robe to the top of her brown head scarf.

'You said the woman on the bus was a redhead with nickel-gray eyes,' Fromme said. 'This woman has dark hair and brown eyes.'

'Contacts and rinsable dyes,' Louis said.

'It's her,' I insisted. 'There's no doubt in my mind.'

'How can you be sure from this angle?' Hoskins said. 'You can barely see the right side of her face.'

'When I close my eyes, I know they're the same person,' I said. 'This picture should be given to every media outlet in the country.'

'That won't happen,' the magistrate said. 'This woman has rights. If you're wrong and we say she's a suspect, we could be destroying her reputation.'

'And putting her in harm's way,' Hoskins agreed.

Incredulous, I said, 'So you're not going to use this?'

Fromme said, 'We'll pass the photograph along, and your thoughts on it, but I highly doubt this will become a focus of the investigation unless some other evidence comes forward to support it.'

'Like what?' Louis demanded.

'Another picture would help,' Hoskins said. 'And it would be better if she was caught climbing off the bus somewhere. But again, there are

336

not many public security cameras in France.'

'Someone should check all the cameras around Sevran, at least,' I said.

'We'll recommend that as well,' the magistrate said, and picked up his glass of wine again.

'That's it?' I said.

'For us,' Hoskins said. 'I'm going home and sleeping for as long as I can.'

'You're making a mistake,' I said.

'We don't make the laws,' Fromme said. 'We just enforce them.'

I was still furious when we were a block away, and I noticed Louis lagging behind me and limping hard.

'Have you had that knee checked?' I asked.

'It will pass,' Louis said. 'It always does.'

'Go get it checked. That's an order. You're no good to me like this.'

He looked ready to argue, but then nodded. 'I have an old friend, Megan, who specializes in knees.'

'Go see Megan,' I said. 'Or at least go somewhere where you can get it elevated and on ice.'

'It does feel like shit,' Louis said.

'Get a taxi. I'm going for a walk.'

'How can I contact you?'

'I'll buy a phone and text you the number,' I said, and left him there.

Chapter 93

I wandered out of the Batignolles neighborhood and headed south toward the river. The sun had broken through the clouds and it had gotten quite warm – easily in the high seventies. Coming upon a phone store a few blocks later, I bought a disposable Samsung and texted Louis the number. I also asked him to send me the picture. It appeared almost immediately, along with the news that Megan, his doctor friend, was going to see him at once.

'Good news,' I texted back. 'Keep me posted.'

Given the violent events of the prior night, a surprising number of Parisians were out walking or jogging along the Seine. I didn't know if they were defying AB-16 or just ignoring the group and its threat.

Twenty minutes later, I stopped across the river from the Eiffel Tower. Calling up the picture, I looked at the woman and wondered if she and AB-16 wanted to topple the Eiffel Tower and all the great monuments of Paris. It had been Hitler's plan once. Were they really out to obliterate French culture like that? Were they really out to see Paris burning?

Those questions put me in a foul mood and I walked on, thinking that I needed to eat. The Plaza was a few blocks away, and there were several cafés from which to choose. But before I decided, the phone I'd just bought rang.

'Louis?' I answered.

'Louis told me to call, Jack,' Michele Herbert said. 'I hope that was okay.'

'More than okay,' I said, feeling tension drain from my shoulders. 'Would you like to have lunch?'

There was a pause, and then she said, 'I'd like that very much.'

I hailed a taxi, giving the driver the address of a café that Michele Herbert had suggested in the 6th Arrondissement, not far from L'Académie des Beaux-Arts.

We got there at virtually the same time. Just seeing her made me forget all about terrorists and bombs and burning horses. For an hour, anyway, I wanted to put it all aside and find out more about her.

But when we took a table, all she wanted to talk about was the night before and what I'd seen and done.

'You were a big help, by the way,' I said. 'That guy, Epée? I followed him to the factory that burned down last night and that horse statue. Did you see it?'

'All of France has seen it,' she said. 'Is he in custody?'

'Not that I know of,' I said

Between breaks to order food, I told her the rest of it.

'You saved that cop's life,' she said, shaking her head.

'Anyone would have,' I said.

'This is not so,' Michele said with a dismissive

flick of her fork. 'So what then? You went back to the factory? You saw the horse burn in person?'

'I did.'

'Though I hate to admit it, I thought the sculpture and the way it burned were brilliant. Was it as spectacular in person as it was on-screen?'

'Awe-inspiring, and unforgettable,' I said. 'I guess that was the point.'

'Point taken,' Michele said. 'So what will happen tonight? Will AB-16 attack again?'

'The police and army better assume so.'

That seemed to upset her. 'I want to fight them, but I don't know how.'

'I hear you, but this is a national security deal now.'

'The government pursues leads?' she asked. 'That is the word, isn't it?'

I nodded. 'I'm sure they are. But they should be looking for this woman.'

Getting out the phone and calling up the picture, I said, 'Even though she looks a lot different here in the robes and head scarf, I think she was the same woman I saw on a bus just before the Sevran explosion.'

Intrigued, Michele took the phone. She looked at the picture blankly at first, but then her facial muscles twitched and she enlarged the phone so the face of the woman filled the small screen.

For several moments, the art professor gazed at the picture, blinking as her other hand came slowly to her lips.

'My God,' Michele whispered. 'Why didn't I see it last night?'

Chapter 94

12TH ARRONDISSEMENT
1:10 P.M.

A taxi dropped us down the block from our destination.

Michele looked nervous. 'What if I'm wrong?'

'Then we walk away,' I said.

'And if I'm right?' she said.

'I take a picture, we walk away, find the police.'

The art professor chewed the corner of her lip.

'You said you wanted to fight them,' I reminded her.

That pushed her over the top. She led the way to a four-story apartment building that had recently been sandblasted. She rang a bell and waited. She rang again, looked back at me, and made a 'What do I do?' gesture.

An older man exited the apartment building. Barely giving us a glance, he walked away, the door closing slowly behind him.

I grabbed the door before it closed.

'I can't be part of a break-in,' Michele said quietly, looking after the old man.

'All you're doing is knocking on a door,' I said, and then told her what I had in mind.

She was doubtful, but went inside the building and started up the stairs. I went back up the street, counting doors – seven – and hung a left and then a quick left again into an alleyway I'd seen on the Google Maps app on Michele's smart-phone during the taxi ride over from the restaurant.

I counted rear exits and found scaffolding set up behind the seventh building. The workers appeared to be on break, so I started climbing. As I did, I noticed a Dumpster beneath the scaffolding and flower boxes behind it.

When I reached the fourth floor, I texted Michele. 'Knock.'

I heard a dull *rap-rap-rap* coming from one of the windows. The shade was drawn. The window was shut and locked.

I checked the alley again and looked over my shoulder at the building behind me. I had the place to myself.

I drew the Glock and used it to bust in one of the windowpanes. Reaching in, I tore down the shade and undid the latch.

Then I climbed inside, gun first.

Chapter 95

The apartment seemed to be a home for hoarders. I stepped in on a toolbox wedged between stacks of newspapers and magazines. A hodgepodge of broken furniture was piled along the walls. There were dozens of lidded five-gallon buckets too – stacks of them.

Rap-rap-rap.

I picked my way through the mess, threw the

bolt, and opened the door.

Michele slipped in and I shut the door behind her.

'I don't like this,' she said. 'I shouldn't be here.'

'All we need is a picture that confirms it. And then we go. But all this crap? Does it make sense? It feels like a storage unit for a slob.'

'Think of it as a supply warehouse,' Michele said. 'These are materials.'

'You're the artist,' I said, and then found the kitchen, which was tidy and uncluttered.

There were still droplets of water on the insides of glasses sitting upside down in a rack. Used very recently, probably within the last hour.

But beyond that, there was nothing on the counters or cabinets, and no pictures – no touch of home at all. For all the junk in the outer room, the mind behind this *was* ordered and operating in a stripped-down fashion. Whatever this place was, it was not a home.

That feeling hung with me when I returned to find Michele in the storage area with the lids off several buckets filled with metal parts, nails, and short lengths of iron rod. Seeing the contents, I became single-minded and walked down the hallway to the bedroom and the bath. I was positive we were in the right place; now we just needed to prove it.

In the bedroom I found stripped twin beds, two empty dressers, and bare walls. Except for a few hangers, the closet was also empty. And there was a bleach smell in the air. This was either the lair of someone who swept tracks or more likely someone who'd just cleared out.

'*Merde*,' I said.

'Gone?' Michele asked as she came into the room.

'Probably for good,' I said.

I took a step and raised the bedroom window shade, throwing light across the wood floor. By the discoloration, I could tell that there'd been a rug there by the bed, and by the scratches, a chair and table of some sort up against the wall.

I mentioned it, and Michele said, 'Drafting table.'

I pushed up the sash, looked out the bedroom window, and saw that the apartment below had a window box with churned earth and freshly planted flowers. Something small and golden that I couldn't make out sparkled in the dirt.

But I was more interested in the Dumpster in the alley directly below the window. People who leave places for good throw away their trash and whatever else they don't want before they move. I squinted. Was that a piece of a cell phone down there?

Intending to go back to the alley, I wandered into the bathroom, finding it also stripped except for a short stack of newspapers on a shelf by the toilet.

The papers were months old. Two were classified sections with circled ads for what Michele said were flea markets and junkyards. The other three were folded and featured partially done crossword puzzles. There were doodles of stars and geometric designs around the puzzles of the first two sections.

But there were no stars or boxes around the

344

third puzzle. Above it, however, there was a crude doodle in black felt pen that didn't make sense. But when I turned it upside down, Michele's breath caught in her throat.

'It's a study of a horse's leg,' she said. 'And look at the way it's drawn. That's *the* leg and rear haunch, positioned much as the statue of Al-Buraq was.'

I immediately took a picture of the sketch and sent it to Louis Langlois and Investigateur Hoskins, along with a text that read, 'Drawing of Al-Buraq's leg,' and the address.

I hit send, and we heard the dead bolt thrown.

Then the front door swung open.

Chapter 96

For me, everything became simple then. Whoever was coming into the apartment was part of AB-16, and given the group's actions until now, I had to assume they were armed, dangerous, and ready to kill, which meant I needed to be just as ready and just as deadly.

Setting the newspaper and horse drawing aside on the vanity, I motioned to Michele to stay quiet and not move. Then I slipped to the transom and listened to footsteps that entered, and stopped. The front door shut.

I took a peek and saw a big woman, short blond hair, dressed in hipster black. She had one of the bucket lids in her hands.

Which meant if she had a gun, she couldn't go for it easily. It was my opportunity, and I acted, stepping out into the hallway in a combat crouch, the Glock braced in two hands. We were no more than twenty-five feet apart.

I couldn't remember how to say 'Get down on the floor,' so I yelled, *'Asseyez-vous!'*

Sit down!

She jumped in alarm, twisted toward me in panic. I yelled at her again. But instead of going to the ground, she whipped the plastic bucket lid at me like a big Frisbee. She must have had mad disc skills because the lid came whizzing at me with surprising snap and accuracy. I had to bat it out of the air, which gave her the chance to flee.

'Damn it,' I said, and raced after her down the passage.

I should have slowed down, taken my time. Instead, I barreled into the choked living area like a stampeding bull. The blonde darted down the entry hall at the same time I caught motion to my left and was immediately hit with a spray of short sharp bits of metal.

Most of the shrapnel caught me on the right side of my face, and only reflexes prevented a piece from blinding me. It cut into my eyelid and blurred my vision. I lunged right, trying to get out of range so I could turn and shoot.

But when I tried, I tripped against one of the big buckets. By the time I regained my balance and was fighting for a sight picture, it was too late.

Haja Hamid had me dead to rights.

Crouched behind several stacks of magazines that covered her chest, she was aiming a pistol with a sound suppressor at me.

I froze.

And she tapped the trigger.

Her bullet smashed into the exposed grip panel of the Glock, just below my thumb. It was as if an electrified sledgehammer had hit my hand, causing it to close and inadvertently pull the trigger, discharging a round before the pistol slipped from my useless fingers and fell to the floor.

Even in that crowded space, the sound was deafening, disorienting. Blood was blinding my left eye. My right hand had gone completely numb. And from wrist to shoulder, my muscles twitched and my bones burned.

I realized that Haja was shouting at me, and that in shock, I'd gone to one knee, holding my useless arm. She came at me. The blonde returned. She shouted, but Haja couldn't hear, or wasn't listening.

Haja was getting a better angle. Maybe she'd aimed for my hand at first because she wanted to find out how much I knew before killing me. But my gun going off had ended that idea.

The shot would bring the police, and she had to be gone when they came. She would kill me now to cover her tracks. I could see it in her nickel-gray eyes when she stepped out from behind the stacks of magazines, raised her pistol, and aimed, two feet away, no more.

'Haja! Don't!'

Those were the first words I heard clearly after my gun went off, and they hadn't come from the blonde.

Michele Herbert was standing in the mouth of

the hallway, afraid, but insistent when Haja turned to her.

'Don't shoot, Haja! It's me, Michele!'

Seeing Michele surprised and broke something in Haja. Her arms, hands, and pistol began to sink.

It registered in my daze, and once again my marine training kicked in. I let go my damaged hand, and lunged at her.

My left shoulder hammered the side of her left knee. Haja crashed sideways. Her gun went off as she fell. I went frantic then, and scrambled up on top of her, straddling her legs. I saw her pain and hatred of me, and the fact that she no longer had the pistol.

But she'd found a nasty chunk of metal, and swung it hard at my head. I blocked it with my good arm, stunned at the raw power of her blow. Then she bucked against me. With her iron-worker strength she damn near threw me off.

Then she hit me in the face with the butt of her palm, caught me right under the jaw, and rocked me. She cocked back that hunk of metal again, meaning to finish me off.

Flinging out my left hand again, I caught the inside of her elbow, and then used the only other weapon I had.

My head became my hammer. I swung it with every bit of my remaining strength and felt my forehead crack and crush the bridge of her nose.

When I lifted my head, she was addled, and there was blood gushing from her nostrils. But I hit her a second time, just to make sure.

Panting, drenched in sweat, my face slick with

sweat and blood, I heard something, and looked to my right in time to see the blonde. She gripped a three-foot piece of angle iron, which was already in full swing at my head.

Halfway through the arc, I heard a thud.

The blonde hunched up and let go of the iron piece. It flung through the air, clipped my ear, and hit something behind me. Dumbly, she looked at me, and then down at her chest before going down in a breathless heap.

'Jack?' Michele said weakly. 'Help. Me.'

I pivoted. She was sitting up against a piece of busted furniture. Haja's pistol was in her lap, and her hands were clasped across her belly and blouse, where a dark rose of blood had bloomed.

Chapter 97

14TH ARRONDISSEMENT
6:12 P.M.

Sharen Hoskins pulled her car over in front of La Santé prison. She climbed out, came around the back door, and opened it for me.

I was in handcuffs. My face was swollen and held together by thirty-two stitches. A black patch covered antibiotic cream smeared over my sewn eyelid. My arm was in a sling, and my spiral-fractured wrist in a cast.

A dull throb had returned to my fingers and lower forearms as Hoskins led me, Juge Fromme, and Louis Langlois toward the security entrance.

Louis's doctor friend had figured out that he'd slightly dislocated the head of his tibia, and had snapped the bone back into place. But it was still so sore he could only walk as fast as the magistrate's top speed.

My chief concern, however, was Michele Herbert, who was still in surgery. I had put her there, gut shot, and it was killing me. The fact that I was walking up to prison doors instead of in vigil outside the operating room was killing me too. To my way of thinking, you owe a person who takes a bullet for you, and then saves your life by putting a bullet through someone else.

Two high-level French intelligence officers met us on the other side of security. The shorter, balder one introduced himself as La Roche. The taller, paler one told us his name was Rousseau. Both were probably operational handles.

'You are here as a courtesy, Morgan,' La Roche said in perfect English.

Rousseau said, 'Despite the fact that you broke enough laws to get you thrown in jail for thirty years, you risked your life multiple times to catch Hamid, and France owes you that much.'

'The handcuffs necessary?' I asked.

Juge Fromme cut the intelligence officers off before they could reply, saying, 'The minister of justice himself says those cuffs are staying right where they are until Mr. Morgan is placed on a jet leaving France.'

La Roche shrugged.

Admitting defeat, I asked, 'Has she said anything?'

350

'Hasn't had the chance,' La Roche replied. 'You busted her up pretty good, but the doctor says she's coming around. They're moving her to an interrogation room as we speak. Investigateur Hoskins? We'd like you to conduct the initial interrogation, along with Juge Fromme. All on tape, of course.'

Hoskins said, 'Why me? Why not some big counter-terror expert?'

'Because this began as a murder case,' Rousseau said. 'You know the details better than we do, so I want you to question her about the killings at the same time you ask about her accomplices, and their future plans.'

'Back and forth,' said La Roche. 'Keep her off-balance. If we have questions, we'll text you to come out of the room to hear them. Can you do that?'

'I'll try,' Hoskins said, and the magistrate nodded.

Soon after we started walking, Rousseau moved beside me and said, 'There are a few things I don't understand.'

'Only a few?' I said, wincing at my sutured and bandaged cheeks.

'Two, then. How did Professor Herbert know Haja Hamid? And how did you track her down so fast?'

As we made our way through the ruined halls of the old prison, I explained that Haja had attended the academy of fine arts on a scholarship for one year. Michele Herbert, an upper classman at the time, had been Haja's student adviser. She described Haja as an angry woman right from the start, someone who made life difficult for just about everyone she met. At the same time, she was passionate about her art, and had gravitated to metal sculpture and welding almost immediately.

Haja, Michele said, liked to play with fire and hammer heated metal, as if she were burning and beating her inner demons when she was working. After the first year, she left to go to a welding school.

'Haja told Professor Herbert that she'd learn all she needed to know there,' I told Rousseau as we reached the ultra-max security wing, where Ali Farad, the imam, and the others caught up in the AB-16 conspiracy were being held.

'Haja dropped off Michele's radar when she left,' I went on. 'The last the professor heard, she'd gone off to work somewhere in the south of France. When Michele saw the picture of the woman outside the mosque and recognized her, she called up the alumni office at the academy of fine arts, and asked if it had a forwarding address for Haja on record. There was one, and I blundered us into the hornet's nest that got Michele shot.'

'I know her surgeon,' Rousseau said. 'She's in good hands.'

The other intelligence officer asked, 'Did the professor know what Hamid was angry about back in school?'

'Michele didn't know,' I said. 'Haja wasn't the kind who opened up.'

'Did Herbert ever hear her speak of hating France, or supporting radical Islam?'

'She remembered Haja as happy to be in France,

glad to have left Africa, so Michele figured her anger was personal. And Islam? Michele said Haja was adamantly nonreligious, and apolitical. Do we know exactly where she's from, by the way? The professor couldn't remember.'

'Niger, in sub-Saharan West Africa,' La Roche said. 'By birth she's Tuareg, a desert nomad. On her citizenship application she listed no religion, and her occupation as 'welder and artist.'

We stopped near two doors guarded by counter-terrorists.

'People do change,' said Rousseau. 'Investigateur Hoskins, Juge Fromme: your job is to show us how much. Give us five minutes to get in position, and then go in.'

Chapter 98

The French intelligence officers led us into a soundproof booth that faced a two-way mirror into an interrogation space turned ICU.

Wearing a prison gown, Haja Hamid sat semi-upright in a hospital bed. She was lashed to it with restraints. An IV ran into her left arm. Her nose was bandaged and the rest of her face looked as though it had plowed into a brick wall. You could barely see her eyes for the swelling.

A nurse was taking her vitals. Haja had refused all pain medications.

'I want a lawyer,' she told the nurse, sounding like someone with the worst cold in history.

The nurse ignored her.

'I want a lawyer,' Haja said again. 'I know my rights.'

The nurse continued to ignore her. When the door opened and Fromme and Hoskins entered, the nurse immediately nodded and left.

'I want a lawyer,' Haja said.

'In due time,' Fromme replied, painfully moving into a chair.

'I know my rights.'

'You don't know your rights,' the magistrate said firmly. 'You have committed murder and acts of terrorism against France and her people, so the normal rules and rights don't apply. You'll see an attorney when I say you can.'

'Which means the more you cooperate, the sooner you see your lawyer,' Hoskins said, taking a seat by the bed.

'This is wrong,' Haja said.

'So is killing innocent people because they represent the best of my culture,' Fromme said.

Haja said nothing for several moments before spitting out her words. 'France is doomed no matter what you do to me. The Prophet's warhorse is in the skies and the dark Muslim horde is coming for you. You are already in a state of siege that will not end until France and all of Europe are taken.'

'That's your goal?' Hoskins asked. 'An Islamic republic in France?'

The sculptor hesitated, seemed to come to some decision, and then nodded. *'Inshallah.* We are willing to martyr ourselves to see that day come to pass. Every one of us. And our numbers grow

354

every day.'

'She's brazen,' Louis remarked on the other side of the mirror. 'Hasn't denied a thing.'

Hoskins said, 'Did you know Henri Richard?'

'The opera director?' Haja said rather quickly. 'Not personally, no.'

'Never came into contact with him?'

'No.'

'Who killed him?' Juge Fromme asked.

'I don't know,' Haja said. 'Things in AB-16 are kept cellular. We often don't know what other cells are doing for the cause.'

'Who do you take orders from?'

'Allah,' she replied.

'On earth,' Hoskins said.

'As it is in heaven, I take my orders from God.'

'Did Allah design the graffiti tag?' Fromme asked.

'An instrument of God did,' she said.

'But you built the statue,' Hoskins said.

'I was an instrument through which Allah expresses himself. If God wills it, it shall be done.'

The magistrate seemed to tire of this line of questioning, and returned to the murders. 'Did you kill or participate in the murder of René Pincus?'

'Me? No. I'm guilty of the statue and nothing more.'

'Bullshit,' I said.

'You were seen leaving the scene of a bombing,' Fromme said. 'The witness, Jack Morgan of Private, is willing to testify.'

'I've got nothing to say about that,' Haja said.

'I'm sure the prosecutors will have a lot to say

about it,' Hoskins snapped. 'And whose body burned in the linen factory fire? Was it Paul Piggott? Epée?'

Haja's puffy eyebrows rose at the question. 'I have no idea who that is, and body? Some bum must have snuck in after I left.'

Hoskins looked irritated. 'Is this a game to you?'

'No,' the sculptor snapped. 'This is war.'

Chapter 99

In the observation booth, Rousseau, the taller intelligence officer, said, 'That's one war you are going to lose, bitch.'

Haja asked for water. While Fromme poured it for her and held the cup and straw to her lips, I remembered something from earlier in the day.

'Do you have access to the list of evidence seized at her apartment?' I asked La Roche.

'It's still being processed,' he replied. 'From what I understand, there was so much stuff the floors were about to cave in.'

'I told La Crim about a busted cell phone I saw in the Dumpster beneath her bedroom window,' I said. 'Has anyone analyzed it yet?'

La Roche pondered me a moment, and then said, 'I'll find out.'

He left the room, and was not present when Hoskins said, 'Were you involved in the killing of Lourdes Latrelle?'

'No,' Haja said. 'That was another cell of believers.'

'Minister of culture Guy LaFont?' Fromme
asked.

'No, though I heard it might be coming.'

'From?'

'Amé, my dead friend, and martyr.'

'You're referring to the blonde who died in your
apartment? Amé Thies?' the magistrate asked.

'Who else?'

'Where did she hear that LaFont might be
assassinated?'

'Can't help you. She had the contacts. I didn't.'

'I don't believe you,' Hoskins said sharply. 'You
need to start leveling with us if you want to have
some chance of seeing daylight ever again.'

Haja responded smugly, 'You can't offer me
hope, *madame investigateur*. I know my fate and
accept it as any true believer would.'

'Were you involved in the death of Millie
Fleurs?' Fromme pressed.

Haja almost laughed. 'I can honestly say I never
heard a thing about her being a target. Jacques
Noulan? Maybe. But not Millie Fleurs.'

'You're again saying another cell was responsible?' Fromme insisted.

'Your guess is as good as mine,' she replied.
'And I need more water.'

Neither magistrate nor investigator moved a
muscle.

'You deny me water?' Haja asked. 'That's
torture. That's what that is.'

Hoskins's lower lip curled inward. She stood,
poured Haja more water, and held the cup out to

her. As Haja sipped through the straw, I started thinking about how she had been angry, not religious, and apolitical when Michele knew her.

What had turned her to this? When was that moment?

Hoskins set the cup on the bed stand and sat back down, asking, 'You regularly attend services at the mosque in Barbès?'

'Not regularly,' Haja replied. 'But at times.'

Fromme asked, 'Is the imam part of AB-16?'

She didn't answer at first, but then said, 'Al-Moustapha? Of course he's part of it. And Firmus Massi. How do you think we communicated? Through FEZ Couriers. We're all part of AB-16. We're all out to change France. And we're all willing to spend time in jail because we know it won't be long before the prison doors are thrown open and we are rescued by the mob.'

'Ali Farad of Private Paris?' the magistrate asked. 'He in AB-16 too?'

'A great soldier of the revolution,' Haja said.

I didn't know why, but in my gut I didn't buy it. Then again, I didn't have to buy it. A jury did, and on these counts Haja sounded confident enough to convince one. One thing was sure now: Ali Farad faced life in prison.

La Roche returned to the observation booth, and his partner filled him in on what Haja had said. La Roche glanced at me and Louis as if trying to decide whether to kick us out. Guilt by association.

Instead, he said, 'Nothing on the phone, Morgan. They found both pieces, but no SIM card.'

Frustrated, I forced my attention back to the

interrogation, wondering once again about the source of Hamid's anger during her time at the academy of fine arts. If she was a terrorist from the beginning, a sleeper sent to France, was showing anger back then carelessness on her part? Or an inability to mask her hatred of France?

Then again, Michele had said she believed Haja's anger was personal. Was the anger connected to her willingness to join AB-16? If yes, I decided, the source of her anger had to be deep and violent.

Back in Africa, back in Niger, did someone French murder someone close to her? A sibling? Or was Haja raped at some point? By a Frenchman? Was she beaten or had she watched someone close to her beaten? Was she...?

Stark images from the week before flickered in my mind.

Now *that* would be enough to make her angry, wouldn't it?

I thought so. Very angry. Spitting angry. Maybe in a constant rage at what life had done to her. But is it true? Simple test, right? But say it *is* true. How does that translate into her being willing to spend her life in prison for the...

It dawned on me then.

'What if there's another explanation?' I asked Louis and the intelligence officers. 'What if we have this all wrong?'

'What are you talking about?' Louis said.

'Text Hoskins and Fromme,' I said to La Roche. 'Tell them to come out.'

Ten minutes later, we were all gathered down the hall from the interrogation room, and I was finishing up explaining my theory and the evidence that supported it.

The French intelligence officers looked skeptical at best, but I could see that Fromme was chewing it over, and Hoskins was keeping an open mind.

'Doesn't hurt to ask,' the magistrate said at last. 'It's either true or not, and she sure can't hide a thing like that.'

Chapter 100

We watched from the booth as Hoskins and Fromme reentered the interrogation room.

'I've cooperated,' Haja said. 'Can I see a lawyer now?'

'A few more questions,' the magistrate said, sitting on a chair to the sculptor's right and leaning over his cane.

Hoskins, who stood on the other side of the bed, said, 'Michele Herbert described you as angry when you were at the academy of fine arts.'

'I don't remember that,' Haja said.

'Was it your hatred of France that made you angry?'

Haja paused and said, 'Maybe. I was disgusted with the decadence of Paris.'

Fromme said, 'So you came to France already a radical follower of Islam? Is that right?'

'It was my fate. Part of my calling.'

Hoskins reached into a folder and took out an

eight-by-ten photograph. 'Is this you?' She held the picture up to her, and even through the swelling, I could see shock registering.

The *investigateur* saw it too and said, 'You didn't know Henri Richard was taking pictures of you two having sex with him dressed as a priest and you in a robe and hijab?'

'I don't know what you're talking about,' Haja said. 'That's not me.'

Hoskins said, 'Do I need to use force? Strip-search and photograph you myself? Or do I spare you that indignity?'

The bomber and sculptor closed her eyes.

After several long beats, Fromme said insistently, 'Is that you, madame?'

'Yes,' Haja said at last. 'It's me.'

'Who did that to you? Who mutilated you like that?'

'It doesn't matter,' Haja said, opening her eyes.

'Oh, I think it does matter,' Hoskins insisted. 'I think it matters a great deal to you. I think your castration is the source of your anger.'

'I stopped being angry about that a long time ago. It was the will of Allah.'

'That's how you react after having your clitoris cut off because of Islam? You think it was right and proper for your father's religion to lop off one of your body parts so you could never enjoy having sex?'

'Islam is submission,' Haja said. 'Submission to God's will. Once I submitted, I was able to see the rightness of Islam. It's what I fight for.'

'You want an alternative explanation? One that Jack Morgan is floating?'

At hearing my name, Hamid shifted and said, 'What's that?'

'Morgan thinks it's possible that you're fighting for something else entirely,' the *investigateur* said. 'He thinks because of your resentment over your mutilation, you planted evidence against the imam and the others to stir things up, create a mob mentality, promote a civil and racial war in France.'

Haja snorted. 'And what good would that do me?'

'It might just drive Islam from this country,' Hoskins said. 'It might just cleanse your adopted society of the religion that butchered you.'

'Mr. Morgan has quite the imagination, but he is dead wrong.'

'You deny wanting a civil war?' Fromme said.

'I want a coup d'état.'

'How do we know you're not lying?'

'Why would I?'

'Why wouldn't you?' Hoskins cried. 'You lied about knowing Henri Richard. And here we have pictures of him buried in your mutilation, pictures sure to come out in court and make your humiliation complete.'

Haja's hatred shimmered through her swollen features before she closed her puffy eyes and said, 'Burn in hell, bitch. I'm not saying another word until I have a lawyer present.'

Chapter 101

MONTFERMEIL, EASTERN SUBURBS OF PARIS
7:20 P.M.

Major Sauvage left General Georges's evening briefing at a crisp pace, with Captain Mfune hard at his shoulder.

'What are we going to do?' Mfune muttered.

'Not here,' Sauvage said sharply

The major found Corporal Perry, a young, scrawny kid assigned to drive him, and told Perry to catch another ride back to their position. Then he ordered Mfune to take the wheel of the Renault Sherpa.

Tan, squat, and plated with armor, the Sherpa looked like the head of some prehistoric reptile. It was imposing, and people tended to get out of its way the second they saw it. The big machine gun up top helped. It was an AA-52, the machine gun that French soldiers referred to as La Nana, or the maid, because it cleaned up. Sauvage had seen a combo of the Sherpa and La Nana work all the time in Afghanistan. The Taliban ran like hell when they saw them coming.

Mfune pulled the armored vehicle out into traffic and said, 'Major?'

'You heard the briefing,' Sauvage said. 'Haja's staying on story. She's sacrificing everything.'

363

'With all due respect, sir, Amé sacrificed everything,' Mfune said. 'Haja is still alive. Haja could change her mind.'

'She could if she was normal, but she's not, so she won't,' the major reasoned. 'And because of that, the powers that be will have to take her at her word, and act accordingly. In fact, if you think about it, she's in a unique position to convince them that the AB-16 threat is real and growing.'

'Another layer of disinformation,' Mfune said.

'Exactly,' Sauvage said.

'So we do nothing for the time being?' Mfune asked. 'Let the uprising build on its own?'

Sauvage thought about that. It was a good question.

He considered his options for several moments, and then said, 'No, I think it's time we show France what a little fighting back would look like. Get more of the home team behind us.'

The captain said, 'Without provocation, sir? Is that advisable?'

'Of course not,' Sauvage said. 'We'll create provocation, and then *la pagaille*, in the chaos of battle, we'll retaliate. Hard.'

Chapter 102

14TH ARRONDISSEMENT
8:15 P.M.

Leaving La Santé, I was aware of the prison's cold hard walls and the fates of the people inside. Haja Hamid deserved to be in there.

But Imam Al-Moustapha? And Ali Farad?

Though Haja had denied it, I was still entertaining the possibility that her motives were opposite the ones she cited. In that scenario, the sculptor was prepared to suffer, and she was prepared to make innocent men suffer with her.

Juge Fromme broke me from my thoughts. 'As helpful and insightful as you've been, Mr. Morgan, Investigateur Hoskins must now take you to a holding cell until the minister of justice sees fit to deport or release you.'

'This is ridiculous,' Louis fumed.

Fromme growled, 'Carrying a handgun without a license. Carrying a handgun in the commission of a crime. These are crimes we take seriously in France, Louis. Or have you forgotten?'

Louis looked ready to argue, but I said, 'You'll take off the cuffs if I'm in a cell? Get me some pain meds?'

'Yes.'

'Can we go by the hospital first so I can check in on Michele Herbert?'

'That's not happening,' Hoskins said. 'But I'll get you an update.'

We returned to the police car we'd taken to the prison, and I was climbing in the backseat when Louis's cell rang. He answered, listened, and said, 'Here. I'll let him explain.'

Louis hit speaker, and I said, 'It's Jack.'

'Where are you?' Justine asked. 'And where have you been the last day and a half?'

'I'm on my way to jail,' I said. 'And the last thirty-six hours are too complicated to go into at the moment.'

There was a pause. 'What are you charged with?'

'Multiple felony counts. How's Kim and Sherman?'

'They had a truth and reconciliation meeting before she went to Betty Ford. Kim fessed up, told her grandfather everything.'

'How'd Sherman take it?'

'He's grateful she's alive. He also sent over a check this morning for one hundred and fifty thousand dollars, and a note asking if it was enough.'

'That'll do,' I said. 'Transfer half to the Private Paris bonus account.'

'That's enough,' Fromme grumbled from the front seat. 'You're in custody, not business. End that call. Now.'

'You heard the judge,' I said. 'Gotta go.'

Louis ended the conversation. As he put the device away, I thought about how cut off I was without a phone, and what a valuable tool it was for someone in my line of work. A phone keeps you mobile, not tied down to a desk, and yet able to access information when you need it. A very good thing.

And if we were lucky enough to get hold of a bad guy's phone, well, that was like hitting the mother lode, finding the keys to the kingdom. Thinking back to that busted cell phone I'd seen in the Dumpster below Haja Hamid's bedroom window, I felt reasonably sure that it had been hers or Amé's.

How had that worked? Had the burn phone been broken and tossed in the alley, or from Haja's bedroom window?

I shut my eyes, tried to imagine the pieces sailing out the window, falling through the scaffolding, tried to envision the trajectories the pieces might have taken ... falling to the...

'Turn around,' I said.

'Why?' said Hoskins.

'No,' Fromme said firmly. 'He goes to–'

'Haja's apartment. Turn around.'

'That is an active crime scene of a killing in which you are a suspect,' the judge shot back. 'You'll never be allowed in, and neither will we.'

'Then call someone there,' I said. 'I think there's something we missed.'

Chapter 103

SEVRAN, NORTHEASTERN
SUBURBS OF PARIS
10:04 P.M.

The chaos of battle! Major Sauvage thought with growing pleasure and excitement. *La pagaille! It's coming, so close I can smell it. Kill them now, soldier. Vanquish them. Drive them from our land.*

As all this played in his head, Sauvage was pacing inside his command post in an abandoned building, drinking coffee, and monitoring the radio traffic from the six units under him. He was waiting for one of the hot spots to gather wind and throw sparks. So far, however, there'd been little to suggest a repeat of yesterday evening's chaos: the bombing, Haja's burning horse, and all the violence those two masterstrokes had spawned.

He thought of Haja, and knew without a doubt that she *would* sacrifice herself to their cause. She was that noble. She was that committed.

Sauvage admired her greatly. To the extent that he could, the major even loved her, and it made him sick that he might never see her again.

His burn phone rang. Had to be Mfune. Seeing the junior officers inside the command center caught up in their work, he slipped outside. He didn't recognize the number, and almost didn't answer.

Then he did, and said, 'Yes?'

'Chloe there?' a woman said in a voice thick with alcohol.

'You've got the wrong number, madame,' he said.

'You're sure? I punched the number she put in my contacts last night.'

'If Chloe did that, she's either stupid or nuts,' Sauvage said, and ended the call.

The major hesitated, and then hit redial. The other phone rang twice.

'Chloe?' the woman said.

Sauvage cut the call, and went back to waiting for a mob to appear.

It wasn't until shortly after midnight that the first gunshots were reported around La Forêt – the Forest – a housing project six kilometers northeast of his position on the northern border of the Bondy Forest.

The major called Captain Mfune on the radio. 'Take the convoy jammers and triangulate the entire place. I'm coming behind you with two full units.'

'Rules of engagement?'

'If fired upon, defend yourselves.'

'Roger that,' Mfune said, and signed off.

Sauvage grabbed his flak jacket, helmet, and sidearm, saying, 'Let's move, Corporal Perry.'

The major got in the Sherpa, climbed into the backseat, and pushed up the roof hatch.

Taking goggles and a radio headset from a hook by the hatch, the major wriggled up through the opening and got in position behind the machine gun.

Moments after his driver and the sergeant who usually manned the turret gun climbed in, Sauvage's headset crackled. 'Where to, sir?' the corporal asked.

'La Forêt housing project. Patch me into all radio traffic in the area.'

'Roger that, sir,' the corporal said.

They pulled out and headed north.

Sauvage loved his station in life at that moment, riding high above the streets behind La Nana and a whole lot of accurate ammunition. Was there anything better?

The major's brain replayed savored bits of past trips into the chaos of battle, and he felt his body warm. The radio traffic only fed his excitement. There were reports of armed men in the streets around the housing project, and snipers.

In Sauvage's mind, the sniping was more than enough provocation to retaliate with force, regardless of whether someone was hit or not. He trembled with an addict's anticipation then, knowing for certain that he was on the verge of slipping into the familiar insanity and lethal bliss of *la pagaille*.

Chapter 104

LA FORÊT, NORTHEASTERN
SUBURBS OF PARIS
APRIL 13, 12:44 A.M.

Nine seedy totalitarian-style high-rise buildings made up La Forêt housing project. Four sat to the left of a central access road, and five to the right. The project bordered a crescent-shaped wetland. If you made a straight line through the Bondy Forest, it was less than six miles from Les Bosquets.

Some of those AK-47s have got to be here, Sauvage thought as the Sherpa rolled to a stop two blocks from the eastern edge of the project. How many? Five or six at least. But perhaps as many as ten or fifteen were taken out of Les Bosquets, and then smuggled through the woods.

Mfune's voice came over the headset. 'Convoy jammers in position.'

The jammers were state-of-the-art Argos designed to interrupt all cellular and walkie-talkie traffic within five hundred yards. With three of the Argos in place, the housing project was a dead zone, which is how Sauvage wanted it.

'Turn them on,' the major said. 'Shift all comm to C.'

'Yes, sir.'

The headset went dead. The major ducked down

371

into the Sherpa, looked at the gunner sergeant, and said, 'You'll mobilize here as part of the perimeter.'

'Here, sir?' the sergeant said.

Sauvage nodded. 'You're to stop and search anyone seen fleeing that project. If they have weapons of any kind, arrest and restrain them.'

The sergeant pursed his lips and got out, shutting the door behind him.

'Change to C frequency, Corporal Perry,' Sauvage said.

The driver looked uneasy. 'Protocol says B under these—'

'Perry, are you being insubordinate?'

'No sir!'

'Then do as I say,' Sauvage snapped. 'Intelligence indicates that AB-16 may be monitoring police and military frequencies.'

He knew nothing of the sort, but it worked. His driver typed in the new frequency on the Sherpa's in-dash computer.

'Well done, Corporal,' Sauvage said. 'Going topside.'

The major crawled up through the port again and got his boots solidly in the stirrups below before triggering his mic.

'Captain Mfune?'

'Roger.'

'Put two-man teams on every corner two blocks back from the target,' he ordered. 'You stay mobile on that perimeter. Catch the cats as they run.'

'You're playing rat tonight?'

'Affirmative,' Sauvage said.

There was a pause, and then, 'Good luck, Major.'

'Roger that,' he replied. 'Corporal Perry?'

'Major?'

'You're recon-trained?'

'Yes, sir.'

'So you know what a rat patrol is?'

'Seek out the enemy and draw fire, sir.'

'Are you a brave man, Corporal Perry?'

'I'm a recon soldier, sir.'

'Then do your duty. Advance east. Cruise the perimeter of the project.'

'Done, sir.'

The Sherpa rolled toward La Forêt. Sauvage put both hands on the machine gun, swept away in the heightened awareness he longed and lived for.

He felt the way he used to in Afghanistan, when the sky was moonless and armies were moving. He sensed the tension that built before *la pagaille*, waiting for the first shot, the first flare, the first rocket streaking across the sky.

It was where he belonged.

I'm coming home, he thought ecstatically. *Coming home right–*

A gunshot ripped the night. Someone was shooting in the project.

'You hear that, Corporal Perry?'

'Affirmative, sir.'

'Bear right along the perimeter. Take the first entrance in, road or path.'

The Sherpa swung right onto a narrow two-lane road. The streetlamps were dead. A block away, two cars had been turned sideways, bumper to bumper, spanning the street, and set afire. Two other cars were burning and blocking the road a hundred yards beyond, up against the Bondy Forest.

Between the two barriers, a mob of young men guarded the main entrance into the project. Most held knives or machetes, clubs, Molotov cocktails, or stones. Sheets had been hung in the trees. There was Arabic writing on them that Sauvage read easily.

We fight for the prophet's warhorse!

Even better, Sauvage thought.

Then he barked, 'Straight at them, Corporal Perry! Show them how the Sherpa works at ramming speed!'

Chapter 105

With a lurch that threw the major against the back of the turret, Perry buried the accelerator. The armored car hurtled at the burning barrier.

'Brace for impact!' his driver shouted.

Sauvage leaned into the crash as the Sherpa's massive steel bumper blew through the two cars, sending them spinning out of the way.

Perry screeched the armored vehicle to a halt thirty yards from the mob, which had begun to break up and scatter. But ten or more men stood their ground, screaming at Sauvage. They hurled stones and then a Molotov cocktail that burst into flames in front of the Sherpa.

Provocation if there ever was, the major thought. He flipped the safety lever on the machine gun and almost pulled the trigger. But he held his fire and said, 'Straight ahead, Perry. Get them running.'

Perry steered around the fire and accelerated toward the lingering rioters, who turned and fled into the housing project.

'Follow them,' Sauvage said.

His eyes went everywhere, from the youth in the headlights to the dimly lit grounds and the glowing windows of the nearest high-rise, where residents were looking out fearfully.

C'mon, the major thought. *Let's do this.*

But they passed the first building without incident.

'Left,' Sauvage commanded.

The Sherpa rolled into a bare dirt common area between the first and second apartment towers.

C'mon, the major thought. *I'm giving it to you on a plate. Do it or I'm going to lose my faith in—*

The shot came from six or seven stories up in the second tower, and smacked off the hood of the Sherpa.

Defective bullets in lots slated for disposal have a way of not shooting where you aim them, the major thought in amusement. *Especially when they're shot from guns with faulty sights.*

The 7.5mm cartridges in La Nana, on the other hand, were top grade, and its sights sharply calibrated. He aimed the muzzle of the maid where he thought the shot had come from and mashed the trigger.

The machine gun rattled and shook, spitting death at the upper floors of the second building. Spent casings flipped all around Sauvage as the bullets gouged the walls and shattered windows in the general area where he thought the sniper had his perch. In Sauvage's mind, casualties were irrelevant.

There was a deep silence after the six-second machine gun burst, and then from both buildings he heard screams and wails of fear, grief, and agony that all melded into one quivering howl about the injustice of combat.

Well, thought Sauvage, don't harbor fucking Islamic terrorists and this kind of shit won't happen.

'Drive on, Corporal.'

'Major? Are you– '

'Take an S pattern through the remaining buildings, Perry!' he roared. 'We have to know which ones need to be swept floor to floor.'

'Yes, sir!' Perry cried, and drove on.

Gunfire sounded in the distance. Sauvage's radio headset crackled.

'We're getting fire from the north,' Captain Mfune said.

'Engage,' the major said, hearing more shots within seconds.

As they rolled on, Sauvage watched the upper floors of the building he'd just shot at, and saw no one at any window, shattered or whole. That worked in his favor. No witnesses meant that his version of events would be the one accepted.

They rounded the far end of the second building and passed between it and the third, with no shots fired and no one watching out the windows. Even without cell phones, word of his coming had spread. Bullets had a way of transcending all forms of communication.

All remained quiet as the Sherpa drove slowly between the third and fourth buildings and then along the fourth apartment tower's far side, which bordered a swampy area.

But when the Sherpa crossed the lane that divided the housing project in two, there was a burst of gunfire from the second building on Sauvage's right. He saw the muzzle flash clearly as the defective bullets, shot from beyond the Sterling's optimum distance, skipped harmlessly off the pavement.

'Hard right, then left, Corporal,' Sauvage said, already locking on the crosshairs of La Nana's sights.

Perry complied without comment. The Sherpa tacked twice toward the second sniper, who was on the sixth floor, four windows in.

The major was about to shoot when he noticed a woman in a robe and head scarf standing at the window of an apartment on the third floor. She was holding up a cell phone as if photographing or videoing his actions.

Sauvage took careful aim and shot her first.

Chapter 106

For eight full seconds, until the ammunition was spent, Sauvage raked machine gun fire above, below, and on either side of that sixth floor window where the sniper had been.

'Move, Perry! Evasive,' the major barked. 'I'm reloading.'

The Sherpa picked up speed. It wove back and forth while Sauvage fed a new chain of ammunition into La Nana.

Raindrops hit the machine gun's superheated barrel and hissed as Perry took a right around the near high-rise. The major was already locked and loaded when the corporal took another right that put them in a long U-shaped space, with buildings to either side and a third at the far end.

Many of the rioters had regrouped in the common area. As Perry closed the gap between them, Molotov cocktails flew through the air and exploded. Then one of the rioters fired an AK-47 that damn near killed Sauvage. He heard the sound barrier break when the bullet blew past his ear.

The mob turned and fled as one.

'Full pursuit, Corporal!' the major ordered.

Perry sped after the rioters. Sauvage triggered his microphone and said, 'Captain Mfune, I have armed AB-16 sympathizers heading your way.'

He heard nothing in return, but his focus was

378

on that gang of thirty or forty rioters running in the Sherpa's headlights toward the apartment building that formed the bottom of the U. They did what he thought they'd do: split into two groups. The majority went left, back toward the entrance. But about twelve of them broke to the right, including the one carrying the AK-47.

'Cut the small group off!' the major shouted.

Perry swung the Sherpa hard right, accelerated, and got out in front of the escaping rioters before skidding to a stop in the narrow gap between the buildings. Two of the rioters turned on a dime and took off the other way.

Seeing Sauvage training La Nana on them, the ten others, including the rifleman, dropped their weapons and threw up their hands.

The major noted the fear and loathing in their faces, and then pulled the trigger, mowing them all down in a single three-second burst.

'Major Sauvage!' Perry screamed. 'Jesus Christ! Jesus Christ!'

Sauvage ignored him, wriggling out of the turret and jumping off the roof. With his back to the corporal, the major walked ten steps toward the bodies.

'Jesus, Major,' Perry choked out the open window. 'They gave up.'

Crouching, Sauvage picked up the AK-47 amid the twitching corpses, pivoted, and aimed at his young driver.

'Sorry it had to be you, Perry,' he said. 'But this story needs a saint.'

Terror registered on the young corporal's face before Sauvage put two rounds through the driver's forehead and six more around him through the open window

The major reached into his pocket to tug out a handkerchief to wipe the Sterling down. He caught motion back at the open end of the common area.

He looked closer and saw Jack Morgan running back toward the entrance to the project, his arm in a sling. Even at this, the major could tell from his body language that Morgan had seen him turn the gun on his own man and maybe more.

Sauvage threw the Sterling to his shoulder, found Morgan in his sights, and fired just before he made the corner.

Chapter 107

Bullets smashed off the wall five feet from me and sent me into an all-out sprint to get away.

Even with one eye patched, I'd seen it all, from Sauvage's Sherpa cutting off the rioters to them dropping their weapons and throwing up their hands. I saw the major open fire. I saw him slaughter ten young men, many of them teenagers, unarmed and in surrender.

It had unfolded so surreally that I had just stood there in shock and disbelief, shoeless and with mud dripping off my pants, watching Sauvage jump down, pick up the gun, and shoot his driver in cold blood.

Nothing had prepared me for that. Nothing

could have.

My will to survive kicked in then. I'd started running in my muddy stocking feet, and Sauvage had tried to kill me. Safely behind the building, I kept running, not toward the wetland I'd used to access the housing project but toward the main entrance. As I ran, I dug in my pocket for the cell Louis had given me not fifteen minutes before.

I hit send, then speaker, and dodged out into another common area, this one with children's jungle gyms and swings in it. I took a quick look right, expecting to find Sauvage flanking me. But there was no one, and I ran on. The phone started to jangle weirdly. It wasn't working for some reason.

I had to get back to the street. I had to get to protection. I had to tell someone what I'd seen.

Breaking out from behind the building closest to the street, I cut toward a sparse grove of trees that separated me from the entrance. I reached the narrow road that divided the housing project and was forty yards from the exit when Sauvage stepped out from the shadows to my right, his cheek welded to the stock of the assault rifle.

I skidded to a stop, threw up my good hand, and said loudly, 'I'm unarmed, Major.'

'Don't know what you think you saw back there,' Sauvage said quietly. 'But I just can't let you go telling any lies about–'

'I am unarmed, Major!' I bellowed.

'I don't care.'

Chapter 108

Major Sauvage was going to love this moment.

I could see it in his expression as his finger began to squeeze the–

'Stand down, Major!' a man shouted through a bullhorn. 'Stand down and drop your weapon!'

Multiple headlights flashed on from out on the road, catching us in profile, Sauvage ready and willing to end my life and me just frozen there, wondering if this was the end of everything.

The major began to swing the gun toward the blinding lights, as if he meant to snuff them out along with whoever was demanding his surrender.

'This is General Anton Georges. I order you to drop that gun, Major. Now!'

Sauvage took that like a slap. He glanced at me, but then calmly set down the gun on the pavement. He stepped back, stood there. Engines started. Three sets of headlights came toward us, and stopped.

The lights dimmed, revealing General Georges climbing out of another Sherpa while soldiers on foot came in behind him, their weapons at the ready. Then Louis Langlois limped up out of the shadows behind Sauvage.

I nodded to him that I was okay.

'Pistol on the ground too, Major,' the general said.

'Sir,' Sauvage replied, calmly removing the pistol and setting it down. 'This man was inside my perimeter without authorization, abetting the enemy.'

'That's bullshit,' I said.

General Georges glared at me, and in surprisingly good English said, 'You, sir, defied my direct orders.'

I said, 'General, you can put me in chains and you'd be right to do it, but I witnessed an atrocity here just a few minutes ago.'

'He witnessed ten armed members of AB-16 confronting me,' Sauvage said. 'They killed my driver and were trying to kill me when I opened fire.'

'They had dropped their weapons and surrendered,' I said. 'All ten of them. He gunned them down in cold blood, and then took that rifle there from one of the dead guys and used it to shoot his own man, again in cold blood.'

'He's delusional, General!' Sauvage cried. 'This American fool has no understanding of war, of combat, of *la pagaille* and what the chaos of battle can do to your perceptions. Either that, or he is an AB-16 sympathizer.'

'General Georges,' I said. '*I* was honorably discharged with the rank of captain from the United States Marine Corps. I did two full tours in Afghanistan as a combat helicopter pilot. I know an atrocity when I see one.'

Before Sauvage could respond, I kept right on going, poking my finger at the major. 'AB-16 is a charade, General, just like I told you. I'm betting AB-16 was his idea from the start. I'm betting he orchestrated the entire–'

'This is a fucking outrage!' Sauvage roared. 'I will not have my unblemished reputation destroyed by–'

Two soldiers dragged Captain Mfune onto the scene, his wrists cuffed behind his back. He stared at Sauvage as if he were his only hope now.

'I don't know what they're thinking, Major,' Mfune said.

'What have you done, General?' Sauvage demanded. 'Captain Mfune is an outstanding, decorated, and battle-tested officer who–'

General Georges held up his hand and said, 'Investigateur Hoskins? Juge Fromme?'

Several soldiers stood aside, and the police detective and the magistrate stepped forward. Hoskins held a cell phone up in the air and pressed her thumb against it.

In one of Major Sauvage's pants pockets, a phone began to buzz and ring.

'Answer it,' Hoskins said. 'I'm looking for Chloe.'

Chapter 109

In my life I have encountered men and women whose dark stories were written in every line of twisted emotion that squirmed across their faces. But I had never seen a reaction that spoke novels before.

Disbelief. Defeat. Dread. Honor. Conviction. Anger.

All those feelings flickered on Sauvage's face before he went stoic.

'Why do you have my phone number?' he asked.

'That's not your cell,' Juge Fromme said. 'We checked. It's a disposable.'

I said, 'After your accomplice Haja Hamid busted her burn phone, she tossed the pieces out her bedroom window. Two pieces landed in a Dumpster. But the SIM card hit the scaffolding and landed in a flower box a story below. Hoskins called the last number Haja called, and we got you. I recognized that phrase you like to use – that some person is "either stupid or nuts."'

'This proves nothing,' Sauvage said firmly. 'Since I have owned this phone, I have gotten many wrong numbers. As if the number had been used many times. The fact that this Haja person called me is pure coincidence.'

I laughed in disbelief. 'Major, you are without a doubt the most cold-blooded, conniving, lying bastard I have ever met. You, Haja, and Captain Mfune here murdered five of France's finest people to try to set off a war *against* Islam.'

'Why in God's name would I do that?' he said calmly, though the muscles on his neck were stretched as taut as piano wire.

'Because for whatever reason you and Captain Mfune hate Muslims as much as Haja does,' Louis said.

'And because,' I said, 'starting a war against them would give you the opportunity to engage in the kind of atrocity I just witnessed. We've read up on you. We know you were investigated for brutality in Afghanistan.'

'General,' Sauvage said, 'this is slanderous and un–'

'Enough!' General Georges bellowed. 'Major Sauvage, Captain Mfune: you are under arrest for murder, conspiracy, and treason against France, a nation you were both sworn to protect.'

The captain hung his head. But not Sauvage. He laughed scornfully. 'Treason?' he said, and thumped his chest. 'Against France? The country that we love more than life?

'No, General. If anything, the captain and I are France's greatest patriots. We are the only ones willing to see the obvious: that this nation is already at war, and has been since we started letting Muslim immigrants come here in the sixties. Look at the massacre at Charlie Hebdo last year. They want our culture erased, and their numbers are growing faster than ours. Unless people like Captain Mfune and me and Haja Hamid act, France as we know it will be destroyed, and–'

General Georges cut him off, thundering, 'By any definition and despite any intentions you may have had, you, sir, are a dishonor to your uniform, and you *will* be tried for your crimes against your country, against Paris, and against humanity. What you did tonight? We call that genocide where I come from. Cuff him. Get him the hell out of my sight.'

Four soldiers surrounded Sauvage, who stood with his head held high and defiant, glaring at all of us in turn. They put zip restraints on him and pushed him forward.

From the windows of the immigrant housing

386

towers, people began to cheer and jeer and trill like nomads calling in the desert.

The major went berserk as he and Mfune were led away.

'You hear them!' he shouted at us. 'The Muzzies want people like me silenced. They want the great cathedrals and monuments of Paris burned or reduced to rubble and built up again as grand mosques. Our food. Our music. Our free speech. Our culture will be swallowed whole and turned to shit if they're not stopped!'

Ignoring Sauvage's rants as they faded, General Georges marched up to me and said in open fury, 'Morgan, by rights you should be in a brig along with him. You did exactly what I explicitly ordered you not to do.'

I hung my head. 'Yes, General. But I knew you were handcuffed, awaiting your rules of engagement. And, I don't know, I heard the pace of the shooting, and I thought – well, both Louis and I thought – that someone had to come in here and bear witness. So I did.'

'And it's a good thing he did,' Hoskins said.

The general stood there fuming. 'I don't know what to do with you.'

I said, 'Let me show investigators what I saw and where I saw it from, and then I'll go home. When I'm needed, I'll return to testify at my own expense.'

Georges continued to stand there and fume.

Juge Fromme said, 'General, I'm sure the minister of justice will agree to Monsieur Morgan's proposal. He's as sick of Morgan as you are, and wants him out of France as soon as possible.'

The general said, 'It's on the minister, then. After Morgan makes his statement, I want him taken straight to de Gaulle and put on the first plane out of Paris.'

Nodding, I said, 'With one important stop on the way.'

I thought the general was going to punch me.

Chapter 110

11TH ARRONDISSEMENT
8:04 A.M.

Michele Herbert was awake but drowsy when I knocked on her hospital room door. I still had mud all over me and wore a pair of ill-fitting boots that one of the soldiers had given me. I hadn't showered or shaved or slept. I hadn't even been allowed to return to the Plaza Athénée to pay my bill or gather my things. They sent Louis to do all that, with orders to meet me at de Gaulle.

'What are you doing here?' she asked in a weak, slurred voice.

'I owe you dinner for saving my life,' I said, and produced a cup of ice chips.

Michele smiled wanly. *'Bon appétit.'*

'They say you're going to be okay.'

She nodded, swallowed, and gestured at the television, which was on mute and showing still shots of Sauvage, Mfune, and Hamid.

'I saw what happened,' she said.

'Fighting back. You were an important part of it.'

'Too much hatred in the world,' she said.

'Agreed,' I said.

'Not enough love.'

'Double agreed.'

Michele smiled again, and blinked sleepily.

'They're booting me out of France,' I said. 'My jet's coming in to get me in a couple of hours.'

'Your jet?'

Before I could reply, a man said, 'What the hell is he doing in here?'

Looking over my injured shoulder, I saw François, her agent with the crazy hair, coming into the room with a cup of coffee.

'Paying my respects,' I said.

'You almost got her killed!' François shouted. 'One of the greatest artists of her time and you almost kill her!'

'François,' Michele said. 'He uncovered the AB-16 plot.'

'I don't care,' François said. 'He's a danger to you, Michele.'

That seemed to amuse her. She looked at me. 'True?'

'I hope not,' I said, and then caught something out of the corner of my eye on the screen. 'Do you have the controls for the television?'

'Please leave,' François said. 'You're not wanted here.'

'On the table,' Michele said.

I turned off the mute. We watched as Imam Al-Moustapha, FEZ Couriers owner Firmus Massi, and Ali Farad were released from La Santé prison. They each made a brief statement condemning the intent of AB-16, swearing their allegiance to France, and reiterating their belief in nonviolence.

The screen cut away from them, and the anchorwoman quoted other condemnations that were rolling in from around the world against Émile Sauvage and the rest of the AB-16 conspirators. Parisians of all persuasions were said to be outraged at their methods and goals.

After a few man-on-the-street interviews, the anchor said, 'In other news: One man is trying to show that Paris is not burning by simply going on and celebrating in memory of one of the murder victims.'

The feed cut to Laurent Alexandre. Wearing a black mourning suit, Millie Fleurs's personal assistant stood in the middle of her haute couture showroom. It was packed with white folding chairs. There was a large picture of the designer on an easel surrounded by floral bouquets.

'I think what AB-16 wanted was obscene and unthinkable,' said Alexandre. 'All of Paris, all of France, should stand up against this kind of thinking by showing them that our culture goes on. This afternoon, many of the best designers in the world will unveil dresses made in Millie's honor and in defiance of AB-16.'

'Morgan?'

Sharen Hoskins stood in the doorway. She tapped on her watch. I nodded, and turned to Michele. As I did, I saw a model appear behind Alexandre. She wore a stunning black cocktail dress. Millie Fleurs's assistant gestured to it and said, 'This is my contribution.'

'Beautiful dress,' Michele whispered, almost asleep.

'I have to go.'

She roused, looked at me. 'Come back?'

'God no,' said her agent.

I nodded. 'To testify, at least.'

'Call me?'

'Definitely. And you should come to L.A.'

'Not happening,' François said.

'I'd like that,' Michele said, and paused. 'You know you've never kissed me. You've never even tried.'

'I thought you were out of my league.'

'She is,' her agent said.

'You're not,' Michele said.

'My bad, then. It will never happen again.'

Then I leaned over and kissed her tenderly.

Chapter 111

11:18 A.M.

On the ride out to de Gaulle, I relived that kiss over and over, wondering when I'd actually get to see Michele Herbert again. We could Skype and see each other, of course, but I meant to actually hold her, and kiss her more than once, and learn her story by heart.

My eyelids drifted shut in the backseat of the

sedan that Hoskins was driving. Juge Fromme sat beside her, determined to see me aboard my flight and gone.

I drifted into a buzzing sleep, right on the edge of consciousness.

Images from the past few hours slipped by me: Sauvage ranting as the soldiers dragged him away, the look on Hoskins's and Juge Fromme's faces when I showed them the massacre site, Michele's wan smile when I left her, and then Millie Fleurs's assistant gesturing to the black cocktail dress.

'Morgan?' Hoskins said, waking me. 'We're here.'

I looked around in some confusion at the entrance to the private jetport at de Gaulle because the image of the black dress lingered with me. And I didn't know why. Then I flashed on a drawing of the dress, and Millie shaking that swatch of black fabric the one and only time we met.

Something about it all clicked, and I said, 'I don't think AB-16 was responsible for Millie Fleurs's death.'

Hoskins and Fromme twisted around in their seats. 'What?'

'There's another suspect you should consider,' I insisted. 'Her assistant, Laurent Alexandre.'

Fromme scowled, but Hoskins said, 'Why?'

'The morning before she was killed, I saw a drawing of the dress that Alexandre later said he designed in memory of Millie. It was on his desk.'

'Okay...' Fromme said skeptically.

'Millie had this piece of black fabric that she said she was using to make Princess Mayameen's little black cocktail dress that night,' I said. 'But when we found her, there was no such dress on the mannequins. One of them was bare.'

'So maybe she just decided not to make the dress, and Alexandre used the fabric in her honor from his own design,' Fromme said.

'I don't know,' I said. 'Millie was adamant that the dress had to be ready first thing in the morning. And the princess told Louis and me that she'd gone to Millie's workshop after the club specifically to see that dress.'

'Seems thin to me,' the magistrate said.

'What do you think happened?' Hoskins asked.

I thought a moment. I spotted Louis limping down the airport sidewalk toward us, pulling my roll-on.

'Alexandre designs the dress,' I began. 'And maybe Millie just doesn't have a good idea for a spectacular cocktail dress that evening, but then she sees her assistant's design, and she steals it for her own.

'Alexandre kills her in revenge, and pins it on AB-16. He even uses fabric instead of spray paint to form the tag. He comes up with the idea of a fashion show in Millie's memory. The dress is his again to make a statement in front of the best designers in Paris about the woman he murdered.'

Hoskins looked at Fromme, who shifted uncomfortably before saying, 'We would be remiss if we did not look into your theory, Monsieur Morgan.'

'It's been nice getting to know you, but I think I've overstayed my welcome,' I said, and opened the back door to climb out.

'Morgan,' Hoskins said.

I stopped, looked at her.

'Thanks,' she said. 'For everything.'

'Moi aussi,' Fromme said with his hunched back to me.

'My pleasure,' I said, and got out and shut the door.

'You look like shit,' Louis said.

'Appreciate the vote of confidence,' I said, yawning. 'The jet here?'

'Already refueled,' he said. 'They have a shower inside you can use before you go. Your clothes and shaving kit are here, and your passport.'

I showered, shaved, and dressed in cleaner clothes. Louis had nodded off in the waiting lounge.

'Time for me to leave Paris,' I said after waking him.

Louis stood and threw his arms around me. 'You are a hard man to contain, Jack Morgan.'

'Thanks. I think.'

'No,' he said. 'This is a great compliment, a–'

His cell rang. He looked, raised his eyebrow, and answered. 'Justine?' Louis listened, and then handed me the phone. 'She wants to talk to you.'

'You caught me about to board,' I said. 'Can this wait until I get back?'

'No, actually,' Justine said. 'We just got a call from General Santos with the Rio de Janeiro Olympic authority. He's nervous that Brazil isn't handling security for the games well at all, and he wants Private involved.'

'That's not what he said after the World Cup,' I said.

'Things change.'

'The games are in what, less than four months?'

'Fifteen weeks, Jack,' she said. 'Which is why I'm afraid you're not coming home to L.A. Tell the pilot you're bound for Rio.'

Acknowledgments

Private Paris could not have been written without the gracious assistance of many people. First and foremost, our deepest gratitude goes out to Paris expert and author Heather Stimmler-Hall for guiding us, opening doors, and introducing us to the right people.

Thanks to Detective Nicolas Gouzien of the New York Police Department and Detectives Luc Magnien and Eric Trunel of the Paris Police Prefecture for patiently explaining 'La Crim,' the French judicial system, and the racial tensions in the eastern suburbs.

Jean-Manuel Traimond took us into several public housing projects in the suburbs and helped us to understand the forces behind the volatility in those areas.

At the War College, we were greatly helped by Rear Admiral Marc de Briancon, Brigadier General Christian Beau, and Colonel Thierry Noulens.

Chef Cristophe Saintange with Chef Alain Ducasse brought us into the world of three-star Michelin cuisine.

We learned about Parisian high fashion from Laurent Dublanchy, Stephanie Coudert, Eric Charles Donatien, and Eymeric François.

Isabelle Reye at the Academy of Fine Arts helped us. So did hotelier Nicolas Bourgeois and Parkours expert Thiboult Granier.

Léttitia Petrie and Emmanuel Schwartz were kind enough to take us inside the Institute of France and explain how it works.

The staff at Plaza Athénée, especially Elodie, could not have been more helpful.

Any mistakes are our own, and to one and all, *Merci beaucoup!*

The publishers hope that this book has given you enjoyable reading. Large Print Books are especially designed to be as easy to see and hold as possible. If you wish a complete list of our books please ask at your local library or write directly to:

Magna Large Print Books
Magna House, Long Preston,
Skipton, North Yorkshire.
BD23 4ND

This Large Print Book for the partially sighted, who cannot read normal print, is published under the auspices of

THE ULVERSCROFT FOUNDATION